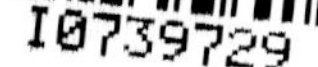

A Woman OF DESTINY

A Calypso Novel

By

ROSELLE THOMPSON

EAGLE PUBLICATIONS

Published by Eagle Publications
P O Box 66050, London W3 3EU, England.

A Paperback Original
First published in Great Britain in 2014

Cover design by V3Creative Designs

ISBN 978-0-9542325-1-1

A CIP catalogue record for this book is available from the British
Library

Printed in Great Britain by IngramSpark
Paper used by Eagle Publications books are made from wood grown
in sustainable forests.

This is a work of fiction. Names, characters, incidents and
dialogues are products of the author's imagination or are used
fictitiously. Any resemblance to actual people, living or dead,
events or locales is entirely coincidental.
www.eaglepublications.co.uk

CONTENTS

		Page
Preface		i-x
Prologue		1
PART ONE		
Chapter 1		7
Chapter 2		34
Chapter 3		68
Chapter 4		108
Chapter 5		136
Chapter 6		165
Chapter 7		181
Chapter 8		189
PART TWO		
Chapter 9		222
Chapter 10		240
Chapter 11		253
Chapter 12		265
Chapter 13		287
Epilogue		304
Glossary		310

A Woman of Destiny – A Calypso Novel

Author's Preface

This novel has a generic sub-title, which alludes to a particular evaluative approach to reading the text – as a *song* (calypso) and a *book* (novel). The term "*Calypso Novel*" therefore suggests that a **fusion of these two genres** (the calypso or oral narrative and the written text); exist within this book. The reason for this perspective is that the book or *written text* presents the narrated stories as calypsos, regarded as *oral* genre. In other words, it is possible to relate to this fusion because the narrated/spoken stories are also written down to create the literary text and together, they bear a resemblance to the oral characteristics of calypsos in general.

However, the simple descriptive subtitle, "*A Calypso Novel*" in this book "*A Woman of Destiny*" belies the complex nature of the narrative structure of the book. It is an experimental approach that challenges the conventions of the Caribbean literary canon, by incorporating characteristics of the calypso into the text, as a way of honouring Caribbean forms of expression. Such an approach creates new, hybrid forms of expressions and opens up new possibilities for the reader, when reading Caribbean literary narratives.

What we have as a result, is a novel that can be improvisational and digressive, flashing backwards and forwards, teaming with the vibrancy of Caribbean life, as it presents the Grenadian folks in a landscape that can never be taken at face value. Therefore, tolerance is needed to understand the underlying, structural significance of the thematic approaches through the lens of calypso music. This will help the reader to adapt him or herself to the expressive powers of the calypso in the narrative and to appreciate the new possibilities that it presents for both author and readers of the text.

i

The background to calypso music is associated with carnival and carnivalesque forms of revelling and lifestyles. It is said to have derived from several linguistic backgrounds; meaning a joyous song *"carieto"*, or drinking party or festivity. Additionally, it is referred to in French (archaic) as *carouse or carrouseaux*. During the process of Anglicization of the language in the Caribbean region, the word *"caliso"* was used; Spanish for a topical song. It is also referred to in West African, Hausa, as *Kaiso*; when used to express approval and encouragement, similar to *bravo* in applause. Many early calypsos were sung in French Creole by an individual called a *griot*.

The role of the griot, rather like a travelling musician in West Africa, became known as a *Chantuelle* or singer, and eventually the word *calypso* was born, sung by a Calypsonian; who sang of situations in society as he/she saw them. This brief etymology already suggests a fusion of origins or elements, into one region, which have had an impact on the lives and expressions of people in the Caribbean.

From the 1930's Caribbean, to our present 21st century, the word *"calypso"* embodies all of the above definitions and more. One of the main characteristics of the Calypso is the significance of its oral transmission. Communication is realized through face-to-face contact with a live audience and singer. The song is presented by a Calypsonian/singer, who functions as a person whose job it is to, not only sing joyous songs, but *"tell it like it is"*. This means that as the *'people's mouthpiece'*, he/she presents orally, **all** aspects of the society in song; which also simultaneously documents (in a fusion of generic forms – oral/literary/performance/electronic media), the cultural, social, political, and economic history of a place, via its musical framework.

But the *sweet* calypso music we enjoy today, played by steel bands around the world, performed in front of various jovial, dancing crowds, is essentially a bitter-sweet cultural golden nugget; having been born from a *bitter* experience during colonization, slavery and plantation days. Similarly, rather like the *sweetness* of sand, sea, blue skies and paradise-like landscapes in the Caribbean, men and women in the novel (and in real life), have had to experience the *bitterness* of leaving their offspring behind, to venture off into unknown territories, in order to find a better life and/or ways of improving their lot; despite the ensuing unpleasant consequences.

Therefore, the many voices in the novel, led by the narrator, are as varied as the number of origins and inputs that make up the calypso, and are reminiscent of the characteristics of its musical genre. These voices are the different characters, whose individual dilemmas function as a calypso/song that is sung throughout the novel. They wander in and out, improvise, and play with relationships; have solo, duo, trio, quartet and group percussionist experiences between sounds; through their own authentic voices.

Whether, praying, speaking, fighting, cursing, gossiping, killing or through the innocent wanderings of the children's voices, they juxtapose incongruent musical ideas in innovative ways in the novel's structure. Through these, the reader must pick up on the narrative 'beat' or lose the novel's 'rhythm' totally. This makes the act of creating and producing more important – a priority over reader opinion.

This *Calypso Novel*, is set in the early 1970's, with a focus on a Grenadian village in the Parish of St. Andrews - *landscape*. It validates a sense of place, mood, and projects the vitality of characters that populate it, as essential to the plot of the calypso tune – *the audience*. However, that Grenadian village is also symbolic and representative of any other Caribbean island village, which experienced aspects of the main themes in the novel – Caribbean extended families caring for children who have been left at home, whilst parents migrate to the metropolis – UK, USA, Canada or elsewhere, in order to seek betterment abroad and the resultant complexities experienced by all those involved.

The main characteristic of the calypso is *communication*. Communication, in the case of this novel, is realized by a narrator/composer, in engagement with a 'live audience', or its readers. Whether with our without lyrics, episodes within the narrative are reminiscent of the musical genre as they '*sing*' the life of the people via performance, speech-making, folk and religious transmissions, *ole talk*, storytelling, gossip or giving the *lowdown*. Additionally, this is done through whatever varieties of the Grenadian vernacular is projected; Grenada Creole, French Creole or *Patois* (pronounced *pat-wa*); or Standard English, as they are uttered among the different generations within the novel.

In establishing a strong sense of place, every aspect of our senses is engaged, observed by the narrator; as she presents the village as something that's not only physical, but one which soothes, gives comfort, hope, peace, forgiveness and restores. *"As I stood there the beauty of the place punctuated my thoughts with flashes of our childhood exploits and the glory of those days."* Later, she tells us *"I took in deep, fresh, breaths of air, soaking in this spiritual renewal and my mind became sanguine once more."* Therefore, the landscape has a number of impacting qualities on a person's whole being; emotional and physical; cultural and spiritual. *"I drew fresh courage from the quietness of the place."*

Later, we are invited to engage our feelings and feel the breeze as she narrates, *"the rustling leaves in the gentle breeze soothed my spirit and whispered the need for comfort and hope, peace and forgiveness."* However, that same landscape is also steeped in cultural beliefs where, *"many had already feared the tree's association with death, evil and the belief that there, lost souls who are unable to rest in peace, roamed the land of the living"*, because *"the silk cotton tree was a symbol of witchcraft. Obeah men, we were told on storytelling nights, could catch a person's soul and nail it on a silk cotton tree."*

The descriptive language used is meant to deliberately communicate the landscape in highly visual, imagistic and regenerative terms. We see this each time the landscape is described, down to the minutest details, how the houses are arranged, the Junction and its environs, the activities of mad ants, the reminiscent downpour, or women washing clothes in St. John's river; are characteristic of the calypso genre and its conformity to giving details, within its musical framework.

The most obvious allusion to the calypso musical genre is the examples of 14 calypsos presiding over each chapter in the novel, as a way of honouring the past oral master-Calypsonians of the musical genre. These early Calypsonians are among those who have maintained a determination and insistence, through their repertoire, on giving respectability to the calypso over the past 100 years, so that we can learn to appreciate it, with the current global significance it now enjoys.

A case in point is that Steel band music is taught in British and other European schools, as part of their curriculum brings, as never before, calypso and pan music to the fore; widening its global frame of reference. The early calypsos existed at a time when singing them was unpopular; when they were censured or banned because the lyrics, whether interpreted as negative or positive, were used to influence political thought and sway the mass population into action. It can be seen that the calypso lyrics embodies subject matters that document the whole spectrum of life, as it is lived in all aspects of society; thereby giving the Calypsonian's repertoire an *archival function* within society.

So like a Calypsonian, the narrator in *A Woman of Destiny: A Calypso Novel*, tells us like is; by becoming *"the people's/readers' newspaper" or "mouthpiece;"* documenting all aspects of her landscape/society in her story/calypso, throughout the novel.

- The fight between Jean and Dessima
- Gospelypso:(an off-shoot of the calypso) in the village church services
- Sukram's murder and the ensuing drama
- Mark's death – a village in mourning

V

- Verna, Christopher and the fiasco in England
- The dilemmas of immigrant Grenadians in Britain
- The *Man-of-words* at the narrator's Farewell
- Grenada's Independence
- The sapodilla incident and the English Headmaster's corporal punishment
- The village children's innocent discussions based on hear-say
- The corrupt *"African priest"* - castor oil purge and the women's curses
- The funeral of the Caribbean/Grenadian returnee
- The mother's experiences at work in England
- Gossiping and family dilemmas about pregnant unwed daughters
- The holiday experiences of the youth in England
- The Queen and the Duke's visit to the Caribbean region
- The fathers who don't look after their children and the mothers who 'father' them

Symbolically, and in order to do so, Joanne is aided and is given a *rite de passage* by her elder Calypsonians, to 'sing' through her dilemma/song, as they themselves had done in the past, or are continuing to do today.

In *Chapter 1*, we learn instructively of "a mother's duty", *Chapter 2*, we are educated on the "bewitching", "fascinating", "throbbing, "absorbing" calypso rhythm. *Chapter 3* presents a warning to Mothers on bringing up their daughters; *Chapter 4* sings a caution on the need for solidarity and love for one another; *Chapter 5* sings of the dilemma of Caribbean migrants in London; *Chapter 6* inspires determination and allegiance to Britain as the motherland. *Chapter 7* presents inequality in society and *Chapter 8* takes you back to the occult religious forms of obeah or witchcraft, being practiced in the region. *Chapter 9* advocates love for vagabond fathers, regardless of their shortcomings, while *Chapter 10* speaks politically; tongue-in-cheek via parables, of what voters' actions should be, regarding the inefficiency and ineffectiveness of those in power. *Chapter 11* personalises the effects of colonial history on the region; *Chapter 12* informs the populace of the vagaries of migration for those who've left the Caribbean and *Chapter 13* presents regret, in a kind of diasporic 'blues', for those who have left the Caribbean to settle in London.

There are numerous digressions, tangents and flashbacks as the narrative weaves back and forth between late 1960's and early 1970's, with a densely populated collection of characters in the two different landscapes (Grenada and London). These present an idiosyncratic narrative structure of the novel that alludes to the influence that the genre of calypso music had on the author. Her lack of participation in carnival festivities intensified her interest in it and made her acutely aware of its traditional value and implications, despite being instructed to the contrary.

She tells us in chapter two, that despite her family's rejection of this aspect of Grenadian culture, her interest in the calypso/carnival intensified. It confirms the power of the calypso to influence thoughts and actions; especially since rejection of the popular calypso lyrics had pertained to a priest taking part in carnival one year. The lyrics which suggests breaking all religious boundaries and joining in the bacchanal, gave licence to the listener to do likewise, *"If the priest could play who is we"*?

According to her overtly religious family, this was somehow blasphemous. Therefore, as children, they were banned from showing an open interest in or taking part in the yearly carnival festivities. Conversely, this brought her closer to this island's tradition, and in this context, calypso music can be seen to disrupt lives or present a challenge to the status quo.

Likewise, in the context of this novel, the calypso musical structure could disrupt the reader's conventional approach to the literary text. In other words, as with calypso music in society, the narrative structure of *A Woman of Destiny: A Calypso Novel* could disrupt expectations that the reader has developed while reading conventionally written texts. The difference in the book's narrative structure calls for a distinct reading strategy, where the musical framework is the inter-textuality of the text. So the reader of this novel must take his or her cue from the calypso musical genre, in order to understand the most effective ways of evaluating the text.

Joanne's story is her calypso being composed, and it includes the essence of the whole 13 calypsos enshrined at the beginning of each chapter. Her repertoire exemplifies a calypso composition in the making – beginning with a *solo composition*, when she introduces her song in the Prologue. As a master Calypsonian herself, her dialogue/story is her art-form. In her *backing musical band*, many Calypsonians are given a hearing, as in a *calypso competition*. Some *speechify* (as in Joanne's farewell event); demonstrate the *competitive and linguistic mastery* element of the old Calypsonians.

The church congregation, at the beginning of the novel, projects the *call-and-response* structure of some calypsos, evidenced by Revered Blackman's prayer in the church service. With the novel as a whole, the *bass percussion instruments* are provided by the men who are hardly audible, mainly around the rum shop; with *bass solos* playing in and out of Joanne's *medley* to either *praise or abuse*.

These are mixed in with the *alto and soprano percussion* of the mothers in the *calypso band*. They are very vocal, loud, sometimes playing as *solos, duos* (Irene and Gran-gran; Gran-gran and Miss Mattis, Cleothilda and Irene), or as a *whole syncopation*. We see an example of this musical composition, as provided by the initial introduction of a *two-piece band/duo percussionist* provided by Dessima and Jean in the fight. In their *mêlée*, they were joined by *bass instruments* (men's intervention) and added to by a *whole band of instruments;* played by the men and women who intervene and stop the fight. The *bacchanal* the fight produces is carnivalesque, reminiscent of the *calypso performance* in *carnival*.

Whereas the creativity of Joanne's calypso is most demonstrative of group effort in its creation, seen in Part I of the novel; Part II evidences a return to solo creation in an unknown territory or landscape (England). There the *solo pieces*/stories present quieter *rhythms,* with a *slower pace;* returning to the *solo lyrics* or the voice in engagement with the main narrative/calypso. All the other competitive elements, we saw in Part I, the support of the *band/family* and landscape in her formative years, have given way to a *single voice* in the main narrative/composition, and we regain focus by listening, via the reading, as to why the whole composition/story began in the first place.

Joanne's composition began as a solo, and 'as it was in the beginning' (just as with all the difficulties and struggles the calypso encountered to survive), Joanne's determination, staying-power, and insistence on form, structure and content, is what she has learnt, will see her through 'to the end'. Born out of a bitter-sweet beginning in the Caribbean, she must learn to manipulate both elements, guided by those who were part of her beginning (Gran-gran and Irene, her master Calypsonians), to end with her own composition as she sees fit.

Therefore, *Joanne's solo,* 'as it was in the beginning', suggests that the characteristics of the forerunners of today's calypso, still exist and therefore it will continue to every narrator/Calypsonian's 'end'. However, the idea of an 'end' here is elusive, suggesting several possibilities by its open-endedness and will be analysed according to what one makes of her *calypso composition/her narrative,* as she concludes in her Epilogue.

With such exemplary characteristics, forged by the making of the calypso, it is highly probable that the novel title – *A Woman of Destiny,* will be a reality for Joanne, as someone who has learnt the art from her calypso-masters (past griots); that she will realise her villagers' prediction, and become their *woman of destiny.* This, we can surmise, would be achievable whether she encounters, *censorship, ban, praise and abuse, or approval*; she has become a griot in her own right; a mistress Calypsonian, who uses her song/story to "tell it like it is" but fading out on a certain note, with a question, as the *music trails off* in the Epilogue.

An overall approach is for the reader to appreciate and understand the work conceptually, without getting bogged down with the small details of literary theories that attempt to categorise, within existing frameworks. Such approaches can be limiting and can distract one from comprehending the overall significance of the work, thereby minimizing its value within both the Caribbean and general 'literary' canon.

Furthermore, this *Calypso Novel,* with its folksy vernacular, may dislocate readers of the traditional novel, or may cause frustration, by slowing down the reading pace, as he/she comes face-to-face with the fusion of language varieties uttered as Grenadian vernacular.

However, being the authentic voice of the folks, it is important that the reader does not try to fit the proverbial 'square pin in a round hole'; (especially if the 'square pin' is innovative without an acknowledged past): but must instead, be open to the new perspectives that the novel offers. Each time the reader engages the story or 'hears' a calypso within the narrative, each variation or variations should convey a richness of perspective, if only to invite the reader to marvel at the sonorous nature of the language of the folks, and its consequences in the text.

The appearance of the calypsos at the beginning of each chapter, (some of them over 80 years old); still function as presiding forces of our ancestral *griots,* and confirm that this form of Caribbean artistry, is an ongoing process or *continuum* of creative development. They span over 500 years of Caribbean culture.

Finally, my view is that this **Calypso Novel** facilitates critical thinking, when seeking to explore the complexities of Caribbean 'literature', Caribbean life, as well as responses to life's problems; by examining the layers which have contributed to their making.

Roselle Thompson

PROLOGUE ...*"As it was in the beginning....*

"For the benefit of those who didn't know
Calypso is our heritage from long ago
But many of the puritans in this land
Against the singers took a stand (!) cant understand
They hate to have their linen washed in public
So they devised this scurvy trick
To apply pressure strong and viberous
And attempt to take our music from us."

Atilla the Hun (Raymond Quevado)

"Ashes to ashes, dust to dust!"

There was no weeping or wailing among the gathered brethren to drown Reverend Blackman's solemn and shaky voice, as the thick clumps of brownish-red earth were tossed over the coffin. But the speed of the grave-diggers signalled the apparent departure of the dead from the land of the living. The Reverend's small, dark and bony figure was dressed in the customary long, black gown. Purple sashes, decorated with embroidered crosses at each end, hung over the gown. This completed his matching mitre which bore a similar design. Clearly *"the man of God,"* was distinguishable from the crowd. He stood at the head of the six-foot, brass-trimmed, wooden box, with his worn Bible in hand and spoke with a seasoned voice of courage; the message from the *"Good Book,"* as he made his benedictory pronouncements.

"I am the resurrection and the life. He that believeth in me though he were dead, yet shall he live."

At the same time, the Mothers of the church were singing mournfully:

The grave-diggers plunged into the red and brown sticky mound of dugout earth, placed at the mouth of the grave and in unison, they obliterated the sight of the concealed corpse; fast, faster, faster still. Mother earth accepted irrevocably, this travelled remains, as the last juncture in mum's cyclical journey here on earth.

The sun had cast weak shadows under the canopy of leafy green foliage overhead, which gleamed like filigree emerald lace. As I stood there, the beauty of the place punctuated my thoughts with flashes of our childhood exploits and the glory of those days; the precious days of my youth. I took in deep, fresh, breaths of air, soaking in this spiritual renewal and my mind became sanguine again. This soothed my senses which were only slightly marred by the reality of this funeral. The shadows from the waving, lacy, foliage rose and fell on the gathered congregation around the grave.

Many attendees had found places to stand as they quietly observed the "foreign" funeral. There was no bawling. No woman had tied her belly. There was not the customary, painful and emotional appeal to the Divine to return the beloved one, now! The immediacy of pain and hurt; shock and loss were almost absent. It was the kind of "quiet" funeral that many in the region were growing accustomed to. It was also a typical situation of those sons and daughters of the soil who had sojourned in far-off lands; only to return to their native land at the point of death. Many had not been back since leaving for betterment abroad. However, they ensured by request, that their battered, worn-out remains be returned to their homeland for burial. This had become a common feature for the expired, migrant, Caribbean-returnee.

Irene Bernadette Theresa Thomas, was swallowed into the bowel of her Maker, while those dressed in black and white with purple, walked the land of the living. They uttered condolences, reminisced and were also philosophical about the inevitability of this fact of life which must befall everyone.

A daughter had returned Home having passed away. This had been the case with many of the fifties and sixties migrants to England. Irene's family received her with the usual sadness but glad that she had requested a return to her native soil to be laid to rest. Her only written wish was to be 'buried under the silk-cotton tree,' which was near to the mango row in the village.

Many had already feared the tree's association with death, evil and the belief that in this spot, lost souls who are unable to rest in peace, roamed the land of the living. Yet, it somehow stood to reason in some people's mind, why this spot was a good choice. Many had whispered their doubts as to whether the Holy Saints her namesakes; Bernadette and Theresa, would grant rest to the sister. Those who did not know her well in the last few years had remembered her as a young child growing up in the tropics. She was the apple of her parent's eye and their youngest offspring.

Time had healed the shame that her early pregnancy had brought on her parents at the tender age of 15 years. She was regarded as a comet – a would-be *woman of destiny* they had surmised, who had fallen from grace. Their great expectations had been denied and it was from this beginning that Irene's steely characteristics took root.

Going to Trinidad soon after her child's birth, was her way of maintaining her freedom and abandoning the child that had been blamed for 'cutting her off in her prime.' Her settled stay in England after her year's sojourn in Trinidad had softened the blow and her absence from the village environment helped to quell the incessant gossip. It assisted time in healing the hurt and shame that the family was forced to endure.

I remained near to the wreathed-covered grave, whilst the mourners and brethren who were supporting each other in sorrow, eventually left for the house. There, further gatherings in honour of the dead, were to take place. The Reverend uttered his solemn *Words of Comfort* to me, "*The Lord Jesus Christ said, let not your heart be troubled, sister.*" He gave me a sympathetic tap on the shoulder, as he too made his way to the direction of the house. The bulk of the crowd had dispersed, leaving me understandably, to reminisce in silence, under the silk-cotton tree.

I drew fresh courage from the quietness of the place and stood there surveying this tropical landscape. The rustling of the leaves in the gentle breeze soothed my spirit and seemed to whisper the need for comfort and hope, peace and forgiveness. I breathed in the air again with long, deep, peaceful, breaths. I remembered my dearest, sweet, Grandmother, or '*Gran-gran,*' as I and all the other children in the village used to call her. It was a fitting term of endearment, for one of the most beloved members of our family and community. She had died over 15 years ago but remained in my heart, as a spiritual guide and friend to me.

"If you're watching, Gran-gran," I whispered, masking the secret conversation while pretending to arrange the floral tributes on the grave; "Look after your little one, who today has come to you."

The quietness of the grave spot was unnerving. My black veil felt loose, so I tightened it. Afterwards, I stood next to the flowers on the protruding mound and watched the remaining few figures in black, white and purple, disappear completely out of sight in the distance. I sighed with relief from the burden-some years, and the roller-coaster experiences with the interred. Nostalgically, I decided to cast my mind BACK - BACK into time; remembering and reliving the eventful pages of this, now closed book. I reflected on the few humorous passages, the thrilling, the suspense and emotional pages; as well as the plain indifference of many of its chapters.

I remember only a few months ago, when I was back in England, how exhausting it was coping with Irene's illness. It included rushing to and from work, then to and from the hospital; barely stopping for food on some days. This daily punishing schedule climaxed into sheer exhaustion and anxiety, which I was forced to saddle all alone. I remember too, the many times I had actually fallen asleep on my bed fully clothed with coat and shoes on, too tired to self-care because of exhaustion.

My twin sisters had gone away - one to Canada and the other to Africa. They did not seem to care about their mother or my desperate need for their physical, emotional and financial help. Yes, they had sent letters to me. Many good wishes were expressed and I had read them when they arrived, glossing over the meaningless platitudes to search for any offer of help. Finance was needed but moral support came instead. They should have been at home physically to take their turns in making the trips to visit mum at the local hospital I thought but letters with sympathetic words came instead.

Standing here now in this tropical shade, the branches of the silk cotton tree shimmer and dance in the breeze. Unlike them, I shiver and fold my arms around my chest, as if to block out the coolness of the wind. The leaves seem to whisper their commiserations. I guessed that their condolences were promises of my future peace. Momentarily, as I replay the events that led up to this date, my thoughts go BACK, BACK, BACK, BACK, BACK to the West Middlesex MD2 Ward for the elderly, in England. There mum, as well as many confused patients who had become senile, was spending her last days. They seemed lost in their apparent second childhood, as they displayed their '6th stage of man.'

PART I

Chapter 1

"A good Mother always does things constructive
To help her children is her objective
No matter how poor she happens to be
Her duty she'll perform assiduously
Without the shadow of a single doubt
They'll feed you, clothe you, and remain without
Send you to school to be educated
So that in days to come, you'll be respected."

Lord Caresser (Rufus Callendar)

"Irene, your daughter's here to see you!"

The nurse was bellowing with the hope that the slightly deaf Irene would hear her, prior to my entry. It could have been due to deafness, irritation of having to be bothered with visitors or just plain uncooperative determination, but Irene certainly did not stir. This charade was a situation that I had become quite used to.

The bent figure of an emaciated woman covered with a black shawl, was crouched on a wooden framed commode chair in the corner. She was oblivious of time and her surroundings. She seemed lost in her world of disappointment, unfulfilled dreams, much of it through her distorted and revengeful lust for mastery over those around her. Here, in her world of oblivion, time was now the master who dominated - not her. He mocks her now just as she had manipulated others, gloried in their downfall or orchestrated many a catastrophe in her attempts to control destinies.

Here, in the Common Room, sat the authoress of her own misery, made to tolerate the continuous replay of her life's malevolent deeds in her head; whilst locked in her own somnolent world of hell. Her seeing eyes are now dead but the pictures of life she now relives are mentally vivid, alive, painful and pathetic. They serve as a punitive reminder of the emotional terror she had once inflicted on others.

The air in the Common Room was filled with the stale lingering smell of urine, coupled with strong disinfectant. The putrid smells of worn bodies, with leaking passages, were from those who were no longer able to conceal their dignity. Instead, they did obeisance only to old age and senility.

The Common Room also had a sense of commonality among its confused occupants. Lily, who was often clapping to sounds audible only to herself, hummed rousing wartime British songs. She sometimes la-la-la-ed to the melodic tunes which she heard in her head. Dressed in a wrinkled, floral, long-sleeved top and skirt, with an over-washed, worn-out Marks and Spencer pastel-green cardigan, she had a childlike hairstyle that completed her animated appearance.

She was a small, white woman, whose disfigured knuckles made her clap awkwardly, those joyous songs which she sang. Often she would show off the weeping sores on her legs just above her contorted bunions. This was because she wore shoes which continually bruised them, instead of wearing her pink open-fronted slippers. This situation gave her increased attention from her Carers. She loved putting on make-up and would dab lipstick onto her upper lips, so that it reached right under her nostrils. On her cheeks she smeared red blush so that it created large red patches that made her look like a marionette in a side show.

In the same room, was sixty-five year old George. He sat

in his wheelchair, spinning it around with apparent new-found excitement. He would constantly talk loudly to an invisible companion who he called his 'friend,' about a fire he was once rescued from. His children had bought him the wheelchair and therefore it was his personal possession. He was obsessed with riding around the Common Room in his own chair and he made sure that not a soul touched it. The only time he was contented to leave the wheelchair, was when he gave his consent for the transporter to be parked up at night.

George had a wrinkled, black, face with heavy greying eyebrows which matched the grey hair on his head. His lips protruded over his false teeth which were intact. Some say he really can walk but he refuses to, in order to enjoy the pity and attention he got from those around him; especially the nurses. He appeared well enough and many a nurse could be heard screaming with laughter because of his unadulterated sexual innuendos and attempted 'physical' advances. It was said that George often showed them his penis but when faced with indignation and a rebuff from the staff he would retort; "It's me legs that's sick, not me head!" That was indeed a debatable point, because George constantly talked to imaginary people and fabricated his grandiose exploits in fantastic stories. In fact, most people said that he was suffering from "delusions of grandeur."

"I met the Queen once, man," he told me when I had enquired after his health. "She shake me han' too!" he blabbered. "Well ah tell she ma'm, you can try me anytime!"

My eyebrows, automatically raised in a cautionary surprise, caused him to defend himself.

"Well ah figure she may need a real man sometimes, so me, I aint bashful, I offer she help!" he mused cheekily in a heavy Trinidadian accent.

I smiled a broad smile and George was satisfied although he was more used to getting rip-roaring, bellyful of loud laughs to his harmless jibes.

"Ben, come here, let me do up your flies," the Care Assistant called.

Ben passed round the room like a naughty boy on skates. He was touching everyone and everything with delight; almost as if he had just discovered his sense of touch. Ben was a 70 yr old from the North of England, who wore a pair of creased trousers and an un-tucked shirt. He did not seem to hear the Care Assistant and it seemed she was quite used to this situation. The fact is, he made no attempt to respond to her and she made no real attempt to do up his flies either. It was a childish game, involving naughty 'grown-up' children.

Ben had one remaining tooth at the upper front of his mouth so that he resembled a toddler, who had just cut his first tooth. His hair was unruly and his shirt was constantly out of his trousers. He had no visiting relatives and he dribbled constantly in a semi-conscious smiling state. Ben used to be a truck driver up North, is all that is known about him.

Joyce, on the other hand, looked well dressed. She was an aggressive English woman with short dark-brown hair and brown eyes. She was constantly clutching a white, 1930's style handbag which she jealously guarded, as she sat glued to the TV screen. She was perhaps fifty years of age or more and she looked out of place among the other patients. Joyce was always clean and unpredictable. She was known for her violent outbursts which often required the help of three or more people to calm her down. Once I saw her attacking a nurse whilst yelling out at her.

"You black horse! Don't touch me!" she yelled. "Help! She touched me, the black horse!"

The Care Assistants and Key workers had rushed to the scene of the outburst, knowing full well that it was one of Joyce's usual moments of rage. They say that Joyce, who came from Liverpool, was emotionally traumatised. I was told that the mishap which had sparked her off had begun a long time ago, when her husband ran off with her best friend and neighbour. Her obvious mistrust of others was at first difficult to understand; not only for the staff of MD2 Ward, but also for other patients and visitors. There was no telling who would be the next victim of her unpredictable outbursts and it was clear that she raged against women more than she did against men.

I had been witnessing this private hidden world of MD2 Ward for the last 18 months. At first, I was surprised by the 'otherness' of the place. "So this is where they keep them!" I had said to myself, newly awakened to the fact that the occupants had been carefully separated from 'normal' life, to exist there until their terrors and nightmares finally ceased to haunt them. Here, they could pass unnoticed by the outside world, before going to that place beyond life.

Mamie sat there bent over her chair, uninterested in me or anything else around her. She hardly responded to anyone but like a robot, would roll her eyes to show surprise; sometimes to record her annoyance or to refuse what was being offered to her.

"Mamie! Mamie! It's me!" I bellowed. "How are you today?" I questioned, touching her silvery grey head and stroking the much-wrinkled face with clenched jaw.

I pitied the contorted face of pain. But was it pain of sorrow, of forgiveness or pain of hate? I often wondered which. The days grew longer and longer and she battled on defiantly, staring into space. I sat silently, accompanying the sad figure of mum, and then I remembered the other times too; 30 years of nostalgic memory, so much a contrast of today.

ح

My first introduction to "Mamie" was through my grandmother, a majestic-looking woman - her mother. To me, Gran-gran, as we called her, was a female warrior; confident, seasoned and strong. Her name, which was Catherine Braveboy, had resonances of bravery and courage infused with her background of the fighting Ashanti spirit. She lived in the village of Belair, near to Gutt, St. Andrews, Grenada, in the Caribbean.

The village was an array of thinly populated galvanised-roofed houses, which rested on stilts made of wood or concrete pillars. They looked like painted, pastel-coloured boxes, trimmed with white among the green leafy surroundings. Each house was demarcated by its own muddy path, which made its snake-like way through the bushes that eventually led to a yard. The yards were made up of tough, reddish brown earth and stepping stones marked off the individual territories that surrounded the homes. Golden apple, governor plums or damsel trees stood tall above hibiscus fencing and competing to reach the sky; privatized each owner's territory.

The one main road which accessed these houses had no electric light. Along this road, Miss Ivy's grocery store and Septimus' rum shop were strategically positioned, so that each one could be reached with ease. The road led to a T-junction branching off to Gutt on the left and Hermitage Post Office, as well as the doctor's surgery, on the right. One of the things which made the junction popular was Mr. James big house and a Friendly Society Hall. They were the junction's major landmarks. This Society Hall was the local social hot-spot, which occasionally had a local dance with live music or community meetings and religious services held by missionaries from Canada and England.

A Seventh Day Adventist Church was next to the Friendly Society Hall; convenient for its congregants who tried to woo the ungodly to seek refuge within. The church was a stone building, just like Mr. James' house, with glass windows and a toilet that flushed. It stood amongst the buildings, constantly competing for an audience, whether there was a village dance or not.

Mr. James was a mulatto; a man of mixed race who Gran-gran called *beke*. I thought it was because he looked like a white man who was baked to a rich brown colour in the sun. However, half-white and very rich, he had a car, a truck and as most of the bourgeois people did, he sold bananas, cocoa and nutmeg. He was the main contact with the white visitors who seldom came to the village.

On these occasions Auntie Meena would often bake cakes, bread, little delicacies and give them to Mr. James to assist in his entertaining, on behalf of the village. This was unwritten village courtesy and everyone knew Mr. James. He was regarded as the main man of the area for all worldly matters; spiritual matters were firmly the remit of the Christian brethren in the village.

The junction therefore was the village hub. It was also a meeting-place where men hung out. There in rum shops, they discussed their various dreams and ambitions and young boys listened to them. Occasionally, it was there that boys met disobedient girls who had sneaked away from their homes, in the twilight of the evening; ultimately, to get up to no good. The junction's multi-faceted use meant that missionaries with their gas-lamps, which drew fire-flies to dance around them, also drew some stray wanderers to the open-air, evangelical, roadside meetings. It was on those occasions, fervent pleas were made to non-believers and backsliders alike; *"To Repent! The kingdom of God is at hand!"* The faint responses of *"Hallelujahs!"* and *"Amens!"* from the trickle of a crowd would often sound lonely and unconvinced.

But the junction had a reputation for being the place where young men tried to lure young developing women to their sexual traps. It was also where old men, boasting about themselves in their stories of sexual accomplishments, occasionally succeeded in wooing another man's woman as a result. There, young men imitated the 'big talk,' and 'big dreams' of the older men.   Conversely, older men expressed regrets and commiserated with each other for their past failures. Fully saturated with the Grenadian *fire-water* or River Antoine rum; they would become garrulous with glib, lamentable, stories about their lost loves, lost chances, lost hopes and lost dreams.

But this was during the days of my youth. Surveying the tropical landscape as I am now, while standing near to mum's grave, I feel compelled to reminisce over the happenings of the past 30 years. Like watching a video, I had often reminisced about Grenada during my time in England. During those moments, I used to challenge my memory recall by mentally pressing life's *'replay'* button; *pausing* now and then to savour some sweet memories or *skipping*, as if to *fast-forward* the memories I chose to forget.

Right now my mind races back to my happy, youthful, growing years; as I use the peace of this moment to indulge in the nostalgia of both pleasure and pain. Hopping on to the memory train, I bask in the Grenada of my childhood and really long once again, for the pleasure that its innocence gave. I long too, for the communal world of my youth and the safety and the feelings of love, which dependence on family and the community bring. Right now, memories are a profuse, lively and comfortable book of refuge. I now select and turn the pages of the past, and recall the last 30 years; with instant gratification.

ع

At the delicate age of 10 years, I had learnt to shoulder responsibilities – the kind that as a young girl, you were expected to take on; small daily chores around the house. This included cleaning, fetching water or fire-wood, learning to wash my own clothes, being fully active in church activities and doing school work with all my might! Not so today, because for the entire day, me and Gran-gran will be on our own. Auntie Meena had said so.

Aunt Meena is preparing to go to town. My cousins, Catherine and Claudette, are going to the river to wash clothes. My chores in Aunt Meena's absence, she had said, was to stay at home and make sure that the water, which she had put into a huge tub in the sun for Gran-gran's mid-day bath, will be just the right temperature to wash away the pain from her painful joints. Mid-day, the perfect time to test the temperature, was the time when the sun would be at its hottest overhead.

The tub of water was put in its strategic position, in order to catch the full force of the morning's sun. Some selected bush, considered to be medicine, was added to the water. There, the water will remain and be warmed incrementally throughout the morning, as it pays homage to the spherical fireball above.

My job was to put enough *careila* bush and *bois den* spice leaf, with some *black sage* in the tub. With the right blend of this homeopathic remedy, I would put them all together in the water, vigorously agitating them until the water turned a dark green colour. When Gran-gran eventually gets into this tub, I would be expected to rub the water's goodness lovingly, all over her. I was taught to sap her joints and soothe that glistening, grateful, Grenadian frame. Without fail, I rubbed her with the herbally-infused 'medicine,' which I learnt was good for pain, rheumatism, colds, soothing hurt emotions, and loving the one who I had always regarded as my mum.

But my young 10 year-old world was full of questions. It was how I learnt about things around me. As a Grenadian child, you learnt by observing, listening, apprenticing, and experimenting. Questions were not asked, since they were not encouraged. In fact, asking questions can sometimes be regarded as being downright rude! But today I broke the rules. It was done by firstly gauging its appropriateness and testing the general atmosphere to figure out if it would be allowed. I wanted to ask questions because there were things I needed to know. Gran-gran, I reasoned, was the one with who I could take a chance to suspend the rules with. Indeed, her answers often helped to put my youthful, puzzling view of the world straight. Aunt Meena, on the hand, who was strict, did not approve of questions whatever the circumstances!

"You ask too much questions!" she would often retort.

"Children must be seen and not heard," was her justification. This would sometimes be alternated with, "Ask no questions you get no lies told!"

Now this always made me wonder what strange lies grown-ups had to tell children. Why were we, the silent wonderers of cryptic sayings, left in our young dark world to puzzle everything out ourselves?

"Yes, there must be some dark lies or secrets hidden by

parents that children must not know about," I concluded.

Of these secrets all our families were conspirators because Daisy, Jean, Gloria, Yvonne and Dessima and other village children, all had the same retort from their parents. They too, must be 'seen and not be heard,' except in church.

In church, you were called on impromptu, to perform some small task, such as give a talk, present a welcome speech, explain a biblical passage or say a prayer. Life was the church, and the church was our stage. This is why my heart skipped with beats of excitement at the thought of being left alone to ask Gran-gran the many questions I needed answers for; before Aunt Meena returned home from town. The thought of Aunt Meena being out of the way, made me sigh with anticipation, because I would certainly know more than I did yesterday.

I had woken up early this morning and said the customary morning prayers and went to collect water from the standpipe, which was 800 yards away. It was five thirty in the morning but Joanna, Yvonne and Daisy were already there. The aluminum buckets clanged as they were put noisily on top of the concrete stand to accept the frothy waterfall, as it gushed impatiently out of the pipe. Noisily at first, in the hollow receptacle, the water pelted down into our buckets. Then, quietly it accepted the foaming liquid, as it bubbled and fizzed to the top. Reaching the top it overflowed with quieter resignation.

Each bucket rang out the same tune with clang, hollow, foam, fizz, and overflow! Sometimes the water jerked and splattered or appeared to cough, in its urgency to drain out the desperately needed liquid. The pressure of the early morning water was stronger at 5.30am in the morning than any other time during the day. Later in the day it was known to trickle, or sometimes even stop altogether from the increased daytime demand. Therefore, fully accepting the logic of our first chore of the day, we chatted and planned our day's activities at the stand-pipe. We went backwards and forwards, to and from the stand-pike, filling buckets as we stashed our family's supplies for the day's needs indoors. Our duty demanded that all work had to be done before the sun came up and before we went to school.

Dogs barked in the distance, some cocks still crowed and radios were beginning to broadcast, "*The Voice of Prophecy*," - an early morning religious programme, on air from America. Mr. Zephryn, a neighbour, was already chopping wood for his fire, while his wife sang along with the radio choir, "*sweetest name on mortal sound, sweetest carol ever song, Jee-ee-sus, Jee-ee-sus, Jee-ee-sus!*"

The aroma of cocoa-tea with cinnamon spice filled our house as Aunt Meena made the breakfast. She fried bakes and salt fish and she too hummed her own hymn.

"Joanne!" she called.

"Yes Auntie Meena!" I answered quickly.

"You pick the *careila* and the other bushes?"

"Yes Auntie."

"You put it in the tub?"

"Yes Auntie."

"Mamie clean clothes press?"

"Yes Auntie."

"Don't forget to put oil in her hair. Ah leaving some bakes here. Make sure you make tea for her before I come back."

"Yes Auntie."

"Get some more wood, rinse out the tub, wash her vest and panties, put it to dry and part her hair in four when you plait it."

My orders for the day were given in quick successive commands. My tasks were set and there was no arguing with that - always accepted in quiet submission, total obedience and life rolled along. You did not cross her path; no, not at all! One day she had hit Ann with a big stick across her back, saying, *"Who cyan hear must feel!"*

I was also a victim of the big stick once because we had sneaked out to Gutt Junction and loitered with what she would call *"good-for-nuthings,"* instead of going to where she had sent us. Of course, Aunt Meena being Aunt Meena did not trust anyone so she secretly followed us. As we had no idea we were being trailed, we did what all the other children usually do; in Aunt Meena's words, we were *"behaving ungodly."* So when she secretly witnessed our loud singing, dancing and proclaiming *"the road make to walk on Carnival day;"* she sneaked up behind us and dished out licks like sharing rice and peas on a Sunday morning, with the big stick she had carried.

Obviously, she assumed that she might have had a need for the whipping stick and as she rained down blows, hitting us willy-nilly, we roared. We screamed and vowed, through the loud tears, never to do it again. Promises were made fervently with the contact of each wild stroke, as it connected painfully with our backsides, legs, arms – wherever it landed!

The day was already beginning to get very warm as dawn gave way to the rising silver sun from the horizon. The village became alive with noises rising to a confusing crescendo. Hens were clucking, donkeys were braying, neighbours could be heard shouting to crying children, punctuated with the odd laugh from nearby houses. This communal orchestra was often added to, with a carnival of radio programmes, as each neighbour's radio competed for the loudest, clearest sound. The myriad of radio sounds were either American soul, American Christian morning worship, the BBC World Service or Radio Antilles.

I could hardly wait for Aunt Meena to leave for town. She was fully dressed and had already made breakfast as well as our lunch, so I waited impatiently. Eventually the bus which was going to take villagers to town came at 7 am. It was laden with colourfully dressed passengers, who were constantly fanning themselves because of the already threatening heat. It collected town-goers on its way down the main road through the village, at intervals along its pot-holed street.

Nearer to the road, the various "*mornings and howdy-do's*" could be heard among the adults as they entered the bus in its usual stop. Here, those journeying to St. Georges would board, assured of a seat all the way to town, as well as a guarantee of a seat on the return journey home.

"Good mahning, good mahning to all," Brother Charles said, greeting the passengers as he entered the bus.

"Mahning Brother!"

"Good mahning Brother Charles!"

"Howdy-do Charles," chorused the various responses within the waiting bus.

"Howdy do, Bro. Charles," Miss Mattis piped singularly, intent on starting up a conversation with Brother Charles.

"The family awright?" enquired Brother Charles.

"Well yes, we dey," came the reply then she lamented. "We not too bad, jus' the rheumatism in me knee and shoulders, stiffness in me legs."

"You take *fever bush*? Drink it with a little *Scotts Emulsion* in the morning. Dey say it good," the confident Charles advised.

"Well, I done try that already - still have to t'ank the good Lord I alive, noh?" Miss Mattis replied.

"Well yes, praise God!" Brother Charles affirmed from the back of the bus.

"Good mahning, howdy do to all," affirmed Miss Ruby, as

she stepped into the bus.

The passengers chatted and fanned themselves as they settled jovially for the journey. One by one, villagers joined the waiting bus; clean, confident and expectant.

"Miss Mattis you dey, howdy do?" Miss Ruby called in a jolly tone, addressing her neighbour. She squeezed past everyone and made for a space next to Miss Mattis.

"Well ah dey, Makomen," came the reply. "I ain't troubling nobody," she teased laughingly.

They were all in good spirits and the bus driver cranked up his engine as they sat squashing one another. Sweaty arms touching floral cotton clothes; powdered faces oozing beads of sweat and the mixed smell of Limacol and perfume wafted through the wooden transporter in the morning breeze. The passengers continued to talk of familiar aches and pains, their last night's dreams and letters they had either expected or received from relatives abroad. Fully loaded, the bus whizzed down the broken tar macadam road with urgency, to its destination in St. Georges.

Saturday churchgoers to the Seventh Day Adventist Church walked briskly on both sides of the road up to the junction. Taxis tooted for business as they cruised down the road for ambitious travellers and very soon, the village atmosphere became quiet. It felt as if Gran-gran and I were the only ones left behind.

Our little house stood on concrete pillars 50 yards away from the main road. A damsel tree fronted the little path of red earth, interspersed with one or two big stepping-stones that led to our home. Around this sanctity were *sweet bush, careila* and *black sage*, to the left of our house. Gran-gran said that *black sage* was good for fever and colds.

"*Careila* cleanses the blood," she had told me one day. "That *bitter-bush* over there is good for your inside and outside too," she would tutor me as we walked past. I was coached about the varieties and cures from our land and I learned to recognise the natural herbal remedies by sight. The *lemon grass* which she tended behind the house was good for tea and slight fever. They were all close at hand, Gran-gran's medicine chest - a potent garden of island remedy; growing natural, respected and free in our yard.

A *golden-apple* tree stood at the back of the house and to the side, facing the main road, was a short *avocado pear* tree. A *governor plum* tree was close to our house and it was like a magnet to passing children who constantly picked the fruit. The *jump-up-and-kiss-me* with its red flowers was to the left of the house. As children, we used the colour of this juicy, red flower to smear the bitter red colouring, as pretend lipstick, on our lips. We also rubbed it onto our finger nails, staining them as pretend nail varnish.

Hibiscus and *bougainvillea* formed a little hedge fencing in front of the house next to the *damsel* tree, which bared its rugged roots into the earth. The naked roots looked like the model of a spider, whose legs were permanently stuck in the brown earth. Under this tree we had often sat at nights listening to 'Nancy stories' and occasionally, we dug holes while playing in the earth. The area around this tree looked worn and tired; terrorized from our constant, rough and energetic play.

Gran-gran and I sat in the verandah at the back of the house pounding cocoa. The huge, stone mortar stood in the middle of the small room like a big fat barrel with a hole in the middle of its belly. It was ready to take the smooth, dark, crispy beans as they were tossed into it. This ageless monument from the past, had survived the many years of our island's political and social alteration. It was a relic of plantation days, just like the huge grinding stone which was forever parked up at the back of the house. They had been around for "as long as I can remember," Gran-gran had told me. I looked at the mortar and ran my palms over the cold, defiant hard stone and wondered what thoughts had encouraged the smooth, deliberate hands of its maker, to fashion such an island archetype.

There, always in the corner it stood; unbroken, unblemished, and untouched by Time's constant changes. Like the grinding stone, its partner, it stood watching and witnessing the passing of years, the passing of men and women: the ruled and the rulers. It stood there still, like a granite soldier on duty for life.

Our tête-à-tête began as Gran-gran pounded the hard wooden pestle onto the cocoa beans. She crushed them in the mortar until they became a greasy, smooth black mass. It was her task for today and she sat as usual, in front of the cold, round, stone-tub, caressing the pestle as she intermittently changed her grip on it to pound the coco beans. She pounded and pounded the beans relentlessly; cracking and crunching them as she did so.

The next lot of beans was tossed into the mortar and she pounded and pounded as if to revenge some mental experience or to obliterate some present un-welcomed thoughts. The pounding and bashing of the beans was invigorating; it made her sweat with exhaustion or pleasure. Carefully, I watched her moist coffee-coloured face give birth to beads of sweat as they raced down her face, stopping momentarily at the tip of her nose; then swiftly meeting other droplets in their watery race, they climaxed at her chin, before drip-dropping onto her cotton frock.

My job was to mop up the sweat from her face each time her skin expelled the watery trickles that ran into her eyes. However, she moved that pestle up and down into the mortar with such determination and vigour, that at times, it was difficult for me to catch the swiftly rolling droplets. Now and then, armed with a face-flannel, and when I could skillfully avoid obstructing her pounding rhythm, I would stop their bold watery journey as they raced down to her chin just before they fell onto her dress.

Her beautiful silvery-grey hair was parted down the middle of her head showing four plaits; two on each side at the front and two on each side at the back. Her neck was held taut and looked strong with each bounce of the wooden pestle. Just like a robot, Gran-Gran crushed the helpless cocoa beans with the pestle into the mortar until the mixture formed a thick, brownish black, squeezable lump. This very aromatic, pulpy mass was patted and eventually rolled into a big shapeless lump. From it, Gran-gran tore off small amounts which she rolled between her palms into balls. Afterwards, she carefully placed the balls onto a tray lined with banana leaves, where they were left to become hard.

The sun was up in the sky, dominating the island with its hot and punishing rays. The water in Gran-gran's tub sat still, in quiet submission, while the fireball above took vengeance on the baking earth and simultaneously infused the water with its heat. Then our tête-à-tête began.

"I didn' know my father," Gran-gran told me. "Hard work kill him on *beke* plantation. He worked hard-hard; ah don' even remember what he look like," she said thoughtfully.

My day's lesson had begun, so I sighed with contentment.

"Do you have a picture of him?" I asked.

"No chile," she said soothingly, "Our people didn' take pictures. In dem days you had to survive. Food come firs' and we didn' have camera."

I nodded in a grown up way to show that I understood.

"Only *beke* have camera," she added as an afterthought.

"What did he do? Ah mean my great-grand father," I asked, probing further.

"He had a mule, a big strong mule. The bes' mule in Gutt and that Mr. McDonald did like him too," she continued animatedly.

To me, it sounded a little odd that 70 year old Gran-gran was still calling someone "*mister.*" Age was indeed respected but always from younger to old generation. Gran-gran was not younger than Mr. McDonald. In fact, he was the son of a White Scottish plantation owner; formerly *Master*, now *Mister* McDonald. The years after slavery had not changed that. To Gran-gran he was, and it seems always will be, "*Mister*" McDonald.

I listened intently, sometimes feeling too young to ask probing questions, in case it was considered over-stepping the mark, but I wanted to know more. Luckily, for the moment, Gran-Gran seemed to be comfortable with recounting her past.

"Was Mr. McDonald a good man?" I enquired, wanting the precious time with her to continue in more conversation.

She was silent for a short while. She seemed to be considering what answer to give me. This response was not as spontaneous as the others, and right now, her eyes did not level with mine as before.

Her head was still bent and the moist brown parting in her hair now looked like a T-junction in the middle of her head. As she looked up, her mouth showed signs of secrecy. Her lips pressed each other as if to say "lips are sealed." She looked at me and her sad cataract eyes were a greyish brown. As the head of our family, Gran-gran was less talkative. The children, meaning our parents, did the arguing but when reasoning and good sense was required, she was called on. This was usually to either add her seal of approval or impose a final judgment on a debatable point. She often did this in parable or in *patwa*, murdering the broken-French words as her own and curtailing children's eavesdropping.

I've come to realise that she used the *patwa* to give adult advice or when some personal things needed to be said among adults to exclude our young ears. Perhaps this was one of her most personal moment. I could sense it, because right now, there was certainly no *patwa* for me! Instead, she pursed her lips and looked at me with flickering eyelids. I had not seen her eyelids flicker for a long time. Today, they jerked and danced, almost as if to shut off or stifle the memory of trapped, emotional pain located there.

The last time I had witnessed similar eyelid tremours, was when she had heard about the death of uncle Clyde, her oldest son in England. At that time, she looked as if she wanted to bawl out loudly but some strange unseen hand had seemingly clasped itself over her voice-box, baring the explosive sound she wanted to let out. Instead, the overwhelming pain had travelled to her eyes. Her eyelids had flickered and danced and rebelled; trying to squeeze tears from her eyes. Eventually, when the floodgates were opened, voice found itself, she leashed out a bawling that was no longer restricted. She had groaned as if she was wounded beyond measure.

Today, it seemed that I had awakened yet another sad and painful memory, so my heartbeats were thud-thudding loudly in my chest for fear our session might stop. After a brief moment, Gran-gran said that Mr. McDonald was kind to her family after her mother had died.

"Very kin'," she stressed, when she had regained emotional composure. She gritted her teeth as she often did when stressed and continued talking. I know she had quickly skipped over the pain and papered over the hurtful cracks of her life. Instead, she glossed over the details and continued with her flow of answers to my questions.

"You see that saddle under the house in the corner?" She quizzed, cheerfully changing the subject. I nodded.

"Well ah keep it there. The mule done dead and gone and ah have nothing, so ah keep the saddle."

I wasn't surprised. That saddle has always been there; nobody talked about it or bothered with it. It remained there quietly just like the mortar and grinding stone; relics from the past that stood there voiceless but reminding.

The sun was moving fast to the overhead position and I went round the back of the yard to inspect the now greenish water in the tub. It was warm and the green *careila* bush and its herbal companions which I had put in earlier, now lay limped and resigned. I began to squash the vine together, then vigorously rubbed the handfuls of squelching bush before I squeezed them. I continued to scrup-scrup the soggy leaves with my palms until the limped, crumpled vine had oozed out all its green goodness into the tepid water. The herb-infused, emerald-green water was now ready for Gran-gran's bath.

As I bathed Gran-gran, I recalled my thoughts about the people, including Auntie Irene, who had left the island for England. I was only five years old then but certainly not too young to be puzzled and feel hurt the day the boat left St. Georges harbour. That morning, no one had told me when Auntie Irene was finally leaving the bus. I did not see her go. That is why, despite promises of sweets and future trips to town, I had cried loudly, deafening the passengers on the bus all the way home from the harbour.

I had been thinking about England for many weeks. Those who had left seemed to have gone forever. Before they left there were many weeks of talking, planning, praying and crying, as Auntie Irene prepared to leave the nest.

Her older brother, uncle Clyde, had died over a year ago in

England. "The cold kill him," I overheard my Aunt Irene telling Miss Letisha. England's cold was blamed for all kinds of ills and without the details of the death, it was the standard conclusion. Ironically, despite the bad news, Aunt Irene was also preparing to go to England and a good *bon voyage* send-off event was planned.

Preparations for the send-off brought all kinds of confusion to my five year old mind and the biggest bombshell of all was the fact that the woman I had always called "Auntie Irene" *was* really my mother and not Gran-gran! Everyone in the village, young and old, had called my mum 'Aunty,' so did I, and as a result I followed suit, never calling anyone 'mum' or 'mother.' However, the night before the departure, my mother had bathed me and promised that I would not miss anything, since she was going to make sure that I woke up in the early hours of the morning for the long journey to the harbour in town. By going there, she had said, I would be able to witness her departure.

Splash! Rub! Splash! Rub! Water was poured over my head like a mighty waterfall as the bowlfuls were splashed onto my head. The water rushed from head to toe, forming multiples of streams down my body, legs and hands and collecting in the dented enamel basin in which I stood. Big hands rubbed my face, sliding, speedily with one quick brush-stroke over my entire face, squashing my eyes, nose and mouth together. Another bowlful of water came cascading down.

"You must listen to what Mamie say," she said.

Splash! Rub! Rub! Wipe!

"I'll write letter to Meena."

More water was poured in this ceremonious fashion and each bowlful was preceded by an instruction.

"Learn your work good in school to pass your exams."

Splash! Rub!

"Remember you must have a *destiny*!" she stressed, then cleared her throat.

It was the first time I had heard the word "*destiny*" but there was no time to ask what it meant. She continued swiftly with what seemed like her last rite, by splashing water, rubbing and cleansing me, in preparation for bed.

"I'll send for you when you get big." The last words.

Splash! Splash!

As quickly as it had begun, my mother's instructions were over and so ended the brief moments of her dutiful activities.

After the instructions, came the equally ceremonious rubbing down with coconut oil. I was smeared with quick dabs on to my face, smoothed and loved momentarily. Then my arms legs and back too were stretched and pampered. The last quick care was over and we were finished.

My sleeping clothes were put on and immediately I was put to bed, while the commotion in the dark night continued. Excitement, crying and farewells followed as neighbours and well-wishers came to the house to give their last *words of comfort*. Following protocol, they gave comforting words to Gran-gran but for Auntie Meena, came words of wisdom to "*Be strong on the other shores*" and "*Go with God's speed*."

"Sister Irene, I wish you God's speed!" Brother Littleman called out.

Everyone called him "*Brother Littleman*" because he was a 'brother' in the Baptist church, which was practically our family church. Others sang, "*God be with you till we meet again*." The tone had the same monotonous drool, rather like a funeral song and I didn't like it. It scared me because it made people cry. Men gave the bass and tenor, whilst the alto and soprano were blended a-cappella-style in the, "*Till we mee-ee-eet, Till we mee-ee-eet*." As they sang, sniffles could be heard at the next line, *"Till we meet at Jesus feet."* But Auntie Irene was strong and she showed no signs of weakening. There certainly was no changing of her mind, no reversing the status quo and there was to be no change of heart; to England she was bound, in the morning.

Quickly, gaining composure after the tearful line, the men and women embraced in the most respectful way. Both persons would put their arms together then clasped them together at the chest; then fully stretched out to the side; whilst neck-to-neck they would meet to the right and left. Afterwards, together they would be fully outstretched upwards above heads, then come downwards, before clasping together again at the chest. In such a manner, the familiar Spiritual Baptist courtesy completed the parting farewell. There is no doubt that the sound of the church bell ringing and the smell of burning candle would echo in their memories, until the time they will meet again.

Gran-gran did not get ready. She was not going to the harbour. She had cried before in church and was not crying now. Auntie Irene had packed her suitcase and it laid on the table, waiting for her departure. The grip, as everyone called the suitcase, had four aluminum corners which shone in the darkness like giant cat's eyes; whilst the white label which was taped in the middle, looked like a square mouth. The filter of light from the other room reassured me and I tossed and turned in the bed, waiting for the quietness that would lull me to sleep. Through their whispers and sniffling, I heard Blackie, our dog, yelp after a loud angry voice had probably hit it. Afterwards, I fell asleep, dreaming that I could fly.

Passengers bound for England were dressed and ready in the early morning. The special bus arrived and stopped outside our house but it was still dark outside and the light from the house lamps cast giant shadows on the partitions from the moving figures of everyone in the house. Some moved hurriedly, like dancing silhouettes in a game of hide-and-seek, as bodies crossed the light intermittently, then disappeared.

Soon the night had given way to early dawn and the grip was taken down from the table and fastened to the roof of the waiting bus and I felt a little confused, not knowing exactly what was going on. They had put my best clothes on and I sat on the chair, looking like the English child in my reading book, dressed in a blue can-can dress, white ribbons, white socks and black patent shoes.

I sat there and tried to imagine what being in England would be like. I had read my favourite English book so many times that I could remember every word on each page. Everything with the slightest connection to England was of interest to me then and I had fantasized what it must be like for that little girl surrounded by children standing around an ice-cream van, to the sound of "ting-a-ling-a-ling" in England. I sat in the corner swinging my dangling legs and pretended that I too was going to England. Then big strong hands grabbed me and placed me on soft warm laps in the bus so I held onto the back of the seat in front of me.

The early morning air was fresh and nearby cocks crowed repeatedly to the echoing of other cocks on Murray Hill in the distance. Despite this, the village was asleep as the special bus with migrants for England made its way to the harbour in town. There, they would board Her Majesty's Ship for an onward 21-day journey to Southampton, England.

The bus had reached the harbour-side for some time before I woke up to the sound of laughing and chattering from people who were rushing backwards and forwards outside. It was already first light and the harbour was active. A giant ship stood on the sea in the distance with strong masts, surrounded by small yachts. They bobbed up and down on the water, welcoming the rising sun in the horizon and the silvery sky around it. Auntie Irene had gone with her things to get ready for the big boat; that's what Auntie Meena had old me; though I could not see her. I became anxious and I began to cry because no one had bothered to wake me when we had arrived here.

"Wait you'll see her in a minute," Miss Mattis said, trying to console me.

There were only three people on the bus - the driver, Miss Mattis who was an old lady from the village, on whose leg I now sat and me. I was crying louder now because I wanted to see the passengers for England again before they left. I struggled desperately to recognise the many bodies hurrying with quickened steps outside. Shadows of people came and went and then lessened. I strained to see where Auntie Irene was but there were too many faces. There were too many colourful clothes, felt-hats on men's head and women waving with gloved hands. They were in their best dresses, wiping their sweaty foreheads with handkerchiefs. They chatted, smiled and greeted each other. Their straightened hair-dos glistened in the new light, as they fanned themselves furiously. I could not see Auntie Irene.

"Look over there!" the driver said, pointing in the direction of the boats with strong masts.

"There she is - she's waving! Look over there, wave to her," Miss Mattis coaxed.

Although I could not see her, I waved. I could not tell which wave was my mum's, as everyone in the distance was waving at the same time. Handkerchiefs looked like colourful flags and the sea of smiling faces, laughter, talking and tooting of horns caused instant confusion in this early morning carnival. The boat belched out mouthfuls of black fumes from its hollow chimney, then it boo-hoood loudly, as it shifted slowly away from the pier.

There was cheering as the noise reached a crescendo. Then slowly, the noise lessened as the boat distanced itself from us. Further and further it moved away from the pier and then in no time, the performance seemed to be over. The travellers to England had taken their last bow on Grenada's stage. It was as if applause had died down with the boohooing of the ship, as it signalled its last farewell. It was also as if on a stage, the curtains had come down to signal the end of this present Act and Scene.

Chapter 2

Attila the Hun (Raymond Quevedo)

I rubbed the *careilla* once more, squeezing the limped leaves to a pulpy mass, daring its efficacious power to infuse the sun-soaked water; then Gran-gran stepped into the herbal preparation. She sapped her wet shoulders repeatedly as if to drive out the arthritic pain there. Then I began the bathing routine by rubbing her back. The green water lovingly formed a glistening glow, caressing her body, enriching, curing and strengthening it. I had learnt just where to rub her and also what amount of pressure to apply; especially in areas where Gran-gran had said it made her feel good. She closed her eyes and hummed a hymn as I cared for her.

The ritual washing over, she got dressed and went to sit inside on the edge of the bed, where I was instructed to rub *Thermogene* into her shoulders, sap *Bay rum* into her ankles and some *Limacol* was dabbed behind her ears and chest. The rest of her body was oiled and massaged. The brown, elasticized skin, had nurtured years of resistant ageing flesh and now it continued to live on, to teach and to exist. I rubbed coconut oil into the painful bunions and gently massaged and soothed them, before I proceeded to cut her tough toenails.

Gran-gran was careful where the cut pieces of toenail went and I gathered them into her hands. It was as if I had to give account for each and every cut piece of nail which she then wrapped carefully in a leaf or held in her warm fist.

Her clean clothes were fleecy and warm too: a brown two-tiered skirt reaching above the ankles which matched her long-sleeved bodice. The bodice was buttoned down the front and it fell below her waist. The outfit had its own cloth-belt which she tied at the front and moved to the side to hang there. When she stood up, the starched, crispy white, petticoat just showed about half an inch of delicate filigree lace, decorating her glistening oiled feet and she looked thoroughly satisfied. Her face too looked revitalised, reflecting a feeling of inner peace, which radiated with contentment on the outside.

"Part it in four," she told me, as I combed the silky, silvery hair.

I had teased the plaits with the pointed end of the comb and undid them so that they looked like crinkly, curly segments. I combed through them, being careful not to tug or pull on any knotted ends. Her curly hair was called "*dougla*," meaning of mixed breed. I combed the soft shoulder-length waves repeatedly. Then using the big tooth of the comb I gave little satisfying scratches here and there in the scalp or wherever she asked. She closed her eyes as sleep nudged her intermittently through the combing.

"When will the boat get to England?" I asked her. Although her eyes were closed I didn't want her to go to sleep. But it was obvious that my gentle combing was sending her into a place of sweet repose because she was nodding off to sleep. But I needed her to be awake and we had barely begun my planned catalogue of questions for the day.

"Gran-gran, the boat," I repeated, but there was silence, so I deliberately scratched the middle of her head hard to wake her. She woke up immediately and complained that I was being too rough with her head.

"When will it reach England?" I asked again.

"Reach what?" she asked. She obviously had not heard a word I said earlier.

"Auntie Irene and the boat to England," I reminded her.

"Oh Ho! Well that boat go take 21 days - three weeks. Englan' is far away, chile."

"Twenty one days? How will they get out and do things?" I asked in disbelief. I could only imagine their situation as compared to what Justin, Emma's brother, had told us a jail was like.

ع

Justin told us that he heard the men talking outside Mr. Zephryn's rum shop about what prison was like, when the news about Sukram had been announced on the radio. The news was that Sukram, a crazy Indian man, had harpooned Itran, his best friend, when they went fishing. Apparently after killing Itran, Sukram then hacked off his friend's head and carried the bleeding, horror throughout the streets of Belair, saying, "I catch a big fish today." Everyone bawled fearfully, making signs of the cross, whilst gathering their children, dashing into their houses and furiously slamming their front doors behind them.

Sukram had become insane and everyone was uttering variations of, "Oh My God!" shocked at the nightmare before them.

"Bon Je!

"Papa Gawd, oh!"

"Gade mize-mwen, noh!"

What drove Sukram to commit such a heinous crime was not untypical among adults in the Caribbean in general. Unrequited love, betrayal, disappointment, unfaithfulness, those hurt by children being born out of wedlock, and women discovering their own children's extra siblings from their partner's undeclared, or *outside the basket* relationships; was common. Sukram, it seems, had similar issues with his wife and best friend, which resonated with the fear of being turned into a cuckold. He therefore took evasive action that was guaranteed to land him in jail for life.

Some time before this horror, Sukram had heard gossips about Itran and his wife Lola but Lola had denied it. She swore her faithfulness to her husband by telling him that she would cut her neck on a block, if she had to, in order to prove her innocence and loyalty to him. Itran had sworn too, on his mother's grave, that he did not have a relationship with Lola, stressing that he could never deceive his best friend. Feeling satisfied to hear all this, the two men renewed their life-long friendship; by reminiscing about their good, old days together. During this emotional upheaval, Sukram had secretly prayed for the gossip to be false. He did not want to believe there could be any truth in it and confessed to the other two, that he felt bad inside, for having listened to such 'wild rumours' in the first place.

Nevertheless, as time wore on his thoughts nagged him and he continued to feel self-conscious and secretly hurt. He was never sure when people looked at him whether they had been talking about him. If anyone remained quiet in a conversation it unnerved him, so he consoled himself, more often than usual, in Grenada's finest rum. Increasingly, he had found it difficult to live with the very thought of his wife and best friend cheating on him. Therefore, to satisfy his curiosity and to regain his waning confidence, Sukram decided one day that he would follow the pair, instead of going to work.

It is rumoured that on this particular day, having followed his wife Lola to a hidden spot in the nearby Estate, Sukran saw her and Itran making love below the cocoa trees. His shocked eyes followed them as they came out from behind the bushes. Lola was quickly doing-up her dress-buttons at the front and then she dusted herself while Itran fussed with his fly-zip.

Afterwards, Sukram mischievously grabbed at her and she playfully ran away from him, so he ran after Lola and they looked like children playing hide and seek. The two lovers laughed when the chase was over; unaware that Sukram had been spying on them. As a result, he became emotionally distraught and turned to drinking large quantities of rum every day. Being helplessly drunk, the depressed Sukram would often cry in the rum shop. There, his drinking pals would commiserate with him and make suggestions as to what they would do, if it was them.

How Itran and Lola had deceived him! The part of him which had refused to believe the gossips deeply pained him; whilst the nagging voice that had condemned them, laughed and jeered at him. It made him look like the fool that he was afraid of becoming - the laughing stock of the village; a cuckold!

"Oh Gawd! Oh Gawd!" he was heard saying on the day he had seen them together. Shock had overtaken Sukram and he held his chest as if he had suffered a heart attack. Afterwards, he went to the rum show to drown his deep sorrow in very large measures of rum. They said that his eyes went wild with rage and he began to talk to himself but mostly he cried repeatedly, "*Not my Lola*!" and "*Not my best friend*!"

Even before the verdict was passed in Court, neighbours had tried to reason with Lola. It was her fault they had told her. She had provoked the man to commit murder. The radio announcement later publicized the verdict of the crime.

"Today in court, forty-year-old Sukram Cheema was jailed for life, for the murder of Itran Joseph of Paraclete, St. Andrews."

Lola could not deal with the guilt and horror of the situation. She banned her belly and bawled for days before taking their three children and running away to live with her sister in St. David.

So Sukram went to jail for life. Emma's brother told us that he heard that jail was bad; the worst place to be.

"You don't get to come out; you eat, shit and sleep in the same place and nobody cares if you sick or die. Cooped up like a cage animal!" he said as he tutored our attentive ears.

ع

I had imagined Auntie Irene and the people going to England to be cooped up just like that, since they could not really turn back. There was only one way the boat could go and that was forward. But it was true, they were locked up somewhere on the big ship, as it seemed to re-enact a second Trilogy. Theirs was a journey of reversal; like new slaves, eating, sleeping, shitting and being sick in the same place, on their way to England. Some would make it there, find a job, a home and come back home rich. Others would not. It was common knowledge that a few of those who had found England too tough to exist in, if they were lucky, could escape to America with the help of travelled friends or family there. Few had, for different reasons, died in England.

Gran-gran was fully awake now because she slapped a

handful of sand-flies that were stinging her right ankle. This caused my greasy fingers to lose my grip of the plait, and the weaving strands slithered out of my hand. Eventually, I tucked the completed end into the body of the plait and Gran-gran's shawl was put around her shoulders, forming a tie in the middle of her chest. She sighed with relief when I took the familiar book from the shelf. The large print seemed to jump out from the front page of the battered-looking manual, *WORDS OF COMFORT* it advised. It had been my job daily, to impart such guidance by reading them out aloud to Gran-gran. This I did, as soon as I was old enough to read.

Gran-gran positioned herself in a comfortable corner in the verandah, so that she could see all who went by along the road, in front of our house. People from cars waved to her or tooted their horns. She sat there like the Queen of Sheba; black and comely, clean and contented. Just then, Miss Joseph's voice could be heard greeting Miss Cleothilda in the house nearby. She had finished her morning task at the local estate, which was cutlassing grass under the cocoa trees, in readiness for the picking of the cocoa pods.

Miss Joseph was a tall, skinny woman, wearing black Wellington boots. She held a cutlass in her right hand, just as the men did and a small cocoa basket was cushioned on her head by a *kata*. This *kata* was a thickly folded piece of cloth in a circular shape; used to ease the hardness of the basket and the heavy weight she carried on her head. Miss Joseph's *kata* was very thick and it made the basket on her head look as if it was doing a balancing act over her small head and long neck.

Her damp, sweaty clothes were stuck to her sweaty body and she looked as if someone had just thrown a bucket of water all over her. Her face glistened with the rows of sweat which were trickling down it and she stopped in front of the gap between the road and our verandah. She relieved the weight of the coca basket by resting it under the damsel tree and wiped her wet brow with the back of her hand. Then she sat in the coolness of the shade and fanned her body with her loose skirt, so that it rose and fell, making balloons of air underneath her.

"Makome!" she called out to Gran-gran.

"Howdy do - Howdy do!" Gran-gran replied.

"Wha' happenin' dey?"

"Well ah dey, just the rheumatism in the shoulder, lancing me night and day but still ah in the land of the livin', God be praised," Gran-gran reasoned.

"Amen!" Miss Joseph pronounced. "You try *soft candle*? Is dat what de give me ah ease-up. My son sen' and tell me to buy cod liver oil. Well you know how things hard with him in Trinidad, but he sen' me a little change to buy the cod liver oil."

Then she swiftly continued, "Eh, it real good!"

"Well, dat's good. But me, papa me't! It ent have nothing better than the bush remedy and a good bush tea noh!" Gran-gran declared.

Gran-gran had already tried soft candle and she told Miss Joseph so. She had tried the Bay rum and Thermogene, before she tried *pepper-leaf,* and *bush tea*; her own concoction of *bois den leaves, cloves, black sage, spice sticks* and *ginger*. These had brought her complete relief she had said. That's why they were the preferred remedies. She swore that bush medicine was better than any doctor's medicine.

"Young people just don't know what good for them when dey sick," she said and Miss Joseph agreed.

I was sitting on the floor in front of the Gran-gran, ready to read the "*WORDS OF COMFORT*" from her book, but she nudged me to go and get a cup of cool water for Miss Joseph.

"Ay-ay! Chile you dey!" Miss Mattis said, addressing me in surprise. "Go and bring your Nenen some water. God will bless you," she coaxed.

Promptly, I disappeared from the verandah leaving the two women to gossip freely.

"So you hear Boysie dead eh," said Miss Joseph.

"Eh heh! Boysie who?"

"Boysie for Miss Flora, behind the corner in Soubies. They say he take a stroke and by the time Miss Flora run outside for help, when she come back, he well dead, man."

"Well ah sorry to hear dat," Gran said, propping up her chin with her hand and resting it on the banister of the verandah.

"Uh huh, the funeral is day after tomorrow in the Anglican church in La Bay. But you know, when God call for us too, is so we have to go," Miss Joseph reasoned.

"Yes! Yes!" Gran-gran agreed.

I was in the kitchen now and the women's voices lowered into a whisper.

"Listen noh, I hear Letisha belly big!" Miss Joseph whispered.

I pretended to rattle the pan-cups to convince the women that the noise was drowning their confidential mutterings from my hearing.

"Eh heh? What a way children does bring shame on their parent's head, instead of raising their nose."

Gran-gran whispered back then continued, "Well you know you make children but you doh make their mind and I been through de same shame myself. Papa Gawd self see ah did try me bes'."

"And mama oh! The girl aunt *didn'* know eh! Is hear, she hear it from *ole talk* and put question to the girl. Ah hear she bawl and bawl and say she doh want no children playing big ooman and breeding under the same roof as her, because it's not respec'ful."

"Bon Je, gade mize non!" Gran-gran replied.

"Well Cousin Seeviny had to hold Jean down to stop her beating up Letisha, in case she add more disgrace by killing her own sister child and the baby in she belly at the same time. I hear she vex, vex, vex with so much shame. She say she can't eat, especially since the girl mother is all the way in England. She 'fraid they will say the woman let her daughter go astray."

"Well ah sorry to hear that eh," Gran-gran answered then continued. "Well, when my own chile had her turn, ah did guess something was wrong because when I was washing clothes, I me-self, didn' see no clothes with blood for a month and a half. Instead, she was eating green mango like a cow, and playing shy-shy when mornin' time come."

I returned with the water and so did a temporary flourishing of *patwa*.

"Pale *Patwa*, petite moun ka rive," Gran-gran had quickly warned her that I was coming and Miss Joseph automatically replied in *patwa*.

"Se kon ca tout moun an famina-a ye."

Poor Letisha, her family had a bad reputation for this kind of disaster and that's what Miss Joseph told Gran-gran.

But I knew some *patwa* too, yet it was amazing how the grown-ups always thought that when it suited them to talk to us in *patwa* we would respond and when they needed to exclude us from their conversations, we would somehow wipe out all knowledge of the island language from our minds. It was like a game and everyone played it.

"O t'ank you chile," Miss Joseph said to me, as she took the cup of water.

She spat out the piece of straw that was at the corner of her lips, and then took the cup of water from me. She drank the water at such speed that after four "Gluck! Gluck! Gluck! Gluck!" The water disappeared down her throat to a satisfactory, "Aaah!"

"So you say the funeral is day after tomorrow, ah go try and pay me respecs," Gran-gran told her, trying to make out that the issue with the deceased Boysie was the only subject of their conversation.

"Maybe Telfa could drop me down dey, so we go meet up," she concluded.

The conversation had become awkward with me standing there quietly with nothing more to do. Miss Joseph gave Gran-gran some yams, four green bananas and some sweet potatoes from her basket. She then busied herself with fixing the bundle. She unfolded the *kata* and folded it again, as she prepared to toss the basket on top of the circular cushion on her head.

"Well Makome!" she said, "Since mahnin' ah on me feet."

Miss Joseph grabbed the basket with a tight grip and tossed it on top of her *kata* and her head and neck received the heavy weight. With the bundle firmly on her head and the cutlass in hand once more, she made her departure.

"God willing, we go see tomorrow."

"Awright, Awright Makome! Walk good," Gran-gran replied.

Gran-gran sighed as Miss Joseph left. Deep in thought she stared across the road into the leafy green distance, then shook her head. That tell-tale, 'I-can't-believe-it-how-disappointing' head-shake, was common among all the women when they heard bad news. I offered her the waiting *WORDS OF COMFORT* and she became composed again. I read her favourite passage repeatedly as she had instructed: "THE LORD JESUS SAID LET NOT YOUR HEART BE

TROUBLED. YE BELIEVE IN GOD, BELIEVE ALSO IN ME."

By the fourth repetition, I looked up and Gran-gran had fallen asleep. She was breathing gently, her arms folded, head bowed and her chin resting on her chest. I covered her legs with a cotton sheet and finished the line in case my movement had woken her up.

"IF IT WERE NOT SO I WOULD HAVE TOLD YOU". I read the last few lines deliberately, slowing down the pace, "I GO-TO- PREPARE-A PLACE-FOR YOU-AND-I WILL-COME AGAIN AND ..."

Then very quietly, I closed the book and tip-toed out of the house, leaving her undisturbed and peaceful.

I went outside and quickly rinsed the bathtub and washed her underclothes, just as Auntie Meena had ordered. Then I left them to dry on the line. Gaily, I skipped out of the yard to look for my best friend Emma.

Emma's house was about quarter of a mile away from ours. Her mother had also gone to England the year before Auntie Irene. We did everything together. Often swapping stories of what we would do when we eventually joined our mothers in England.

I sprinted up the road and took a short-cut through the trace; a narrow gravelly path through a mango row, which led to the next couple of houses. Everyone used the trace and it was well-known because it saved time going along the main road. It was lined with a variety of tall mango trees, their green leafy branches forming an archway like a giant umbrella, towering above the path. Behind these trees which formed a boundary, were all kinds of cultivated crops; gungo peas, cocoa, nutmeg, banana, bluggoe, yams and plantain. One or two avocado pear trees were on the left hand side of the trace and a little ravine which was surrounded by healthy calaloo patches ran at the bottom of it. It belonged to Mr. Mitchell.

Mr. Mitchell had been to England, having lived there for seven years. He had bought eight acres of land, while in England, which his brother had taken care of for him. Now, having returned from England, they both work on the land. Although Mr. Mitchell was kind and generous, his neighbours still secretly helped themselves to his crops without asking. A deeply religious man, his attitude was that 'the Lord would always provide abundantly' for him. For this, he prayed and sang very loudly in church on Sundays.

As I walked briskly up the path, I could see Justin, Emma's cousin, approaching. He was 12 years old and was always making sweet eyes at me. Once he confidently told Emma that when he grows up he would marry me. I had laughed at the thought, though I felt flattered that anyone could feel this way about me because I was not as attractive as Emma.

I was a lonely child, surrounded by people but yet alone. I did not have many friends because our family was deeply religious and as a result, we lived an over-protected life style. No running around with boys or having them to call out to us when the elders were around us. It was considered undisciplined and disrespectful to our elders. So ultimately, girls eyed boys and boys eyed them back; taking every secret opportunity to hang out with them, if they could. That's why the talking and intimacy was left for times when boys met girls and girls met boys behind their parents back. So I cherished Emma as a gem of my youth.

One rainy day when the three of us were inside their house sheltering the heavy downpour and Emma's back was turned, Justin had squeezed my small, painful seed-like breasts. The pain had made me squeal so I bit his hand. I was proud of my newly developing chest size, though they looked like two huge seedy bumps. I checked their size daily, prodding at the size of the slowly growing mounds; each time speculating how much they had grown. My friends' bodies were changing too and we discussed the changes daily in the school playground.

We swapped stories about whose thighs were thickening, ways in which others had experienced having their monthly periods and the noticeable tell-tale stripes behind girls' calves which signaled they had become a "young woman." This was the signal that boys read, the girls thought. Yet the boys knew that girls were instructed not to talk to them on first having their periods. Conversely, and as a result, it seemed to draw them to girls more; as bees to honey.

So girls wanted their hair straightened after their periods, to show that they had become "big". At the same time, parents attempted to prepare their daughters' approaching signs of womanhood, by forcing them to wear childish dresses with bands that tied at the back, as well as socks and shoes. No straightened hair was allowed. It was felt that these ploys kept the inquisitive wandering males at bay.

As Justin reached me we both stopped.

"Emma home?" I enquired.

He winked at me and then said, "Uh huh!" He moved towards me with an imitated step forward and he stood right in front of my path, defiantly staring into my eyes. That boy just like to *moless* people, I thought to myself.

He was a cocky boy who prided himself on telling us what the grown-up men had often talked about. He copied their speech patterns and always talked with a blade of grass in the corner of his lips. He also spat frequently, especially when he felt he had our full attention. Justin's mastery of male mannerisms and the unfettered level of freedom which his dad had given him, though considered by others as too much, had impressed us.

"That boy is *a Thomas*!" his father once said outside the rum shop one day, slapping Justin proudly on the shoulders and boasting to his rum-drinking comrades.

"He's a real *Thomas* man!" he told them, as if to convince himself of that too. Usually, if his wife was within hearing distance, he would make sure that she heard what he had to say by speaking loudly, so that she also received the liquor-induced instructions via his advice to Justin.

"Bwoy, tell your mother to get you a good, strong pair of leather shoes and learn to walk straight in them. Nobody go say a *Thomas* cyan walk good in leather shoes. When I was your age man, I didn' wear no *Washicon*! I always used to smell sweet, with a straight part in my hair and had clean clothes on me. And you should've seen me, bright too! Nobody did know about Shakespeare, Blake and Wordsworth more than me noh! Nowadays, dem fellas talking 'bout Rasta living in mountain and going back to Africa."

Then he sucked his teeth with a long, loud, "Stupes!"
His dad's friend piped in, "Dat's true, man! The fellas and dem playing reggae and singing shit too, not calypso any more."

"Yeah man, in those days we could sing calypsos and *had* to know how to write poems; like that poem, em...em..," he hesitated, searching frantically for the words.

"Yes, I know the one you mean: *The boy stood on the burning deck, whence all but he had fled.*" Justin's dad's utterance of the pure Standard English sentence sounded foreign. Then he turned in the direction of his son and interrogated him.

"Bwoy, you know that poem?" he enquired, looking seriously now at the boy.

"Yes daddy!"

"Yeah man! You *is* a *Thomas* for sure!" he declared happily, as he murdered the English verb.

He took another swig of the measure of rum without a chaser. Then noisily he rested the small glass down before continuing his lament.

"Etymology, phonology, syntax, prosody," he said, holding his head with both hands, as if the stop a confusion inside his head. Then he looked down on the table searching for more run. His linguistic mastery was given further utterance by the third or fourth swig of rum and as always, he would regress to a time in his youth – that of his hopes, successes, failures and regrets.

Justin was growing up like him; pompous, overbearing and a know-it-all. He traded on his father's boastful predictions that he, the young *Thomas*, was going to be a lawyer. "Yes liar, not lawyer!" we used to tease him and he would run after us, threatening to hit us.

"Don't go and work on the land below no cocoa tree bwoy!" his dad advised him. "Get away from all these rum-heads and vagabonds it have around here. Put something in your head, then you wont have to dirty-up you hand, working on anybody land."

This was his constant advice to Justin. Clearly his perceptions of the rum-heads excluded himself, because he figured that a *Thomas,* despite present circumstances, was considered above all ridicule or wrong!

"Look at Cleveland!" he said to Justin, who by then was standing alongside his dad and being slapped on his back again with heavy hands. Trapped in this situation, Justin was made to listen to all his dad's drunken ramblings.

"Cleveland done gone and leave us here in this place!" he said with a loud stupes. "Man he could ah never do better than me in school, with his *crapo-go-to-church* hand-writing. Noh man!" he said indignantly.

"Cleveland is a big-shot now though!" another rum-head interjected in Cleveland's defence.

"You hear that bwoy!" his father continued. "A *big-shot* lawyer - in America. That's what this young *Thomas* going to be man!" he said pointing to Justin. Then he took the last mouthful of his rum and with a final heavy slap on Justin's shoulder, he advised him.

"Bwoy, go home now," he concluded. "Get out your books. Learn to read and spell good – You're a *Thomas*. You hear me? A *Thomas*!"

"Yes daddy!" Justin confirmed obediently.

Everyone mimicked Justin after that drunken prediction because his father was used to repeating the same information very often. Moreover, Justin was already acting as if he was our boss. So we teased him the more, "Liar! Lawyer!" and usually he would run after us to hit us. Lately though, Justin's chasing was developing into more than a kind of childish game. His growing interest in me was nothing to do with play-fighting, so I always shoved him away briskly. However, I liked his wide, mischievous smile and the way he stared into my eyes, before surveying my chest and then grinning. It sent ripples and bubbles of excitement inside my body and I stifled the tingling feeling inside me, by pretending not to be the slightest bit interested in him.

Now, as Justin was walking up to me in the bushes, my heart thumped loudly and I was filled with a mixture of excitement and fear of being alone with him.

"Hi lawyer!" I called smiling nervously.
He stood in front of me, staring fully into my eyes, just as the men did to the older girls. He was smiling deliberately as if he was about to do something mischievous. There was a kind

of understanding between our eye-talk and I stalked him with my eyes too, waiting for his sudden move. Then, as he was about to grab me, I dodged him behind a tree; running and laughing loudly. I was glad that I had outwitted him by anticipating his move.

I ran away and he chased after me in the hot sun; darting in and out of branches that were slapping my face and chest until I reached the clearing. The clearing was an open space; a few yards away from the open road. I teased him even more because I had outrun him when he tried to catch me. I knew he would not want to come any further, for fear that someone might see him.

"Catch you next time!" he yelled and went back towards the trace.

"Oh yeah! You try!" I teased.

I crossed the road and ran into their yard, calling out for Emma. Emma was one year older than me and she had a sister called Phyllis who was 15 years old. I always felt that Emma was a lucky girl because she was allowed to go to School concerts and could sleep over at her cousin's house, if it was too late to go home. As for me, Aunt Meena certainly would not entertain anything of the sort!

ع

One year, I was given a leading part in a cultural concert, which the school was putting on, for some missionaries from Canada. My part was to recite the *Welcome Speech*. These missionaries came every summer. They would often organise a programme of activities for all the children in the village. The activities included sewing, embroidering, making models and various Bible learning competitions. Aunt Meena knew that I desperately wanted this part. Additionally, my school friends had told her that they would look after me; being the smallest pupil in our school.

They had all said that I looked cute in my folk costume but Aunt Meena said that I could not go. I begged as if my heart would break; to no avail. After much pleading Gran-gran agreed that I could go, but only if Aunt Meena agreed. She refused point blank and just wouldn't budge! The next few days after her refusal, I tried to appease Aunt Meena by doing all my housework with extra diligence. I had hoped that it would bring a change of heart, but Aunt Meena's answer was still "No."

"What your mother go say, all the way in England if anything happens," was always her excuse.

It was those times that I would hate this mother of mine and England. She was far away but she still seemed to cause much trouble for me in Grenada. So I sulked, wishing she did not exist and swore that I hated her as much as I was beginning to hate England too. My resentment intensified the more I felt restricted, especially when I learnt that Emma, Phyllis and Justin were allowed to go to the next event - Tivoli Harvest Festival. There they would meet everyone they knew there.

People from all other schools went to Tivoli Church. It was big and famous for its Harvest Festivals but we were not allowed to go there. It was a Catholic concern. Ours, minute in size by comparison, was Baptist. There, the other children dressed nicer, they seemed livelier and knew more about worldly things in general. That's how I came to label them as "the talkers" whilst I remained "the listener" meaning; being cooped up with the least to offer in a conversation.

It was also one of the reasons why I also hated the island carnival. Every February, I used to pray that something would happen in the island that would make carnival stop for that year but year after year, despite my praying to God, carnival and its merriment came and went as usual.

When I was younger, I thought that the fearful *Jab-Jab* and *Shortney* masqueraders were stronger than God because everyone was afraid of them and they were always there; returning year after year. The tarred, black, devil masqueraders with the shiny, live, black serpents they carried seemed powerful. So too were the *Shortney* masqueraders with their scary masks and strange costumes which had mirrors that reflected flashes of light every time they jumped up, danced and squirted baby powder all over your face. They made children feel afraid with their grand moves and we were forced to give them money as they jumped up, whined or squirmed in front of us.

Always armed with change to give them, people smiled wryly and parted quickly with their money to the fearsome 'mas.' This action was to avoid the Jab Jab smearing their clothes with black tar, or being frightened by their accompanying writhing, slimy, fearful, serpents.

But as we got older, we were restricted from showing any interest in carnival because people of the Baptist religious faith did not take part in "*The devil's work*," Gran-gran had said adamantly. It was one of the few things that she and Aunt Meena instantly agreed wholeheartedly on. Therefore, instead of going anywhere near a Carnival band, my cousins and I were always sent off into our land near the trace, to spend time worthily; picking gungo peas!

Of course, the peas patch couldn't be further away from the main road. They had intended for us to keep well away from these worldly influences but instead, our interest grew stronger. We listened intently to the different sounds of the music and speculated exactly where, in the village and on which roads, the bands were. Occasionally, we would sneak away from the peas bush to get a view of the passing crowds and bands when we were sure they were close to us.

I often wondered what it must be like, to freely follow a band but only Emma was always able to fill me in. She was allowed to go to the carnival because her family was not religious. She usually filled me in with the details of what she had seen and experienced throughout the whole two days of revelling and merry-making. Any extra news and information that she left out were filled in by Justin and Phyllis; who had the freedom and opportunities to do as they wanted at any one time.

One year, my family became strongly against the carnival, when a popular calypso that was being sung, jeered at the fact that a priest was a masquerading participant in the carnival. The song claims that the priest was seen publicly among revellers in the island event. The newspapers had shown him eating, drinking, and whining up among the revellers. In fact, some say he was even swearing just like any one of the non-believers you could find. This special calypso, "*If the priest could play, who is we?*" was made popular because it confirmed the view that religious license was now given to all people to join in the carnival bacchanal.

The sentiments of the song also informed church-goers that they should take part in the revelling by following the priest's example. So we were banned from singing that song in our house. Furthermore, we were told that such rhetoric's were not for us to repeat, since it was '*the work of the devil!*' But we had also grown to accept the carnival tradition as part of our culture. Although we did not actively take part; it was also our folk tradition and so, as children, we felt no harm would be done!

ع

As I neared her house, Emma heard me calling and asked me to come inside their house. She was scrubbing the floor boards of their best room and had almost finished. Her aunt had gone to Grenville and Phyllis, her older sister, had gone with her. Emma emptied the dirty water at the back of the house. Afterwards, we feasted on some mangoes. There a few varieties in a basket under her kitchen table, so we helped ourselves to *mango Lung, Starchie and Grafted*. After that, we went underneath their house to engage in our usual role-playing.

Their little painted wooden house looked like a coloured box on concrete stilts. Gran-gran told us that people often built their houses with lots of space underneath, to provide somewhere to hide during storms. However, Hurricane Janet had taught everyone a bitter lesson, Gran-gran had said. It had caused inestimable damage, so that ten years later, people were still fearful of a repeat performance. Those who had space under their houses, at least had a place of refuge where in times of emergencies, they could take shelter there, many had reasoned.

But at school, we were told that the hurricane had crushed to death, some people who chose to shelter underneath houses. Nevertheless, grateful for our own special space under the house, Emma and I role-played our fantasies. There, we planned and discussed how, in the future, we would continue to live near to each other in England.

We often role-played pretend scenes of our visions of what life in England would be. They were wild imaginings and our imitations were hilarious. We adopted a posh accent, with a toffee-nosed attitude and instantly changed our appearance by

55

making out we had high-heeled shoes on. We did this by sticking suitable sized stones underneath our heels with black tar. Then we decorated our ears with the curly parts of the flowering pumpkin vine, so that the spiral floral bits hung around our ears and dangled just beneath our ear-lobes as long-dropped ear-rings.

After that, we would smear crushed *jump-up-and-kiss-me* flowers over our lips, licking off the light bitterness of the red stain and finished our *'English'* look with also smearing the red stain on our fingernails. There was no mirror, Emma commented on my looks and I criticised hers. Then, with hands on hips, we chatted.

She was more talkative than I was and more imaginative too. Generally having a little more freedom than I did, Emma was more versed on worldly things, so I learnt well from her. I took in whatever she said; hanging on to her every word. As such, I needed to see Emma everyday to catch up on news and gossips, since she had become my 'eyes' in the outside world.

Much of my time was spent going to church on Saturdays and Sundays, to mid-week prayer meetings, going to school and staying at home. No deviation was allowed from this daily routine. It began with morning prayers, collecting water from the local standpipe, going to school and then back home.

The evenings generally included more collection of water if needed, help with collecting firewood but the obligation of being inside the house by 6pm, was never relaxed. After dinner in the evenings, more prayers followed then we relaxed. Later, perhaps a storytelling session would take place in the moonlight, underneath the damsel tree. If visitors came there was generally a feeling of relaxation and only then was it possible to by-pass the strict rules. Girls chatting with boys were forbidden, especially if the boys were older, and without deviation, girls were required to be at home by nightfall.

Aunt Meena used to say, *"close at hand, keep the wolves at bay."* If a girl was caught calling out to a boy or a boy calling out to her in the presence of an adult, there would automatically be a guaranteed slap in public.

"I'm going to have two children," Emma announced in our role-playing session. "A boy and a girl," she finalised, when she had my full attention.

We both laughed and she stuffed a piece of old cloth underneath her dress skirt, cupping the bulky bulge so that she looked pregnant. We imitated the grown women by putting our hands on our hips and assuming adult postures. Smiling up at her I replied, "I want one child - a girl. And I will dress her up everyday in socks and shoes with ribbons and can-can dresses."

"What you think she'll be - a doll?" Emma asked laughing at me.

"Not a doll, but dressed up just like the English girl in my reading book," I replied in earnest.

"Wow! Really?" She asked, looking a little more serious now.

"Yes and I'm going to dress myself and my house up every day. I am going to have servants like the Kents and the McDonalds too," I announced with finality.

Emma looked at me in disbelief.

"You? Servants? But the Kents and the McDonalds are *beke* people. How you go have servants when you're not half-white like them?"

I stared at her.

"You don't have fair skin and long curly hair for a start," she stressed. "Servant?" she said waiting for my reply. I remained quiet but resolute.

"Ki servant sa?" she asked and just like a grown-up, she

sucked her teeth loudly.

"S-T-U-P-E-S!" Emma's suck-teeth was challenging, loud and long.

Shifting uncomfortably from where I stood in front of Emma, I was silenced by the reality of her questions. I stood there not knowing what to say. Emma was always able to reason better than I could and just now I had no answer for her.

Emma's rhetoric was sometimes too grown up for me and I searched for words to fill this void. Then I fidgeted with my side pockets, where I found two *Chicklets*. I put the chewing gums in my hand and held them out to Emma as a peace offering.

"You want some?" I asked and it broke the silence. With relief, we chewed noisily and blew bubbles so that when a large bubble burst on Emma's face; covering her nose and upper lips, we roared with laughter. This laughter was a grinning mask that helped to ease the difficulty of questions, when life could not readily provide the answers.

"Ha- ha- hai!" I laughed.

"Woo-ooy!" she jeered, and eyeing me said, "Doh make me laugh noh!"

After a couple of hours, the sun seemed to have disappeared and rain was being made up in the cloudy sky. I eyed the threatening clouds with suspicion and decided I had to sprint to our house to pick up Gran-gran's clothes which were hanging on the line. Aunt Meena had left me in charge and would not have expected me to be pondering such '*Big Women Things*,' as she would have called them. Failing to get home before the threatened downpour, would mean that I would have to give an account of how the clothes had got wet, when I was supposed to be in the house. Moreover, I would be forced to give an exact account of where I was when the rain was falling.

I felt a couple of cold, isolated, drops of rain on my sleeveless arm and began to run towards our house at once. Others, who had been warned by the one-one drops of rain and the darkened sky, were quickly pulling clothes off their lines or grabbing them off fences or nearby bushes, where they were catching the sun's heat. The wind began to blow and trees swayed from side to side hastening the rain. At the same time, their branches seemed to quarrel with each other, in competition for the noisiest leafy commotion. Thunder cracked then rumbled in the distance and the face of the sun over the village, was completely swallowed up by the dominating clouds.

From the hill, at the top of the mango row, the sun could be seen miles away over selected areas in the distance, where it had chosen to linger before giving way to the threats of thunder and downpour in our village. I reached the yard just before the rain began.

Like bullets attacking the ground, it drenched the baked, gaping earth, soaking its open fissures, pushing the sun-filled leaves down and over-watering the dry grass. Water was busy everywhere. It dripped furiously from banana leaves; busy in its single-minded rush to collect at the sides of roads and form in little streams that seemed bent on some preordained mission.

I was lucky to rescue Gran-gran's over-dried clothes and to push the firewood under the long pieces of galvanise at the back of the kitchen. Thunder cracked again and lightning flashed intermittently, as the rain pelted down onto the sun-scorched, waiting zinc-furrows in the roof. Afterwards, the water met inside the bamboo gutters and hurried down wooden spouts. There it formed a heavier stream, then tumbled noisily into the waiting oil drum directly under a spout.

The water made a hollow sound in the empty containers. As it fell, the melody syncopated on the pitch road, on the galvanised roofs, in a small ravine at the back of the house, in an old pan cup outside the kitchen window, and on a variety of the surrounding outstretched leaves.

Such an orchestration was always a lullaby to my ears, and often I would sit in the comfort of our house, and look through a nearby window to wonder at this tropical gift. Today, as with all the other rainy days, I witnessed the *'showers of blessing'* as Gran-gran called it. She was also not at home when the rain began and it was my hope that she had not been caught in the downpour.

I sat mesmerized by the dominance of the water and how it had forced itself on everything in sight. As it landed on the waiting earth, it had busily created its own routes, gathering in strength and size, as the multitude of streams converged anywhere they forced a path; to form their own junction. Though they followed some man-made paths, at the same time they drifted along the routes which served them best, as they drowned insects and helpless little beasts.

I sat there wondering at this and every downpour, trying to imagine how much more severe Hurricane Janet could have been. I speculated on the enormity of the watery hell which many people, we were told, had gone to or suffered from in 1955. I pondered on the versions of the Hurricane Janet stories we had been told.

Was it karmic retribution on a village locked in its history of social depression, political ignorance, economic depravity and religious blindness? The ritual *Saraka* feasts to the African ancestors and the *Shango* supplications were frequently made to the God of Lightning, on everyone's behalf. The Baptist and Seventh Day Adventists revivalist fervours had preached repentance and the need for forgiveness. The Catholic "Haile Marys" too, had petitioned to the Mother, for cleansing and clarity on the villagers' ways of life. Yet, the only answer was reminiscent of an angry God, who was intent on punishing his erring children with Hurricane Janet.

٤

One story-telling night, Gran-gran was the first person to tell us that not all stories belonged to Anancy. We had heard the story of Hurricane Janet several times too, but the seriousness with which Gran-gran had told it, made us quieter than the usual hilarious responses to Anancy, the Master Out-witter. For us, Anancy was a star of comedy but Hurricane Janet was an enigma.

The night of Gran-gran's *Janet story*, we had all sat around the main steps to our house in the moonlight. The full moon was casting its reassuring beams over us; inspiring our storytelling tradition and drawing us all closer to each other. The moonlight blocked the giant shadows from trees in the yard, making the night seem friendlier, so Gran-gran sat at the top of the stairs. Her feet were resting on the first step and she covered her shoulders as usual, with her favourite woollen shawl.

All the neighbours' children had come to our yard and we sat in a haphazard fashion; not quite making the circle we had intended to form. Emma had brought roasted corn and she shelled them slowly, whispering "*Ship Sail*" games to me. She closed her fist, concealing the grains of corn and when it was my turn to guess how many she had hidden in her closed fist, she signalled by calling out.

"My ship sail, how many men on deck?"

My part in the game was to tell her how many grains of corn were inside her clenched fist.

"Twenty!" I whispered.

"Nope!"

She opened her hand, counted the corn and all fifteen were tossed into her mouth to continue the incessant chewing, which had started 10 minutes earlier. We played "*Ship Sail*" for 5 minutes more because she had also given me a roasted corn. I shelled the warm grains into my hand to call out my "*Ship Sail.*" If Emma could guess the correct amount of corn in my closed fist, it meant that I would have to give them all to her. If she failed to guess how many I had in my hand it meant I would get to keep my corn and eat it. This would continue until the corn cob was empty.

Also in the yard where we sat, Phyllis and Jacinta were roasting cashew nuts on an open charcoal fire. As the curly nuts were tossed in the hot coals, they fizzed and noisily spat out flying oil, making the fire dance and blaze. The nuts became a multitude of individual flames in the open fire. Each flame rose momentarily, as the oil was purged out of it. Then, when the intense heat had sucked the oil dry, it left the nuts looking like blackened bits of curly coals. Afterwards, the girls pounded the nuts on a stone to extract their sweet, kidney-shaped kernel and the broken pieces were collected in a large wide-mouth jar.

During the morning, Aunt Meena had promised to patch corn to make *asham* which Gran-gran liked, because the roasted grains were too hard for her ageing teeth. We mixed the powdered corn with sugar, and from a plastic bag, we sucked the bulging corner through a hole, taking in mouthfuls of the sweet, powdery, corn mixture and feeling quite relaxed.

There was no strictness now and everyone was in good spirits. Friday night, which is story night, finds the sleepy village usually teaming with vitality - laughter, singing, joking, cursing and philosophizing. Children played games or told riddles but above all, stories were the highlight of the pre-weekend joviality.

"Tell us the story about Compere Tigg and Compere Zaen, please Gran-gran?" I requested, now that everyone was animated but attentive.

"Noh!" said Jacinta, "How 'bout Anancy?"

"Me, I hear enough about Brer Anancy, tell us about Hurricane Janet then," I requested again.

"Yes, yes, Cosmos and Pa Jim," Daisy reminded them. Everyone laughed hilariously at the very thought of the well-known comic duo, during the time of the Janet Hurricane fiasco. Therefore, agreement for the Janet story was made unanimously.

Gran-gran took cue.

"All you skinning teeth now, but Janet wasn't ah easy hurricane noh! All of you could ah die," she said soberly.

We settled down in comfortable places and those who cleared their throats did so quickly, voices became quiet whispers and Gran-gran began.

"Well, Janet come with one mighty punishment, taking those who she come for, and leaving a real mess in this place. All where you sitting now was covered with water up to where I'm sitting." We looked at one another in disbelief.

"When, Gran-gran?" someone asked.

"When? Let me see," she repeated, pausing to think. Now let me see," she said pointing to Daisy. "You were two months old."

"It was 1955!" I yelled.

"I tell you dat's one t'ing nobody in Grenada can forget. De hurricane mash-up everything. De radio did tell people to go to a nearby hall and all school send children home early.

Well not everybody have radio and in any case, how will dey go and leave all their t'ings behind?"

She had asked rhetorically, so we listened in silence. Her manner of speaking always commanded the utmost respect for an elder and in return, it was simply our job to listen.

"Those who could ah find nails, did nail-down windows and bar-up their doors; hoping and praying they would pass the time and Papa Gawd would spare them."

"Yeah Cosmos couldn't pray!" someone yelled, laughing and the whole group laughed again.

Aunt Meena had prepared the *asham* and she distributed it quickly and sat down next to Gran-gran. The moon moved only slowly, causing the shadows behind us to move also. Crickets could be heard dominating the nightly sounds in the darkness around us; the temperature was comfortable and we felt good.

"Well, papa oh! Ah did hear when roof start ripping off houses and trees falling around, all lights go out and all man frighten. And Rain! Man rain fall like never before. Wind pulling you - throwing everything at you and around you." Gran-gran paused for a moment and then continued, uninterrupted.

"Wood and all kind ah thing was flying about; everything in the house totally mash-up. As for Cosmos and the grand-father - dem two really, really lucky to be alive!"

"Ha-ha Hai!" We laughed out loudly at the thought of 'the comic duo,' as they were later branded in the village.

Gran-gran shook her head, in remembrance.

"Yes is true," said Aunt Meena, joining in the storytelling and taking up where Gran-gran had left off.

"As for you Emma, your mother put you in a grip and she close you in it! You was a baby - let me see, about 3 to 4 months, ah t'ink. The t'ing is, she nearly get a fright too because in the dark night and flooding everywhere, dey lost the suitcase. Everybody end up under you mother house; sheep, pig, goat, chickens - all man Jack and their brother, was sheltering in the same space under the house."

"But papa mwen ooh! Those who praying, prayed; some telling others how much they 'fraid and worried about everything. Some crying, some bawling, but the wind and the rain and thunder and everything, was mad like hell outside. I hear that in Moyah, a galvanized roof flying out, cut a man neck right out! People all over the place confused, trees falling on them, some even get buried under their own houses but we were lucky."

There was silence everywhere again, as attentive ears and eyes were fully focused at the front; where Aunt Meena and Gran-gran were sitting. Gran-gran resumed the Cosmos story.

"Well, this Cosmos now, he was Catholic, not Baptist like us and when desperation take them, his father call out, Cosmos! Cosmos! Cosmos, you doh hear ah calling you?"

"Yes, Pa Jim!"

"Cosmos! Get up and pray!" he yelled.

"Pa Jim, what to say?" pleaded the terrified son, and everyone roared at the humour this seemed to have caused at the time.

Aw, poor thing!" some said in response.

After having heard the punch-lines so many times before, everyone mimicked the two men and chorused together; "Say Haile Mary! Mother of God, pray for us!"

Everyone laughed at the top of their voices, not at the predicament of the men but at the comedy of their exchanges in the life-and-death situation. The humour was created by the way the story was always told; each time evoking the same hilarious response.

Luckily, for Emma, they had found her in the grip below

a piece of board in the bushes. Aunt Meena said that the suitcase was soaking wet on the outside but the thick material had prevented the inside from becoming too waterlogged. Like baby Moses, Emma was recovered the following morning very much asleep and unaware of death's close call during the night.

Those who had been living near to rivers were washed down to the sea, we were told. After Janet subsided and left, the many homeless and destitute islanders were given 'hurricane' relief of free food, clothes and speedily built prefabricated homes, called *Janet houses*. They were hastily given as compensation for their lost belongings and shattered lives.

This memory was re-lived on story-telling nights as oral history; woven with folktales of myths and legends. This was maybe to provide warnings of similar occurrences. However, for us it provided comedy; being far removed from the reality of the past situation. People, it was stressed, felt more prepared now, but too much rain and overflowing rivers tend to bring back anxiety and sad memories and possibly a little fear of what could be again. The post-Janet children; all young and free, were untouched by such anxieties, and laughter now reigns where weeping and wailing once walked.

"You see," Gran-gran said to Aunt Meena, while pointing at us,

"You hear them - it's true dey say teeth doh always laugh good t'ings."

With her parting proverbial wisdom, she was finished.
She pulled her shawl even closer around her than before and announced to Aunt Meena,"*Il fait froid maitainent.*" She was feeling cold now, she informed in her patwa, and this was a signal for her to leave us for warmer comforts inside.

Those were unforgettable story nights.

Now, as I mentally re-live the watery tale, the rain has stopped but the drip-drop dripping everywhere continued for some time. Slowly, my mind returned from daydreaming about stories and the Hurricane Janet memories, to the present moment. Muddy water glazed every single path and the leaves everywhere resembled polished rubber plants.

Then, as if to mock us all, the sun came peeping out, momentarily. Shyly at first, then showing its mastery too, it remained up in the sky, emitting its fire, for a short while once more. It was not long afterwards that it overshadowed the rainbow which had appeared also and then it disappeared. I shuddered at the sudden weather changes but felt reassured that the rain had stopped and everyone could now be let out of their hiding places once more; spared by our most powerful friendship with nature.

Chapter 3

"A warning to Mothers
Better keep your eyes on your daughters
From the age of seven now, they are wise
And the immorality they try to equalize
Don't let them out of your sight
These forced-ripe men they are too bright."
Lady Iere (Edna Pierre)

I was 11 years old when Africa was introduced to us. It came in the guise of a priest; tall, black with bushy beard and smelling of camphor. He had come after many talks of independence and Grenada's new national anthem. He arrived like a prophet, preaching African spirituality, African language and African habits.

He had come as swiftly as the English Queen and Duke had left. Except, they had come in a blaze of triumphant pomp and circumstance, and he was like an obscure ship passing in the night. Like a prophet, he had a short reign. He preached, made friends as well as enemies and in the end; luckily, he was spared his crucifixion. The African coming contrasted with the English Empire-inspiring figures' brief sojourn, and it was the latter which people remembered most.

The Empire figures signaled the mellow fading of their lengthy dominance because a new process was afoot. Many school children had been part of this new process, and when we had been asked to enter a competition to compose the nation's new national anthem, I felt sure I would win it. I loved hymns, especially the rousing ones we used to sing. They were my favourite songs, the ones that Aunt Meena and

Gran-gran' had given their permission to sing. Not for us the smutty calypsos and songs with too much worldly emphasis.

With zeal, I had visualised what it would be like composing a song like our school song. It is the one we sang very often, especially on Fridays at School. Friday was for me a 'lazy' school day, since it was more activity-based and less serious than the other four anxious days.

It was my view that the winning song would have to be a rousing song like *Men of Harlech*, so I set out to imitate it.

> *"Men of Harlech in the hollow,*
> *Do you here like rushing billow?*
> *Wave on wave that certain follows*
> *Battle's distant sounds:*
> *Loose the folds as under*
> *Flags we conquer under,*
> *The placid skies now bright or high*
> *Shall launch its boat with thunder,*
> *Onward 'tis our country needs us*
> *He is bravest, he who leads us...*
> *Come on everyone let us answer the call..."*

This was reinforced in my brain by Aunt Meena, who often sang it out aloud as she worked. She used to leave out the majority of the words and sometimes the song just did not seem to make sense.

> *"Hart of oaks are our ships...*
> *We always will be ready,*
> *Steady, boys steady!*
> *We'll fight again and again, and again!"*

But I imitated the strength and vigour of the sentiments the song offered, and juxtaposed it with Aunt Meena's favourite words. This way, I thought, I would be able to decide what the bestt approach for my anthem should be. The song of the Empire inspired in us a soldierly attitude of fighting for something big; solidarity with England we were told - the Mother-country. The Queen and the Duke had come to remind us of that.

The day of the Royal visit on Empire Day, we were given free cakes, a choice of sweet drinks and our own free Union Jacks to wave. In our school, teachers, especially the Headmaster, made threats about the quality of our appearance. If we looked less than 100% perfect, each teacher and Form Prefect had his permission to make sure that the right punishment was given. They had to ensure that each child was greased, combed, perfectly uniformed and clean enough to join in the Royal celebration.

The Queen and the Duke, we had seen daily in the school's photograph on the stage; large and imposing like the Union Jack which accompanied it. There they stood, silently watching, monitoring, disciplining our behaviour and directing our history. The Queen confidently stood with her wooing smile of youth, as if to say "So nice, *my* people!" and the Duke standing next to her seem to reply with "'Tis true!"

We had practiced the welcome-song a million times and were drilled like soldiers in the hot mid-day sun. Rows and rows of children-soldiers, walking to the left-right! Left-right! beat before the resounding, "'TEN-TION!" The drilling was delicious to the English Headmaster and he reveled in the mastery over us, his Queen's subjects.

He licked his lips, pouted his stomach and took his own quick-march in his head then shouted, "Left-right! Left-right! Left-right!" With head held high, he shouted arrogantly then headed for the entrance door. Our teachers, who were in front their classes, marched after the headmaster, as they took the "quick march!" cue from him. Everyone marched until all the natives learnt the routine correctly; by going in and out of the school building several times.

On the day of the Queen and the Duke's arrival, people came from everywhere. They came from St. Patrick's, St. David's, St. Andrews, and St. Johns - in fact, not only those parishes because the whole island had answered the call.

"But what was *Harlech*?" I kept asking myself.

Aunt Meena had told me one day that it meant "brave West Indian men going to fight for England." She was unable to offer further expansion on the subject, so concluded that I had asked too many questions. I pondered on this even more. Perhaps Jamaica, Trinidad, Barbados and the rest of the West Indies had sent *Men of Harlech* too. Nevertheless, that was the sentiment I proposed to imitate in my composition - people with a fighting spirit, a sense of pride, the kind who would inspire others.

Calypsonians had sung to spur the people on; increasing the tempo, giving the low-down and spreading their own gospel of celebration for the Royal visit.

> *"Ding Dong darling, the Queen and the Duke coming,*
> *Ding Dong darling, everybody rejoicing*
> *Man is true, they say they go jump up to*
> *And join in the bacchanal for this Carnival."*

Our behaviour and manners were polished, so were our smiles. Two weeks before the event, when Mr. Jessup arrived at school, in his Land Rover, he was dressed in his ex-army uniform. He wore British Army khaki-coloured gear, completed with a beret which was cocked to one side of his head. He did this performance every day before the visit, to remind us of our duty. He too, was performing his duty. The white, blonde, blue-eyed schoolmaster, an ex-Army General, was sent by Britain to Belair Government School, St. Andrews, Grenada, to educate subjects in the colony.

Our semi-final dress rehearsals seemed like the real thing; held in town with all of the islands' schools, created excitement, anticipation and speculation. The island was in a royally-inspired upheaval.

Mr. Jessup was a patriot and it was his general knowledge quiz to the whole school each Friday morning, which made me ponder about the word "*Harlech,*" in our *'Men of Harlech'* song. The quiz was always about world-wide affairs and it was good. I was given a *Student's Companion* as a General Knowledge prize once, so I tried to memorise the contents well. However, having searched it from cover to cover, I knew that *Harlech* was not in the book. What or where was Harlech? Who were the men of Harlech and why were we singing about it with such patriotic fervour? I asked myself several times.

I asked Gran-gran who said that maybe they were the men who had marched in St. Georges, having answered England's call to go and fight for the *Mother Country*. She remembered she had seen during the war, many people who had volunteered and had joined many other West Indians from the Caribbean islands to go and help England fight.

All these thoughts and questions had come back to me since the call for entries to the island competition. I had spent many nights, trying to think of words in the candlelight of my bedroom that would inspire my composition. I was determined to meet the deadline which was drawing near. I was confident. I believed that I stood a chance of winning the Island-wide competition; despite the fact that none of my friends were interested. They felt that as children, we did not stand a chance against the whole island. I was perhaps too naive to consider the competing strength of the whole island in the competition, so my general response was to blatantly dismiss all negativity. Instead, I laboured tirelessly, trying to make the lines of my song rhyme.

ع

One evening when I was sitting under the damsel tree in our yard, battling with the words on the page, willing them to do my bidding, Justin's father passed by. He was staggering from side to side as usual; spitting as he did so, followed by his mangy dog which he cursed.

On reaching me, he said he found it strange that I was sitting by myself, so he enquired why I had not gone to play with the others. I told him that I was not going to play until my masterpiece for the National Anthem competition was perfected. In fact, it is also what I had told the others. For most people, my determination seemed like a joke and this made me even more determined to succeed. At least, this was the situation until this moment. Justin's dad destroyed my blossoming confidence with his cruel opinion of my creative spirit. As soon as I told him what I was doing, the horror of his reply stunned me.

"You?" he said in disbelief, pointing his finger at me and watching me cross-eyed. He then scowled and made the longest sucking teeth noise I had ever heard.

"S-T-U-P-E-S! You! You!" he mocked in disbelief. "You could never win that competition!"

He was clearly drunk but this did not lessen the impact of his cruel language. Then he continued, whilst still staring at me.

"S-T-U-P-E-S! In fact, you could never pass ah exam!" His mouth was cocked to one side in scorn, and his red blood-shot, rum-eyes leered at me.

He had pronounced the final sentence cruelly and coldly; punishing my ego and deeply hurting my pride. There was a sinking feeling in my stomach, caused by the dancing butterflies that seemed to be in there; to rise and fall with fear. Those painful words nagged me. My hands quivered and my breathing quickened though I attempted to steady my racing pulse. My lips twitched and the prickly heat which the hurt feeling brought to my face, made my eyes fill with tears, so that I saw everything around me in a wobbly, watery blur. The water gathered in my eyes then it rolled down, unchecked on my face. Then my whole body shook uncontrollably with shock and hurt feelings. Alone there, I covered my face in shame with the palms of both hands, before letting out a stifling cry.

I lost faith in my newly developing zeal.

Justin's dad was cruel and his tongue had done his bidding. It was a mischievous tongue; bragging about Justin's future, quarrelling with his wife, arguing with the other men openly in the rum shop, or lamenting about his failed hopes and dreams.

These were his favourite pastimes. Justin's dad felt he should be the only person to talk about knowledge. But he had only reached Standard Seven in school, and instead of going on to do further studies, he had fallen madly in love with a well-to-do *mulatto* girl. Aunt Meena had said that his family was a bright set of people and although he was one of the brightest, he had brothers who had travelled abroad; all doing better than he was.

As a young man, Justin's dad had wooed Jessica; a pretty, young, slim girl, whose parents had great expectations for her future. Her fair half-white skin, long curly hair and connected family, meant that she could get a job in a bank. Barclays Bank was full of people like her. Maybe she could have become a *"Pupil Teacher"* after she finished Standard Seven; better still, someone like her could easily emigrate to England or America. Emigrating was the favourite choice.

Jessica had the right appearance and qualification to succeed in the future. I often heard that she was from a *"Big hefe"* family connection. But along came Justin's dad; a tall slim and talkative fellow. His name is Egbert Thomas, but as children we just called him "Justin's dad." With his big-sounding English words and his knowledge of poetry, this smooth-talking saga-boy had swept poor Jessica off her secured half-white feet.

He too, was bound for America, to follow in his brother's footsteps. It was almost one hundred percent certain that Justin's dad would go to America. His brother would send for him. Life there sounded attractive to him and he had already begun to emulate American street-talk, in sentences which either began or ended with the word *"man."* He acted as if he was already in the *"US of A,"* as he often called it.

One night at a local dance in the Friendly Society Hall, Jessica had drunk more than a little taste of rum. She was already feeling heady from the stares and sweet eyes which Egbert was making quite openly at her, while he showed off all night to the other girls. He was dressed in a nice open-necked shimmering black shirt, showing a chest that was adorned with a gold-plated chain, which had been sent to him from America.

Wearing black and white patent shoes, a handkerchief that was deliberately sticking out of his back pocket, Egbert's smooth, coconut-oiled words were sweet to Jessica. The words anointed her feminine feeling, and opened her repressed passions, so that in their close dancing to the sound of saxophone being played in the band, she lost sight of correct decorum as well as their individual visions for their future.

By the time the evening's bacchanal was over, the seeds of a changed future for them both were sown. Pregnancy swiftly curtailed Jessica's parents' plans for her. Similarly, Egbert's wings had been clipped and therefore he flew no further than over the village pastures, settling down to make do with some kind of frustrated, regrettable, bitter, unfulfilled life.

Jessica's father had threatened to kill Egbert because he had 'spoiled' his daughter. So with the help of his brothers in America, Egbert was able to build a house for them before the baby was born. By village standards, he had still done well; giving Jessica a roof over her head and making an "honest" woman of her, by marrying her. Her father never forgave Egbert and would never acknowledge him as *real* family because he felt he was not good enough for his daughter.

"A worthless rum-head, *saga boy*," the girl's father had described Egbert to the helpless Jessica.

"Daddy I know teeth and tongue must meet but it happen already noh!" she reasoned.

It had surprised the girl's father that she had taken on grown-up characteristics that he had not witnessed before, so he retorted, "Yes, maybe is dat what killed you' mother, God rest her soul. What ah go do now?" his quivering, half-drunk voice asked.

No one knew the answer, so silence reigned supreme. It was always best that way, while deep thoughts and ancestor wisdom, self-pity, pride, shame, feelings of loss of face and anger battled for pride of place. Often her father had cried publicly, for his two, sudden losses and the worst was the village gossip that never seemed to go away. The rejection and frustration drove Egbert to find solace in large quantities of River Antoine rum. It helped to drown his pangs of regrets and reproaches and made it easier for him to accept his lot in life.

Therefore, Justin who was Jessica's younger brother was expected to be the 'saviour' of their family name. Everyone expected him to do something that would "*raise their nose.*" Justin, it was expected, would be the role-model that would represent the future *Thomas* generations

That moment of Justin's dad's severe criticism had shaken me deeply and my budding creative endeavours died a sudden death. From then on, I refused to let anyone see me writing for the competition; mainly because each attempt to do so recalled the mocking echoes of those cruel words in my ears.

"You could never win. You could ah never pass an exam!" The predictions ripped through me like cutlass cutting down sweet cane. After that, no more encouragement could be stirred up from inside me - just fear, self-pity and hurt. He had wounded my pride and I vowed never to speak kindly of him again.

ε

It was perhaps two years after the incident with Justin's dad, that the African priest came to our village. I didn't know his name, who had brought him, or how he came to our village. But this Black Scholar seemed to have impressed Gran-gran and Aunt Meena. Everyone in the post-independent village had become deep thinkers and Africa was talked about more than England.

We had our own flag with meaningful colours representing the sun, sea and luscious vegetation. The map of Grenada was printed and embossed in mock gold on our free medals and our anthem was changed. The African priest had come to bring more changes.

"Yes, yes, the children must learn about their roots man," Uncle Charles said to the priest, agreeing to his suggestion to teach us our African roots. To make matters worse, being a priest seemed to automatically give him a license to enter into our sanctity, our domain, a home full of females; since we owned the village church.

"Our children are our future, we have to teach them good and with God's help they'll reach to higher heights and deeper depths,'" the priest preached to Uncle Charles, who had absorbed every word and responded enthusiastically.

"Amen Brother!"

Until the priest's arrival, the only priest in our church was Reverend Blackman. He was a short black man, going bald with grey sideburns and he wore glasses. He was the Priest in the St. Johns Spiritual Baptist Church, for as long as I can remember. He had been ordained in Trinidad and he often wore a black suit except for his purple sash and long white-robe which he wore at funerals. The purple sash had embroidered white crosses at each end and it always reminded me of death.

No wedding ceremony had ever taken place at the St. Johns Spiritual Baptist Church. It seemed foreign to our Baptist church area. The few who had such nuptial aspirations and were from the surrounding areas, got married in Tivoli Catholic Church; which was a big, imposing, brick building with fairly large grassy grounds. It stood in the middle of the three surrounding areas, networking its tripartite location - Tivoli, parts of Hermitage and La Poutrie.

It was where everyone wanted to go, because dressed up in their special Sunday clothes; they eyed each other up and down, in their post-mass gatherings. It was also where they gossiped and competed for the best-dressed churchgoing outfit. Some had even passed the St. Baptist church to travel three miles on foot, to visit this packed Catholic Church. The church in Tivoli had many seats; a big grassy space outside to hang about in and a white priest.

Apart from the precious little money which the congregation had, they brought offerings of eggs, fresh fruits, best pieces of meats and lots of other food to the priest. He thanked and "blessed" them, to which they grinned shyly and genuflected while saying *"Thank-you Father."*

The St. Johns Spiritual Baptist Church, by comparison, seemed a nonentity. A very small breeze-blocked building, it had six benches. There were three benches on either side of the aisle with a seating capacity of perhaps 40 people. A covered table and a two-tiered platform formed the altar; which was the focus of attention, and this interrupted the square space. The altar was dressed in pure white starched cloths, brass candle sticks with white candles, vases of fresh flowers and most importantly, a bell was placed to one side on the altar.

There were six wooden windows in the church; three on either side of the building and these were held open outwards by long wooden sticks, as stoppers. A galvanized roof covered the entire structure. The church was often in a state of disrepair, with the odd hole here or there in the roof. It was frequented by a few bats which congregated there. They clung to the ceiling rafters; sharing the wooden beams with quick-spirited, common lizards. This dark and scary presence of God was one of my weekly chores to clean and refresh.

It was there that I changed the altar cloths early each Sunday morning; having ironed and starched them myself on Saturday. I cleaned out the vases of old flowers and scraped the candle-wax from the white cloths. I was often alone there, dutifully doing as Gran-gran and Aunt Meena had ordered. After being groomed in the church in this way, my next step would be to take my place on the altar praying and reading the word of God. My grooming had started with reading from the *WORDS OF COMFORT* and occasionally offering a prayer, when asked to do so by Reverend Blackman and Gran-gran.

Gran-gran was proud to see me 'at the front' and she encouraged it in whatever way she could. Mr. Blackman too had felt relieved of the burden of having to take the whole three or four-hour long services. He therefore gave us sections of the day's service to be responsible for and was glad to witness the enthusiasm with which I did my part. One day he called me aside and suggested that as a future *"Woman of Destiny,* I should form a Sunday school to teach the remaining children of the church.

"*Sister* Jo-Anne," he had said as he addressed me and I felt I had suddenly graduated. The word "*Sister*" was not used for children.

"The Lord has got a work for you," the Reverend advised, "And when He call you, like Samuel in the temple, you must obey. Since you are a *Woman of Destiny*, our new Sunday school is a job that we are placing entirely in your hands," he pronounced with finality.

This was both a suggestion and an order, to which I had to agree. Gran-gran said that it was a good opportunity and a great job for me to be "in front of things." My only consolation was that I was given a free hand, so I planned to improvise as I went along, as long as my sessions represented elements of a Sunday school.

Subsequently, I rose to the challenge and seized the opportunity to enjoy the limelight. It was also an opportunity to be focused on something worthwhile, in order to stop the mental echoes and re-echoing of Justine's dad's derision of me. My new job gave me fresh impetus and a strength that helped me to create my own affirmations. I used them to counter-attack Justin's dad's opinions of me and create more personal zeal.

"I can and I will pass my exams!" I affirmed repeatedly with; "I will be somebody! I will be a *Woman of Destiny*!"

But sometimes the derisive echoes seemed louder than my affirmations and I would sulk and feel sad. During the moments of sadness, I tried to be defiant in order to show Justin's dad that I really can do something and be somebody; even right here in the village.

My attempts began as an initial struggle but soon the efforts soon grew into a kind of growing strength; slowly at first, then with practice, it became stronger. Afterwards, those occasions of strength gave me hope and I felt that the goal of being a *Woman of Destiny* was not going to stop here. It would continue somewhere else in England, where Emma and I had visualised our rise to great heights would be.

ع

So Africa walked into our church that Sunday morning, towering over the short Reverend, looking quite confident. He wore a replica of Rev. Blackman's funeral robe but it was completely purple. On his head, he wore a matching round purple hat which had an imposing cross at the forehead. He looked like a Jewish Rabbi with a long, black, bushy beard and black curly hair, which hid most of his face. His eyes and mouth seemed as if they were the only moving parts on his face, surrounded by this mass of thick hair. His quick, sharp eyes flashed around the room with interest; pleasantly surveying the young children, as they walked one by one into the church. Their protective parents accompanied them all.

The few regular members had come dressed in colourful clothes because they had been warned, *"A stranger would be in our midst."* Rev. Blackman was the most excited I had ever seen him, and the adult congregation shared his enthusiasm, like children themselves.

On this hot Sunday morning, the ladies came armed with real fans and Bibles in their hands. Some wore glasses which they used only on special occasions. Mother Sayee, a Senior Mother of the church, like Gran-gran, was in top form as usual. She was dressed in her red, white and blue head tie. This was matched by her three-tiered, puffed-sleeved dress, also with red, white and blue layers. Her pure white apron completed her dress, so that she looked like a proud Matron on a very spruced and cleaned ward.

Gran-gran too, looked smart and her pure white head-tie matched her blue and white dress which was hidden behind a beautiful white lacy apron. The ladies did not usually have to wear shoes because when they were filled with the spirit, their agile movements were natural and controllable; shoes seemed a humbug.

Today, they wore their ballerinas. The men wore crisp and clean short-sleeved shirts and their hard-skinned palms were greased and shiny. Girls and boys mirrored their parent's cleanliness because we are told in parables that "cleanliness is next to godliness." Additionally, everyone was on his best behaviour, as they solemnly greeted each other. Though they had laughed, talked and joked in the most familiar way during the week, on Sundays these men and women assumed a formal posture; respectable and Godly.

"Mahning Brother Charles," said Sister Jomen.

"Ay, Brother Little, everything awright?"

"Yes, yes! God is good."

They took their pews, fanning themselves furiously against the rising heat. Those who had been standing at the entrance earlier had hugged and kissed as they met one another. Now, as the start of the morning's service drew near, the hand-bell was made to let out its piercing rings. The deafening noise rang in the nearby village to signal the start of church proceedings. It pealed among the congregation, intent on driving out any uninvited evil spirits from the four corners of the building and instilling a mood of reverence.

For it was in the four corners, that Mother Sayee would ring the bell most furiously, for minutes; after which she walked to various areas up and down inside the small church, ringing as she did so. She began the ringing from outside the front door then she proceeded to ring, causing loud peals up and down the aisle.

It was also a ritual symbolic ringing; intent to cleanse the atmosphere and rouse the ancestral gods to draw nigh to the Christian God, and collaboratively grant them a hearing.

Mother Sayee poured water libation in the four corners from the main vase. It was supposed to purify the sacred space. White candles burned in the four corners, crying wax and spilling the hot liquid over the chalky white inscriptions on the concrete floor. The inscriptions looked like African hieroglyphics and each one seemed different. They had been drawn there when Mother Sayee was in the spirit, which they say, gives her utterance. It was during those spirit-filled moments, that she would write these inscriptions down, prophesy and warn the members against what her spiritual eyes had seen.

The African priest and Rev. Blackman were on the platform. The priest was behind the *mercy-seat*, which was his special chair on the altar. He shut his eyes and the congregation hummed, *"Lead us heavenly father lead us."*

There was no musical accompaniment apart from hand-clapping. The hum-hum-hum rose in intensity, with the increased pealing of the bell. This spoke a meaningful, spiritual language to them. It helped to put them all in the right frame of mind for the day's messages.

During the humming, one by one, the members saluted each other, as well as their guests. They began from cheek-to-cheek, hands outstretched to the individual sides; above the head and finally clasped in front. Finally, they curtsied to each other. The greetings of the whole congregation lasted for at least 15 minutes, until everyone had a turn to salute. After that, Reverend Blackman held up his hand for a pause, and slowly the voices in unison, dropped, became quieter and then stopped. Then reverently, he raised both his hand in a symbolic surrender and with head facing skywards, he began.

"Brethren, let us pray."

Everyone knelt down on the cold concrete, hands also outstretched, some armed with Bibles in them and their eyes closed.

"Let us t'ank Gawd for keeping us still in the land of the living," he began.

"Amen!"

"Papa Gawd, we t'ank you bringin' us here today," he continued and "Hallelujahs" rang out from the fanning congregation.

"Lawd, we want to t'ank you too for the Brothers and Sisters here today; for health and strength."

"Yes Lawd!"

"An' Lawd we have so much to t'ank you for we doh know where to start."

"Hallelujah!"

Rev. Blackman had faced the altar and was kneeling with a burning candle in one hand and a bible in the other. He began to sweat.

"We want to t'ank you Gawd for this country of ours, Lawd," he began.

"Yes Lord!" the congregation responded.

"For Ministers of the gospel."

"Yes Lawd!"

"Women in child birth, the sick and the helpless."

"Amen Lord."

"The lame, the blind, the deaf, those in prison. Not forgetting our Sisters and Brothers by the way; those who're backsliding. Those in institutions, leaders of countries and leaders of the Gospel."

"Yes, Hallelujah!"

"Lawd, we bring you Mother Sayee, Lawd. Help her, and anoint her body. T'ank you for sparing her from sickness."

"We t'ank you Lord!"

"Mother Mitchell, Lawd, our dear sister, strengthen her weak body. Sister Meena and Sister Mary too Lawd, not forgetting Brother Little, Bother Benjamin, Sister Jomen and the many little brothers and sisters here Lawd; protect them from harm and danger, sudden death and accident."

"Hallelujah! Amen! Do Lord!" Here the responses were more enthusiastic, louder and more pronounced as it referred to us; the growing innocents.

"Lawd we musn' forget sister Irene, sister Mary and Brother Raphael all the way on England's shore; walk with them, direct their every step and continue to grant them travelling mercies."

The list was always long and impressive. Everyone and everything was included, maybe for fear that to miss out something or someone would render them unprotected or show the person praying to be weak, and unfamiliar with our preferred method of prayer.

Praying was a skilled art-form, never needing to be rehearsed or written down on a list. The overriding criterion was that it had to come straight from the heart. The prayers were always filled with spiritual fervour and with the ability to uplift the supplicants.

The Reverend's voice then changed. He slowed down and his new pitch was deliberate. There was a little hush from the congregation as they showed perfect interpretation of his deliberation and he continued.

"Papa Gawd we haven't got a lot to offer but these few words of our mouth and the meditation of our heart; let it be acceptable in thy sight. We know you are coming to make the crooked paths straight and the rough ways smooth for us."

"Yes! Amen!"

"So we want you to hear us Lawd and especially for our Brother here, all the way from the other side of the world in Africa, give him utterance and strength, Lawd."

"Do Lawd! Do!"

"Go before him in all his ways, and watch his steps."

"Lawd you know Satan is always busy, bruising our heels and mashing our toes, but we know you will hold us up with your powerful han'."

"Yes! Hallelujah!"

At this point, the congregation broke into song. The bell rang furiously, echoing their agreement with all that was being offered, so that together in song, they made supplication on the Priest's behalf. Clapping, dancing, shouting and more bell-ringing followed, while Rev. Blackman, still on his *mercy seat* in front the altar, continued to pray. He was unimpeded by the increased volume of voices, dancing, jumping, clapping and members being filled with the Holy Spirit. Some of them got utterances and they spoke in tongues while the Reverend still continued with his prayer. He came to an end after they too, had come to a physically exhaustive end. They had climaxed at the same time.

The African priest followed suit, praying eloquently, with a less sing-song tone. His beginning was impressive. It was an unknown language and profuse *Amens* and *Hallelujahs* did not interrupt it, as he invoked the African ancestral gods. Confidently he took the *mercy seat*.

"Abalachiony, Bessiami, Yemetanah, Semai, Icadus, Tempta, Fecadus, Indehonetchre, Indehon, Bemeda, Tahon, Yehlit, Yaselalimoo, Amen."

His *Amen* was re-echoed enthusiastically by the expectant crowd and then he broke into English, finishing his short prayer and his impression was made. Each member followed in turn with prayer, starting with the 'Mothers' who were the most senior or the church elders. They were the passers of wisdom, tradition and discipline. Seniority was revered and greatly accepted by all.

Each person went down on his knees on the cold concrete to pray. After the 'Sisters,' the younger women or those who were recently baptized followed suit. This was done in rotation of age in an unspoken, but accepted church protocol. Then it was the children's turn. We took up our places at the altar. There, all forms of shyness were shed; so too were ideas of being grown-up or feeling too 'big' or above this type of life-style.

As children, our dread was to be seen in action by passing friends or boys who had shown an interest in us. There, whether you liked it or not, you did your part. You prayed, armed with candle in one hand and bible in the other because it was the place where all inhibitions were lost. It was in this air of holiness that we learnt why the African priest had come to be with us.

"We are all one people," the African priest had said, thumping his fist on the pulpit banister, the whites in his eyes flashing against the black.

"Africa, Grenada and Cariacou, Trinidad over yonder, Jamaica and Barbados," he continued, begging God for mercy as he made his regional pleas for the Caribbean. The women continued to say *"Yes!"* and *"Amen!"*

Later, we were told that he would be teaching us our African roots. Undoubtedly, ninety per cent of the congregation did not know what aspects of our roots were going to be taught but they welcomed him with open arms and sent us all to his cultural lessons punctually, daily, with no absenteeism.

As usual, I cleaned, brushed and prepared the church building for those after-school sessions which had to be finished before 6 o'clock, when all children especially girls, were expected to be indoors. Being the little Sunday School Teacher, I was introduced to the African priest and daubed their expected *Woman of Destiny*, so he made a bee-line for me. At first he genuinely assisted and gave me ideas for the Sunday school and taught us to say prayers in African language.

We all learnt to make the sign of the cross in African, counted ABC, and sang some African children's songs. We were willing students because it was the talk of the village - something new, a gossiping point and he was branded an extremely patient man, a good teacher. He brushed his beard with his hands often, whilst clearing the hairs around his mouth and we clung to his every word.

Our new linguistic acquisition of African knowledge was the envy of all the surrounding non-Christians and soon they too sent their children to join our church-children for the extra lessons. The village took on a new life as children became more obedient. Men and women too were on their best behaviour; since there were less wife-beating or swearing big, dirty words.

The African priest had come all the way from Africa and they did not want to show him their bad habits. Rum-drinking during the weekday was only prevalent on Fridays, when the stranger was bound to be located in the church for prayer meetings. Being there he would not be mingling with them locally and after all, Friday night was the night they had licence to drink and get drunk. It was their earned right after working very hard on the land all week.

Big succulent chunks of fried fish covered under new table cloths were brought to him; thick fried coo-coo pieces with ochras, roasted breadfruit, succulent avocado pears, freshly grated cocoa tea and milk stout with eggs and spice were also given. He was spoilt like a chief, being offered the villagers' best. Everyone was grateful, the children were learning new things and boastfully, the Priest basked in the glory as he displayed, through his devotees, his knowledge and ability of effective 'African' spirituality.

Proudly, we were made to stand up in front of audiences or passers-by, to display our new-found mastery of 'African' linguistics and though no one really knew the precise interpretation of what we were being taught, everything was taken at face-value. It was good because it sounded very good. He had won everyone's confidence; he was a star and Africa was good.

The Priest was punctual and become over-zealous with his time-keeping. Sometimes he arrived an hour early, before the start of our lessons. Each day, he seemed to arrive at our house earlier than the next; during which time he was overfed, praised endlessly, put on a pedestal and could do no wrong. After that, he accompanied or followed me to the church even before I got the chance to clean, dust and drive out occupying bats. He helped, encouraged and praised me as I worked. Like a protégé he was pruning, he helped and supported all my efforts.

The attention felt good and my ego rose to great heights because I was the lucky one to get extra tuition and got the chance to learn new words that no one knew as yet. I was keen and felt privileged. But 'Africa' turned sour when he made me stand too close to him in those pre-lesson sessions, so that he could put his hand up my dress.

While he did so, I was made to show-off to passers-by, who sometimes stood and listened then left. No one would have guessed or believed the catastrophe which was going on inside the church building! After all, we were safely inside our church, and they the ungodly, were outside. There we all were, children who were expected to be safe from harm and danger in the sanctity of God, being molested inside it!

He would cleverly position himself on a chair next to where I was standing, furthest away from the front door but near to the altar. Viewed from the front door, I probably looked like a young student being taught by the most patient and caring teacher; putting in 100 percent of his efforts. There, in front of God's eyes, the 'African' priest's big, clumsy, fingers rummaged inside my clothes, frightening me to death. Baffled and frightened at the thought of how he had forced this strange manliness on my innocence, I wanted the priest to stop.

I had slowed down my recitation, with gaping mouth, shocked at the advantage being taken of me but he made me continue to recite my African verses in the silence that threatening. I was bewildered and this reduced my recitation to a staccato style. But he eyed me sternly and deeply; his angry, defiant eyes willed me to continue and dared me to stop.

Now and then he squeezed my painful, seedy breasts; having first checked for prying eyes. My heartbeats thumped loudly and threatened to jump out of my chest and yell STOP! But the fear of this camphor-smelling priest was real. Afterwards, he tried to compensate for his naughtiness, by calling on me to stand up in front of the class the next day, to repeat some of the new words and verses he had already taught me before anyone else.

This new ploy of his became the envy of the other children; that is, those who were not yet his victims! Foolishly, and jealously they accused me of being his favourite because of his selective tactics. They resented his interest in me and to his delight; demanded that they too should be given the same treatment! He grinned and agreed that each week he would take a different person for one-to-one tuition or maybe two girls at a time.

I recalled the many times the Reverend had prayed for the protection of this "*Man of Gawd, who had come all the way to Grenada, to teach us, the helpless ones, so that we can be strong in times of weakness.*" That is what was preached each Sunday and no one denied it.

But as luck, experience or maybe both would have it; Gran-gran was becoming uneasy with the difference she was beginning to notice in my attitude. She was always very observant and attentive to changes around her. Or maybe she had smelled a rat and just needed time to catch it!

"Joanne, what's the matter wid you?" Gran-gran asked, offering me sugar-cake.

The crackly, crunchy, roasted, peanut and fudge mixture was our favourite treat - hers and mine. For us, it was considered a special treat from anyone who was thoughtful enough to offer it.

"Nothin'," I muttered.

"How you mean nothin'?" she replied, "An' you refuse sugar-cake. You never refuse sugar-cake before," she declared.

I was reading my history book and the pictures of Homo sapiens were quite boring but I pretended to be interested. I held a fixed stare deep into the book, past the words on the page into nothingness. Gran-gran may have noticed that I was sighing repeatedly, while pretending to read.

"Maybe you have the fever. Come here, leh me feel you."

She did the usual; she felt my forehead and under my neck.

"How you feelin'?" She asked frowning and fixing her dark brown eyes in mine. Her furrowed brow looked puzzled so she coaxed further.

"You want to tell me somethin'?"

I could have blurted out the whole awful truth and the confusion that I was feeling but then I remembered the "*Man of Gawd*" and the reverence they had all bestowed on him. Instead, I tried to cope with a short, quick answer.

"No Gran-gran."

"Maybe a drink of fever bush will do you good. You probably catching a cold," she suggested.

I had looked up and saw her eyes searching mine. As she surveyed my face, she seemed as if she was about to ask me something, then as quickly as she had thought of it, the question was immediately retracted. Perhaps her better judgment sensed it was not the right question, time or approach.

I sat there and continued staring at the page of Homo sapiens in my book for ages. I was sure she knew that nothing productive was taking place, because I had not turned a page for nearly half an hour!

"Well you better go in you bed," she advised. "Ah go bring you some bush-tea for you."

She left me inside the room and immediately made no secret of her worries to Aunt Meena, who had just finished grating coconut to make oil.

"Somethin' worrying Joanne, Meena."

"You mean she sick, mama?"

"Well there's all kinds ah sickness but she's sickin' 'cos of something."

"Last night I watch her tossing, turning and talking in her sleep. Right now, she sitting dey trying to look as if she reading, but *ki read sa*? Her mind is restless and worse than that, she doesn't seem to want to go to the church! Ah doh know what the priest go say. Ah just know, a few minutes ago, she actually refuse sugar-cake!"

"Now you know that somethin' have to be wrong for Joanne to refuse sugar-cake," piped Aunt Meena.

The two women paused and then Aunt Meena whispered, to make sure I could not hear them.

"How you mean?" Gran-gran asked.

"Well the Priest did say she was the brightest, a real leader and now maybe it's someone else turn; it's probably even jealousy," Aunt Meena whispered.

Gran-gran remained silent and then she sighed.

"Ah doh know, that chile is not herself. And is not her menses either. She don' see no blood yet? Somethin' wrong somewhere for sure," Gran-gran concluded.

Ten minutes later, Gran-gran brought the bush-tea; *black sage* leaves, mixed with *lemon grass, ginger* and *bois den leaves* with *cinnamon spice* sticks. The dark liquid was piping hot and extremely sweet. I stared at her as she handed me the steaming cup; wondering if she would ever guess what had happened. She was quiet for a moment, maybe expecting some comments prompted by the tea, but neither of us said a word.

Earlier that evening after school, Emma and I had talked about the horror of the situation. I learnt that she was also a victim of the Priest. Although she was a little worldlier than I, she seemed just as confused and was nearing tears as we talked. We were walking up the 2 miles from school together, behind the first crowd from the school to our village. Usually, we were the first to reach the village; full of chatter, laughing and mimicking the teachers, teasing one another and recounting our daily antics.

Instead, today there was heaviness and awkwardness between us. We weren't interested in role-playing our usual grown-up routine. The laughter and gaiety of our innocence had given way to burdensome moments of silence. Our innocence was interrupted by the priest's deceit of our families and the unwarranted experience that we now shared. It dampened our spirits and confused our minds.

"Mamie used to say if anybody interfere with you, tell Auntie," Emma spoke finally as we walked, breaking the silence.

"I s'pose so," I said. "Maybe all of us should tell at the same time, and then they would believe us together."

"He have no right to come here and play God!" Emma blurted out. "Ah go tell me Mamie!" she said finishing her outrage with renewed confidence. She was referring to her mother in England.

Strangely, I too had often said the same thing when hurt. It was that familiar way of consoling yourself, using the threat of telling as a deterrent against whatever troubled you; the consolation of telling your mother, all the way in

England! But this was never of any use, apart from just helping to nurse the wound of being left in the care of others. Psychologically, it meant that there was always that *someone*, somewhere that you could turn to; albeit in thoughts and wishes only.

Complaints of injustices therefore remained in our thoughts, waiting to be unburdened when we got to England. But answers were needed now and we needed to find a way of coping with the present situation.

"You tell Phyllis yet?" I asked Emma.

Phyllis had not attended any of the church activities with the Priest. She had said that she was, 'too old for this kind a thing,' and refused to have anything to do with it.

"Noh, not yet, ah cyan tell her inside the house. S'pose Auntie hear me, then its licks for me on top of all this problem."

"You planning on telling?" she asked me.

I shrugged. "I aint planning on it but I might have to," I told her, not making too much sense.

We continued walking on. Locked in our own private thoughts, silence engulfed us, except for the clicking sound of our slippers; slapping our heels with each step in the long journey home. The road ahead which lay like a long, grey ribbon was flanked by the dense, thick greenery of the land on both sides. Just now, the familiar landscape did not inspire us with a solution, so we each focused silently on how we were going to unburden ourselves from this sordid affair.

"Hey what's going on?" Justin shouted, as he jumped out from a nearby bush and slapped us both on our backs. As if from nowhere, the boy had sneaked up, to frighten the life out of us. Locked in our fears and deep secrecy, we were furious that he had scared us in this way.

"Stop it you fool!" Emma snapped. "What's wrong with

you? Don't ever do that again!" she warned, looking wild and mad with anger at him.

"Eh-eh, ah only playing, doh get so pectus girl," Justin replied, trying to calm her down.

My heart was beating fast from the sudden fear, mainly because he had frightened us so suddenly, when we were already full of fear with our own personal thoughts. My nervousness from the sudden fright made me attacked him verbally too.

"Boy, you crazy?" I screamed at him.

Justin was surprised at our unusual outbursts. He realised that we were obviously not in the mood for jokes, being so unexplainably angry with him. He looked puzzled and surprised as he spoke.

"I ran all the way to tell you that ah hear the Priest have a secret," he retorted angrily, "And the two of you behaving as if I done something to you."

"What secret? Who tell you then?" we demanded, bombarding him immediately with question after question; hardly giving him a chance to answer the first one.

Our spirits sank, as our facial expressions showed the horror we were feeling about our presumed exposure. However, Justin being Justin *Thomas* realized that he now had the upper-hand. He used this opportune moment to play on our curiosity. He held us in suspense, nursing the moment for as long as he could. We felt worse, our secret must be out! Who, among anyone we knew, could jester and tease us, faced with such a predicament? Only Justin! We needed to know exactly what he knew about us, so we continued to demand more information. Justin played us along all the more.

"Now that kind of information's not for little girl's ears," he teased, "So I really shouldn't even be telling you," he said, secretly eyeing our responses.

"Well don't then!" Emma snapped.

"C'mon on Justin, stop playing around and tell us noh!" I begged.

"Well you see, when a smart man like me, get to know certain information some people don't know……," he said slowly, teasing even further and breaking off in mid sentence.

We pretended not to be interested for the sheer anger and frustration he was causing. We were greatly anxious to learn more, and quickly; so to get Justin to react quickly we called his bluff. We tried to walk away and pretend to be disinterested in his information. It worked. Without a captive audience, Justin needed to re-gain our attention, so he quickly got to the point.

"Well you know that priest, he aint no priest for a start! And he aint no African, either!" he finally blurted out.

"What!" we both chorused simultaneously, facing Justin squarely.

"What you mean?" I questioned.

"You sure?" Emma asked.

"Sure? Sure, I am sure. I sure 'bout everything," he said boastfully and instantly the *Thomas* attitude returned to rear its ugly head again.

Emma and I looked at each other; eyes and mouth opened wide in disbelief.

"Well, my information came from ah good source," he said confidently, refusing to say any more.

"Good source, who's your good source?" Emma insisted, and with an assured audience of two, Justin settled back into his teasing routine again.

"Papa Joe say he sure that the priest face look familiar."

"What else did he say?" I enquired.

"Well, he say the priest look a bit changed. Like he

change-up himself - you know, the bushy beard all over his face and the long priest gown, an' all that."

Papa Joe was a trafficker, who went from Grenada to Trinidad each week with a boat, selling fruit and vegetables, in exchange for the groceries he brought back for his shop. Everyone said that Papa Joe had a good spirit guiding him because he always survived the rough waters in *Pick'em Jenny*. This is where most people went overboard and those who were lucky enough to escape this watery hell, vowed never to venture into those parts again.

Papa Joe was the *griot* of the ghostly stories surrounding *Pick'em Jenny's* mysterious, rough waters; where it was rumoured, people and whole boats went missing too. *Pick'em Jenny* was our mini Bermuda Triangle, but Papa Joe was fearless. He was a literate man who always brought back many old newspapers with him from Trinidad. A fountain of worldly knowledge, he was always able to tell the men in the rum shop what was happening around the Caribbean; meaning Trinidad mostly.

"Oh Gawd, oy!" we both chorused. This new shock had doubled the confusion we were already feeling.

"What you saying! He's **not** ah priest and he's **not** ah African?" Emma asked slowly, stressing on the "*not,*" in order to be doubly sure we had heard him correctly.

"Look!" he said warning us, "I didn' tell you anything eh, so don't go and call me name!"

With that, Justin ran away, back into the bushes; leaving us standing there more perplexed than we were before he came along.

ع

For the following week, I refused to go to clean the

church. Instead, each day I either feigned sickness, complained of fake belly-aches, or volunteered to take food to blind Mr. Zachariah, who lived about an eight of a mile away. Gran-gran had always done the job of carrying food to Mr. Zachariah herself, so it's not surprising that she became very intrigued by my new-found interest in such an extra chore.

She swung into an immediate plan of action to get to the root of the puzzle. To cure my belly-aches, she ordered castor oil with vermifuge in it from the doctor's surgery in Sauteurs. It was the worst kind of purge or laxative medicine. Then to add insult to injury, she sent me to collect it. The thick heavy oil looked threatening and choking in its dark-brown bottle. It caused my stomach to churn, at the very sight of it. I shuddered.

"She probably have worms," Aunt Meena said, believing that we had eaten too many mangoes and fruit lately.

"I try warning them about sucking too much mangoes; a dose of castor oil will bring down the worms," she said in her short, sharp, to-the-point way.

Gran-gran agreed and they planned to give it to me early on Saturday morning. This was to give the medicine enough time to work through my system. I would have to be fit and well by Sunday for church-going, and for school on Monday. Although I dreaded the castor oil like no other thing in the world, I dared not tell them that I did not need *that* sort of purging. I certainly could not bring myself to tell them the truth as yet, because it would cause uproar in the home and village.

The thick castor oil was a clown jeering at me from within the dark bottle, daring me to tell. I felt sick each time I leaned the bottle from side to side, to follow the medicine's painfully slow movement within. Being given castor oil during mango season was a purging ritual which children were accustomed to. I fiddled with the screw-on top as I leaned it on its side, trying to make the thick slime inside stir.

On Saturday morning, Aunt Meena ceremoniously held my nose back and ordered me to drink the castor oil.

"Open!" she said sternly, as she pushed the first tablespoonful of the castor oil into my fully-salivered mouth. I gulped it in two swallows at first, but with each swallowing action, I felt like vomiting the slimy oil. Each time I heaved and fought the combating oil, my stomach threatened to expel the disgusting laxative.

For the second spoonful, Aunt Meena ordered me again to open my mouth. Obediently, I did so. The castor oil touched my tongue so I swallowed quickly but could sense my stomach trying to fight back. I motioned to bring it up again.

"Hold it!" she warned, so I swallowed repeatedly, forcing the purgative to stay down in my stomach. I gulped again and again through clenched teeth. It was in my interest not attempt to bring up the medicine; otherwise more castor oil would have been ordered and given. I swallowed and shivered, closing my eyes as I did so. I swallowed again, scorning the taste of the nasty purgative, until the threatening vomit eventually subsided.

Soup was promised for the day and the thought of it made me feel better. I visualised the customary plain water soup which consisted of Irish potatoes, macaroni, dumplings rolled into little balls, pieces of salt beef and tiny tanias cut up in half; all with a touch of salted butter with chive and thyme. Thoughts of the impending soup immediately made the smell and the taste of the castor oil vanish from my mouth. After that, began the waiting for the evidence of worms to appear.

Gran-gran was intent on seeing me at the forefront of everything and it concerned her that I did not want to continue with "*my calling*" at the forefront in the Priest's activities, as a would-be *Woman of Destiny*. I know that she did not want to lose face with the Priest or the members in general but it bothered her that my future status was being affected by something that was perhaps unknown to her.

She had taught me many little prayers to say just as she had often dictated letters for me to write for her with obedience. However, right now I seemed to be balking at the all-important *"duties,"* and this was blurring her vision of my prominence. She was alerted when she noticed that I was *'lagging behind'* as she called it because I made excuses and subtle attempts to sit in the back row of the church instead of the front! But Gran-gran was an experienced woman with wisdom; a veteran in life's battles, she was a vigilant General for those in her charge. She proceeded to conduct her own reconnaissance before planning further attacks in getting to the root cause of the 'problem.'

One day, she cleverly called me to read to her from the customary *Words of Comfort*. This I did with eagerness. Yes, she smiled, clearly pleased that at least, this little important job was not affected by my new attitude. The real test was to make me read twice the normal amount for that day and strangely, she did not fall asleep while I was reading to her. She was happy with this but not totally satisfied. There was a continued, strange look of searching; a deep surveying in her puzzled dark-brown eyes that made her remain calm and resolute. She was silently working out her battle plan in order to ensure the final victory.

Often, deep in thought, Gran-gran would grit her teeth and appear to be very far away, maybe in England, where Aunt Meena was; in Trinidad, where Uncle Feelan was or Aruba where Sister Aresina was. Her mind appeared to wander across different periods along her 70 years time-line. Today, she was somewhat disconcerted about the affairs presently at hand in Grenada, so she searched for the solution by encouraging discussion.

"Nex' week you comin' to town wid me," she announced.

A brilliant psychologist she turned out to be because that was bait number one. Her unprecedented announcement was a shock to me, since I was the one who often had to plead, beg and cry relentlessly, for her to let me accompany her on her journeys to St. Georges. In any case, most of the times her answer was "No." I had accompanied her before and those times were wonderful memories, therefore she stirred up a great excitement in me, for further open discussions.

Journeys to town were special occasions. There was the brightness of the town buildings, the many cars and buses and the business of taxi drivers, hustling and jibing with potential customers – it was a joy to witness. The market-place too with its kaleidoscope of colours was very memorable, as women and men bartered for the best prices for their land produce. Most memorable was the frightening, steep descent on Market Hill. This sharp decline to the town was made more frightening by the shimmering, deep-blue, scary sea, waiting below. They were forever vividly etched in my memory.

Gran-gran made those monthly visits to town to pay, by installments, for land which the family had bought many years ago by installments. The carefully folded land papers were always wrapped up in a cloth which was tied with a string and kept in the most sacred place, near the Bible in a little grip. Amongst the confidential package was the *Friendly Society Savings Book*, some camphor, money which had been tied up secretly in another piece of cloth. There was also a black and white photograph of Aunt Irene in England, sitting on a wicker chair, in an English photographic studio. Gran-gran had always handled the land papers with a kind of reverence, probably comparable to the handling of a winning jackpot lottery ticket.

The last time she had taken me with to town was important because she needed to show me what to do, in case anything happened to her. Her reasoning was that I would know where her 'business' was located, to help deal with it. When we entered the Land Payment Office, two fair-skinned Receptionists greeted us. They looked dainty, with straightened hair, cutex on fingernails and both wore bright red lipstick. One or two white men in short-sleeved shirts and ties looked relaxed in the solar-heated room, despite the revolving electric fan overhead.

Grand-gran admired them. She took on an air of importance, which showed confidence; after all, we were land-owners. She responded to their greeting and conducted the transaction. As soon as the business dealing was over, Gran-gran took the opportunity to instruct me.

"Dese people are '*Big*' people," she whispered. She cast her eyes on one of the Receptionists battering her manual typewriter as she typed and motioned to me to look. As promptly as we walked out of the Land Office, she made an announcement.

"When you grow up I want you to be a typewriter, like dese girls." A look of determination returned to her face. "One day you will be a *Woman of Destiny,*" she said, in the same way that Reverend Blackman and Miss Joseph had proclaimed it. She looked at me for confirmation. I nodded and I knew what she really meant was that she would like me to become a Typist. However, although I agreed to be a *Woman of Destiny*, no one had explained what it entailed.

"The people inside that office are *big* people?" I asked since I was unsure as to why they were considered "big."

"Yes, dey are *Big* people," she said then continued. "You see them fronting job - they clean and tidy - dey "*Big*."

It was her constant vision of going forward, being someone '*Big*' that she held for me. So far I had appeared to be steering in that direction, as far as she was concerned; that is, up until now. She had felt sure that the church and my Sunday school position was proof of my climbing up the ladder. That is why my recent balking at my calling disturbed her visionary quest for me. It made her probe even further.

"You know old Mr. Thomas say he can hear a lot of things about England on his radio."

England was the subject. She had plucked the brass strings of delight to my ear, and bait number two was steadily on its way.

"Ah, see a radio in town last month. Ah pay nearly all the money for it. Ah only have one more payment to make," she continued calmly. My eyes lit up.

"We will take it when we go to town," she confirmed.

Gran-gran was a master at her brand of psychology and it was working. She could see she was giving me a shock after the suggestion she had made so far, and my big eyes opened wider at each offering. I had become animated, evident by my incessant chatter and new-found happiness.

"We go listen to BBC World Service on the radio," she promised, then continued. "You know dey tell you what happening everyday all over the world," said Gran-gran.

She coaxed gently, as she watched my expressions of real delight. So bait number two was proof that my interest in going further and learning was still confirmed. Bait number three was designed to get to the heart of the matter.

"Dey does talk about Africa on the radio too," she told me casually.

I had appeared half-interested and she guessed that perhaps I did not hear, so she repeated herself. To be respectful I pretended to be interested, by mouthing wryly, "Africa on the radio, too?"

Gran-gran continued, "You know dey say people here in the islands really come from Africa."

I remained awkwardly silent and did not volunteer any information to keep the conversation going. Maybe she had expected me to offer some information about the new knowledge I had gained from the African Priest but instead, I questioned her about the radio.

"What colour de radio have Gran gran? When I grow up I want to be an Announcer, like the people in it." I said this in order to obliterate Africa from my mind, hoping that my new and additional ambition would delight her.

She frowned a little, realising that something deep within had struck some chords with her sense of uneasiness. Her eyes twitched again, that awful twitching of painful realization. I believed just then, she knew all that she wanted to know. The probing stopped and she remained silent for a while before speaking again.

"You eleven years now, yes?"

"Yes and December will make me twelve. Emma is 13 and Daisy is twelve. I am the last one."

She probably even knew what the word "*last*" implied, so she kept the conversation going.

"Yes they turn into young women now," she replied and dropped the subject.

It was common knowledge that the girls had become young women, having seen their first monthly periods; they now needed to be kept closely in sight and it was what all the women felt and 'preached'. During the days which followed, Gran-gran insisted that she should help me in the church.

"Two hands make work light, and quick," she reasoned.

Such encouragement worked and I agreed to resume my duties again. She often used to let me go ahead of her into the church and soon afterwards, she would pretend that she was taking a little walk up the road. Alone, walking slowly, though stopping constantly after a few steps; she would stop with hands behind her back, to rest, think and survey the surroundings. I had watched her on many occasions when she stopped to admire nature, as she stood in the cool shades of trees to rest before taking weak steps to complete her journey.

She was like a protective angel of mercy; the ones in heaven that Reverend Blackman said were watching over us. On reaching the church, she would sit at the back; watching, surveying, learning and judging. The African priest did not really know what to make of Gran-gran's unplanned presence and it was evident that he felt awkward. He seemed uncomfortable and instead of his quiet, confident posture, he became nervous. Each day she did the same thing; Gran-gran sent me ahead and the priest followed. Then she appeared, promptly after him and sat quietly, observing and noting his proceedings.

His feeling of guilt and unease made him take his job more seriously or so it seemed, and he shouted at us constantly or criticized us unjustifiably. He was confused and his guilt was giving him away. Gran-gran was fighting him in her own silent, 70-year-old way. She used psychology and her years of experience to beat the 32-year-old priest at his foolish games. Her presence was threatening and it haunted him; especially as he did not know whether his foul deeds were exposed or not.

He showed more dedication in his endeavours to teach us and he appeared to work hard; squeezing every ounce of knowledge he could muster from himself to us. It was too late; the spectating Gran-gran was wise. She was not convinced with his antics and she knew that he was showing off and could read between his performances and reality.

It was not long after Gran-gran's meeting with all the elders in the church and village that the priest left us. Rev. Blackman had announced it on the priest's last Sunday morning service.

"Lawd, we bring you our dear Brother, who must leave this village to take his knowledge to other shores."

"Yes, Lawd!" the congregation answered loudly.

"Lawd walk with him, guide his footsteps and teach him to walk in the right way."

Rev. Blackman had laid emphasis on the words *"right way."* Everyone, it seemed, knew exactly what he had meant.

"Amen!" the congregation responded heartily and deep within my heart, my own "Amen" was the loudest, the biggest, and most relieving sound of all.

Chapter 4

"First we must learn to love one another
Be generous and kind to one another
Cherish and love your mother
And cast thy bread upon the water
Don't be misled and act right away
It is a solid foundation we are bound to lay."
Lord Beginner (Egbert Moore)

"Jo - anne! Jo - anne!"

"Yes, Gran gran!"

"Whe' you come from? You didn' hear me calling you?"

"No, Gran-gran."

"Ah tell you, what you head lead you to do," she said angrily, "You backside go pay for it, you know!"

Gran-gran was more vigilant and anxious with me since the priest left our village and she had become somewhat more obsessed with my movements. She was either calling me to identify my whereabouts or following me after she sent me on errands.

The priest's behaviour in the church among all the girls was given a post-mortem and it was clearly evident that all the women became somewhat more paranoid over their girls. The fear of what could have been for them and us was real. It was tied up with their hurt feelings of being taken-in by a twisted "brother;" a wolf in sheep's clothing. At the same time, it belittled their judgment and reduced the quality of their unblemished authority among their children.

A sense of shame prevailed over their trust in the stranger. They were shocked that they themselves had been consenting parties in sending their lambs to the wolf! It seemed to prick their consciousness and constantly agitated them; so that they became excessive in their attempts to make amends.

Aunt Meena took turns with Gran-gran to marshal us. When Gran-gran was not on duty, Aunt Meena would be doing the calling and threatening. Between them, we didn't stand a chance of falling by the wayside.

Whilst Aunt Meena was away, thre was a joint effort of preparing our lunch, Monica, my cousin peeled the yams. Yvonne and I peeled the green bananas and sweet potatoes. The fish which we added was already seasoned and left to be marinated by Aunt Meena before she left the house. After marinating for hours we fried it and prepared the meal quickly and with precision; in order to keep the peaceful atmosphere.

Blackie, our meager-looking Labrador, was given the discarded fish gills and guts, as well as the left-over food. It laid on the dry ground, with outstretched legs and head in the hot, red, dust; looking like a wounded animal, it panted quietly in the shade.

The sun had come up blindingly hot, causing the prevailing heat to shimmer, sizzle and dance in the distance. The cane leaves brushing along the back door of the house, reminded us that the wind was still blowing as we sat quietly on the verandah. There was nothing pressing to do and the afternoon heat made us feel lethargic and sleepy, after our heavy lunch of ground provisions.

Earlier, a few people had passed our house on their return from their daily tasks on the local estate. They looked tired and worn-out from their morning's work on the land. All was quiet and peaceful except for Aunt Meena. She seemed restless and agitated since her talk with Daisy's mother at the junction earlier today.

Aunt Meena was not very demonstrative in matters of affection. There was no time for emotional exchanges; no "I love you's" and certainly no loving embraces. Love was outward defense against threats from outside our family circle and she did so most vehemently. This was especially so, if a situation presented itself and warranted public retribution.

Aunt Meena had long, curly hair, which most of the times was in two thick black plaits that reached her shoulders. She was slender and her big eyes were set sharply in her dark-brown, skinny face. Her mouth was sharp; always ready with a hardened expression to scold someone. She also had a seriousness which made it difficult to approach her with anything insignificant. Whenever you did have to go to her, it was often either for a reprimand, to answer to some charges or face the whip or the belt; both of which she yielded with constancy.

Her neck was small and her collar-bone was always prominent in the thin shoulders above her small breasts. She worked hard on the land which she cultivated for her sister and brother in England. Buying land in Grenada was one of the main aims of most migrant travellers; in preparation for their return. But she called our land, *"The Garden;"* because it was where she sowed seeds and planted enough food for our need. Aunt Meena always took the surplus food for sale in Grenville market on Saturdays.

She was a shrewd businesswoman, sharp with her tongue in her rebukes for those criticizing her method of sale or prices. This was often quick and effective. But she had her regular customers; therefore, her small cottage-garden business thrived. Each season she sold whatever fruit or vegetable was available and when I had accompanied her to Grenville on such occasions, which were few and far between; it was to help her oversee the piles of her produce on sale, as she bartered and bargained with her difficult customers.

The ground provisions were often displayed like pyramids in a kaleidoscope of competing colours and she proudly used her seasoned charm, her confidence and knowledge of her goods, to attract her customers. She seemed serious all the time but when she laughed, it was clear and loud; like a hen cackling. Aunt Meena would tilt her head backwards as she cackled, showing big, strong, ivory-looking teeth and wrinkles around her eyes. It was sometimes nice to hear those bellyfuls of laughs from Aunt Meena, but as children we also found it difficult to judge their exact meaning. We were sometimes unsure as to whether those laughs were really happy laughs or not. This is because Aunt Meena could also be seen making those same bellyful laughs, even before she seriously dished out licks as punishment to us.

The reason is, when she was very angry, it was also possible to hear such a laugh and the quickness with which her temper changed made us always on guard. The kind of control which she had over us was the same kind of control she had over her customers. She had a kind of school teacher's austerity which helped her to survive. It was her strategy to help her perform the tasks of looking after a child on behalf of departed mothers and fathers to some foreign shores. She was especially watchful over me, since I was left in her care.

Perhaps the most common role in Caribbean families was probably being totally responsible for some other Caribbean migrant's child or children; a burden which made it difficult for the women to relax totally. It would seem that others judged the quality of their protective care as representative of the quality of their character. The status or position they held in the community and their ability to rear their own siblings and family members' siblings, were daily assessed by the whole community. The villagers were the daily judges; presiding over surrogate women and children left by their absentee parents.

Aunt Meena's face was always serious. She seemed more serious today and it often troubled us because it was an indication that one, if not all of us, had done something to merit her displeasure. Whatever the misdemeanor, the result would definitely be punishment with the belt. Today, we had behaved well but her mournful humming soon aggravated our afternoon composure. When she could contain herself no longer, she called us into the kitchen where he was.

She interrogated all of us. My cousins, Monica, Yvonne, Lydia and I stood in front of Aunt Meena like suspects on trial and we were afraid of her impending wrath.

"That Priest touch all-you?" she asked.

No one answered immediately. We stood looking at the ground at our feet, avoiding her gaze; terrified at what telling the truth might bring. Often telling the truth would bring a reprimand anyway. The fact is, it was the same illogical routine if we did something wrong at school and had been beaten at school for it; the usual repercussion would be, you would be given another beating at home. This punishment at home would be given for having been punished in school in the first place! Such was the inexplicable kind of grown-up reasoning, which we had all learnt to accept.

We each discovered that through the priest's short reign, we had all fallen prey to his fiendish ploys. In retrospect, we wondered if we had told our families about it, how they would have received the information. For each one, the threat of more retribution was a reality and this deterred us from even trying to speak. It was a fact, many parents had turned their children into liars; having been forced into making choices between telling the truth and lying to literally save their skins. Justin said that we had developed the wit of Brer Anancy and we had jeered at him, but maybe there was some truth in the boy's reasoning.

"All-you don' hear ah talking? Open all-you mouth before licks take all-you backside!"

She was armed with a leather belt this time. She stood as a very present threat so Monica, the oldest, spoke.

"He touch my tay-tay."

"He wat! That nastiness, touch your breast! Is Gawd alone what save him. I woulda cut 'e blasted neck, Papa Gawd himself know."

Aunt Meena was reviling him. She looked wild with rage and we could tell that her anger was not one hundred per cent directed at us - a rare thing. However, we were standing in front of her and she had a belt, so it was possible that anything could happen; we were on guard.

"You, Yvonne, what he do you?"

"He just say if I let him touch me, he would teach me some new things," Yvonne said fearfully.

"That wretch! Pli maliwells!" she said in Patwa, spitting furiously on the ground and pronouncing her broken-French curse on him.

"The same han' he put on all-you, is the same one that will stay cock-up when he dead. Is La Croix that will have to break and straighten it in his coffin!" she retorted, walking up and down in her rage in front of us.

As Aunt Meena ranted and raved, I stood there trembling. I could hardly wait for her to pause for me to speak. She was wishing she had planassed him with her cutlass, with more uttered curses on his name.

"He put his hand under my dress," I blurted out quickly. She became like a mad dog, hopping and cursing. Obviously, she seemed more mad the fact that the priest seemed to have gotten away with murder.

"That low-down, dirty, dog; somebody go give him a good buss ass," she prophesied.

"May Gawd punish him," Aunt Meena said, spitting repeatedly on the ground in anger again. She cursed him, again and again, as she chewed up the broken French words.

"Pli maliwells!" She continued cursing him in patwa, then warned; "He better don' let me start on him wid me *goat-mouth,* noh! You know goat-mouth does bring poison prophecy!"

If the priest had been there to answer to the various charges, his crucifixion would have been one hundred percent certain. All the women in the village were horrified. They got together and made the sign of the cross in the red dust and regrettably pledged that if they had known, they would have surely cut the priest's neck.

"And he better don' put it past us yet. Because we go look for his ass," Daisy's mother confirmed.

When the realisation of what could have been really hit Aunt Meena she sat down; forgetting that we were standing in front of her, she muttered to herself.

"Bon Je', look at me crosses noh! S'pose you mother hear that in England? She go say ah let you go astray," she said turning to me.

We stood there silently. Her question needed no answer. We had been told to call the priest "*Uncle*" – our cultural respect for an elder amongst us and demonstration of Christian values. Older women were called '*Auntie,*' and older Men, were called '*Uncle.*' Senior members in church were '*Mothers,*' '*Sisters*' and '*Brothers;*' based on seniority of spiritual attainment.

"Look how innocent people could get ah bad name noh!"
She said this, lost in thought, obviously referring to herself.
Then Aunt Meena stood up and straightened herself.

"All-you mus' open all-you eye, eh!" She was calmer now
and with an unusual concern, she spoke in parables.

"Not all flesh is good meat; same way not all people good
people - you understand?" she said, trying to help us reason
with her.

"An' ah want all-you to promise me that if anything like
that happen again, nex' time come and tell me or all-you
Granmother. All-you hear me?"

"Yes, Aunt Meena," we chorused.

"Stop this *Auntie Meena* business right now! All-you is
big enough - in fact, too big to keep calling me *Auntie*." With
more annoyance she questioned, "So all- you doh know I is
you mother?"   She said, surveying Yvonne and Monica's
face.

"Yes," they both said coyly.

"Yes who, then?" she retorted.

"Yes mamie," said both girls, sounding rather strange with
their new expression.

She was my aunt so I repeated after them, "Yes, Aunt
Meena."

Aunt Meena was bent on putting all matters straight
immediately. She had been caught; out-smarted by a crooked
'christian.' Secretly, her new attitude indicated a kind of self-
blame for a situation which needed instant reformation. It was
an inducement for us to confide in her. She made us sit down
while she explained.

"Ah want all-you all to understand that all this saying
'*Auntie*' for everybody is good because when all-you was
small, we encouraged it. But it's good when family is close

together; we teach children how to respect the older ones. But now, all-you is grown children now."

Tradition and culture were giving way to a new kind of thinking because a new situation had emerged that demanded change.

There was a tickle in my throat but I dared not cough. I held back the scratch and swallowed several times, while my eyes watered because of the throaty itch. I shifted uncomfortably several times, puffed my mouth and made little attempts to stifle the rising, loud, cough from the tickling throat. There was no point in openly clearing my throat, in case it was misconstrued as a rude gesture. A drink of water was the perfect answer but we had to stay put. We had to stand and listen to Aunt Meena's long spiel, for fear of instigating some instant punishment.

The atmosphere was already dicey and there was no point in tempting fate further. I swallowed my saliva several times and eventually it helped to quell the throaty riot. Yvonne sniffled and every now and then she would look up, to catch our gaze from where she was digging her toes in the dirt in front of her. Monica was older, she was attentive and she kept Aunt Meena's gaze steadily.

"Now you know that is not everybody you see is ah good *uncle* or ah good *auntie*. From now on, there's nothing wrong in saying *"mister"* or *"miss."* We have to draw the line and change things up to suit our ways nowadays." Aunt Meena became the school teacher and she instructed further.

"The word *Uncle* and *Auntie,* from now on, is only for your blood relatives. All-you hear me?" Aunt Meena said, making sure that what we were about to receive would be clear to us.

We nodded profusely. Then she turned to me with individual instructions.

"Joanne, you have to stop calling your mother *"Auntie"* too. She is not your *Auntie Irene*, she is your mother. All this confusion we cause all-you, we mus' straighten it out now. You children have to understand from now on."

She lectured us, as we remained silently, attentive in front of her; letting her vent her anger till she graduated to a much calmer pitch.

"In fact, Joanne you must start writing to you mother. It's about time you start calling her *Mamie*. Our family size is big, so ah have to tell all of you, who is who."

Then Aunt Meena became emotionally melodramatic once more.

"Only Papa Gawd knows when he go call me, and those who behind have to take care of the others," she said.

Maybe she was thinking out aloud. However, for Aunt Meena the macho image must remain, so she stopped herself, sighed and checked us.

"All-you understanding me now?" she asked, revived by her new plan.

"Yes, Aunt Meena," I said.

"Yes Mamie," the others chorused.

We were dismissed to go inside and wash up and get ready for bed. Aunt Meena continued muttering and cursing by herself in the kitchen. We were spared the customary blows, so she vented her feelings on the helpless pots, pans and pancups instead.

We did our homework, had our wash and sat indoors; feeling clean and relieved by the warmth and safety of being inside our house. Gran-gran was in the bedroom. She made me recite *'The Magnificat'* to her from her Bible, and the others listened too. *"My soul doth magnify the Lord and my spirit hath rejoiced in God my saviour."*

When her *WORDS OF COMFORT* was completed, we said the customary prayer, in unison with Gran-gran.

> *"This night, as I lay down to sleep;*
> *I give the Lord my soul to keep."*

Meanwhile, Aunt Meena was sitting in the darkened verandah, thinking and pondering; letting the defeat that all the women felt, come up and haunt her mind. There, concealed in the darkness, the shame was easier to accept, so she allowed the night to console her.

The few weeks which followed, found everyone resettling back into normal routines and the vigilance subsided gradually, in time. We all looked forward to *Gloria Saturday*, which was the Saturday within the Easter weekend; the next event from our childhood calendar.

ع

Gloria Saturday was predicted to be the time when there would be lots of crayfish in the river. It was the Saturday after Good Friday, and despite all the prevailing old beliefs, we went to the river to wash clothes. Some said that because it was the day after Christ's death, the river would turn to blood so they preferred to spend their time in prayer. Those like us, who went to church on Sundays, felt that we were not trespassing on our Sabbath day, so we generally did as we pleased on Saturdays.

Emma, Daisy, Monica and Lydia went washing too. Armed with big bulky parcels of dirty clothes like a big bun on top of enamel basins, we made our way to St. John River, where we also met the St. John women and girls doing their weekly washing. It was a female environment and if there were boys in the vicinity of the river, it was primarily to make

118

some sweet eyes at the girls or whisper secret plans behind their parents back.

The river was one of the main tributaries in the northern Parishes of the island, which ran its course over many miles before reaching the sea. As such, it was located among mountains, through the rich fertile lands which produce cocoa, nutmeg, bananas, spices, and ground provisions; amidst thick, dense vegetation.

The clean, clear, water meandered through the greenery; often making whistling music around big stones or at times, depending on its flow, barely whispered its presence. The water sometimes collected in huge basins where it would remain silently, threatening and undisturbed. Rainfall in the mountains at the source was often a problem and most people had to contend with the danger of St. John's River bursting its bank; swelling with the dirty soil-eroded water and killing those along its course.

It had been rumored that one hot day, during the dry-season, when everything seemed perfectly normal and the villagers were baking in the heat, unknown to them rain had been pounding the mountains very heavily. They were unaware that the vicious, overflowing river had burst its bank, and had engulfed many people and animals in its path.

The muddy river water had raced along, sweeping everything in its mad fury, breaking small trees, shifting big granite stones and crushing whatever stood in its path. A lot of vegetation was destroyed. The river had, in some areas, altered its own course, flowing over some bridges and making roads impassible. It overflowed where concrete, which formed bridges, had caved in or washed away by the forceful pressure of the angry water.

It had washed houses that were nearby and some had exaggerated that the water level was so high, that it had come up to the 40 ft high St. John's Bridge.   It was rumoured that water had covered the road and made it impossible for anyone to travel between Hermitage and Upper St. John! Though I had believed the stories about the water's destructive power, it was harder to be convinced that the overflowing river had reached the height of the bridge. I pondered this each time I had occasion to pass that way home from various errands.

Since then, no one really trusted the river with its innocent looks. Decisions as to whether people went there to wash on any given day, was first preceded by surveying the quality of clouds over the mountains, in order to predict the river's behaviour for the day. As a child, I was frightened by the river's history; the dreadful possibilities of more silent destruction, and the appearance of the silk cotton tree, which stood near its bank.

For many, the silk cotton tree was a symbol of witchcraft. Obeah men, we were told on storytelling nights, could catch a person's soul and nail it on a silk cotton tree. The giant trees, which were often located near to the water, seemed to grow hundreds of feet high. Their long spidery roots, like robotic prongs that had been fighting the years of watery revolution; looked ugly and appeared haunted.

A basin of water often collected around the imposing tree. So too were old clothes that had been washed down with old rotting fruits and vegetation, leaves, twigs, broken branches, shit and whatever filth was deposited further up in the never-ending stream. So the river and the silk cotton tree were twins of evil and they were blamed for many misfortunes in their vicinity. As far as the silk cotton tree was concerned, it was the worse of the two evils; since Cosmos' grandfather had a fatal car crash near the bridge. The vehicle had plummeted over the bridge and crashed in front of the silk cotton tree, causing the fatal accident. This had instigated many superstitions that gave rise to a lot of our childish fears.

Rumours were rife that the tree claims human lives in order to have survived over the centuries. Much blame was attached to the tree for the bodies that had gone missing in the river. This tree was reputed to suck people into its body by means of its web-like roots; in order to feed on human blood for its longevity. So with such prevailing folklore, it was no wonder we were frightened to go past or even look at the tree.

Our rustic village life was pervaded by folklore and all life's little mysteries were given some supernatural explanations. The forces of nature were all powerful, bringing men to their knees and the control which they displayed over the folks' lives, made it impossible to accept scientific causes. None of life's phenomena was accepted as a consequence of man's causes. The land was life, producing life, it nurtured life but at the same time, it also controlled life by taking life. It did so as and when it pleased. Its partners in crime were the other forces; wind, hurricanes, flooding, rain, sun and crop disease. Each one had the power to inflict on us, its own brand of punishment and as potential victims, we were at their mercy.

So on *Gloria Saturday*, those who preferred to believe that the fish were plentiful in the streams, sought to prove it with exhaustive flurries of activities. Their aims were to leave the rivers or sea, loaded with the unfortunate little beasts in order to perpetuate the age-old myths.

It was early when we arrived at the river. The crystal clear water hissed and fizzed around the stones, sometimes forming miniature waterfalls. It appeared clean, innocent, and pleaded purity; since no one else would have begun washing in it as yet, anywhere along its banks. We knew the early morning water was cold, so we sat on the biggest flat granite stone talking and planning what we would do, after we had washed and put our clothes to dry.

Slowly, the coolness of the morning began to give way to the warmth and encouragement of the sun, and we began our washing tasks. Each person chose a sizeable stone on which to rub and scrub the clothes. Therefore, around each big stone, was an unspoken but defined space, which included the nearby bushes along the banks or beds of pebbles. As these were not in the water's path we used them for drying areas. After dipping our feet sheepishly into the cold water to test its temperature, we settled into our positions for the next two hours.

Basins with soapy water held the soaking whites on one side, while the non-white clothes were scrubbed with an empty corn-cob. They were battered, squeezed, poked and prodded before being submitted to the day's sun. The scrup-scrupping of the soapy clothes against tightened palms agitated the dirty areas and each item in turn received its rub and scrub treatment, before being carefully placed aside to dry.

Emma was quieter than normal. She had whispered earlier that there was something she needed to tell me.

"Auntie get letter yesterday," she whispered.

"Yeah? Something happen?" I asked, noting her seriousness.

"Noh, noh, we'll talk later," came her quick answer.

I watched her and noticed that today she was deep in thought and she worked diligently, slapping the clothes and showing very little interest in our chatter about searching for crayfish later.

"What happen to you then?" I asked jokingly.

"Eh? How you mean?"

"Don't worry with her, now she's going to England," Daisy teased, "She probably feeling better than us now."

The bombshell was dropped. Emma didn't look up. She avoided my surprised gaze and rather than our excited predictions about going to England, she seemed so sad now. My heart beat fast and I pressed her with urgency for an answer.

"Is true? You really hear from your mother? She send for you?"

Emma did not share the same urgency for an answer, so I coaxed her.

"C'mon on' she's joking right!'" I laughed nervously.

I couldn't bear the thought of not having Emma there and right now, she was taking too long to calm my sudden irritation.

"Awright!" she snapped. "I don't know for sure. Auntie say she get letter from Mamie and they making plans, something to do with the laws in England wanting children to join their parents before they turn 14 years."

Our previous role-playing and fantasizing about going to England was fun, this reality was not and secretly, I didn't want Emma to go before I did. She was my best friend, my support, and the thought of her not being there frightened me.

Daisy cut in, "All you think England life is easy?"

"How you know?" Lydia asked her, "You ain't been there."

"Ah have good ears, ah does hear things," she said, "And I always read letters Aunty Dinah send from England."

She slapped the trousers which she was washing, dipped it in the water then twisted it, by swirling one end of it in the water until it looked like a big fat twisted snake. Then using her knees to grip one end of the twisted snake tightly she wrung and wrung, forcing the clear water out of the khaki garment. The 15 year old looked older than she was and she adopted grown-up mannerisms because she was allowed to wear a bra, when most girls were not.

"Auntie Dinah lives in a place called Paddington in England. She's always saying how things hard. You know I hear that at times you can find up to three people - all of them strangers, living and sleeping in one room!"

We looked at her with interest and she was not smiling. Daisy was always quietly observing, and learning from what she saw and heard; now our attentive posture encouraged her to continue.

"You know Auntie says that in England nobody would believe the kind of things happening there. She say some England people put up big signs saying "NO IRISH, NO DOGS AND NO COLOUREDS" in their windows, so you cyan get a place to stay. Imagine that, some even slam doors in people face when they ask for a room to rent to live in!"

"You sure you read that in a letter?" Lydia asked her, "Or you make it up," she mused.

"Make it up? How ah go make up something like that? Ah doh know 'bout no Irish and ah doh know 'bout no rooms," defended the girl.

"I thought everybody live in a house in England," Daisy said.

Some of us sat silently near to Daisy's stone, waiting for her to continue and others nodded their agreement that she could not have known about what she was telling us, unless she had read it. Daisy continued as we listened.

"Anyway, Auntie say you should see women fighting for space on a cooker to cook before the gas they using run out. She say those who cooking will be cooking while some bathing and others playing their Blue Spot music loud, loud. But the worst thing is they have to put money into a gas meter. The trouble is, those who did not put money still want to use up the gas, so sometimes you could be bathing and then the gas finish."

"What!" we exclaimed.

"Yes," she confirmed with confidence, "Hot water stop on you man! You have to run out of the cold bathroom and put clothes on you."

"Eh-heh?" Lydia grunted in disbelief.

"Me, I can't believe that could happen in England," I said, "They have a lot of everything there!"

"Look girl, here in Grenada, we free. Look you can bathe in this river. You think it bad. It's not as bad as bathing in a bath of dirty water and no water to rinse your body," Daisy said.

She suddenly seemed very knowledgeable about a lot of things that Emma and I had not even considered.

"Woy-o-yoy!" Phyllis remarked in disbelief. "You mean a big place like England they doh have a river to bathe in and clean themselves? That's nastiness man!"

Daisy, it seemed, had focused on every little detail of her Auntie's letters from England, much to our amazement. Afterwards, Phyllis added her own news.

"It must be true, because you know that Mr. Mitchell who have land in the mango row? Ah hear he say that once when he was in England, some people called Teddy Boys beat him up with some heavy boots; mash up his mouth so now he have to wear false teeth."

We all turned to the girl, with her amazing stories and listened attentively, while she continued.

"And I hear he say, all he was doing was going home from the hotel where he used to clean and wash up plates."

We were transfixed on the girl's face as we listened in the silence.

Phyllis continued, "I hear they say Mr. Mitchell didn't say a single word to them although they cursed him real bad, saying they go give the nigger a real bashing."

We gasped noisily and she continued.

"You know the man have cuts on his body and the false teeth to prove it! He say since that time, he decide he not staying in England because in those days, England people want to hurt you because you coloured."

"Eh eh? What kind a thing is that?"

"Well, he say the worse thing about England, is when people leave here as teachers and nurses, some of them going all the way to England to wash shit, clean people house, make up bed and wash dishes!"

Phyllis had now become our social informant, so we kept listening to the confident girl.

"Never mind the big *hefe* people they used to play here, when they go to England, they not doing anything better. Well yes, they come back here looking nice to fool us. But right here man; take it from me, we real good ah telling you."

The time was quickly passing by and a few others had come to the river to wash their clothes. They had taken up their places at other big stones. A few scrup-scrupping and slapping of clothes were already taking place but our interest was greater in the stories about England than in washing. Daisy was intent on keeping the centre-stage which she had, so she continued.

"Ah hear a person does dress up to go to work in suit and nice clothes, but what you think they going to do? Maybe sweep train station, wash dishes and they going back home afterwards well dressed up again in their suit, just as if they went to town!"

"But England nice too man," Lydia defended. "Look at Miss George when she come back for a holiday, she's nice and fat. She always look happy and she have some nice clothes! An' let's face it, she does send money to mind she children, don't she?"

We nodded.

"Look, what you think paying for Glenna and Bernadette school fees at the convent school - England money!" Lydia concluded her input; glad that she could offer us information we did not know about.

Lydia, like Daisy, knew more about England than the the rest of us. It was obvious that we could do with learning from them, so they continued to swap information at will.

"If you can't burst peas in a place, to cook you rice and peas, then it can't be all that good," Daisy reasoned.

"How you mean? Why they can't burst peas in England?" I asked.

"Ah tell you they *can't* burst peas there," Daisy insisted, then continued. "Auntie said they have a kerosene heater, to make the place hot when it cold. When they don't want to use the cooker, or if the gas finish and nobody have coins to put in the meter, they have to burst peas on the kerosene heater."

"Ha, ha, hai! Woy-e-ee!" We all laughed, surprised at the backwardness of the place they were describing.

"Listen noh, one day, she say she put dry peas on the little heater and the whole day, from morning to night, the pot cock-up on top the heater, boiling and boiling and the peas never burst!"

Everyone laughed. England had seemed like an unbelievable place and although I had heard all their discussions, I did not want to believe these absurdities about the place.

"So what you mean?" I asked Daisy, "England is worse than here? Why people going there, then?"

Daisy did not answer. No one answered because no one knew the answer to that question.

"Well is go, Emma going, she will write and tell us better, eh Emma? You will send and tell us how England is OK?" they all asked.

Emma had said nothing throughout the whole conversation because what we had both just heard was vastly different from what we had often imagined. It was certainly different from what we had role-played when we were alone. Which details were real and which were fantasy; no one knew. Being unable to confirm the details and having already lost a lot of time talking, we concluded that enough time was spent on the conversation and everyone dispersed to their washing stone, to continue washing their clothes.

Back at my stone, I was a little angry with myself because I did not know as much as the others. My mind went back to Aunt Meena who, after reading the letters, always told me, *"You mother write; she send and say hello."* No details of life in England were discussed. I felt angry that I had been by-passed information but more so, that I had never seen the inside of a letter from England.

Often, we had picked up the air-letter-forms from Hermitage Post Office, and the oblong blue and red rimmed onion-skin envelope was just passed on to Aunt Meena, who read it in her own time. Disturbed by this new knowledge of England, I vowed to sneak into the house when no one was around, to search for the letters from England. I wanted to see for myself if what the girls had said was true.

I now decided that I should write to Mamie Irene in England in order to have my own replies. I did not want to be mentioned in a letter which was generally addressed to the whole family. It was a new feeling of determination and protest because for the first time, I felt that I would need to be more forceful and more self-assertive. I was about to lose Emma, my eyes and ears in the outside world and I suspected that it was the knowledge of this fact and of our eventual parting; which made Emma so quiet, and me so sad.

Six years had gone by since Mamie Irene had gone to England. The passing of time had made her seem less real to me. She had become like a phantom; like Santa Claus, who had the ability to send presents and nice things. She was there to make my requests known to buy my books for school, new uniform, a dress to attend a wedding, Christening or Harvest Festival. For Christmas, the delight was being able to receive pretty balloons, a mouth-organ, a flute and most important of all an English doll. I often requested one with blue eyes that moved, with long blonde hair, fully dressed with little socks and shoes on.

Aunt Meena had said, "Now you getting big, write you mother, send and tell her how you doing in school."

I wrote often, with the help of Gran-gran but Mamie Irene had never written a personal letter to me. The six years had spun a great chasm over what I remembered of her since the parting at the age of five. Each passing year had made her seem less real, existing like a pen-pal; a memory which was not fantasy, but a fantastic means of achieving a goal, going to a bigger and better place when I got older.

Soon our washing for the day was over, and our plan for the big fishing-spree afterwards was to prove that the *Gloria Saturday* myth was true. Everyone agreed that the superstition was true because we had caught a lot of crayfish. As usual, we headed home for the crayfish soup cook-up. We had caught all types of our favourite - *Booke, Cacadow*, and lots of little transparent crayfish from among the reeds. Our next mission was to mix these little miscreants with small round cornmeal dumplings, pieces of green fig, sweet potatoes, salt-butter, chives and thyme, onions and whatever else was available or took our fancy; to make the tasty brine.

This expectation always climaxed the day's washing event. It made the long hours of toiling over the stones in the river and suffering the blistering sun a worthwhile compensation. Invariably, we also picked seasonal fruit that we found anywhere along the riverbank. Those who could not fish accompanied those who could, in order to help perpetuate the mythical quest. But in this way, it also meant that everyone was employed in some kind of useful activity to produce our loot of the day.

The judicious sharing was expected to come later after the cook-up. We would wait for the food which often took a long time and during its cooking, it was usual to hear exaggerated stories in grandiose styles about how our bounty was gathered. Thoughts of the impending cooking activity pervaded our minds and it always made our weary steps up St. John Hill with the heavy washing loads, more bearable. The hill was steep and tiresome, a cursed last-lap to negotiate, after a long day's washing in the river.

However, what mouth-watering expectations we had of our day's ending, was instantly marred by the bad news which we heard on our journey up the Hill. It quickened our steps, leaving us severely shocked and frightened, as we hastened to our houses. A tractor had killed little Mark during the day. The news cast a fear in our hearts.

٤

On enquiring what had happened, we were told that earlier in the day, Mark and his friends were hopping on and off a tractor which was making its way through a short-cut; on its way to Cariere Estate. It was a childish prank and we had all done it several times; running after the tractor, hopping on for rides, challenging the mechanical monster's ability to plough through the toughest and roughest terrain to carry us. We often did this as we hung on, branding our activities as ideal measures of excitement and fun. The monster's wheels, with its deep patterned furrows, made the unmistakable tractor-wheel prints in the soft mud, as it squashed rotten leaves, soft pulpy earth, twigs, and insects in its path.

Mark and the other two boys with him had been riding on the back of the tractor, while its driver was unaware of their foolishness at the back. The tractor hit a gravelled path suddenly, causing the vehicle to swerve and bump so hard that the boys were thrown off their comfortable grip of the machine. Mark was unlucky. The jolt threw him on the monstrous wheels and his leg was quickly swivelled by the merciless prowess of the machine's tyres. It left the helpless, shattered body of the boy bleeding profusely, staining and marking the brown earth.

The manner in which this story was told and retold pained everyone, so that repeated heart-rending bawling and wailing followed each recount. Everyone had exclaimed, "Oh Gawd!" and the disbelief of the accident with questions of, "Why Papa Gawd?" were sent heavenwards, and appeals were sincerely made.

"Lawd, Gawd! Have mercy on us!"

Mark's mum, on hearing this, was instantly shocked into unconsciousness; doubling the state of confusion in the home and adding to the familiar sounds of pain. The rest of his family had to band their bellies tightly with thick, wide cloths and they bawled. The mournful wailing, night after night, disturbed my entire being. There was such confusion, shock and mournful wailing in the village that it saddened everyone sorely.

For seven days and nights the women bawled and screamed, disturbing our sleeping, our waking, and our minds. I became anxious and frightened. This first-hand brush with death was not experienced by any of the young children of the village before. We were confused at adult helplessness, perplexed at their pleading to God, numbed by the open, excruciating, painful displays of the women; who had all become emotionally very distraught.

Mark's family was so deeply affected by the uncontrolled display of intense emotions that many of them had to be physically supported by other women from the village. The shattering predicament rendered them incapable of being able to stand on their feet unaided. Gripped by this state of extreme emotional trauma, the death of little Mark had brought on other little deaths; death of our childhood innocence and death of a village - its sense of peace but also its jovial routines.

The robust matriarchal figures, who had been 'mothering' and 'fathering' their children had become temporarily, children themselves. They wailed helplessly, sorrowing over a community loss; over a family torn apart, having felt cheated by Provident. They were angry for being robbed of their little male cherub. There was no doubt also, that our childish composure and confidence in the fact that all was permanently well with the grown-ups, was now quite shaken.

A sense of loss had touched every person's heart and those who did not know Mark or his family very well, came from near and far; having heard the death announcement on the radio. They came to commiserate, to support, to cook, to share, brought food, and took turns in helping others who were also paying their respects. Some came just to weep and wail in support. It seemed as if the whole of little Grenada had converged on our village over this most sad affair.

All the village children were fed, and supervised by women who had naturally taken over the usual role of community mothers, and we were left to spectate freely and witness the village's pain. Mark's mum, who had become hoarse, having lost her voice though the loud screams, constantly passed out. Her husband, shocked and confused at the loss of his only boy child, appeared dumb and robotic; while Mark's sister and aunts were wild and uncontrollable with bawling.

They bawled as if the relentless noise would change the mind of the Seer and Knower of all things, and make Him send their little Mark back from his apparent sleep. Unashamedly, they questioned God through a plethora of "Whys?" Their open appeals seemed to suggest one thing; they wanted a Divine reprieve for the return of their beloved little one!

We, the village children, did not easily understand this experience of death. We listened to the various versions of how the fateful event took place for weeks after the funeral. As a result, we gave the Mango Row a wide berth for a very long time, because we were frightened to pass by the bloodstained path, where the accident had taken place. We were more frightened that the boy's soul might still be there and the superstition about such sudden horrible death confirmed our fears.

The sound of weeping and wailing remained in my ears for many weeks and I was afraid to walk alone, especially when darkness fell. It was due to the memory of the repetitive sounds of dogs howling, when the women's bawling dominated the atmosphere. It was also the mournful singing that frequently trespassed on my thoughts in the night; forcing me to read Gran-gran's *WORDS OF COMFORT.*

I had found no real comfort in her book because the words could not penetrate my mind to comfort my racing, pounding heartbeats or stop my nervous feelings. But the act of reading the book occupied time, which would have been spent thinking over and over about the fatal accident. It had given me some distraction, especially when no adult was around, because the whole affair caused a lingering fear in our hearts. This had become obvious because since Mark's death, all the village children became insecure when they were not in the presence of adults. Many children did not venture out much. Instead, they preferred to play only in areas where adults could be viewed from a distance.

The women's vigil, before the funeral, had lasted until Mark's relatives, who were abroad in England, Trinidad and Canada, arrived in Grenada. The day of the funeral seemed to exacerbate all pain and the migrant relatives also displayed their brand of sorrowful mourning for the child. The level of melancholia was more marked at the moment La Croix's hearse pulled up outside the family home to take Mark's body into the house.

The sight of the funeral hearse in the village intensified the fear of death for me. The colours of black, white and purple, and the increased number of people from everywhere around the island, heightened the fear and intensity of the unknown phenomenon; which made the village children hurdle together for group comfort.

Unlike the adults whose duty it is to visit the dead, as children we had grouped together earlier to discuss whether or not we should go and see Mark's body, when it was brought to the house. Although we did not all decide to go, it was with a strange mixture of bravado, inquisitiveness and trepidation that we trod up the gravelled path which led to Mark's family's yard.

One by one, we filed into the house to see our little pal. The sight of what was there to represent him and his big toes which were tied together by a string, sent shocking waves of extreme fear through my body so that amidst the women's screams, the milling crowds, the smell of death, confusion and a choking, heady feeling; I wet myself.

I was so overcome by the horror of this sight that I ran out of the house. Running at top speed and heading for our house, I dogged branches, stumbled and refused to check the tears which were rolling down my face. I ended up in Gran-gran's lap. She had paid her respects to Mark's family earlier in the day. Gran-gran was sitting in our verandah, rocking backwards and forwards, as if she was consoling herself also. She seemed to be lost in deep thoughts of remembering.

I sank down on my knees in front of Gran-gran and looked into her sad eyes. Hers was the sad grayish-brown eyes of a mother who was remembering her own loss; that of her son in England who she was not able to mourn or bury herself. I hid my face in her dress and then cried loudly and uncontrollably. I sobbed as if my heart would break. It was the only incident of death that I had experienced then. Additionally, it was one that left an indelible mark, not only on my mind but also on those of the villagers, especially the women. It was an experience which resonated with the strength of their courage, humanity, and capacity of feelings, as well as their sense of real community.

Chapter 5

"Many West Indians are sorry now
They left their country, I don't know how
Some left their jobs and their family
And determined to come to London City
Well they are crying; they now regret
No kind of employment that they can get
The city of London they have to roam
And they can't get their passage to go back home."

Lord Kitchener (Aldwin Roberts)

It wasn't until Christopher Smith, a little 4 year old from England, was deposited in Grenada that I wondered about the reality of the situation in England. I thought about the plight of those who had left our island; their fate and their lucky chances of being abroad. The fact is, Christopher's dilemma had raised many queries. Why were children, who were born in England, being sent to Grenada to be raised by relatives? Surely it should be the other way round, I thought! After all, we were accustomed to the idea that people left Grenada, not sent back to it. Why were they sent from a land of plenty and 'bigness' to an environment where everyone just seemed to benefit from the cargo cult? The general idea perpetuated in the region was that 'small' was not so good.

The opportunities of going somewhere 'big' like England, Canada and America, from where one could send boxes and crates of goodies back to the islands, created new concepts of wealth. It was the cargo-cult that everyone wanted to become converted to. As a result, many migrants who were abroad were preyed on because of greedy demands from squandering relatives who extracted money and goods from them with impunity. The reason for this is that it was felt certain that a bottomless pit of plenty was available freely and laid in waiting in the big countries. The misconception was that you just had to travel there to collect plenty of money and goods; put it into boxes and airmail envelopes, then send it via BOAC and BWIA to the West Indies. However, Christopher was not cargo yet he was sent to Grenada from England. His appearance in the village was an enigma and as children, we felt sorry for him.

Christopher was usually dressed daily in his long-sleeved shirts and long trousers and he wore socks and shoes in the Grenadian heat! It was an attempt to keep out the sand-flies which attacked his smooth, fresh, English blood; causing masses of oozing sores to erupt over any visible areas of his skin. The fight was to save Christopher's legs and arms, because his face was already attacked, making the boy look as if he had chicken pox. Where the flies could not venture to punish the poor boy's skin, the intense heat from the sweltering sun did. Christopher's situation was not helped by the smelly drains near their house. They harboured the starving mosquitoes that attached the helpless little boy.

Whether attacked by sand-flies or mosquitoes, they caused Christopher to suffer and soon his skin looked as if he was suffering from yaws. His socks and shoes, which he could no longer use in the hot sun, had to eventually give way to the Grenadian fresh breeze; in an attempt to let the sores heal naturally. The need for natural healing and the fight to keep the attackers out was a battle Christopher would not win either way. Therefore, when the long-sleeved shirts and long trousers were finally ditched, Christopher's skin became the mosquitoes and flies' playground. Unlucky for the boy, the situation got much worse before it got better.

After earning his scarred appearance, a kind of blight on many a travelled person's skin, the flies eventually left Christopher alone. It was as if they were now content, that they had enough of him and needed fresh fields to plough. So with his tropical identification marks; a fate many children from England suffered in the tropics, Christopher blended into the locality. Later, having become quite used to his new environment, he was able to shed all his English clothes and run around with other topless and shoeless children.

Perhaps it was the reversal of the migratory movement which baffled me most, and I constantly wondered why Christopher had been sent to Grenada. Verna, his mother, a former teacher from Gutt village, had left for England the same time as Mamie Irene. My curiosity was satisfied one day when a gossip between Miss Mattis and Cleothilda in Grenville, provided the interesting background to Christopher's unplanned appearance in Grenada.

"She know how hard things is in Grenada and she still send the poor chile here," Cleothilda gossiped to Miss Mattis.

The women were in Grenville Market, standing next to Aunt Meena's stall. Cleothilda had taken Christopher to see Dr. Japal for asthma, which the poor boy had also developed since arriving in Grenada.

"Eh-eh, you ever see the light!" The women said, puzzled at the English child's predicament.

"Well dey say some Jamaican man clip Verna wings," said Cleothilda.

"Is so?" replied Miss Mattis, as if to say, *tell me more*.

"Well, you know how she used to play big *hefe* and scorn everybody round here. She go all the way in England and breed for a Jamaican good-for-nuthin," Cleothilda told her.

"Woy-o-yoy! *Papa-mwen* that is stupidness!" Miss Mattis replied.

"A real damn fool! Like brightness get to she head!"

What followed were two loud "Stupes!" Each woman had given a real long, suck-teeth, then Cleothilda continued.

"Doh study her noh. She send a poor helpless little thing like that here."

"And look at she old mother," Miss Mattis said, sounding irritated and angry. "You doh think Verna should ah really feel sorry for she mother? The poor woman is not strong enough to manage grandchildren in her old age."

"And you know, ah doh say ah laughing now, but Verna did used to siddown and laugh at other people here; playing she was too damn good for them. Now look, she onions brown until they burning!"

Cleothilda too, had become agitated with the situation but continued to offer more information.

"Yes things too hot for her to handle up dey. England is a big place and they say the man that breed her already had a woman he was minding in Jamaica!"

The two women's tête-à-tête became intense in their exchanges of views, so Cleothilda continued.

"Look noh, he fool Verna while she was living with him as man and wife, saying she was the *only* one and the stupid woman believe him!"

"Ay-ay! What is dis?" enquired Miss Mattis.

"But when Verna hear the cry, the Jamaican woman just turn up unannounced, on their doorstep in England!" said Cleothilda, in a surprised sing-song voice.

"What you saying?" asked Miss Mattis, bending her inquisitive head closer to her gossiping partner.

The *lowdown* was in full flow, so Cleothilda continued in a whispering tone.

"Yes! Listen noh, that Jamaican woman start to beat de man up, licks for so. Ah hear she throw some heavy cuff, punch and kick on him, just like a man! As for Verna, she didn' wait for her turn, she take she chile and run like hell!"

"*Sesay mwen,* dat's bacchanal in England, *oui!*" said Cleothilda, relishing in the news.

"Yes, dat's real *comese,*" Miss Mattis concluded.

I could not help overhearing the women. Despite whispering occasionally, they generally did not show any caution with me and Christopher within earshot of them. I was sitting in front of Aunt Meena's stall and Christopher was scratching his arms and stamping his feet with annoyance, at the flies which were buzzing around him. He looked as if he was about to cry. His cracked lips were very dry and he looked hungry and lost. He stood there trying to drive the flies, as he waited patiently for his aunt gossiping Cleothilda.

The woman knew all her sister's personal details and it was aired on Grenville Wharf. Verna, it became clear, had no one in England to look after the little boy, so poor Christopher was dispatched to the next best place that his mother could think of – to her sister Cleothilda, in Grenada.

"Eh! Eh? Poor thing!" said Miss Mattis.

"Yes *Makomere,* that is the situation and that's why the poor chile now end up here in Grenada."

The two women shook their head, with the customary, "*well-would you-believe-it?*" sentiment then parted.

ع

This was just the beginning of Christopher's story. Later on, Aunt Meena told Gran-gran that Verna's story began when she was introduced at a Blues party one Saturday night in a place called Ladbroke Grove, to a fellow named Manny Smith. It turned out that Manny had nowhere to go because the landlady where he was living did not like the way he was eyeing her at every given opportunity in their house. He used to smile too often. The habit of saying *"Morning"* or *"Evening"* is not common in England, and the woman, being unaccustomed to such etiquette, mistook Manny's felicities for romantic interest in her! She herself was clearly developing feelings for Manny which she could not handle, so when her emotions had got the better of her, she told her husband that Manny had been making advances at her. Manny became homeless and jobless because he was promptly kicked out of the house.

The opposite was the case for Verna. She had a job as a chambermaid at the Mayfair Hotel; a sharp descent from her schoolteacher days in Grenada. However, it still meant that she had a job when many other West Indians were struggling to get one. She was lonely and a bit carefree, so when she met Manny one day and he talked sweetly to her; it was not long before Verna was making plans for the two of them. She decided to leave the room which she was sharing with two other women; a Dominican and a Trinidadian, to set up home with Manny. Both women had warned Verna against such a rash move. They told her that she didn't know Manny well enough to make such a decision but Verna was lonely. Having being surrounded by women all the time, she said that she longed for male companionship so she took the plunge.

Manny, the saga-boy, told her that he had fallen in love with her the moment he had laid eyes on her in the Blues party and she believed it. They both found a room on Verna's two pounds and three shillings a week wages. Verna paid their rent, one pound and six shillings; whilst Manny promised her the world. She helped him to buy cigarettes and the Stones Ginger Wine, which they bought each week to drink with their friends. They lived in Kilburn in a damp, dark, basement room quite happy and contented.

On weekends, they would congregate with other Caribbean compatriots at Blues parties or around someone's place, to listen to music on their Blue Spot gramophone. They played cards, dominoes or just chatted about life in England. Life seemed good to them because Verna had a little money from which she occasionally sent two shillings a month for her mother back home. All was well and soon Manny found a job in the same hotel as Verna; getting the same wages as she did so things generally improved for them.

No migrant minded the cold, so long as there was somewhere warm they could return to; somewhere to turn a key in, go inside and lie down, after working like a donkey and feeling dog-tired all day.

One day, Manny told Verna that his mother was sick back home and needed to send her a little change for the doctor's medicine. Poor Verna had no reason to doubt his sincerity because he was treating her really well. They both dressed well, they bought nice things and when he wasn't with the boys, they went to the cinema together. So altogether life was good for Verna.

She soon became pregnant. Manny took it in his stride and acted as the perfect unmarried husband. He took care of things when she was not able to stir from her heavy pregnancy. He took charge of things when she was in hospital and welcomed them home. Not long after they brought the baby home the landlord, an Irish man, told them that he didn't want children in his house. He said that he didn't mind them because they were the best rent payers he had ever had but he couldn't have them in his house with children.

Manny had taken the responsibility bravely. He had to find some other room for them. When he was not working, on his day off, he went out in search of a place for them to live. After working on the long day-shifts and at weekends, Manny took every opportunity to comb the area; knocking on doors, and looking for a room to rent. It was hard. Doors were slammed in his face and whatever racial abuse he suffered, he dismissed them without retaliating, for the sake of Verna and the child.

One day, on one of those cold, bitter days after his night-shift, Vernon met a schoolmate on Kilburn High Road. His luck was in because he was told where a 'room to let' was available. The two men gladly exchanged addresses and talked after short reminiscences and it was felt certain that Manny would get the room, since the house belonged to a sympathetic Jewish man. Later, Manny got the room and they eventually settled into their new home.

The friend who Manny had met was so excited to have met a fellow Jamaican; he wrote to his family in Jamaica telling them of the good news. Back home in Jamaica, they were pleased that things were going well for their countryman in England so they boasted about the news. It was then that Claudine, Manny's ex-girlfriend, got to know about his whereabouts in England. When he had left Jamaica, Manny did not know he was going to become an absent father because he had only known Claudine for one week.

So seizing the opportunity to claim her man, Claudine was able to get Manny's address. She wrote to him informing him of his baby girl! This gave her the opportunity to extract whatever she desired from Manny materially and the baby was used as a bargaining chip. To Claudine, Manny was her very own personal Santa Claus. She demanded food, clothes, and money from him, as often as she could get a letter out of Jamaica and receive a reply in return!

Manny secretly bowed to her every demand for money, which were profuse and at times, threatening. In England, things were going well between him and Verna and he felt that he could not possibly tell her about his predicament to destabilize their home, so he used the idea of his mother being sick and the need to send money to her as an excuse. However, little did he know that Claudine was gathering the money he was sending her, to pay for a plane ticket to join him in England.

Meanwhile, Verna, Manny and their child continued to live happily in their new room, which was in a large three-storey house. The house had other tenants from other parts of the Caribbean. There were people living above them on the upper floors and people living on the floors below; yet everyone seemed content to mind their own business, in order to get along in peace. Their old friends ran a *Susu*, using weekly "*hands*" in a money-partnership. It was set up to pool sums of money together, which they then gave to each other in turns, every week.

This old form of community banking helped each of the occupants of the building to become more financially independent. Before too long, the tenants were able to talk of buying their own homes and sending for their children from back home. Verna and Manny contributed to the *Susu* and they talked about marriage because Christopher was getting older. They were fortunate, to be able to baby-sit Christopher by taking turns because of their shift jobs at the hotel. Verna babysat the child during the nights and Manny during the days, when Verna was at work. They were contented with each other until that fateful day when Manny answered a surprised knock on their door.

They were not used to having visitors and certainly not during the week, but Manny opened the door to find a big plump girl, who he instantly recognized as Claudine. She was standing there waiting for a jolly welcome; grinning at Manny and expecting him to be ecstatically happy with her presence. Instead, Manny's shocked response left him speechless with his mouth gaping. Thinking that he was too surprised and shocked to let her in, Claudine barged her way in and walked into the room only to come face-to-face with Verna and little Christopher. That day was the first and last time Verna had seen them.

That night, after overhearing the women tell of Verna's story, I decided to look for one of Aunt Meena's letter from England. The details of the predicament in England whetted my appetite for more. I had now heard a different side about life in England and was beginning to piece together what I had heard that day from Daisy in the river, and what the women had been recounting. Since our talk in the river, I had at least discovered where Aunt Meena's "England letters" were hidden, and was waiting for an opportunity when I could be certain that I would be alone to read the letters then put them back without being caught.

ع

The day's market sales were going slowly and we waited in the sun, which had come out as hot as usual. As the hours sped by, the various conversations and gossips flowed like oil into a drum. I was looking forward to the evening which would bring an end to the tiresome day. The sea around Grenville wharf became rough with the inland tide; crashing against the walled barrier near to the jetty. This signalled the end of day and as the sun set, most people talked to bus drivers about their homeward journey and departure times.

We hurried to get on the bus going to Gutt. The bus driver made a circular round to nearby streets then back to the waterfront, tooting the horn to attract attention and instigating hurried movements from villagers. The driver parked the bus

145

for approximately 15 minutes more, as he prepared for our departure. Sugar, flour, fresh fish, *lambie,* some frozen chicken and salted pork, formed the bulk of our luggage, which was stuffed into a crocus bag and tied to our luggage in the minute space. All other luggage was put on top of the crowded roof of the bus, where the space was shared by many other travellers.

All passengers for St. Andrews area climbed in, sweaty bodies, squashing sweat-stained clothes, amidst a collection of the day's other smells. The open wooden transporter looked like a pregnant centipede, as it made its way around La Bay, in an attempt to collect its last unboarded customers. The horns of many vehicles, all using the same strategy, orchestrated around the wharf to attract passengers' attention. Consequently, it signalled the fact that we were about to leave Grenville.

There were few children on our bus but we had to stand and give up our seats for the adults. We were either being squashed silently, suffering from the crushing legs and arms of the grown-ups, which were intertwined around us. No child sat when a grown-up could be seated, even though it meant that particular adult would be squeezing their posteriors into a space that was too small for them. As long as a person's rear end could squash into whatever shape the space offered, they were happy to let the upper part of their bodies suffer the consequence of any obstructions it happened to come into contact with.

The nightmare on the bus was the constant swaying and straining at corners and having to hold on tightly to the back of the wooden, bench-like, seats in front of us. As children, we swayed and strained and straightened, to avoid losing our grip and falling sideways. However, the wooden bus swerved madly around curved corners, seemingly without the control of brakes; to the sound of the clutch-pedal flapping from the driver's sandalled feet.

The only thing we had to do was pray that another bus, with an equally reckless driver, travelling at the same speed or using the same road space, was not coming from the opposite direction towards us. For each traveller on board, getting home, under whatever condition, was the most important consideration and the driver knew that.

We reached the village in late dusk but the night was falling fast. We had stopped at a multitude of request stops to let out passengers as we went along and being nearest to Gutt Village, which was the terminus, we were among the last to get to our homes.

The evening was a normal Saturday routine for those who had gone to town. It means that we had to endure cooking our supper late into the evening. It was a regular occurrence and the customary frying of fish after market day was a habitual scenario. I had bought some sugar cakes and Paradise Plum sweets for Gran-gran and she was glad. They were her favourite treats and she smiled, having had us safely back home.

"How you pass the day?" Gran gran asked Aunt Meena.

"Well, La Bay was brisk. God is good. Ah sell the yams to a man from Trinidad. The banana, mango and *sour sop* didn't do too well at first. Banana doh have good price. As for mango, it plentiful - everybody sellin' and nutmeg is only 10 cents a pound. The best price was for the zabocas. Some white people wanted more from me. Now, I figured out they could be people buying in order to sell again, because they buy up every single one and then ask for more!" Aunt Meena recounted animatedly.

"Hear them noh. Any more avocados?" she mimicked. "One of them say avocado, the other say pear and I saying zaboca. What ah confusion this morning!"

"Ha Hai!" Aunt Meena laughed loudly. "You see even zaboca turn pear and avocado now," Aunt Meena mused, as Gran-gran listened.

"Anyhow, dey all gone. Next week, God willing, ah go bring more!"

She concluded her summary on her market day, so in the convenient silence which followed, I piped in.

"Ah see Christopher and Miss Cleothilda," adding my information too to Gran-gran.

"Eh heh?" Gran-gran grunted.

"Christopher have wheezing on his chest, so they went to see Dr. Japal," I told her.

"Dat little bwoy leave all the way in England and come here to catch asthma, poor t'ing!" Aunt Meena said sympathetically.

Night was falling fast, so in the dark night, Aunt Meena cleaned the jack fish she had bought. She rubbed them with lime and rinsed them well. Our dog Blackie got his treat of the week; the discarded fish guts and he ate it with gusto. While Aunt Meena was tossing the fish into a bowl of seasoned flour, before frying them, my cousin Monica and Yvonne were helping to split the wood for the open fire. They were going to roast breadfruit.

I helped Aunt Meena to fan the fire in the coal-pot and the iron pot glistened on top of it, with the hot oil in it. She placed the floured fish into the pot and the coconut oil sizzled and danced around the fish, as it became yellow immediately, from the curry powder that was mixed in with the flour. Together, we prepared the dinner, helped by the light of a hurricane gas lamp. Then we all sat down to eat.

Saturday night was always more brisk than any other night in the village. The meal over, we sat in the verandah, bellies filled, tired but contented. As we sat there we acknowledged the various "howdy-dos" from animated villagers who were passing up and down the road outside our house. The sky was a big sheet of black material, with shimmering silver eyelets for stars. In it, the moon shone brightly, playing games of hide-and-seek, as it peeped out now and then in the night sky.

There were muffled sounds in Cleothilda's house next door, and the Gregory's voice could be heard singing in the distance. Both husband and wife were leaders of the Seventh Day Adventist Church choir, practicing for the next day's service. Intermittently, the bright, elongated, beams from vehicles lit up the pitch black street. Headlights appeared as two enormous moon-shaped eyes, moving like unidentified objects in the distance at first, before they became recognizable as they reached us. They were the vehicles of Saturday night revellers. Many whizzed by in their haste, to make the most of the early night's hours, as they sped to their weekend fetes.

Lethargically, we lazed around in the verandah, quietly passing the after-dinner time. It was then I chose to go inside the house to pursue my quest; to find a letter that would tell me more about life in England. As I walked past her, Aunt Meena reminded me that she needed to hem Gran-gran's petticoat for Sunday morning church. She asked me to fetch her biscuit tin and thimble.

The square biscuit tin was on the table next to her bed, so I opened it. This box contained all Aunt Meena's odds and ends; sewing and embroidery threads, a thimble, needles on a card, pieces of lace from dresses she had sewn for us, a pair of scissors, together with different sizes of buttons, hooks and eyes and zips. I found the thimble which she had sent me to fetch, but while looking I saw a letter. It was underneath the general odds and ends. As I rummaged through the tin some more, I came across more letters. It was not important which one I read first, so in my nervousness, I grabbed the first letter my hand touched and stuffed it into my dress pocket.

All the letters in the tin were addressed to:

MEENA MITCHELL,
Hermitage Post Office,
Upper St. John's,
St. Andrews,
Grenada,
West Indies.

I was satisfied, I had achieved my goal. I briskly returned with the tin, thimble, together with a spare reel of thread, taken in my nervousness, which Aunt Meena did not ask for.
I later busied myself with my Sunday School preparations or so I had made out. Instead, in the quietness of the bedroom, pretending to look at my work, I opened the weightless air-letter form. I had positioned myself at the furthest corner of the room, so that if anyone came in, I would be quick to conceal the letter without detection. I fluffed up my pillow in readiness for the task. Then half-lying on my left side, I crossed my legs, took a deep breath and began to read.

Say Meena,   *"12th February 1961,*
How is the family, I hope fine. Greetings to you, in the name of our Lord Jesus Christ. How is Joanne and the rest of the whole family? What about Mamie? I hope she getting ah ease-up from the arthritis. I pray God give her health and

strength and long life to help you with the children. Right now things over here are tough but ah get a little job and as long as God give me health and strength everything will be alright. Is thanks of a girl I met here last month that help me get a little factory work with a company called Firestone.

They did stop taking people but when somebody left the job, she beg the boss for me pretending I was her cousin. The boss tell her he agree to give me a try at the job because she herself is a good worker. So I trying to hold on. You know England is not like home. When you don't work, you can't eat. At least, we have plenty of food in Grenada. We may not have plenty of money and meat but we can eat. Here you don't know people and nobody to give you a little help like we used to do at home. So when the little money I had was finished, for many days, is walk, I had to walk to the Labour Exchange, looking for work in the snow.

Well that day, I sure is God that speak for me to meet this girl from Sauteurs in the Labour Exchange too. When ah hear a woman talking to the man there, I said to myself that's a voice from home. Blessed Jesus! I thought. It was good to hear someone from home. So we talk and that's how she was able to help me.

This place have plenty meat, big houses but you just don't know what the feeling is like when you have no body to sit down with and have a bellyful of laugh and find you little help when you need.

England is good for work and thing but papa mwen, when you see I make five years here is back I'm coming, oui! I just want to see Joanne do well in school and get a little money together for her education, its only so she can be a woman of destiny to help me in my old age. Girl what about Uncle Tom and Nenen Mattis? When you see Nenen, tell her I send and say hello. I don't want her or anybody saying that her only God-child turn ungrateful.

I enclose a little change to buy the schoolbooks and things Joanne need. Give Mamie some change in her hand. I hope Joanne will get a scholarship. As long as she listening to you and Mamie she will be okay - God is good. I must close this letter now because it's late and I have to get up at 4 o'clock in the morning to go to work. As for Calvin he is okay for now. He get a job he don't like, so now he talking about studying law - you ever see the light? A big man like him, leave all the way in Grenada and come here saying he going to study. How we go eat? Well chutes, you know man is man. Care Joanne for me. I will write again soon. Take good care of yourself, and tell everybody hello. I close in Jesus name, Your sister Irene"

After I had finished reading the letter, I sat in an upright position. There was nothing immediate to say or think about the contents of this letter. The night had grown thick with blackness and the quarter moon had moved beyond the bedroom window. The noises in the streets had lessened. On the bedroom table, a candle burned in a glass-holder and the flickering flame cast a huge circular shadow on the ceiling. Like a projector, the light magnified an inquisitive moth's shadow, as it flitted and danced in front of the yellowish beam.

I continued to think of the discovery of a new kind of England and momentarily, I felt sorry for Christopher; the Grenadian people in England and for Emma. But somehow, secretly lurking in my heart was a wish that Verna's experience was isolated and not the general experience of everyone who had travelled to England.

I wanted to believe that Verna was unlucky and although I felt that Christopher was perhaps more unlucky, having been sent away from England, I believed that somehow all would be well. Not everyone has the same fate, I told myself.   I forced myself to believe that Emma and I had got it right so I willed this kind of reasoning into my consciousness.   I wanted to believe that our past fantasizing and role-playing were more closely aligned to the truth of the Grenadian experience in England.

I sat there thinking of what I had heard, baffled now with the pros and cons of going to England. My doubts and counter-doubts danced like a sea of confusion in my mind. They rose and fell like waves on a stormy sea. I sat with my schoolbooks to distract my wavering thoughts. Books, I reasoned, must be more accurate than people. What Phyllis had told us in the river could have been exaggerated, I reasoned. I tried to stifle the contrasting thoughts and instead I swapped the negative hearsay with an imagined, positive, creative, visualization, of the place that I had learnt about only in books.

ع

Preparations for Emma's departure were made in the two weeks that were left. The reality of parting caused a strain in our friendship and we felt awkward in each other's company. Occasionally, we avoided subjects which were related to going to England. I tried to imagine how I would cope without my best friend and maybe she was also trying to imagine how she would cope in a land that had strange habits and dilemmas. The fear and reality of parting paled our once-happy imaginings into insignificance. The realization of our separation brought an instant end to our fantasizing.

However, it made our last weeks together more precious than before.

I clung to our every action, relishing our closing chapter together; carefully documenting our every move in my mind, so that the memory of it would remain indelibly written there. I wondered whether Emma was consciously doing the same because she appeared quieter and more deliberate in her undertakings.

The weekend over, Monday morning saw Emma and me travelling to School, on foot, to Bamboo Bridge. The three-mile trek in the cool, fresh morning seemed full of promises for the day. As we walked, we talked about the painful vaccination which she had been given on her left shoulder, as part of her pre-travel requirements.

Emma looked like a clean shiny penny, with hair neatly combed into two big plaits, glistening with hair oil in the early sun. Two white ribbons dangled at the end of each plait, like Christmas decorations. Her face was clean, with bright round eyes, showing white teeth that had a little gap between the two big front ones. Her oval light-coffee coloured skin glowed and she walked with the confidence of a promising young future; as if all will be well with the world and us.

I know Emma was especially proud of her non-creased milky-white, Terylene blouse which her mother had sent to her from England. She had said so. It revealed white filigree lacy vest underneath. Her navy-blue accordion pleated skirt with the brilliant white blouse, was punctuated by a black belt at the waist. She wore white socks and shiny black patent shoes. The school tie; the navy, nylon symbol of authority, with its red and yellow stripes, identified her and completed the secondary school uniform - a proud member of S.A.A.S.

Each girl carried her school identification with pride and St. Andrews Anglican High School colours consciously showcased its ambassadors among other pupils. This was in contrast to the nearby Convent school in the vicinity of the market square. Each pupil was a microcosm of the school, bearing the inward and outward marks of her school's identity. She was also expected to take her individual responsibility for the whole school community at all times.

Today, Emma walked proudly with her leather handbag that she carried in her right hand. It made her look like "*S.A.A.S. Pupil of the Year*" and I was proud to be her best friend.

The vaccination she was given before travelling had caused a painful, lumpy, swelling on her arm and she complained about the swollen gland in her armpits. We talked about the photographs that were taken in a studio in Grenville for her passport and of an affidavit which had to be done to change her surname. Our conversations had become strangely civil; staccato in nature. Our chatter had lost its general sparkle, vigour, laughter and our carefree attitude seemed to be quelled by the impending departure.

Emma's manner seemed like a rehearsal for a performance that she felt uncertain about. And somehow, I wanted to believe I could almost hear her subconscious reasoning. I wanted to hold on to our laughter and gaiety, as trademarks of our beautiful friendship, so as we passed a sapodilla tree, I pointed out the laden tree to her. I reminded her of our shared disgrace, when we were both at primary level in the Belair Government School. The memory of the incident brought back a squeal of laughter from us and we were our old selves again; mimicking the incident and reminiscing at the folly of our wild primary days.

"You remember teacher Zoe!" she laughed, showing those white teeth and happy smiling eyes once more.

"That man? Nobody could forget him," I replied, also becoming animated at the instant recall of the sapodilla disgrace.

The sun was coming up hot and we pressed on. We said several *"Good mornings"* to a few passing workers on their way to work at the local estate. The workers took purposeful steps to their destination and we walked at a similar pace, knowing that if we did not, we would miss the connecting bus at Bamboo Bridge to Grenville. For this we would certainly be in trouble for not being disciplined enough to be punctual.

As S.A.A.S. pupils, we upheld discipline as if our very lives depended on it. We had been used to the adherence of school rules since we were made to believe that they were not separate from our general manners and etiquette, but part of our whole development and make-up whether at home, church or school.

The experiences of younger days had imprinted these on our subconscious, so that we were made to feel accountable for every action, as individuals. This in turn, reflected on our immediate families, as well as on extended relations (that is either our Godparents - called in *patwa*, *Nenens* and *Parens*); our school, our church, the village, our Parish, our island, the Caribbean and the race. That's why the sapodilla experience could never be forgotten.

ع

At the age of ten, we used to behave like tomboys. Emma and I used to follow the boys in the village, taking part in every prank. We used to whizz down on coconut bats over hills, make go-carts go at great speed with the slimy, gluey, stuff made from young grated coco-pods. We used the slimy gluey to lubricate the axles and this made them go down hills at tremendous speed.

The boys played marbles and so did we. They made *gazoo-cork* rollers with steering wheels, competed in spinning top competitions and competitively climbed all manner of trees; so did we. So one day feeling, particularly adventurous and wanting to test our developing craftiness to the limit, Emma and I decided to break the school rules and commit a cardinal sin. We skipped the lesson after lunch to go and hunt for fruits. Our aim was to return to school by afternoon break, before it was home-time. We knew that some boys had done this in the past, and had got away with it. We ventured to do the same, defying our awesomely strict teacher Zoe's fearful discipline, as well as his ability to detect our daring misdemeanours.

That day in school, we had sneaked out and ran among the thick green leafy surrounds of our playground, deep into the bountiful paths which formed its border, to pick at whatever fruit we could find. Guavas were nearer to the school but they were not as sweet as the ones in Mr. Franklin's land further away. There we ate our fill, feasted on the soft seedy pink pulp of the guavas, before going on to the sapodilla tree.

Our behaviour had nothing to do with hunger, as it was after lunchtime but our crazy streak made us reckless and willful. We stoned the sapodilla tree, gaining immense joy from our mastery over the little brown fruit. With each stone we threw at the fruit they fell as helpless victims to our growing strength and skills. We competed against each other for the most perfect aim in hitting the fruit on the tree, causing quite a lot to fall to the ground.

Later, we became aware of a barking dog and immediately were alerted to someone who was approaching in our direction. Perhaps it was a watchman, employed to oversee the land but we did not stop to find out. We ran, diving through the foliage and thick undergrowth, bruising our arms against the branches which slapped our faces and bodies, in our furious attempts to hide. The barking sound got nearer and we lay in the bushes, breathing deeply, sweating like pigs and looking like hunted fugitives.

The sound of the dog was coming nearer and we were wild with panic and fear, with bruised, dirty knees, and bits of old dried leaves in our hair. Our palms were pressed against the cold earth as we lay on the ground; with faces downwards. As we waited, we mentally willed the catastrophe not to happen. We heard the school bell ringing to signal the end of break and knew that our plan was going to be fruitless if we did not get back to the playground in time to go inside with the other pupils. I thought of Aunt Meena going wild with rage, the shame of my family, my God-parents, Mamie Irene and I continued to imagine the would-be chain of affected people. I closed my eyes to shut out the dialogue in my mind, which was turning me into a shaking, nervous wreck.

We lay there trembling. The dog continued to bark profusely and then miraculously, the sound lessened. It appeared to move away from our direction, as if the chase was after some other target. The barking echoed in the distance and we were relieved to be able to get up, brush ourselves and head for the schoolyard. We were sweating profusely, dishevelled, but lucky to have been back just in time. We grinned and sighed with relief at our near misfortune. With relief, we mingled with the other children, certain that we had got away with it. We were secretly ecstatic and full of glee. Our challenge had been brilliantly executed and we felt lucky that we had succeeded without detection.

However, the next morning in assembly, I felt I had died a thousand deaths. Teacher Zoe had orchestrated a better plan. He was made aware of our 'crime' by Mr. Franklin the sapodilla owner, , who had given him a big, round, old butter tin; filled with the young green sapodillas that we had destroyed. It was the evidence of our 'crime.' That old tin was rusty and it looked ridiculous but it was made to look innocent and respectable by the most beautiful white embroidered tea-towel that was draped over it! This situation became a hell on earth. We were caught! Teacher Zoe, the trickster, was Brer Anancy jeering at us; though his face was as serious as a judge.

Emma and I did not have any idea what was in the tin, on teacher Zoe's desk, when we had entered the classroom earlier. It was given pride of place in front of the class before assembly, while the attendance register was being taken. It was not until during the school assembly, when we were called and signalled to stand at the back of the whole school in the assembly, did we begin to realise that something sinister was about to take place.

Mr. Jessup, the English headmaster, stood to attention on stage in his khaki army suit, next to the Queen's picture, admiring the young attractive teacher, Rosamond Williams. She was playing the piano, to signal the start of the morning's hymn-singing. The five hundred students of the school, who were arranged in class groupings, reflected the levels of attainment in this educational setting.

The older students, from Standard Seven, were positioned to the sides and the back, near to the balcony. They looked as if they had outgrown the school. Psychologically, they were placed nearer to the steps which led to the exit, and this seemed to reflect their imminent departure. They would be the first ones to leave at the end of the school year. The rest of the school ranked in a pattern, which indicated the length of time, they would remain in the school with juniors positioned at the front.

Moving up over the years the junior pupils would learn, as disciples, to appreciate the value of commitment to their education and discipline; until they are ready to leave the school. That is the reason why the higher classes were standing proudly at the back and the lower classes to the front. ABC classes or Reception children had their own assemblies downstairs. After a year or two, they too would climb the steps to the hierarchy of the educational ladder.

The morning hymn was sung and in the fully-uniformed, expectant crowd, isolated coughing could be heard. We all stood up straight to attention, waiting for our next order from Mr. Jessup. During the hymn singing, Teacher Zoe had collected me and Emma from the front of our class. He gave Emma the beautifully covered rusty tin to hold, and then positioned us to walk down the long aisle from the back of the hall to the stage. The stage was Mr. Jessup's throne. There he stood as his majesty over his subjects, about to make his proclamation.

The proclamation came as a bolt of thunder and lightning when he announced that the subject of the day's lesson was *CRIME AND PUNISHMENT*, and that Emma and I were going to be the subjects of that example. Emma and I were summoned by him to come onto the stage.

Everyone was a spectator in the deathly silence which followed, as we both marched timidly down the hateful aisle, onto the sacrificial altar. There we awaited his majesty's wrath. We looked like knights disgraced and dishonoured; about to have the order for our heads. The covered tin of sapodillas resembled the concealed decree that would justify our punishment. Like fools, we were made to parade in our own crucifixion.

The indescribable shame which we suffered was a lesson to deter any would-be criminal or any potential miscreant from doing the same thing. Moreover, the six leather strokes, which we were about to receive after Mr. Jessup's long spiel on 'punishment,' would discourage any future craving for rampant behaviour and indeed for picking other people's green sapodillas. There we stood, through the thematic lecture, with the tin of sapodilla; the subject of our crime.

Mr. Jessup stood stiffly with his serious blue eyes under his khaki beret. He was about 6 feet tall and he looked like an Army General about to give instructions to his eager hangmen for an execution. The silence was cruel. Emma and I stood side by side on the raised stage; displayed there before the entire school. The tin shook in her trembling hand, as tears rolled down her cheeks.

The prickly heat which rushed to my face caused my eyes to water too and I stood there beside her. I was afraid to raise my hand to my eyes to wipe the tears, so the whole room seemed like a watery blur. My hands were hot and sweaty, with expectation of the communion with the thick, stinging, heavy, leather-belt we were about to receive.

"These two little miscreants are shameful examples of our school!" Mr. Jessup bellowed, pointing at the two of us.

There was no "hear-hear!" but I felt that Teacher Zoe had echoed it mentally. He looked smug, satisfied that we were being punished for his own loss of face with Mr. Franklin; the sapodilla owner. The other teachers, who were standing by their classes, also looked as if they were saying "hear-hear!" hoping that our example would act as a deterrent for their developing tear-a-ways.

"They are charged with breaking the school rules!" Mr. Jessup pronounced.

The graveyard silence that prevailed was a mockery, as he continued.

"Coming from this school, they've let each one of you down!"

Mr. Jessup was a stern dictator who was feared by the children of the school. No one wanted to face the leather belt which he was happy to use to show his supremacy. He pouted his mouth, stuck out his chin and quick-marched across the stage, from one end to the other. Afterwards, he turned sharply to face the assembly and bellowed.

"They have disgraced our school's good name and recklessly destroyed other people's property!"

The charges were publicized and the atmosphere in the building was thick with tension. Then in a fury, he whisked the embroidered tea towel away from the top of the tin and this made Emma jump with fear. The young bruised sapodillas heaped in the tin, were having the last laugh. They appeared to be grinning at us, and the tears rolled, unchecked, down both our faces. An immediate rise of whisperings echoed but died as quickly as it had risen, for fear of Mr. Jessup's reaction to it.

"Lack of discipline!" he bellowed, pouting his lips again.

His lecture about punishment came to an end and his final words of, "Who can't he hear must feel," signalled an end to his morning's lecture. For me and Emma, it signalled the beginning and publicity of our corporal punishment. He made me put the white, lacey, tea-towel back over the corroded tin, in front of Emma and the whole school. I did not see the expression on her face because of the blurring tears in my eyes. Emma was told to put the tin down on his 'throne' and Mr. Jessup reigned as the majesty supreme.

Slowly, he flexed his muscles in the deathly silence that followed, and then grabbed his weapon; our rod of correction. He stretched the leather belt to its full length with both hands in readiness for our corporal punishment. He straightened it, feeling the thick, familiar, pliant, weapon, before he proceeded to fire his shots. He walked up to me first. He took my hand and held it out in a straight line in front of him; my palm facing upwards. I looked like someone begging for manna from heaven.

He lined up my dropping hand and straightened my waiting fingers and he stepped backwards to judge the length of his aim. Then, confident of a perfect strike, he lifted up his hand with the belt, above his head. Determinedly, he summoned with all his might, the greatest physical strength he could muster and then he rained down the strike with full force. It impacted on my palms with FIRE!

A stinging hot cracking blow, like the breaking of a sapodilla branch, rang out; making my trembling hand hot, stinging and tingling, with the prickly heat of fire from the repeated blows. Three were counted on the first hand and then he made a stern order.

"Next!"

Not wanting to break the momentum of his pushing routine, I held out my other hand quickly and in his line of perfect fire, he reigned down the terror of his whole body, full strength, onto my next waiting, trembling palm three more times. The six vicious strikes I received were over. Hot, scalding, tears rolled down my face and my whole body shook with fright.

My hands were crumpled, young, green-peas bush, burning in a hot coal-pot fire; screaming against the furnace. My prickly throat was parched with the strained heat of subdued scream, which welled up there; trying to force out a cry, but I refused to let it burst forth and retaliate against the leather belt and Mr. Jessup's cruelty. I remained there quietly dazed, shocked at the power and full force of the bodily blows. I waited until the ritual was repeated with Emma. After her sixth blow, we were dismissed off the stage.

The whole school had witnessed our disgrace and the mental pain we suffered was more severe than the 6 physical strokes we had each received. So much so, that the additional, physical punishment which we later received at home; after our parents had learnt of the incident, seemed insignificant and lighter by comparison. That morning, we had been punished to showcase the result of ill-discipline. We were sure that the lives of the 500 students in our school would be changed somewhat, as ours were, by the shameful display.

Today, Emma and I laughed at the humour and comedy of that old, past, performance because the grinning mask we adopted was now easier to display; as it hid the permanent pain which we had temporarily resurrected. Eventually, we reached Bamboo Bridge, where many other pupils for S.A.A.S. and the St. Joseph's Convent in Grenville had already gathered, waiting for the school buses.

Chapter 6

*"I'm going to stay here in Great Britain
Yes, to better my position
And in case they should tell me "Go"
Bet your life I'm telling them "No"
(Because Britain is the motherland)."*

The Mighty Terror (Fitzgerald Henry)

The village felt strangely quiet after Emma left and it was difficult to manage my many empty hours. Mostly, I did nothing - sat and stared into space or read a book. I constantly imagined what it must be like for Emma in England. But I was not satisfied with my mental wanderings, so I decided to base my imaginary sessions on facts, which I would get from more of Aunt Meena's letters from England. Feeling lonely, without Emma, I often thought about my own departure and I frequently wondered when that time would be. I remained attentive for feedback or any news of the place.

The first letter that I had sneaked out was already put back in Aunt Meena's tin-box of odds and ends. So this time, I had no qualms in taking another. My intention was to go through each letter at my own pace, in my own time; under the pretext of studying and without anyone noticing that the letters were missing.

One day, I took the familiar red-and-blue bordered envelope, addressed to Aunt Meena, and concealed it between the leaves of my *Student's Companion* book. The bright orange handbook was every student's study 'bible' or according to our teachers, so it should be. As a result of this kind of thinking, studying it was greatly encouraged. My plan was that this book would become the hidden carrier for the letters, while I pretended to read from the book.

I felt certain that everyone would approve of my interest in the book, so I separated the tell-tale envelope from the folded letter; making it look like part of my school work. Ironically, I had unconsciously put the letter between the pages marked "*Civics,*" so it was with a measure of instant guilt that I recoiled from the words of the title on the page: *"OBSERVANCE OF CERTAIN ACCEPTED STANDARDS OF CONDUCT AND BEHAVIOUR."*

Directly underneath the title the introduction explained further: *"We owe it to society to refrain from anything vulgar, indecent or immoral as regards our conduct."* After reading this, a pang of guilt caused my pulse to race so I slammed the book shut. It was almost as if the words and my guilt were speaking to me, especially because I had taken the letter without asking.

I recovered quickly from the guilt, compelled by my stronger desire to learn about the happenings in England. I consoled myself with the thought that I was educating my curiosity but felt more convinced that the letter would soon be replaced before anyone realized it had gone. Letter No. 2 remained partially opened in my book, so I was able to read it with ease.

One afternoon, I sat in our yard under the damsel tree, while three eight year old boys were playing a marble game by the side of the road. It was nice to sit away from them and quite easily block out the noises of excitement they were making while I read the second letter from England.

"May 1962
Dear Meena,

Greetings from England, in the name of Jesus Christ. How is everybody and Mamie at home, I hope well. Generally things not too bad but I had to write and let you know how things is with me, at my end.

Well, you remember after my miscarriage last year, I did tell the doctor I want some birth control, because I didn't want to have to let things catch me unaware like that again.

Over the last few weeks I been suffering from heartburn, so I say perhaps it was wind - you know, eating late at night after work and going straight to sleep, too tired to let the food settle before sleeping. But this morning, when I went to see the doctor, the man examine me and he look me straight in the eye and tell me that I expecting a baby!

You could imagine my shock. Me? Three months pregnant in England! Well, is worried I worried, now, because you know England is not like home. There's nowhere to put down children and run and make a day's work. I'm worried about making children here in this country. The truth is, I really didn't plan to settle long here and it seems I really get caught with this one because I been using the coil; so I don't know what kind ah birth control that is, it didn't control this one. Really that shouldn't happen and the doctor himself was surprised but God knows best. He gives us life, although I know I don't want to put down roots in this place for too long.

The little money we getting here is just enough to hide ourselves in a room, with a roof over our head, buy a little food and every now and then send a change for you Mamie and the children. But what can I do? All the same, I really 'fraid for our situation here, because nobody want you in their house with children and we don't know when the little work we have here will finish, so my heart is really heavy

"Howdy do, howdy do!" a familiar voice called from the
road. It startled me and I jumped from being deeply
engrossed in the letter.

"How is Gran-gran, she awright?" Miss Saraphine called.

"Yes, thank you, Nenen," I replied, "She's inside the
house."

"You studying you book, that's good. God give you brains.
Remember, coming from this place, you need to be a *Woman
of Destiny*; so open you mind and take everything in because
we looking for all-you, the young ones, to raise our nose."

I did not answer Miss Saraphine, since her statement did
not require an answer - it was the usual semi-rhetorical
assertion from adults and close relatives. Her voice and
manner revealed a surety of expectation, as did all adults in
our village.

"Yes, Nenen," I replied.

The leaves of the nearby cane trees rustled as they brushed
against the back of our house. She went inside to look for
Gran-gran. My index finger had formed a bookmarker
between the pages of the closed book. However, the moment
she was gone, I instantly re-opened the pages of the *Students
Companion,* to resume my reading. The coast was clear so I
continued:

*"You see I was never planning on having another child
after all the shame ah give Mamie and Papa when I was
making Joanne. I would ah prefer to get married in any case
to make up for the shame; you know, make things look
respectable. I know I did spoil the family name, bringing a
fatherless child, and I always have the feelings that maybe*

that's what killed Papa, who knows? All the same, it's a heavy cross to bear."

"By the way, you did say in your last letter that Marion, was in Grenville asking to see Joanne. I don't care if they asking about Joanne now Randy, the good-for-nothing, stand by and let his mother say that he could ah never have anything to do with having a child with me and the wretch denied it! He could ah stand by me and own up to our relationship. That way, Joanne would ah have a father and other family to help care for her. What Randy family want to do with seeing her now? Even before she was well formed in my belly, those nastiness did reject her. Anyway, the answer is no! Leopards don't change their spots. Don't forget that! What's not good in the morning cant' be good in the night. So do girl, please don't let them bother the poor child brains now, it will just confuse her.

For twelve years now I alone minding that child and now she's big enough to give me a cup of water, they playing they want to know he now. Ah leaving things to you and I know you can deal with them over there. In fact, me and Calvin getting on quite well and I would want him to accept Joanne as his child when I send for her. She will have to take his name when we get married, so you see I don't want no spokes in my wheel more than how it is already.

The burden I feel with those good-for-nothings, and now this sudden pregnancy just when I'm finding my foot a little, is great. You see Satan never give up! But the good book says that God never give us what we can't handle, so pray for me.

I enclose a little change for you. Buy stout for Mamie and kiss Joanne and the others for me. Tell everybody I say hello and care yourself. I close in Jesus name.
Your sister, Irene."

When I had finished reading the letter, I folded it carefully and put it back into my book. It was a surprise to me to learn of the prevailing silence over my paternal roots. It is true that I was previously a little unclear as to why no one had bothered to tell me who my father was. Knowledge of the whole truth was shrouded in secrecy but the facts were obviously known to the whole village! I sat mesmerized, looking straight ahead of me into the surrounding foliage. The sound of the boys' laughter, during the marble game, rose and fell around me. More laughing could be heard coming from Miss Saraphine and Gran-gran inside the house and my head swooned.

What cruel hand of fate had caused my curiosity to result in the laughing echoes I now seem to hear? They appear to be jeering at my discovery, punishing my inquisitiveness; showing me up as a fool. A lump came up into my throat and a choking dryness gripped the back of my tongue. My constant swallowing were attempts to calm the nervous rush I now felt. Had my entry into the world brought such shame and pain, that my existence was not worth talking about openly?

Had Providence a means of dealing with my heart which was now a stone, for the grief that my short entry into the world had brought both Mamie Irene and our family? My head ached and my pulse raced with the realisation that the whole village knew about the disgrace that my life had already caused. I closed my eyes to stop the imaginings and the mental dialogue which now went on inside my head.

Yet in the midst of this emotional confusion, I experienced a catharsis. It instantly replaced the initial repulsion and my wild thoughts began to subside slowly. Instead, some powerful instinct, stronger than a thirst for education or religion, quickened inside me, at the thought of the pain and sorrow my short life had caused. I felt an instinct of overwhelming sorrow for both Mamie Irene and Daddy Randy; her teenage lover.

They had been caught in a web of love's sweet whisperings. During the one precious moment, they had acquiesced to each others invitation of pleasure and the joining of their two hearts. Sadly, the consequence of this is now a contrast of the present. The reality and history of is that Randy and his parents had disowned me from the start. Both Randy and my mother were teenagers - only 15 years of age when they were both "cut off in their prime." Each parent had previously welcomed their child's stated goal of becoming future teachers.

However, failing to reach parental expectation for successful destinies, my grandparents had demanded that Randolph should marry Irene, their daughter. Randy's squabbling parents flatly refused, saying their son would not have disobeyed them and therefore could not have got her pregnant! Instead of bridging the gap between the youngsters, they proclaimed irrevocable vows to separate Irene and Randy for ever. Consequently, their intransigence had denied me ownership of a mother and a father as well as their joint support and love.

On reading this and subsequent letters, I gathered a good deal of information. What was my response? Well, I felt sorry for the past young lovers. My heart went out to Mamie Irene in England momentarily; urging her own heart to be at peace. Simultaneously, the instinct to soothe Randy's male pride went compassionately out to him; wherever he was. In fact, I had mentally forgiven him and wondered what had become of him.

Sadly, the power of the parents' separation of these ex-lovers had been reinforced during the past 12 years.

Intermittently, it seemed to have resurrected raw pain and anger. This was clearly evident in Mamie Irene's inflammatory remarks in her letter. She had vowed to continue the feud and instructed Aunt Meena to blatantly reject Randy and his family's interest in me. But twelve years had passed and the strength of Irene's hate appeared to still light up the fire of resentfulness and hurt which was still burning deeply in her heart.

I wished that I could now tell them that it should be over by now and that it doesn't matter any more who was to blame. I wondered where Randy was; perhaps lost somewhere in the wilderness of the world, never to be revealed to me. But I felt somehow that amidst this discovery, was hope and possible reconciliation of the two ex-lovers.

How incomprehensible is the new-found feeling of rootlessness that the truth brings! The troubled questions which I had often pondered alone, today was accidentally answered through my inquisitiveness. A feverish quickening of heartbeats pounded in my chest. The mental din of confused thoughts, racing backwards and forwards in my head caused a mixture of sorrow and joy. This informed awakening now created a longing to find a real and lasting solution to the situation.

My feelings of belonging were certainly different now. Gran-gran and Aunt Meena, as well as Mamie Irene's love had, until now, sufficed as parents. However, the new discovery and awareness that another part of me existed somewhere in the world, awoke in me a spirit of compassion, forgiveness and an immediate need to delve deeper to find out more. Earlier, the tiny flame which the new knowledge had kindled in my body was fixed calmly on this need to belong. All feelings of loss and incompleteness quickly passed before me like an unpleasant dream, giving way to a bright new dawn of possibilities.

I was deep in thought and my ears were listening to the distant sounds of the evening when I became aware that Nenen Saraphine was talking to me. She was on her way out of our yard, having left Gran-gran inside the house.

"Chile, ah goin' before it get dark. It turnin' a little cold too."

"OK Nenen," I replied jovially, breathing deep breaths of relief.

Usually, sitting quietly on the ground can often feel quite comfortable but just now the weight of my entire body was pressing down on me, so I shifted to relieve the tingling sensation in my legs and the numbness in my buttocks. Suddenly, the hardness of the ground became noticeable because my thoughts had stopped being the focus of attention.

٤

The contents of Aunt Meena's letter played and replayed in my mind; while I returned consciously to my surroundings. I shifted my body from one side to the other, to relieve the pressure of sitting, by rolling onto my side. That's when my eye caught sight of a mad-ant's nest, and the business of their little world.

I watched the mad ants for ages, with infectious amusement, as the little creatures dominated their territory beneath me. Here, a world was in progress, with ants of some species scurrying backwards and forwards over their little creation; a mound through which they had forged a passage. It looked like a miniature volcano with red ants pouring in and out like brownish red larva, unaffected by human misgivings, trials, tribulations and failings.

173

I kept watching as they crept up the little slope to the mouth of the mound and disappeared down the gaping entrance, in frenzy. The mound was their claimed territory and the earth there was different from the rest of the soil around it. It looked like sandy earth that had been specially manipulated for ease in their ant world. Two large red ants carrying a crumb of bread struggled at the foot of the mound, determined to take their loot to its destination inside the mound.

Other ants followed them, like soldiers guarding their prize with watchful readiness to attack inquisitive invaders. I looked on, thinking that for these little ants, this food was perhaps a week or a month's supply for them. Momentarily, I thought of how they also mirrored human patterns of life - rushing backwards and forwards; in and out, bent on some urgent mission. Whether as workers, carriers, destroyers and hunters all were fulfilling their duties in life.

Here, every movement and deed pre-ordained by the Creator, appeared to radiate power in this intricate creation. It was as if a mirror, the lives of humans reflected that of the ants or vice versa. From here, I witnessed the whole world forming one vast symmetrical expression of love. I realised that each moment for the ants and us was also a gift. The land, the sea and the air too, were expressions of that unquestionable gift.

The struggling ants reached the top of the mound with the bread crumb and disappeared down the hole. In there, some starving ants would be fed, I thought. Some ants too weak to hunt would benefit and pregnant mother-ants would eat; so too would little ants which are being cared for by others. Tomorrow their world would revolve by repeating its daily circle, like ours. Sadly for them, their world goes unnoticed because of their insignificant size, in comparison with the rest of Nature's gifts. The reason is we are prone to step on them in our busy, complex existence; too pre-occupied with our own self-indulgence.

The wind had gone away and the nearby trees were steady now. Everything seemed unusually still. Fewer ants wandered outside the mound, perhaps they were all feeding inside on their loot. The sky and trees and winds too seemed quietly satisfied and inactive. The evening sun was becoming weaker now and it hung over the trees smiling, shining its last weak rays before ushering in the dusk.

I wondered about the ants for a while, then I sat upright and my bottom felt relieved from the cramps. I imagined that some little ants inside the mound; motherless and fatherless like me, were being fed, loved and cared for by the group as they grow up to ponder the workings of their species, their misgivings, their secrets, their complexities and their various expressions of love. A cool, reassuring breeze blew and I went inside to put Aunt Meena's letter back into the tin, before anyone noticed it was missing.

٤

Ten minutes later, Aunt Meena came back from Hermitage where she said she had met Celia, an old school friend. Both women it seemed had been talking at length about Celia's grievances.

Aunt Meena busied herself, as usual, making very quick movements inside the kitchen in preparation for our supper, before dusk fell. Having done all my homework earlier, I watched her as she peeled the brown rough skin off the piece of yam, revealing the hard, slimy, white flesh inside. She put them in a pan of cold water, after cutting them into chunky pieces. Then with skill and experience, Aunt Meena carefully

175

marked open the green banana by running a knife from the top of the stem to the bottom. This made it easy for the green skin to be easily pared away from the white flesh of the banana. The skin appeared to 'bleed' its familiar sticky, transparent glue as she forced her thumb under the green skin, while digging her thumb deeply around it; to push out the long, skinny, white flesh. After peeling all the green bananas, she sliced them diagonally in three pieces and swiftly deposited them into the pan with the yams.

Aunt Meena then scraped her slimy, stained, wet hand with the sharp knife, and was careful not to cut herself. Afterwards she chopped the small, round breadfruit in half. Breadfruit was her favourite vegetable and whether we liked it or not, she cooked it quite often; either roasted, boiled, steamed or fried!

Today, she had two medium-sized ones, which looked like green coconuts and she cut each one in half, then divided the pieces into quarter moon shapes, before applying force with her small knife, to peel the thick, rough, green skin. Very soon the breadfruit, yam and bananas were in the pan of cold water being rubbed with lime to cut the fresh slime. It was the way Aunt Meena usually washed them; squeaky clean each time. She moved with such precision that before long all the peeled food was put into the boiling pot of water on the fire, with a few grains of salt tossed in for the cooking.

The cornflour mixture, which Gran-gran had mixed earlier, was on the table in a clean bowl covered with a tea-cloth. Aunt Meena called me to reduce the flames in the gas stove and to check the boiling pot while she went to fetch the dumpling mixture inside. It was a delight to watch the boiling froth as it rose in the pot, spill over then sizzle as it came into contact with the open flames of the stove.

As usual, it was Aunt Meena's moment to talk to Gran-gran about the day's happenings, since the grown-ups never talked *"Big people business"* in front of children. We heard a lot of our information accidentally and certainly did not question the nature of our eavesdropped conversations. Therefore, filled with the discovery of Mamie Irene's letter, and my already eventful but *'secret'* past, I dared not whisper knowledge of this fact to anyone. It was *"big people business"* and I knew it.

Apart from going to school and learning first-hand religious education, we learnt generally from what we were told or what we happened to hear. I had trespassed into the boundary of adult secrecy and broken the rule of tradition, by sneaking out the letters. For that, my punishment seemed to be a new mental burden to carry on my own. In a similar way, it mirrored what the adults had done, quietly wishing it away, letting time erase the shameful sensation; pushing all hurtful memories into oblivion but obviously to no avail.

Aunt Meena kneaded the thick dough in the enamel bowl and expertly divided the lumpy mixture into small portions to make dumplings. Gran-gran listened as Aunt Meena recounted the conversation she had with her friend Celia, during the course of the day.

"You know I can't believe what Celia say," she began.

"How you mean?" Gran-gran asked, as she helped to roll the dumplings and put them into the pot of boiling water. The two women had their heads bent, looking busy with their fingers as they manipulated the thick dough.

"Well, Celia say she really don't mind looking after the land for her brother because he's all the way in England, but she say she don't want to keep workin' on it for him; if his wife stayin' all the way in England and instructin' her family right here in Grenada to come and help themselves and take whatever they want from the land."

"You mean dey takin' things without askin' Celia?"

"Well, from what Celia say, dey pickin' fruit, taking food, diggin' up yam and doin' whatever dey please."

"Uh huh?"

"She say only last week she catch a big boy up a coconut tree dropping down jellies, she tell him to come down. Then when she confronted him, he just tell her is his uncle land and she alone can't have everything."

"Like dey want to work the land themselves?" Gran-gran put in.

"I don't know but Celia say she will write and tell her brother that if he want her to continue lookin' after the land, he will have to come back to Grenada and straighten things out."

"Well yes, I agree," Gran-gran said sternly.

"I say yes too, because you have to *give Jack he jacket*. If she alone lookin' after the land when he not there to take responsibility for it, then he have to say which one of them he givin' legal power to."

Aunt Meena was always a fair judge and she reasoned well. She continued, "But definitely Celia can't be breakin' her back here, workin' under de cocoa, while her brother wife family comin' and reapin' whatever she plant."

"Ah have to say she's right to get annoyed because two captains cyan rule one ship." Gran-gran continued, stressing her view that, "He will have to come back here and choose."

"Well as for me, I tell her she's right. You see, too many people go to England and as soon as they buy a little piece of land, they expectin' those here to look after it for them, with no payment, as if it's their right to expect. It's not as if they've gettin' a little wage to encourage people."

"Dat is true," Gran-gran said, shaking her head in agreement.

"Really, Grenada people workin' like donkeys in the hot sun out of the goodness of their hearts. The leas' they can do is to show a little consideration."

Aunt Meena was obviously a little irritated for Celia, and Gran-gran nodded her head in agreement.

"They takin' people for granted *oui*! And instead of showin' gratitude, some ah dem givin' people who don't know a thing *about the horse's flesh* to come and do as dey dam well please. So it must mean he laughin' at Celia, while she breakin' her back in the hot sun, under the cocoa."

The whole affair seemed to have annoyed Aunt Meena, so she continued in her complaining voice, until she was satisfied that she had got everything off her chest.

For Grenadians, in fact other West Indians for that matter, owning land was a sacred act of possession. Gran-gran had been paying for hers for many years. The reverence with which she wrapped the land papers, gave the impression that it was like a gift of gold from God; being preserved for generations to come. For some, land was the lifeblood of the family. It brought food, it protected and nurtured; it sustained life, and within it also consumed the dusty forms at the end of our lives.

Yet for others, land was a yardstick, by which a man's social, economic and political worth was measured; his power to influence others, like *beke* had done to them. Most of all, it was a symbol of rootedness, that of belonging and identity; for a person, his family, his island and his race.

Gran-gran, the seasoned elder, was a good listener with many years of advising, judging and making decisions about all kinds of matters; for she had gained the respect of everyone. She listened carefully to Aunt Meena's agitated information then she replied with an almost half-lecture.

"Everybody want to go away and work. Nobody want to stay here and work on the land any more, but it's this same land that keeps all of us alive to this day. Plantation owner, *beke* and bourgeois, all come and go; all claimin' the land, as we work on it for them. No matter how high and mighty they may be, all have to go six foot down and leave the land right here. So I tell you, that land is more than the value of anythin' we know. It worth more than a office; it's more than a plane ticket to England or America and after all is said and done, the bodies of *all man, jack and their brother* must come back to the land."

Aunt Meena had stopped what she was doing and listened intently, then nodded her agreement. The women looked like judge and lawyer, reasoning out a special case. Then Aunt Meena spoke finally.

"Well, ah tell Celia she mus' start off as she mean to go on. She mus' let her brother make some kinda paper to give her power to throw out trespassers, and that will include that lazy *lougarou* family too."

Once the conversation had ceased, they waited; each locked in the quietness of her own thoughts. Aunt Meena and Gran-gran were mulling over the details of Celia's predicament. At the same time, I was pondering my own dilemma; the sordid details of my entry into the world.

The next move, I decided, was to search for Randy's family or find out about their whereabouts. Instantly, I adopted the "*Let bygone be bygone*" attitude; a sentiment that both Mamie Irene and Randy had not yet practiced. This was my sentiments to continue my journey to more self-discovery.

Chapter 7

"...The vagaries of life as they occur every day
Puzzle me, I must say
For on my right we see wealth and luxury
And on the left there's abject poverty
And while some of us are merry and living happily
Others dying in misery."

Lord Executor (Phillip Garcia)

The next day the early morning sun lovingly embraced the dew-covered leaves, making them shine like watery pearls on forest-green material. It was Sunday morning and apart from the odd stirrings in the room next to ours and Aunt Meena's humming, it was quieter than usual.

I was quite exhausted from the night before, lying awake because of my discoveries in Aunt Meena's letter and I was embarrassed by many of the facts. My mind was perturbed with a burden only I could carry; since it would be quite rude and disrespectful to ask any grown-up for an explanation of the information I now had. Since the facts were *"Big people business,"* I knew that I was not *big* and it was not my *business* to trouble them. I lay there pondering the consequences of attempting to find out who Marion and Randolph were. I also wondered where they had come from and possibly where they may be now.

I knew several people from the village and surrounding areas had travelled either to America, England, Trinidad, Venezuela or Aruba; all bent on a mission of economic improvement, seeking the lands whose *"streets were paved with gold."* On matters of the quest to seek out paternal family, I assumed Marion must be living nearby, since she was seen in Grenville, which was our locality. As for Randolph, I imagined him to be anywhere but Grenada; knocking around the four corners of the globe, searching and wondering what had become of me - at least that is what I had secretly hoped.

I lay in my bed turning these thoughts over and over in my mind, finding it harder to think of anything else. I felt like a zombie whose mind had been temporarily possessed by matters from another world, while trying to exist here - muddling through. My cousins, on the other hand, were foolishly arguing over the irrelevance of the '*Solomon A Gundy*' poem.

"Mamie say I was born on a Monday, so I'm fair of face!" shouted my cousin Catherine, showing off her light skinned complexion and slapping her sister Sarah in the middle of her back. Sarah, slightly darker than her, was obviously irritated by the unexpected slap on her back, retaliated with a vicious pinch on Catherine's arm. The girl squealed out, "You beast!" as she held onto the area of pain.

"You're Friday's child!" she shouted, "You must be born to woe, because that hurt!"

Their verbal battles continued as they left the bedroom and ended up in the kitchen.

"This stupidness stops right here and now, this Sunday morning!" Aunt Meena said, scolding them and putting an instant end to their wrangling about last week's school poem.

The girls gave each other a *bad-eye* look as they separated, and I watched them as they continued to mouth their taunting to each other in hushed voices.

Once they were out of sight, I went back to lie on my bed. I drew the bed sheet up to my ears and felt like sleeping again. Tossing and turning as I lay there, trying to get Marion

and Randolph out of my mind, I kicked the cover up because
my toes were sticking out at the bottom. Becoming a little
impatient with the unruly cover, I forced myself to pull it
down with my feet. I became so impatient, that I probably
looked as if I was having a one-man combat with the sheet.
Then it happened.

The first sight of blood - womanhood!   The shocking red
of my first period was not welcomed. The feeling of wet and
the sight of the fresh blood stunned me a little; despite being
watchful and expecting it for some time. Emma, Daisy and
Catherine had all seen their first monthly periods and I had
often listened with great interest to stories of what their first
experience was like. I expected to feel the pain and cramps
that they had talked about.

Emma had told us that her periods were painful because
she believed in the superstition that if someone steps on you
while menstruating, then you will experience painful periods.
Evidently, the girl was sick each month, so she became
convinced that someone at school must have stepped on her
foot and transferred their pain onto her! We had all laughed
at her superstitious rambling but Emma was serious.

"Yes the pain run out from one person foot into yours!" we
said jeering and mimicking her.

"Ha, ha hai!" We all laughed. "Wo-oy! Don't make me
laugh noh?"

Someone ran up to her and dramatized the pain running
away from another person and imitated it going into Emma.
She became very angry, the fact that we had taken the matter
so lightly. It was her aunt who had told her the superstition,
and if her aunt says so, then to Emma it was gospel.

When Emma's own turn had come, it was during our
regular tête-à-tête at lunchtime, at the back of the school
toilets. It was a dramatic moment and such a coincidence

because we had been whispering about the tabooed subject only a few hours before, on that same day!

"What does it feel like having your period?" I asked when the girls had stopped fooling around and was serious again.

"A dull cramp below your belly and then cramp in your legs," said wide-eyed Daisy.

"No, mine made me sick and I vomited all day," said Claudette, "And my breasts hurt me for days," she said proudly, as if the severity of it was the proven symbol of real womanhood.

"You see these stretch marks here," Emma said, pointing to her calves, "They say it's a sign when a girl turns into a woman. Men like to look at you there - you see I have a lot," she boasted.

We had all eyed each other, being careful not to laugh at Emma this time. Their stories of womanhood had intrigued me and I wondered why all the girls had begun to see their periods from the age of eleven when I had not. I had grown impatient, waiting and watching for adulthood each day, looking for that first sight of blood and checking for stretch marks but to no avail.

Today, at the age of twelve and a half, when I had least expected it, womanhood showed her ugly red head; branding me an adult and making me feel suddenly embarrassed and awkward. No one had told me exactly what I should do when my period showed up. Gran-gran and Aunt Meena had not instructed me about what to expect. Though the girls had talked about how it happened to them all, no one had really told me exactly what I should do.

I sat up immediately, squeezing my legs and buttocks, forcing the muscles to wait, while I thought of how best to deal with this grown-up situation. What will I say to Aunt Meena and Gran-gran? I felt so ashamed of myself and instantly shy about how to talk about it. There was no excitement in this as I had imagined, and presently, I did not feel like being a woman. I looked around the room swiftly for something to use and the only thing I found suitable was my face flannel, so I stuffed it into my underwear.

Quietly, I sat there waiting for signs of the strange feelings which the girls had related to me. Nothing similar manifested itself. But I wondered why mine had chosen to come stealing up on me, like a thief in the night. It had come quietly and stealthily. It had crept up on me secretly and caught me by surprise. I sat there thinking of it all, and I wished that Emma was here.

I mingled with the family in a sheepish manner as we made preparations for church. At the same time, I felt quite unclean and aloof with my adult condition. I wondered who I should tell first - whether it should be Gran-gran or Aunt Meena. How was I going to begin introducing such an awkward subject to either of them? I had never imagined myself being in a situation where I would be unable to talk to either of them, especially since Aunt Meena's warning, after the incident with the African priest.

At that time, we had all been reassured that if anything needed to be said, there must be openness, trust and confidence to do so. Today, the embarrassment had seemingly swallowed my speech and I just muddled along in a heightened, mechanical, and stressful stupor. I went to breakfast, to church, had lunch, stayed at home in the evening then went very early to bed. I was too preoccupied with myself to communicate effectively with anyone around me.

The enormity of the dramatic way in which things were escalating in my life, had become too remarkable for me. It had begun with my emotional upheaval sine hearing that Emma was leaving for England. It continued with Emma's departure, then the sudden discovery of Randolph and Marion's existence; as well as Mamie Irene's continued harsh feelings towards them. These affairs seem to compound the roller-coaster emotions in my mind, with the added surprise and arrival of womanhood.

But by the next day I was caught. Aunt Meena had seen me bending down to pick something up and was obviously surprised by the evidence of what she had seen. She surprised me too, by the hard slap which I had received on my bottom for *"playing big"* and not telling them about such an important thing.

Then a multitude of questions were asked in quick succession: When did it happen? How long ago? Who else knows? Afterwards, I was handled like a sick child needing emergency treatment; under both women's protective wings and given a strict warning against the male population.
Aunt Meena, a little agitated said, "This happens to all girls when they become young women. From now on you mustn't talk to boys!"

Gran-gran backed her up immediately, "That means all boys, including the son of that *gros bete!*" I looked at her surprisingly. I knew she was referring to Justin.

"Yes," said Aunt Meena, still irritated and anxious, as she endorsed Gran-gran's comments, "Justin and all those *good-for-nuting* boys it have around here. Stay away from them!"

Aunt Meena had barely finished talking when Gran-gran added to her earlier statement.

"And doh let anybody put words to you. You hear me?"

I listened to the women and half-waited for an explanation of their profuse warnings but nothing more was explained. Why should talking to boys affect my periods I wondered? I was left to draw my own conclusions about the situation. What special words were they likely to put to me? Then once the embarrassment had subsided, I was relieved that the business of womanhood had at least been aired.

Feeling somewhat encouraged by the way in which the women had dealt perfunctorily with the matter, it was with a sense of hope I visualised a possible similar handling of the Marion and Randolph affair. Both Gran-gran and Aunt Meena were less emotionally involved I told myself, and I surmised that perhaps the past twelve years had mellowed the painful memory of their shared shame.

However, deep down, I knew that the task of resolving the Randolph-Marion situation with Mamie Irene and the family would not be easy. Perhaps the strangest aspect of the situation was the silence over the matter, and the severity with which everyone seemed to have conducted the whole affair. They had completely left out all possibilities of my future growing needs. What was more mystifying was their apparent oblivion of my personal development; psychologically and emotionally and my right to know about the truth of my past.

The whole affair had set me pondering a few deep thoughts. Can the flame which once burned the passion in Mamie Irene's heart for Randolph never be relit? Is it not possible to rekindle a tiny flicker of hope for reconciliation between them? Can love which was once so powerfully strong, filled with the purity which had created me, die with such extreme hatred and malice? Can a woman's tender care cease towards the man she really loved? Then more poignantly, I wondered whether the cessation of love had been only with Randolph? It was unbearable to ponder this question, '*Can a woman's tender care cease towards the child she bears?*' for fear of the answer it may unearth. The real question is; can I, the fruit of that once-love-now-hate relationship, be unconsciously included in that cessation of tender care too? Briefly, anger was eroding the self-restraint I had maintained so far and my patience began to ebb slowly.

The noise of the dishes being washed caused a kind of nervous irritation; as if all sounds were trespassing on my struggling consciousness. Images of rebellion and outburst began to well up in my mind. An inaudible voice seemed to be tormenting my soul. It echoed my loneliness, showed me glimpses of being a castaway or an unwanted, isolated and unloved presence. It needed great effort of will to control the impulse which was rising up in me; urging me to unleash an outburst and vent my pent-up frustrations on this grown-up complexity of the world. Then I thought of Gran-gran.

But I had heard with frequency, that God was love, and the voice of panic-stricken anger slowly subsided, giving way to the kind of comfort that I had imbibed so often in Gran-gran's *WORDS OF COMFORT*. The words came flooding in to my mind; penetrating it with peace, so that in a moment I began to regain my composure. The feeling of rebellion slowly abated and I remembered its instruction, "*Let not your heart be troubled.*" Just then, it had become a message of comfort to me. The words permeated my errant thoughts and I felt rescued from premature actions.

Had Emma been here, she would have quickly helped me to reason this situation out more clearly. However, left to my silent, inexperienced mind, the pendulum of emotions swung from despair, fear and panic, to belief in God, the strength of Gran-gran and Aunt Meena, and my hopes of going to England.

Chapter 8

"If you have any trouble you must explain me plain
And please bring you enemy's name
Bring six pint of rum, a suit length and six dollars too
And I will fix your business for you."

Lord Invader (Rupert Grant)

Missionaries had come to St. Andrews Parish during our summer holidays and made it possible for everyone to learn something. We could either memorise Bible passages, learn to embroider the attractive designs which we were shown, or learn to recite and sing English-style choruses and poetry.

Miss Gisbreth was a white Canadian woman, accompanied by another Canadian female, who had come to show the whole Parish the refinements of art, white etiquette and the imitative styles of Canadian Christian elitism. Young and old, male and female; all joined her team in the Friendly Society Hall.

It was every villager's dream to aspire to social excellence and the planned concert at the end of Miss Gisbreth's six weeks in our Parish, gave everyone a buzz. The Canadians loved it. They were Anglicans, not like our local or folksy Baptists. Daily the women worked diligently with everyone creating, teaching, impressing and enjoying the overall interest. And it was with a feeling of great restoration of my confidence, that I accepted the job of reciting the *Welcome Speech* for the planned concert.

People from the areas of St. Johns, St. Andrews and Gutt had come together. Those showing any obvious skill were selected for individual presentations at the concert. However, within the holistic scheme of things, all creativity was centered on biblical knowledge. All sessions began with singing the bible chorus.

"The B-I-B-L-E, yes, that's the book for me. It's God's own word and there is no doubt, the B-I-B-L-E!" rang the theme song each session. The activities were varied so that whatever a person chose to do was always shared with the group at the end of the session - it was called *worship*, which always ended with the theme song.

ع

During that summer vacation, Cariere Estate had a new Overseer. He was a short man, who looked alert and unforgiving. He was not the kind to overlook if you had helped yourself to some mangoes that had ripened and fallen on the ground to rot; or Governor-plums that were so purple and enticing on the tree that you felt the urge to help yourself to them before the birds did.

Many Overseers had come and gone from Cariere Estate, each one starting off strictly; desperate to be seen as fearful supervisors for their absentee English landlord. But then when they later came face-to-face with the reality that the workers, like themselves, were given pittance in exchange for their hard work, they gradually changed. The job descriptions of these Overseers was not only to supervise but they were also engaged in forking acres of land, planting, picking, cutlassing, preparing bananas, and cocoa for exporting, separating mace from nutmeg, sweating and drying wet cocoa beans.

Women too worked huge tasks of cutlassing acres of grass in the hot sun, carried heavy loads on their heads, with very

190

little to make ends meet at the end of the week. Therefore, Overseers, once bitten by the hardship bug themselves, would reduce their initial severity of trying to impress their bosses and instead turn a blind eye to the workers' survival ploys. It was not unusual to see someone taking more than six mangoes home. Some may help themselves to a bunch of banana, or some dasheen, a piece of yam or plantain - all food for hungry children. The Overseer would choose not to see any of this!

Emery's uncle was different. He was a man who had been sent to have no mercy on anyone and as a result, everyone hated him. The enviable Great House which he lived in, had more than 25 glass windows overlooking the road, and the creamy coloured brick and white painted windows, stood among the green vegetation like an ice-cream palace. It had its own tarmac drive. Firstly, huge iron gates opened on to the Great House and electricity powered everything indoors, making it looked like a fairytale castle, imposing its difference on the local natives. The aura of this, the largest house in the whole Parish, forced a kind or reverence, if not fear; on those who had any dealings with it because it outshone anything that anyone had or seen locally.

The roads around the Great House were in perfect condition, compared to roads in the Parish generally. Overall, the stark contrast of care given to the few Great Houses in the island showed where interest was a priority. From each Great House, the roads gave ease of movement to land produce, being regularly transported out of the estates, bound for Geest or other exporting ships to England and the free world.

A couple of months before the summer vacation, Emery had come with his uncle to Cariere. No female companion was among their household, except loud-mouth Jean from our village. She was employed to cook, clean, iron, scrub and serve Emery's uncle. Emery attended Miss Gisbreth's summer vacation activities and he made a point of staring at me often and smiling with his big white teeth. He had no friends in the village and the hateful symbol which his uncle represented, made him, like his uncle, an anachronism in the area. Justin and the other boys in our village teased him and called him a *smiley puss*. He probably knew they did not like him but he seemed not to care how anyone really felt about him or his dad in the Great House.

During Miss Gisbreth's sessions, Emery often sat either in a seat in the row that I sat in or sometimes he would either sit in the rear immediately behind me, or in a seat directly in front of me. There he made it obvious that he was interested in me, without saying a word. He was a misfit, perhaps quite used to being shunned as the nephew of an Overseer; he remained uncompromising in his attitude. He would come into the Society Hall quietly and usually left quietly too when all Miss Gisbreth's activities were finished. He was often collected by his uncle, who usually waited outside to take him home in an Estate-owned vehicle.

On the day of the concert Emery spoke to me. I had prepared my speech and after the great introduction of the concert by Miss Gisbreth, I wooed the hot and fanning audience with my diction, my love for poetic utterances. Being at the forefront of things I enjoyed explicating to the crowd. I believed I had wooed Emery too, because he responded with much wider smiles at the end of the concert.

"You was good," the voice from behind me said, tapping me on the shoulder, so that I turned around swiftly.

"You think so?" I asked awkwardly but pleased with the compliment.

He stood there looking at me fully and as the other boys passed behind his back, they secretly mimicked his smile in a teasing fashion. This made me smile even more in front of the already smiling boy. In fact, Emery may have misunderstood the reason for my increased smile so he made another attempt to talk. We both started off at the same time.

"No you go first," I said.

"Noh, you firs'," he replied.

"You like it in the Great House then?" I asked, attempting to break the ice further.

"Noh and Yes," he replied, still smiling and fully fixing his gaze at me.

"No, or yes? Which one?" I enquired, puzzled at this composure.

"Noh, because it's too big - all those rooms just for two people. A person can only sleep in one room and eat in one," he said pausing. Then when his smile had gone he continued.

"And yes, because it's quite near here and I always look at you goin' and comin' back from school everyday," he said triumphantly.

"You mean you been a peeping Tom, spying on me for two months?" I asked.

He grinned, gleefully, again showing his big white teeth. He nodded his head in agreement and looked quite smug. Just then a Ford Comma truck pulled up outside the Society Hall outside the wide junction. It tooted its familiar horn and Emery instantly recognised the signal, so he made his exit and entered the waiting vehicle.

"Catch you later," he called out confidently, as he departed.

I watched the short boy climb into the familiar truck and sat at the front, next to the driver. He turned around as the vehicle was leaving to blink his eyes at me; displaying a kind of grown-up effrontery which I definitely felt challenged by.

However, I waited with interest, for the circumstances of our next meeting.

The following week, I was filled with anticipation and wondered whether I would see Emery peeping at me through the Great House windows. The thought of it gave me a little feeling of importance. I took more care of my appearance and often walked past the huge, imposing, iron-gates while feigning a lack of interest in the boy; in case I was found guilty of searching for love.

For that first week, nothing untoward happened and I was surprised by the lack of no response from Emery. There was no sight of him, though his uncle's truck often zoomed up and down the road, as it passed us, carrying Estate workers to the junction. From there they would make their own way to their respective homes.

By the third week, I gave up my daily vigil and instead became engrossed in a cultural show in school. This show was led by Mr. Glover, a short, white music teacher, who offered to give me free music lessons.

ع

Mr. Glover was an Englishman; a bachelor with dark rimmed spectacles and hazel eyes which matched his neatly pressed-down, hazelnut-coloured hair. As our music teacher, Mr. Glover chose groups of children for the coming cultural show and organized a flurry of activities for our production.

Aunt Meena did not readily agree for me to have piano lessons with Mr. Glover. I think that in the back of her mind was the fear that I was now "*a young woman*," who had become more vulnerable to danger. Added to this was the "priest" incident at the back of her mind. Overall, she displayed a greater feeling of responsibility for my whereabouts.

I was only thirteen but it was not uncommon to hear of very young girls who had fallen victim to teenage pregnancy. The saddest thing was the fact that those girls were caught before they could say Jack! That was possible because they had not been told about the whys and wherefores of sex education and sexual activity.

Many a strict Christian girl had been trapped by the superficial platitudes of worldly boys. Firstly, they had not heeded the *"Do not talk to boys"* or the *"Don't let anyone put words to you"* and *"Don't show anyone your pantie."* Curiosity and ignorance walked hand-in-hand among them but still the taboo remained.

At first, Mr. Glover had not chosen me for the school choir because during the selection test, I could not make the high-sounding notes on the music scales for the soprano parts. My husky voice was not suitable and because all my friends were chosen, I felt sorely hurt by my misfortune. However, the music teacher was a man of insight. He realised that all my friends were in the choir except me, so my compensation was an offer of free piano lessons, to reward me for my interest in music.

Gran-gran, of course, saw it as another step up the ladder of success towards my becoming her *Woman of Destiny* among the white people. She promptly said 'Yes' to the offer. Aunt Meena was not positive in her response and it created a dilemma. Was she to agree and jeopardize her controlled watchfulness over her charge; or was she to say 'No,' and be responsible for the lack or unfulfilled ambitions of her niece. Worse still, she could be accused of not allowing her niece to develop her natural abilities. She took her time brooding over the decision.

In the meantime, I was beginning to show interest in music and would often rush home to practice playing the pieces by using numbers instead of notes on the ground under the house. We did not have a piano, nor could I see any possibility of ever having one. However, I was often called from my playing the "2-2-2-4, 2-2-2-1-1-, 1-1-2-2-2-3-3-2," in the dirt below our house. My fingers were briskly in synchrony with the music in my head, as they hit the cold ground alternatively; lifting and tapping as I hummed.

Aunt Meena watched with interest. I knew this was making her decision over my budding musical ability harder to curtail, but she remained patient and agitated in her dilemma. She was not an indecisive person. There was certainly nothing she could not do or say if she wanted to. In fact, she was more often than not a rather outspoken woman. Reluctantly Aunt Meena agreed to my piano lessons, but the day she had walked down the school route to look for me, after I had been more than 20 minutes late from school; was the day my music lessons stopped.

I was walking leisurely up the road, strolling with Emery. I did so without a care or concern for my responsibility to the family and for my lateness, Aunt Meena had said. That was the day my musical pursuit, having been nipped in the bud, died an instant death. Restriction re-imposed, I did not see Emery again. He had told me earlier that he often went to La Poutrie, where his family lived. So I assumed that when he was not in the Great House on the estate, it was probably where he was.

Emery and I had a lot in common. His mother and father had also travelled to the United States and he too hoped that one day he would join them. He was a loner and I felt that I could be a friend of his, since Emma was no longer available. Sadly, there was to be no chance of this. Aunt Meena had made it impossible. Gran-gran had very little choice in the matter once Aunt Meena's justifiable reasons were given to her. Furthermore, reasons apart, Aunt Meena was the more mobile of the two guardians, and she therefore made decisions about my movements since she would be the one doing the running around to find me. Therefore, her decisions on such matters were always final.

Mr. Glover was disappointed that my music lessons could not continue. Some excuses were made on my behalf, to do with the long distance of walking after school in the dark. He told me afterwards that there was nothing he could do. The teachers had all lived in the town. For many of them, the school building was a few minutes walk to and from their homes, and this did not put their lives in jeopardy. That was Aunt Meena's justification to Gran-gran for stopping the lessons.

٤

Perhaps it was every person's nightmare in the country; the burden of looking after the children of a sister or brother who had emigrated across the Atlantic Ocean. And perhaps the concern was more intense if that child was a girl who had turned into a 'young woman'. Other added concerns were to do with over-protection and worries about the risk of becoming a potential victim due to ignorance.

But where did our culture get such reasoning from? Ours was a culture that allowed boys to run around freely, unchained; some recklessly, like wolves attacking unsuspecting girls – the sheep. More complex was the thinking within a family who would arbitrate the differences in discipline between their male and female children.

The prevailing macho image had bred *saga-boys* as role-models; yet no one had thought too deeply, it seems, on whom the unchained male permissiveness would eventually prey. It was as if the girls in chastity would somehow miraculously meet boys who would somehow materialise with Godliness and perfection, out of thin air!

The male freedom to conquer was his *rite-de-passage* of manhood, and the females, if they did not get caught; looked forward to fashionable marriages in houses where both man and woman live together with children. The fantasy aspect of this reasoning was a romance of culture that was unchallenged by all: with female acceptance as concessions that marked them off as being victims of their own petard.

This was the reason why Jean and Dessima fought relentlessly one day in the junction, after having strong words with each other, over their individual affections for Teacher Date; a young Apprentice Teacher from Hermitage.

Teacher Date was a slim, attractive and glib young man, whose rising status in the community, as a Probationary Teacher, had exposed him to every girl's admiration; especially those from Standard Seven class. As a young man who was rising to great heights, he was admired by all - old and young, men and women, especially the latter.

The government school Trainee Teacher, most people felt, was a role-model for many young boys. He was also a romantic fantasy of all grown-up girls who fancied him or who felt he fancied them. Teacher Date, as everyone called him, basked in the mutual attention he received. He reigned supreme as the 'king of the saga boys' among them.

ع

Both Dessima and Jean were in Standard Seven and as young women; they competed for signs of Teacher Date's preference of one over the other. It was not known whether he deliberately encouraged the competition but the ensuing drama, which took place at the stand pipe, was talked about in the village for a very long time after the event.

Jean's auntie had a water pipe in their house, so she did not need to collect water from the local standpipe. Her mother was in England and she had often sent money to the family, so they were able to better themselves quicker than most. Jean enjoyed the availability of everything she wanted and the freedom she was given to roam around the village unchecked by her aunt. This meant that she came into constant contact with the local boys who often joked with her and whispered gossips about her illicit behaviour with some of them.

Dessima, on the other hand, was a Seven-Day Adventist church-goer, who had no such chances but she was clever. Her mathematical ability was well-known to everyone and though her family was poor, her manners showed better breeding than Jean's.

The Trainee Teacher was from another Parish, St. Patrick's, and he had often given Dessima, who also lived in St. Patrick's, a lift in his Ford Zephyr car on his way home. This was much to Jean's annoyance. When Jean was given a ride, she made it publicly known but deep down she felt that Teacher Date's interest in her was superficial, compared to the more intense interest she thought he seem to have in Dessima. The girls had no confirmation of any such fantasies from the

Teacher himself but they rivalled each other in ridiculous ways that climaxed one day with a public fight.

That evening at the standpipe, Jean attacked Dessima by calling her a slut. Dessima retaliated by branding Jean a loose whore. Jean was not content to battle verbally, so she pushed Dessima over the standpipe, causing the girl to dive into the muddy area around the pipe. Her bucket, which was under the standpipe collecting water, was filled and started to overflow. The girls were bent on thrashing out their frustrated feelings against each other. Those who had congregated around the squabbling two were amused by their bold, noisy, verbal confrontations. Some egged them on.

"Who you calling a whore?" Jean demanded loudly, squaring up in front of Dessima.

"You! Who else?" Dessima piped up, squaring up even closer in the girl's face.

Some of the crowd looked on in silence. Teacher Date's name was never called, so no one knew why the girls were fighting.

"You calling me a whore?" Jean raged, this time their bodies were touching and their faces, showed eyes glaring viciously into eyes; like two bulls ready in a head-on charge at each other.

"Yes, you and your mother," Dessima yelled, egging the girl further on.

Jean became more enraged. At that point, she felt she now had the license to lose all self-control because her mother's name and integrity was being literally dragged through the mud. Everyone knew that to insult a person's mother was the ultimate in provocation. It was considered an incitement for serious action. Jean took a step back, leapt forward with a charge, then running towards Dessima, she spat in her face.

"Take that," she said. She then swung with her fist around and landed a surprising blow on Dessima's head. She wiped off the spit and eyed Jean wickedly, then ran towards the girl.

"You bitch! I'll tear you to pieces," Dessima warned, "It's 'bout time somebody make you put your tail between your legs. You think you too dam nice!"

With that, she slapped Jean on her face, making the fair - skinned girl go red and wild with rage. Jean grabbed Dessima's hair and twisted her around to that she fell onto the ground. Jean jumped on Dessima and pounded the girl with her fist. They rolled in the mud each gaining superiority at the top intermittently; while the other received the punishing blows below.

They looked like two brown seals covered in mud, unleashing their pent-up frustration on each other in a combat of wills. They were locked in an embrace of vicious rage, rolling all around the pipe in the mud; and thrashing each other to exhaustion. The male section of the crowd was delighted at the physicality of the female spectacle, so they egged the women on. Some appealed to them to stop the fighting. Such a spectacle was uncommon in the village, where women, the transmitters of wisdom and tradition, were supposed to be more circumspect.

The scene had created a noisy spectacle, so when Mr. James heard the commotion from inside his shop, he came out and saw the two girls locked in a bite; Dessima's teeth on Jean's face. He rushed into the ring of spectators and used all his might to separate the two. They behaved like gladiators fighting to the death.

"Stop this stupidness now!" he retorted, holding the two heavy breathers apart.

Dessima being the darker of the two looked like a tar baby with bulging, angry eyes which were now filling up with tears. Jean's long hair all muddied to match her dress, face and legs, looked like one of the Jab-Jab carnival masqueraders; except her face showed a ring-mark of red swollen patch where Dessima had almost bitten off her flesh.

Dessima, trembled with rage and fear, then she spoke.

"She started it first!"

"Look at my face! Yours not staying like that!" retorted Jean, "It's tit for tat!"

And with that, she sprang at the girl from behind Mr. James' back. This time Mr. James was readily assisted by another man; each holding the girls apart and restraining their unquenched anger, until Dessima broke down and cried openly. She was led away from the scene by some people and others led Jean the other way, to ensure that their feelings cooled down without further damage.

Dessima's bucket of water was taken home by kind spectators, to stop her mother from taking up with Jean, where her daughter had left off. The fact is, Jean had a reputation for being a loud-mouth in the village. That girl would curse the priest, if she felt he warranted it, and some said jokingly that Jean would curse Jesus Christ too, if he came down and scolded her!

Those who had walked Jean home, tried to reason with her; since she vowed that the affair was far from over. Some thought it must have been Jean's sense of defeat, for not having overpowered Dessima totally by reducing her to a shameful spectacle. This made her feel more enraged. Her shame was intensified with every consolation that she had received and she walked the last 100 yards home alone, to wallow privately in her hurt feelings.

There was no winner because Teacher Date was unaware that the girls' shameful display was over him. Eventually, his training period in their school came to an end and he left for his next probationary placement elsewhere; possibly to break some other girls' hearts.

ع

But the island was full of *saga boys* or *sweet men*, breaking women's heart, shattering their promises of love and leaving big-bellied girls dotted here and there. Ironically, men fighting over women seem to give them greater feelings of libido; a sense of achievement of male conquest and further qualification. Like bees, they darted from flower to flower, pollinating the youthful flowers as they pass, and in time littered villages with little representatives of their conquests everywhere.

Those women, not wanting to be numbered among the grief-stricken populace, would lock up their daughters; leave them in ignorance of sexual behaviour, for fear that to teach them will encourage curiosity. Some thought that their one command, "Don't talk to boys," would stand their obedient, submissive, little princesses in good stead. Somehow, they expected girls would translate their cryptic commands and be able to reject the developing sexual awareness and the libidinous advances of their male counterparts.

Lucky then, are the daughters who escape the shame that befall the errant few. I thought of Mamie Irene and the letter about her shame and family humiliation. Aunt Meena was hell-bent it seems; on avoiding such dishonour for me, especially since I was in her temporary care. Maybe she prayed for the eventual relinquishing of that burdensome duty. It was difficult to tell, but during Christmas, when we were praying at the table after our carol singing, Aunt Meena's face looked strained. She seemed to have aged recently and I noticed a little sadness in her face when she looked at me.

In the midst of our playful excitement was knowledge of their sad news. Both women had learnt of my imminent departure from Grenada. They watched our childish happiness over our Christmas presents and seemed to stare beyond the present into the future; to a time when I would no longer be with them. Our Christmas presents were simple colourful balloons and noisy flutes which were attached to them, mouth organs, which we could not play, and white dolls with blue eyes with eyelashes that blinked. These were sent to us from England.

As always, the women carried their many burdens silently. Therefore concerns about my migration to England were kept quiet, until it was made public in the New Year. News of my travel brought on a somber mood among the family but the preparations for travel in April escalated, as the days passed speedily by.

The week before Christmas, the letter which had arrived to inform us about the completed immigration papers in England, was collected from the Post Office in Hermitage and brought to our house. However, as usual, the ritual of opening the letters we received from England was performed without variation. Aunt Meena usually placed the letters on the pine dresser inside the house and waited for the comfort and peacefulness at the end of the day before she opened them.

At this time, she was sure that nothing would disturb her ritual opening because by then, all our chores would have been done to her general satisfaction. It was as if she had to be at peace with herself and the world immediately around her before her exposure to England's news. In this frame of mind and with an air of expectancy, she would wash her hands, wipe them dry then sit in a comfortable position before carefully opening the letters.

Aunt Meena never tore open any letter. It was usually treated with respect, handled carefully, as if to desecrate it would be to disrespect its sender. Then she would take a deep breath, clear her throat and begin her silent reading. By the time she had got half way through the page, she remarked in surprise, "Gade mize mwen non?"

Always being close by, Gran-gran enquired what the problem was.

"Sa ki fe`w?"

"Papa mwen oh, petite moun ka ale England!" Aunt Meena replied.

"Ale England," that long awaited phrase, said now with such surprising calmness, increased my heartbeats. I looked up from where I was reading on the floor and say that Gran-gran too, was surprised by the reality of what we had all expected would happen one day, but thought was a more distant reality.

"Bon Je, tout moun ka ale?" She looked resigned to the "Que Sarah," which Aunt Meena voiced under her breath.

Aunt Meena did not publicly shed tears but remained outwardly resolute, with a hardened expression, clearly against any show of emotional displays. I noticed that she gritted her teeth to hold back signs of weakness and instead, withdrew into herself for quiet moments of contemplation.

Gran-gran looked pained and her nervous eye twitches returned; only at this moment, they were more pronounced. She gritted her teeth too and remained sadly silent; biting on her lips to control the screaming inside her heart. I had recognized the isolated moments of voiceless screams, which she had once told me about. She said that they had first occurred during her childhood, after being raped by Mr. McDonald, the white Estate owner.

She made a point of telling me the story one week after I had first seen my period as a means of, not only instructing me on my need for caution against so-called trusted people, but also the need for strict vigilance. She gave me her own cautionary example of the kind of craftiness and trickiness which she had experienced; stressing that such ploys could befall any unsuspecting young woman, since she was unaware of the snares and traps that Mr. McDonald had laid for her.

٤

Gran-gran said that Mr. McDonald had robbed her of her virginity in the most belittling form of servile oppression she had experienced. This had occurred when she was only 13 years of age, because Mr. McDonald knew that she did not have a mother's vigilant protection around her. Her mother had died, leaving her father with seven children to cope with. She told me that she had been caught like a sweet innocent lamb to the slaughter, when she was full of the joys of spring, because she was brought up to obey all her elders.

Her father, who had been left to bring up their seven children, had spent his waking hours, solely occupied with making sure that they had enough food to eat and a roof over their heads, whilst the older girls helped, where possible, to look after the younger ones. Their jobs were to support their father and to ensure that the general running of the house was smooth. But Mr. McDonald had taken advantage of their hand-to-mouth kind of living, by suggesting that he should relieve them of at least one burden.

He had picked Gran-gran because she had a bright outlook on life, and could read a little. Mr. McDonald had given the impression of wanting to help our family, by asking whether Gran-gran could help them in the Great House, just as her mother had done before she died. Wilomena, I learned then, was my great-grandmother's name. She was a first-class Housekeeper who lived up to her reputation of being 'the best maid,' the McDonalds ever had.

On the day that Mr. McDonald chose to rape Gran-gran, she was cleaning out his bedroom. There was no one else in the house, making it easy for him to brutally and violently force his ageing self on her she had reasoned.

"Feel that!" he said, pushing the springiness of the mattress on his bed and teasing her, while she cowered like a frightened lamb about to be devoured by a vicious lion.

"Not like your straw paliass, eh?" he told her, as he leered at her, smirking and fiddling with the flies of his trousers. Her eyes opened wide with horror as she shook her head violently, shocked by her unavoidable trap. She could not run away from his room. She gathered the skirt of her dress closer to her, to protect her innocence and continued backing away into whatever remaining space was available behind her.

"Get down!" he ordered, pointing to the floor while aiming at her. He caught her and in the struggle which ensued, he cupped his hand over her mouth to stifle her screams as he defiled her again and again. The desecration had sent painful shock waves through her body, she said; causing her dry scorching throat to trap the screams there, whilst her eye muscle twitched at will.

She was left to sob uncontrollably on the floor of shame, with a verbal reminder that he was *"the Boss,"* and that no one would believe the story of a starving little oaf like her, against him. Worst of all, should she tell anyone, he had threatened to tell her father that she had played up to him sexually, in order to get special favours. So with that warning, she had kept her mouth shut: silence and the painful memories became her defiance.

Trapped in this way, Gran-gran was ordered to accept the rape sessions repeatedly; each time more vicious than the last, until the day Mr. McDonald suffered a severe stroke on the land, in the sweltering hot sun. The general excuse was that he had not worn his hat in the hot sun. Gran-gran told me that he had set off that day to go and deal with a dispute against a neighbouring owner, about boundaries on his Estate land.

His pale white skin was paler, "as white as a cotton table cloth," she said and, "the top of his head was red like a half-ripe Governor plum, where the sun had tried to roast him as he lay unconscious on the ground."

The stroke that Mr McDonald suffered had caused his face to twist, with paralysis down his left side. This had affected both his left arm and left leg, so he was unable to walk. She told me that she watched the helpless *"couchon,"* as he laid on the same spring bed which he had said was too good for him to sodomise her in and she secretly thanked God for having answered her silent prayers to strike him down with vengeance.

On the day that he had died, 10 months after the stroke, she had felt temporarily guilty for having ever wished for his death and for secretly cursing his very life with Mr. Stan Joseph, the local *Obeah* man. But the memory and voiceless pain had remained within her and she felt that in death, he was the lucky one to have escaped the long suffering, so she reckoned the revenge was justified.

I had listened to Gran-gran in amazement, mostly because she had told me this most personal secret, without the usual adult reservation. It was done in the way that most adults would do; use the experience as an example or extreme form of caution over confidential or personal matters. The old rule was suspended temporarily for my benefit and I was embarrassed as a result of her openness and the intensity of the shame and pain she still carried. She had laid bare her soul's most raw source of pain. Gran-gran, it seemed, was more concerned with my understanding her every word, her motive for showing me the moral behind her story, that she used her wisdom as an Elder and her voice did the caution.

ع

Now as I watched her accepting the "what-will-be-will-be" situation, I felt guilty in wanting to go away to England in the first place. The ritual reading of the letter from England was over, and the plan for my travel was discussed. My mother had suggested a travel date in April, only four months away and various other requirements for travel were talked about. Lost in my own little world of half-excitement and half-sadness, I mulled over the thoughts of having to deal with twin sisters, a stepfather whose surname I would have to adopt for ease of documentation and the discomfort of having to be close to people I had no emotional ties with. I shuddered at the thought.

It was a big step into the unknown; one that I had been looking forward to for ages. Now it had become a reality, the thought of leaving Gran-gran and Aunt Meena behind marred my excitement a little, so that the expected euphoria was exchanged with worries.

Emma's letters did not paint a picture of England's perfection and beauty, as we had both imagined. Her letters were shorter than I had expected and they lacked the kind of excitement that we had shared and visualized here. So it was with trepidation that I accepted the facts. I had four months to get used to the idea of leaving Gran-gran. It took time for me to accept the fact that I would be leaving Grenada for good and all that I had known and loved dearly, to venture into unknown territories. One such territory was living in the home of my family in England.

I had read about the twins - Darris and Darrin - and had scrutinized their faces in the black and white photograph we had of them sent by the family in England. In this picture, toys were strewn all over the floor and in the foreground, figures of two mischievous smiling faces with daring stares, made me feel apprehensive.

I had never seen their father's picture, though everyone referred to him as Calvin. So my immediate alteration from Calvin to "*Daddy*" was going to be a little hard to swallow. I was concerned about having to deal with the reality of a family whose related names, *sister, mamie, daddy*, did not fit in emotionally with my present scheme of things. I secretly resented these being thrust on me. However, I had absolutely no control over my predicament and it became something that I had to accept. It was the way things had to be in order to achieve my dream of going to England, meeting with Emma and living like the English girl in my book.

The subject of travelling to England made Gran-gran talk about her childhood quite often. She related her past sorrow and especially her loss of her young son, who had also travelled to England. No one had heard from him until one day someone sent a message saying that he had died. Speculations about the cause of his death were rife among the villagers whose suppositions of how he had died ranged from Teddy Boys beatings, being starved to death in England's cold weather, being run over by a vehicle or being locked up in a mental hospital. They were far-fetched to an extent, so in the absence of known details, the comfortable conclusion was that England's cold weather had killed him.

Today, those pains were resurrected and multiplied with news of my departure and Gran-gran's physical features gave the impression of defeat. For the first and only time, I really did not feel like going to England because it was causing so much sadness to my family. I continued to read from her *"WORDS OF COMFORT"* more frequently because she needed them. Somehow, I felt she was attempting to hold on to each and every word my voice uttered. She often parroted the verses as I read them to her, in an attempt to restrain her emotions and to physically steady her shaking hands. She read the verses with me and I noticed that she was committing them to memory. It was her strategy of preparing for her own self-support. She learnt them by heart also because her eyesight was failing. It was her way of making those verses instantly available when she needed them.

"You know," Gran-gran said to me after a reading session; "Better it was one of the others going to England instead of you.

Gran-gran was deep in thought, and I could see how my impending event had thrown our world into emotional disarray.

"My time on this earth is not long again," she continued. "Yes, better it was one of the others going and you stay," she repeated, almost as if she had spoken her thoughts out aloud.

I remained silent, feeling hurt at her talking like that and since I could not arbitrate such matters, I listened to her voice repeating her thoughts publicly.

"Still, at leas' when I dead and gone I know you'll be awright. You will be a *Woman of Destiny*, like the big *hefe* people in England one day. I won't be there to see it, but I know it."

Gran-gran was so solemn, I felt like crying. She did not look at me and as she spoke, she stared into the distance. She looked as if she was lost in the thoughts of our impending separation. I felt helpless and guilty because the longing in my heart for England was more than anything I had known. The guilt feeling was to do with having wished my departure into sudden reality; wanting to go away without having thought about how Gran-gran would feel when I was gone.

Such are the childish dreams of children without mature reasoning, to weigh them on the scales of our *"What-ifs"* and *"Supposings."* I did want to be elsewhere and had romanticised the imaginary possibilities and benefits of being in England. However, I had done so without further thoughts of what laid beyond my selfish motives. Emma's letters to me had not confirmed our imagined ecstasy or denied them, so my curiosity had grown more intense. This new opportunity promised a *'grass that would be greener on the other side'* of England's shores. Perhaps I preferred to think that it was nothing else but abundantly endowed in comparison to Grenada.

It was necessary for me to have an Affidavit for travel, so this was done in St. Georges by a Lawyer called Mr. Butler. I then became legally, the child of this Calvin, having been given his surname in the document. So we were going to be one big happy family and I went along with whatever plans were necessary. Vaccinations were done, so too were photographs for my passport. These were done in Grenville in a little studio in La Bay and within the short time available, all the pre-travel arrangements were completed.

Mamie Irene had instructed that I was not to bring anything to England with me, other than the clothes she had sent for me to wear on the day. It was exciting and reassuring to know that everything was going to be new for me.

The medium-sized box which Mamie Irene had sent with my travelling outfit, included a beautiful blue, nylon, puffed - sleeved dress, trimmed with blue and white lace and a lacy blue collar. The dress did not have the customary bands to tie at the back and I was glad. The style looked quite mature, close fitting at the chest, pressing down my breasts, and flaring outwards from the hips, like the hipsters which the older girls in our village wore. There were also two blue slide clips for my hair, a set of gold bangles and gold earrings for my pierced ears and a little white handbag which had a long shoulder strap. Accompanying all this was a white, lacy handkerchief and black patent shoes, which shone with its glazed newness. The shoe was styled with a t-bar front, brass buckle and 2 inches of heels which made me feel quite mature. Also enclosed in the box were blue nylon panties with matching full-length petticoat. There were no socks but Gran-gran and Aunt Meena had vowed to provide this!

"One thing's missing," Aunt Meena announced after we perused the entire contents of this box.

"What it is?" Gran-gran asked.

"Irene seem to send everything except the socks. We have to get some from Teacher Gladys shop."

There was to be no playing *"big woman,"* as far as the women were concerned. Wearing socks meant you were still a child under your parent's control and it was also a sign of proper dressing as far as my family were concerned.

The women planned everything well. My school reports signed with impressive long flowing signatures by Mr. Julien, the Headmaster, as well as each subject teacher; were carefully placed in an envelope alongside the black British passport. Secretly, I longed for the period of "newness" I was going into and I waited for the departure day with mixed emotions.

How the days seemed to race by quickly, leaving me with mixed feelings, nervous anticipation and fear about my uprootedness. My senses became strangely more acute to the simplest things around me. I listened more intensely to the cocoa tree leaves when the wind blew and even the sounds of night crickets and croaking frogs. Subconsciously, I forced myself to absorb everything in the environment in order to recall their very essence at will in the future.

The hymn singing from the Mothers of the church and the smell of burning candle, I imagined, would be indelibly etched on my mind. During the waiting days, I looked at the trees and bushes, with fondness. I surveyed the various textured green leaves in great detail and doubted very much I could forget any of them. Everywhere, the sweet bougainvillea stood proudly waving its final goodbyes forcing its pain and glory on my sight – the prickly thorns as well as the feast of shades of pink, purple and white seemed unforgettable. This was added to by the sturdy flamboyant trees, which dominated the sky. They displayed the flaming red among the nearby green boughs, offering their outstretched leaves of fire to the supreme deity. The kokeyoko, stinking toe, hog-plum, cushu and star-apples; I watched them all with loving gratitude. I tried to convert each detail to a memory that could be etched in my history. I was thankful to the landscape for being part of my young world.

I had taken some of my own things too; Sunday school work, which I had hidden together with my Bible, the commemorative Grenada Independence Medal, which all children were given to mark the Grenada's end of British colonial rule, and my French and Spanish textbooks. The farewell in school was solemn. My classmates were sad but not nearly as sad as the farewell ceremony the family and villagers held for me the night before my departure.

ع

My last farewell was a gathering at home, and many villagers had come to our house. There was at least one representative from each household to express their good wishes, give meaningful last words or advice. Gran-gran and Aunt Meena appeared to be cheerful and seemed strong; as each goodbye and farewell, tore through their emotions like a sharp knife cutting through sweet sugar cane.

"Well Joanne," Cousin Germaine said, "I wish you God speed, God care for you here all these years, so He'll go with you over yonder and will walk in front of you to hold you up if you should dash your foot against a stone."

Such formalities were not unusual. Her eyes became watery and she bid me goodbye with the Baptist farewell. Drinks were passed around for everyone, together with saltfish cakes, fried bakes, fish, and thick pieces of coo-coo, breadfruit, roasted cashew nuts, roasted corn, and a variety of cooked food. The men were offered rum, chased by the customary coconut water; but not in the presence of the children. One or two women drank tiny glassfuls of sherry with cake, as they sang mournful, farewell songs.

It reminded me of a Christening celebration because of the formality with which the proceedings were conducted. However, in this farewell, there was laughter and gaiety but underneath it all, was a seriousness and strong feelings of sadness. Justin's dad had come too, much earlier than most,

215

and was already quite intoxicated by the time the majority of people had arrived. His drunken condition gave him a kind of verbose utterance, so he assumed the responsibility of being the Chairman for the evening's proceedings.

"We have to do things properly," he said. "How come all-you comin' and goin' jus' so? It mus' have a leader to conduct things," he proclaimed.

The self-elected Chairman was doing what he did best, talking under the surfeiting influence of Grenada's River Antoine rum. This caused others around him to suck their teeth quite loudly, irritated by his familiar drunken repertoire.

My friends too, had come to say their last farewell, with their parents and we sniggered secretly or nudged each other knowingly, when something funny or odd made us want to burst out laughing in the adults' presence. Justin was there too, but he stood well away from his father's sight, for fear of being shown up by him.

The Chairman stood in front of the door's entrance, where he assumed his focal point for the ready-made audience. He swayed a couple of times on his unsteady feet and then he began his speech.

"Ladies and gentlemen, tonight we come here to say fare-thee-well to Joanne. Joanne who's going to pass from these meager shores to the luxurious and bounteous shores of England, to meet she mother. The land of King George, Queen Victoria and now Queen Elizabeth the First and Second, not forgetting the Duke. The land that some of us flocked to fight Mr. Adolph Hitler of Germany, for the Mother-Land."

There was loud talking and no one really acknowledged the authority of the speaker and his display of historic knowledge. To them it seemed like his usual, unattractive, intoxicated drool. The result of his introduction was muffled resentment and a profusion of teeth–sucking among the crowd; especially when he digressed into his literary asides.

"I remember this child when she was born," he said.

The general disrespect for him among the gathering was confirmed when someone shouted from the audience.

"You was probably drunk then too!"

This caused fits of laughter and humorous asides but the Chairman was not amused.

*"All-you can stay there and laugh," he said ignoring their jibes. Then he continued regardless of the disorder, as he continued his repertoire.

"I and she mother went to school together. Now, let me tell you about she mother. She mother was a bright, bright woman."

"Well is not she mother here now!" Someone else called out impatiently, trying to silence the Chair's verbal dominance.

"Take a seat!" a voice demanded, but the Chairman disregarded their flippancy and continued.

"Tonight," he said, holding up his right hand for quietness.

"Tonight, Ladies and gentlemen. Etymology, phonology, syntax, prosody. Remember decorum, "D" for decorum. Remember the alphabet. "A" is for attention, paying attention to a speaker. At leas' I tryin' to speak properly. It's for the young ones here tonight who have to follow us eh; "B" is for behaviour, good behaviour. It is the las' thing Joanne should

remember, how to behave herself over there in England, and that means conduct, decorum. Let me see, now where I am – A-B-C-D? OK, now Joanne I could tell, have the voice of a Radio Announcer, bright like my boy Justin in the corner there. My boy, I will compare to Admiral Lord Nelson. Nelson was born in 1750, a great Englishman too. As for you Joanne, I must compare you to.....em.....em; All-you hear 'bout...."

He was stuck for more historical comparison, or any comparison for that matter, and the crowd responded with greater irritation.

"Can Mr. Chairman stop procrastinating and come to decorous order!" Another equally glib competitor had challenged the Chairman, displaying his linguistic mastery of the high-sounding English language too.

This moment was the height of speechifying and the Chairman, who immediately felt challenged, reacted with more competitive energy.

"So Joanne girl, how we feel for you – love. Ammo, amamas, ammatus... I mus' ask you not to forget us, your people, your country. Do something great over there so in years to come, you can come back and help us, not like some of them, who go and give us their back. Now, Time which is master of us all, tempus fugitus says, I must bow and give way to others – Ladies and Gentlemen, I mus' step down for other verbally proficient well-wishers to proceed."

With that, he took a slight bow and sauntered out into the yard for another drink to toast his oratory.

I thanked him. Everyone had roared with cheers and excessive laughter, whistling and spoken relief that the *man-of-words* had finally released them from his impressive-sounding verbose claptrap. It is how some had described his performance when he was finished.

However, this coming together and supporting community members in times of need was part of our tradition and they were used to it. At least, he had reduced the solemnity and sadness of the evening. Everyone agreed that his 'academic' display of the English language had caused lightheartedness in his performance. This had helped to superficially mask the sadness and also lessen the emotionally charged evening.

There was singing, praying, preaching and tears but I endured the evening with a feeling of being quite special and proud of their expressions of love. I vowed to remember everything and everyone and by the time the last person had gone, it was almost midnight.

I was exhausted from the strain of laughing, crying, being attentive and feeling sad for everyone. Each time a speaker had taken the stand and expressed loving words of good wishes, my stomach did some nervous somersaults. I was afraid for Gran-gran and Aunt Meena because I could not imagine fully, how sad their hearts must have been feeling.
However, before I went to bed, Gran-gran called me in private. I thought she wanted to hear her *WORDS OF COMFORT* but instead, she was offering me something.

"This for you," she said.

She placed warm beads from her outstretched hand into mine and closed her fist over them. I noticed that she had closed her eyes, before taking my closed fist and like a priest she gave me her last *Words of Comfort*.

"The world is a big place," she said, looking straight into my eyes. Like a High Priestess, Gran-gran was giving me her own benediction so she continued.

"Never let your heart be troubled. These belonged to my mother, keep them. As a *Woman of Destiny*, focusing on them will help you dry your tears and lift you up in times of sadness. They will bring joy when you have sorrow," she said, quietly and softly, instilling a kind of peacefulness in both our hearts.

I became puzzled by the beads' significance but I continued to listen. Gran-gran looked older and very sad, I could tell that she was finally resigned to the fact that I was really going away and leaving her behind.

I was amazed at the size of the little ivory beads which I had not seen before. She must have kept them in some extra special place because I thought I knew where all her hidden or secret places were. As I looked at them with curiosity, she told me that her mother had made her promise to keep them forever. On questioning her about their meaning, she told me that her mother was an Ashanti warrior. I surveyed the hard round ivory beads which had a hole though them. They looked as if they had been part of some very special link in a decorative, symbolic chain.

"The Ashanti people were good fighters," she said seriously, watching me finger the curious little things.

"Sometimes you have to fight hard to get your way in things – remember the mortar and the pestle over there," she said pointing in their direction.

"Year go and year come, they stay there in the corner, always there when you need them. People born, grow and die and the mortar still stay there, strong as ever. You make it do its duty, pound cocoa, pound yam or banana, make *asham* with corn and things like that – it always there. Generation after generation it helping people survive. Grenada people will never die from starvation."

Her parting *Words of Comfort* was like a little lecture. I listened to them but was unsure about much of their philosophy. To make her meaning clearer, she continued.

"My mother was a strong woman. She did never give up. They say when slave hunters come to catch her, like how they hunt *manicou*; she fight like a tiger, she didn' give up to anyone. Remember that Ashanti woman and pray to succeed in everything. Remember the mortar and the pestle. Be like them; steadfast - don't let anyone keep you down. If you fall, rise again."

I continued nodding fast at her every word of advice, desperately trying to understand the meaning of what she was saying. Then she made her final, heart-breaking statement.

"I won' be here when you come back, but you'll know where to find me - in the little spot of land in Betty. The family's burial spot of land in Betty, as it was called, was where her husband, my grandfather, was buried and she had often shown me the mound when we passed by.

"Go and lie down now," she said, breaking off suddenly to steady her shaky voice.

I clung tightly to her and cried, mumbling semi-audible words between sobs. She held me tightly also.

"Couldn' you come too, I don't want to go and leave you," I pleaded.

She released me physically, with her final encouragement.

"I can't go but will always be right there with you. You have to go; *destiny* is there for you. Go and rest now, a big day is in front of you, when day make light."

PART   II
Chapter 9

"It have some fathers ent good at all
They never mind you when you were small
But never mind how you father bad
If it wasn't for daddy
You'd never, never have a dear mammy.
"I say, remember who, who used to hug and kiss you"
Don't forget you mother and father!"

The Mighty Sparrow (Dr. Francisco Slinger)

Passengers on the BOAC flight to England had woken up to the pilot's voice announcing our descent into Heathrow Airport.

"Good morning, ladies and gentlemen, this is your Captain speaking. We'll shortly be commencing our descent into London Heathrow. We will be landing at approximately 7.15am British time. The temperature on the ground is 12^oC. Please return your seats to the upright position, and observe the no-smoking signs...."

I had woken up with a stiff and painful neck, and nose which felt as if they had been cauterised. The dry cold, air pouring from above my head all night, made me shiver and I sat up nervously, eagerly eyeing the other passengers, as they got ready for the landing.

The up and down dipping of the plane made my head and belly felt as if they were constantly exchanging places. I had closed my eyes to overcome the wobbles of the turbulence we

222

were experiencing. I wondered what would happen to me when I landed and how I was going to recognise anyone or for that matter, how anyone was going to recognise me. The anxiety caused by the enormity and strangeness of the situation made my stomach do leaps and catapults; so that I almost wet myself. The feeling of isolation and being tossed in the air like a feather from a hen traumatised me.

Less than 24 hours ago, I had felt confused during the transition from the LIAT plane which we had boarded in Grenada, to this BOAC jumbo jet which we transferred on to in Barbados. I realise then that I was truly on my own. I had sat for hours in the big open space of Barbados' Seawell Airport, clutching my little shoulder bag tightly; clinging on to the only security I felt was mine, as I witnessed the hustle-bustle of the airport atmosphere.

Confinement to the little space on board this BOAC airplane had created a familiar feeling with the passengers and crew. However, after our seven hours flight, my peace was about to be disturbed once again at our final stop. The air-hostess, who had been supervising me, took my passport and smiled reassuringly, as she completed a little card. My apprehension must have been obvious, so she said, "Stop looking so worried, you're almost home."

Her teeth were immediately visible in her wide lip-stick smile and I gave a nervous, quivering smile in return. My pulse raced and my heartbeats pounded faster when the word *"home"* was uttered. Today seemed so cold and I shivered uncontrollably at the strange chill which prevailed everywhere. It reminded me instantly, of the very cold air-conditioning inside the Barclays Bank in town. This usually made your nose dry and breathing longer and deeper. But the cool air-conditioning in the bank was always nice for a short while and was often only used for a moment's sanctuary from the blistering Grenadian heat outside.

The airhostess could see that I was not appropriately dressed, for the cold made me shiver. She wrapped a little blanket around me, giving the much needed extra layers, to help stop my nervous tremors that were now quite visible. Strangely, my whole body shook, my teeth clattered, my stomach felt queasy, and I held on tightly to my little shoulder bag.

Later, she whisked me off the plane, through long white carpeted corridors and enormously high ceilings; passed queues of quiet people who waited to meet the uniformed, white, serious-looking men at the Immigration Barrier. They did not smile at all. There was no conversation, no *Mahnings or Howdy-dos*. They looked angry and unfriendly and this increased the terror I was feeling inside. My heart pounded faster, the cold air made me feel so alone.

Inside the airport was an arena of white faces jostling, milling and unlike La Bay in Grenville, relatively quiet. They seemed uninterested in anything around them, apart from manouvering their luggage with a purpose and a quickness of steps to go somewhere. Rooted in the spot where I witnessed the comings and goings, I waited to be picked up.

I felt threatened by the sea of unfamiliar faces; very few had brown-skin, a very noticeable fact. My heart felt as if it had skipped beats at the mental terror of *"What-ifs,"* which were now invading my mind. What if I ended up in this strange place, not knowing anyone and find I was abandoned here? What if our letters did not get to England and no one knew I was here? My mind screamed for comfort and reassurance.

I needed Gran-gran and Aunt Meena right now.

I forced my mind away from its feeling of helplessness and terror, while I trembled with fear from the cold weather. I remembered Gran-gran's voice, and her *Words of Comfort* came flooding back to me. Momentarily, I regained my composure with the reserved thought that if anything did go wrong, at least this plane could take me back to Gran-gran and Aunt Meena in Grenada.

Thoughts of the night before in Grenada; the farewell, the expressions of love reassured me and I took deep sighs which steadied my entire frame. Just then, I saw the familiar, tall airhostess, accompanied by a short black woman walking towards me. I watched them intently until I came face-to-face with the fat, round-faced woman.

She was fully coated and she resembled Aunt Meena slightly. With her robust shape, she smiled, showing with a gap between her two big front teeth.

"Little mama," she called me, stretching out her arms to greet me. I smiled and accepted her closeness. She held me tightly to her breakfast-scented coat and whispered, "Everything alright?" I nodded, awkwardly, and released her hold at once. She probed some more.

"Mamie OK? Meena OK?" she enquired in quick succession, with an attitude of familiarity, which I found uncomfortable. I nodded repeatedly, speechless, perhaps because of the coldness of the weather and the unfamiliarity of her voice.

She took my little handbag and we walked out of the airport building into the dull grey day. We entered a black cab, which looked like one of La Croix's funeral hearse and headed in the direction of my new home. The *"WELCOME TO BRITAIN"* sign overhung the long, bright tunnel which took us to my new home.

The stillness of the morning and the biting fierce wind, were England's weather greeting me at Heathrow. Sitting inside the warm cab, I marvelled at the heat around my legs, compared to my tropical clime, where the sun reigned supreme. As the warm automobile made its way to my new home, the heavens opened and the British rain accompanied me in a steady downpour; weak in comparison, to our tropical showers. It smeared the cab windows and obscured my first real view of England in April.

The cab sped past an array of buildings that seemed stuck to each other by one roof, all displaying the same colours. From the airplane these had looked like matchboxes with dull red tops, but now they stood like outstretched concertinas in the fresh morning breeze. The road, which looked like a greyish black glistening ribbon, had various kinds of vehicles, all in a mad rush to their individual destinations. They had overtaken our cab's moderate speed several times, contrasting its unhurried fashion; like spiders overtaking a beetle.

At the front of the cab, the white plump driver with grey hair, sat motionless and composed; looking straight in front of him and the long, wet road ahead. No music trespassed the engine's constant whirring, no radio bleared a song; only the electronic meter's red numbers moved at will. It was keeping the count of fares to be paid; possibly the only thing which mattered to the driver regarding us.

The quietness was unusual for me and I remembered a similar, contrasting journey only yesterday in a small taxi bus, speeding its way with us on board, to Pearl's Airport, in Grenada; amidst a symphony of voices, mechanical and natural.

ع

Those who had taken the bus to Pearl's Airport were travellers who were leaving Grenada, bound for England. They were accompanied by families who were going to watch them leave Grenada's soil. Almost like a calypso, voices orchestrated across seats; the bass of the men, fusing with the alto and soprano of the women of various ages and sizes; occasionally mixed in with the tumbrels and triangles of children's chattering and chuckling. All were overshadowed by the dominance of the radio's steel pans and stringed brass instruments; climaxing to a jazzy crescendo.

The volume of the Grenadian radio had reigned supreme on the bus as usual, and those like me, who were waiting with the uncertainty of the impending departure, were confused by the flurry of activities only a few days before. Then, the dull pain of loss, mixed with impatient expectations, had made me remain quiet. This allowed the radio to trespass on my racing thoughts and it was a convenient distraction. At that time, the Calypsonian's voice of authority rose above the loud talking, forcing us to listen to his lyrical advice, within the confines of the hired transporter.

The lyrics were poignant and I felt as if the words were deliberately chosen for me to listen at this crucial moment:

> *"Remember when you couldn't even walk.*
> *I say remember when you couldn't even talk*
> *But I say remember who..."*

Squashed, as usual, among fleshy adults, quietly being seen and not heard, I listened to the voice of the community, ordering, appealing, musing, reasoning his lyrics, forcing action; as was often the response of adults. This time though, it seemed to be competing with the constant excited chatter.

The bus jerked and swayed, and did not stop to collect anyone in its urgency to deposit its travellers at Pearl's Airport; in time for their departure. I was quite happy for the parting to be over and done with on this painful morning. I needed it to be done with as quickly as possible because there was now no turning back.

There was such a strong desire to hasten this departure that the event made me feel as if butterflies were dancing and skipping in my tummy. It was strange how the voice of the musical prophet should hasten to remind me of my own personal dilemma; evoking the sad predicament of Randolph and Mamie Irene. Thoughts of my quest came crowding into my consciousness once again. How was I going to deal with finding Randolph or even talk to Mamie Irene about him?

Too much had converged on my over-burdened mind and I wanted the radio to stop. I closed my eyes and visualised Randolph and Mammie running in slow motion towards each other in heightened expectation, embracing finally, laughing with the happiest expression of love, joy and triumph. It was a beauty that frightened me also because before I could work out the details of a possible ending of Mamie and Randolph's embrace, the images evaporated with the screeching halt of the bus at Pearl's Airport.

Now, sitting in this quiet British taxi, I remembered how the Grenadian bus had slanted into a slot beside the other buses outside the Airport building, and the stampede of passengers and families pressed and hurried inside.

ع

Yesterday we had gone into Pearls Airport building swiftly, ushered by quick movements and a seriousness of attitude. Workers, who were already very sweaty, fumbled with heavy luggage, as they carried them towards the door marked ENTRANCE. Inside the building, the electric lights overhead had seemed intensely bright, in contrast with the dullness of the morning outside. As the swiftness of movements escalated, I had very little time to know what Gran-gran and Aunt Meena and the others were doing at the small Airways counter. Soon a voice in uniform informed passengers that they should make their way into the waiting LIAT plane. The plane looked smaller on the ground than in the air, separated from us by only the glass partition within the distance of a stone's throw. Here, the small building which had witnessed the passing of men and women bound for betterment elsewhere seemed awesome to me.

"Have your passports and vaccination papers ready please!" announced the steward and he dispensed with pieces of papers by stamping them loudly, as we walked out of the building into the little waiting plane.

Walking awkwardly and waving nervously, I felt emotionally wrecked inside. My new shoes, dress and bag felt meaningless to me now, as I walked away from Gran-gran and Aunt Meena. Moving with the flow of the boarding passengers along the path to the plane, made my head swoon, my throat felt dry and my jelly-like legs followed the crowd. There they stood, our deserted families, all the faces we knew and loved, bidding us farewell into the unknown; waving with handkerchiefs and strong resolute faces. Voices called out, *"God be with you!"* It was too late for crying or turning back.

The moment of separation had come, negotiated and accepted by all.

The breeze blew cool in the weak morning's sun, lamenting Grenada's loss of sons and daughters to a different clime. Swiftly, once inside the plane, I leaned sideways in my corner seat, waving my handkerchief, straining to look out in the hope that they would recognise me. Passengers had entered and filled the empty seats and surprisingly, the pilot could be seen in our little plane; his back facing us. He sat in front of the controls, as he prepared the whining engine for take off. The take off preamble was confusing to me, as I watched the lonely little airport building alongside the plane. In it, I knew Gran-gran and Aunt Meena were feeling wretched inside; perhaps so too were the other families standing outside, witnessing the parting of their dear ones.

Then the little plane shook slightly and the noise of the engine sucking in air rose to a whining scream. It subsided slightly then rose again, noisier than before, as it began to move forward down the runway to the edge of the airfield. I had heard this sound from a distance, throughout my 13 years, and we had daily pretended to chase the iron bird in our childish pranks, waving and shouting, "Come and get me!"

Today, the reality of going made me sad. The plane turned and circled to its take-off position, it stopped with the view of the shimmering sea ahead. In a few moments, the engines bellowed, rising to a deafening crescendo of power, and then becoming more powerful, it bumped along the runway; racing with the wind and swiftly it left the grassy verges behind. Then purposely, it swooped up from Grenada's soil. It rose evenly above the retreating land below, determined to climb to greater heights above the shimmering sea. It leaned sideways, and then straightened as it left the island, bound for Barbados.

The noise and confusion which continued for a whole day, is now in stark contrast with this quiet English setting. The quiet journey to my home in England was reminiscent of a playing field after an exciting cricket game, when everyone had gone, leaving the quiet, lonely pitch in a sort of anti-climax, until the next play-off.

ع

The English rain had stopped and I tried to catch a quick glimpse of the developing morning. As we progressed to my new home, the morning became more alive as the weak sun shone in the sky, inviting people out of their quiet houses, to partake in its moments of rising glory. But in the stillness of the Sunday morning, few people had been enticed out to greet the day.

It was about 10am when the cab stopped outside our orange door. The neighbouring houses had their own coloured doors, flanked by very little green hedges and square bricked front garden walls. Apart from the yellow of budding daffodils, the sparse greenery was a reminder of the recent winter; made more pronounced by the half-bare trees alongside the road. They stood like brown giant remains of a blighted holocaust, alone and sad; as was the lonely, quiet surroundings.

Mamie Irene paid the cab driver and I followed her as she turned a key into number 21. The floral blew wallpaper and the smell of fried bacon felt strange but homely. The room we had entered was small and friendly, boasting Gran-gran and Aunt Meena's photographs on the mantelpiece. My own

231

photo, showed the proud brown and blue school uniform, of my Primary School days, alongside the family's array of memorabilia. A photo of the cheeky-faced twins was also included in the paraphernalia on the mantelpiece. An alarm clock stood in the middle, but a large picture of The Last Supper in full colour with 3-D effect dominated it.

The house was strangely quiet. Mamie Irene drew the heavy floral curtains, letting in the light through the white nets, onto the thick red carpet. There was a sound of movements upstairs, so she yelled, "Darris, Darrin! Are you up? She's here!" She made swift movements to tidy up the room in the few minutes' silence which followed. Calvin my new "Daddy" had come down, bare-feet, looking sleepy and younger than Mammie. He shook my hand, showing big white teeth as he grinned.

"So you're the little lady, welcome to England. It's not too cold today by the look of outside," he said, trying to sound cheerful. I smiled.

"Everybody at home awright?" He enquired further. I nodded. "And you had a good flight?"

"Yes thanks," I said clearing my throat, now that I had appeared to find my voice. I could tell he felt nervous and awkward because he did not stop talking for a while.

"Easter's coming real soon and the sun will come out again," he said.

I nodded.

"Winter does be real cold here. It was cold these last months too. Everybody home awright though?" he enquired again.

During this time, Mamie Irene had gone into the kitchen and then thunder rolled, or so it seemed, as the stampede of feet came charging down the stairs. Then quietly, two bright-eyed identical, round-faced girls entered the room. They sniggered, said "Hello!" then dashed back up the stairs again, with the same thundering sound. They were shy and excited, so I smiled when Calvin looked at me for my approval. Their noise aggravated Mamie, so she scolded them from the bottom of the stairs.

I sat down on the vinyl-looking sofa, surveying the TV, a gramophone, a glass cabinet, with colourful glassware and magazines in a little wire-rack nearby. I dangled my feet and swung them a little as the feeling of "home" seeped into my consciousness.

Calvin excused himself and went to join Mamie in the Kitchen. Much later, the twins returned, washed, dressed and calm. They held their manners in check by strict eye language from Mamie, so that they approached me nervously, together and calmly introduced themselves.

"Hi Joanne!" they chorused, almost as if they had rehearsed the line. They looked at me from head to toe, and I held out my hand.

"Good morning!" I replied, feeling awkward, not knowing whether to be formal or not.

"I'm Darris and she is Darrin," said the replica with the mole on her right earlobe.

I sighed, thankful that I had recognised a distinguishing mark between them, and we wasted no time as we tried to catch up on our years of bonding. The girls took me upstairs to their room, and showed me their belongings. They gave me a present – a beautifully fluffy burgundy bedroom slipper.

"We bought it for you, with our pocket money. We hope you like it," they said proudly. They had perfect English accents which I took an instant liking to.

I thanked them and for the first time since I left Grenada, I was beginning to feel comfortable. They showed me my own bed in the corner of the room, which was opposite a well-made bunk bed. It was theirs they informed me. I sat on my own little bed and swung my legs, feeling good about my own possessions.

Later, the breakfast call from downstairs was answered by thunderous feet going downstairs again; the twins were in front and I followed them. We all sat around the table that was laid in the kitchen. As we ate, the twins made anxious enquiries as to whether they were going to church and their joyful cheers to Mamie's response, made it clear that church-going was not a relished activity. A lot of small talk was made to occupy the short breakfast interlude. Then I posed my all-important question.

"How far is Brixton from here?"
Calvin replied. "Whe' you hear 'bout Brixton? Somebody give you a message?"

"No, No!" I replied, looking at their puzzled faces. "I have a friend there, Emma. I want to go and see her soon."

"Oh, a friend? Yes, soon!" came the reply. Then Mamie continued, "Yes, soon! You have plenty o' time for that!"

As the day progressed Mamie, who had a night job, fell asleep. The twins busied themselves in their bedroom, and Calvin watched horseracing on TV. I surveyed the house, the garden, back and front; peeped at the white neighbours in their gardens on both sides of our house, then went to join the twins.

The room was surprisingly very big for a bedroom. My own side, which had a small bed, a tiny wardrobe, a chest of drawers and a table lamp, created a boundary of my own space and belongings. It was good. I looked through the little wardrobe of clothes I had been given. I loved the assortment of dresses and skirts which, surprisingly, appeared to be my size. To me everything was lovely, especially my very own mirror inside the slender wardrobe-door. I was beginning to feel more at home and I looked forward to the promised visit from other relatives and friends throughout the day.

During the next four weeks, the days wore on, becoming quite routine, and repetitive. I discovered that time was indeed something I had plenty of. Time to stay at home constantly within the confines of those papered walls. Mamie was a busy bee, either rushing in from work in the early morning hours, from her night shift, or rushing out of the house in the late evening to catch the train for her catering job at Heathrow Airport. She seemed to have little time to stand still, to think, cook or talk. Time was not generous to her. Instead, Time chose to give me its excesses. Later, I was to experience that such excesses would add to my frustration of not being able to move freely around the unknown territories beyond our house.

My life revolved around the upstairs-downstairs space of the house; with hardly going beyond the 50ft garden and shed. There was a constant feeling of being penned in by wooden fencing and a padlocked back door. The twins were lucky; they went to school and back and were happy to accept and return to the confines of their treasured, messy room with glee afterwards. The trouble was, having newly arrived in England, I had not been allocated a school; there was a month's wait for a placement by the local education department. I envied the twins' daily school runs, as well as their ready-made acceptance of their routine lives.

Each day I watched Mamie return from work, enquired about the twins, instructed me to get them ready and send them off to school. My job was to make their breakfast, as well as to wash and dress them. My mother was too tired to talk. Often, on returning from work, she would fall asleep instantly on the sofa, with her shoes and work clothes still on.

My life had changed. Caged like a bird, within its domestic compound, I toiled by cleaning, cooking, ironing, scrubbing, and reporting back. Calvin, I had noticed, did very little, except watched TV. Each day he went out and returned with a newspaper, which he seemed to read from cover to cover, before watching horse-racing on the TV. He tinkled with an old guitar, dominated conversations when he talked to his visiting friends and showed very little congeniality between himself and Mamie. I was a convenient go-between, the flimsy link between them – passing a message, carrying out a task and reporting back.

The quiet solemn days were my own, after morning domestic chores were finished by 10am. I read and re-read a small drama book which I had found in one of my drawers; poured over a book of poems, which I had learnt by heart and daily the hours ticked by. Words which I didn't understand, I repeated loudly to myself, until the sound of my voice imitated the twins' accent and then I would smile in front of the mirror. The radio and TV too, became good sources of imitation for listening and pronunciation. I clung to every word, repeating them to my personal satisfaction.

When I had become bored with this personal development, I yearned to play the old rosewood piano which stood in the sitting room corner, but that was not possible. Mamie's days were her nights and vice versa – a strange world it must be for her; sleeping during the days and working during the nights. The house had to be quiet during her day-time sleep.

The sun, peeping through the windows, reminded me of the vast difference in Grenada and I often went trance-like into moments of reflections, recalling memories of laughter, gaiety and energetic fervour. I mentally replayed our many varied adventures of my youth - so much in contrast to my present restricted existence. Oh, how foolish, our childhood pranks and expressions of childish wishes can be. How foolish also to think that England's land greatly surpassed, in everything, the life I had in back home. "Heavenly God!" cried my soul, "I am sorry for saying so, for thinking so, for wishing so." Left in my solitary world, my inner being cried out in sorrow for release from bondage. I needed to go to school, and though plans were being made, they were just too slow. My head ached from the regrettable loneliness and sadness of this little prison world.

Many days I had perused the faces in the photographs with Gran-gran and Aunt Meena. Then, thoughts of my past life there with my friends, my school, my church, my land come flooding back. During those moments, I would tremble uncontrollably, conscious of some painful regrets. I often released the hurt and sorrow through quiet spells of sobbing until my parched throat retaliated with threats of hoarseness.

To live happily, to be full of life and have company, in this lifeless shell was a constant, burning desire. Daily the crying continued, until pity halted with Gran-gran's memorable words. Holding the beads she had given me, the hurt feelings would then subside, so that I could return to my duties with regained composure.

One day, faced with the dire need to do something beyond the home, I volunteered to collect the twins from school and the suggestion was welcomed.

"You know how to get there?" I was asked.

"Yes, I'll mark the way by the white wall at the top of our road," I replied.

I was certain that the white wall, which was at the top of our road, was the only white wall I would see. My need to get out was greater than my need to navigate my journey, so I ventured out at 2.30pm in time for the 3pm collection of the twins from school.

I stepped lightly, gaily, counting the roads without taking any notice of the street names, certain that the place where I had accompanied Mamie before would be easily identifiable. Then panic changed places with my composure, when I noticed at least three similar white walls along my journey. Round and round I walked, becoming more perplexed by my ordeal. I had no idea of the time and determined to do this job right; I persisted to find the twins' school.

I became agitated as I walked down the same roads and lost my sense of direction. I was more alarmed when I realised that the flow of school children in their parents' cars had subsided for some time. I was lost.

The twins would be left behind in the playground and I was terrified of the double consequences – my being lost and the twins being stranded at school. I began to run in a direction which seemed familiar, until I arrived at my marked white wall. My street lay ahead of me, dull and unpromising as ever, as were my spirits, when I realised that I had not been able to get to the school and it had become quite late.

England was quite different from Grenada. You could at least mark your way in Grenada, I thought, even through the thickest woodland. I became extremely irritated. God had blessed us with an abundance of nature. Trees and paths, rivers and banks, tracks and shrubs; all were easy landmarks.

Here, these joined-up brown brick buildings, with their joined-up sameness, showed no imaginative design, and this intensified my anger. I longed for difference – small and large brick house and wooden house, sapodilla, breadfruit, golden apple, governor-plum, mango, paw-paw, hog-plum, cushu and genip! Yes, even rivers and ravines, ponds and lakes, and big, wide, open spaces. Difference was everywhere in Grenada. It was the Creator's unique gift to us; a blessing!

"Stupes! Damn Stupidness!" I said out aloud, "Damn sameness!" I repeated, now cursing loudly and the time raced by.

When I had found my white wall at the top of our road, I cursed even louder, "Dam Sameness!" As I reached our front door, I was filled with trepidation. My heart was pounding loudly and resigned to whatever outburst lay on the other side of our front door, I rang the doorbell.

The sniggering twins opened the door laughing loudly, which increased my feeling of stupidity; especially when I learnt that Calvin had been called to the school to collect the girls. He had deposited them indoors and concerned about my own whereabouts, had gone to look for me. In the meantime, I busied myself with dinner preparation and assisted the twins with their homework as compensation, while I waited.

My mind raced with predicted dialogues of impending scolding, until I was exhausted. The phone rang and my heart leapt. Calvin had sounded relieved that I had, at least, found my way back home. He was pleased that we were all indoors. He would be home much later, he had said on the phone.

Chapter 10

Lord Shorty (Hollis Liverpool)

"Joanne!"

"Yes! Comin'!" I yelled back, over the hollow sound of the bath being filled. I was half-listening for the call because I had become a regular back-scrubber; another chore.

Mum was sitting in the half-filled tub, soaping her slippery, rotund body and humming at the same time. As with Gran-gran before her, I took this opportunity to listen to wisdom, to experiences, to caution, verbal defence and legend but stories in England were always of a vastly different context. England's daily life presented a catalogue of many tales of woe, especially tales of her workplace. I felt as if I knew every single worker in mum's company. Daily, the episodes unfolded; who did what, said what, conspired, lied, hurt, stole and afraid of whom.

There was no contrasting tale, apart from what I had seen on TV, and church-going was not really like church-going in Grenada at all! There was the dreadful silence, the grinning, false smiles, pretence, the meaningless welcome and the intellectual-sounding lectures and accompanying coldness – all was a great surprise to me.

I longed for the Grenadian church noise, the greetings, the bell ringing, the smell of burning candle, the sincerity of the preaching and the attempts to ensure that every word was delivered properly. For a start, every line was repeated, every voice was heard, everyone prayed, sang with fervour, with an animated display of unity that symbolized an attitude of *"Let-us-love-one-another-for-God-is-love;"* these were all displayed in Grenada's hot sun.

I was starved of pleasing contrasts; of laughter, gaiety, and knowledge of what was taking place outside of the walls of my new home. I became increasingly interested in whatever gossip came my way, so I listened intently to the various sagas.

"What about my school? When can I go?" I asked after I had taken the soap to mum's back.

"Well as far as I can understand, the only thing they can suggest to me is some school a good distance away. I don't know anything about it because to my mind you should be going to the Girls' School across the road down here."

"Your Aunty Mary doesn't trust their suggestion. She's been here longer than me so I have to take her word for it sometimes. And you know, most of the time she's damn right too!"

"I don't mind taking a bus to school," I appealed, conscious of the fact that any school, wherever it was located, would be good enough for me because I just had to get out of house. I needed to get into the routine of doing things in the outdoors, just as others did daily. I had outgrown all the interest of stay-at-home-life in Britain; too restricting, that feeling of being caged.

"Well I don't know but Mary say we must avoid something called ESN schools, where the government is chucking all our children. I don't know what it means, she doesn't know too much either but she heard they are not as good as the authorities making out. I didn't spend all that money sending you to good schools in Grenada to have you end up in some ENS school in England," she reasoned, though a little agitated.

"ESN you said, not ENS," I said correcting her.

"Well ENS, ESN, call it whatever you want, you're not going there. We wait this long, we will wait until you can go to the Girls' school down the road."

That was her final take on the whole schooling situation, and that was that.

Her humming had begun and I could tell mum was a little agitated. My cousin Peter, who lived further down on our road, had boasted how he had achieved his 5 GCEs, stressing that they were not CSEs, the lower ranked exams. Mum was proud of his achievement and stressed that she would not be expecting anything less from me! She had said that firmly and finally; signalling the end of all conversations about school for the time being.

It was mum's night off and there was always a measure of excitement on those days because we all watched TV together, or had some special little treats and I felt less of a mini-mum. I could relax and be a child again, while mum did her own domestic chores.

Sometimes parts of my nights were spent watching the big round moon in the incredibly dark star-less sky at night. During those times, I would write poetry about "*What If's*" and recall Emma's laughter, our role playing, think of my missing friends, relatives and the whole village community. On these reflective times, I would make up many games. There was the *self-pity game*, the *I-wish game*, the *one-day-I-would game*, but neither of these had helped much; apart from helping to deal with long, sleepless nights.

When I had some upsetting experiences, I used the nights to recall Gran-gran's *Words of Wisdom* and plan my future strategies. "I will be best of something", I said out loudly one night. Lately, I wanted to be many things, but my overriding thought was of becoming a top Secretary, to be able to type. That's what Gran-gran had meant, the day she showed me the Receptionists in the Landowners Office in St. Georges. However, in order to be a Secretary I had to be the best in my class, and to be the best in my class, I needed to go to a school, which I did not have! And so the pre-conditions filled my thoughts each time; round and round in circles in my head they would go, until I would fall asleep.

Mum seemed a little tenser lately, and so was Calvin. Silence and niceties dominated their relationship mostly though everyone pretended that all was well. I could see all was not well. The thin veneer of Calvin and mum's relationship snapped one night, on mum's night off, when we were all supposed to be sleeping.

A noisy quarrel ensued through a tearful voice. Mum was crying and Calvin talked with controlled anger. I tiptoed to the bedroom door and eavesdropped nervously. This was one of the many strained, silent so-called disagreements and grumbling about money. Calvin's job, which he ran the risk of losing, was due to his absences and conflicts with his immediate supervisor at work.

He visited the Betting Shop daily but swore that his future aspiration was to become a solicitor. Mamie saw it as throwing care to the wind. The worry was about how he was going to sustain our family, once he had happily "given up" his job. Jobs were hard to come by for coloured people in England.

This was always the main topic of Aunty Mary and Mamie's conversations. The talk of work dominated everything – the business of work, the competition for work, the battles at work and the possessiveness of it; all seemed to engulf the lives of the adults around us. As children we therefore learned by listening. Whether we visited friends or they visited our home, it was the most animated subject of discussion. It seemed to me that "*Work*" reigned supreme.

It terrorised the minds of the working few, haunted the unemployed and brought nightmares to those who had a job but were on the brink of losing for whatever reason. Work dominated every conversation, in every family and when the subject of racism was included, it took second place. But it was these discussions which seemed to keep the adults alive; it coloured their mundane existence and appeared to cement relationship among friends and islanders. Having a job seemed to give respectability or status; a purpose to be maintaining a room, paying *su-su*, sending money to maintain families back home or indeed looking after yourself here in the '*Land of Plenty.*'

Landlords, it was commonly known, were unforgiving about pregnancies planned or otherwise – the thought of children in their houses were like bulls seeing red; they threw you out at will. This was so especially if there is a chance of getting a higher rent from someone with guaranteed work. Landlords were also nervous of aspiring coloured people, those who didn't want to settle down to do just any job, but wanted to climb the ladder of success; rather than the till-death-us-do-part, menial jobs. Only yesterday, there was a conversation on the same subject in Aunt Mary's house.

ع

"So Irene, you hear Byron lost his job again!" Aunt Mary broke the silence which reigned over the women's furious knitting needles.

"Not again! I wonder what he did this time," enquired Mamie. "England's not easy. You have to stoop to conquer sometimes," came her fearful warning.

Their bowed heads over the rolls of woolen balls and knitting patterns put them deep in thought and they were worried about their post-migrated situations in England, as well as unrealised ambitions and memories of their childhoods. Their present catastrophes were intermittently mental monologues or aired dialogues over the clip-clipping knitting needles and the loop-and-curl of their fingers, whilst engaged in their favourite past-time.

The women's visual achievement was their own knitted jumpers, cardigans, waistcoats, socks, artistic cushion covers, children's scarves, school items and even colourful thickly starched doilies which decorated their mantelpieces. It was their economies of scales and it enabled them to save on purchasing expensive clothing. Instead, they sent the money home to those who needed it most. They had found a way to deal with domestic life in England, and through the distraction of this art form, it consumed their free time, which was minimal to begin with.

"But Byron don't have *chic nor chac* in England, to worry about like us," Mamie reasoned minutes later, as if she had just spoken her thoughts aloud.

I could tell she had just turned her private monologue into a dialogue and the fury of the clicking needles stopped for a while. She looked at the mantelpiece alarm clock. The women appeared to have awoken from their race against time and their mental battles.

"That's right, if he had a wife and children here to feed and worry about putting a roof over their heads, he would know he have to take what he get," Aunty Mary responded.

"Some of us used to think England had a money-tree, but now reality hit home, you either work or starve," Mamie added.

The women talked as if they were reassuring each other that to do or die was the correct, or only way to deal with problems in England.

"Girl you know, Byron's real problem is that he can't stand being a 'nobody' in England, having to wash dishes when he was a big *hefe* in Grenada." Mamie had ended this reply with big STUPES!!

"Well, let him stay there. How long he will keep up this damn stupidness for? This is not Grenada. There's no breadfruit or yam and peas in the back garden; here he has to eat, and to eat, he has to work first!"

"I know, I know, tell that to some of these men," Mamie echoed with the same annoyance in her voice.

Then she lowered her tones to a whisper, conscious of the fact that I was reading a book, outstretched on the linoleum floor. The twins in the meantime were running around outside, rushing upstairs, or quarrelling intermittently with each other. Sometimes they appeared to be so quiet, you wondered whether they had disappeared for good.

"Calvin is not much different from Byron," Mamie whispered.

"Uh-huh!"

The women's tête-à-tête enabled them to off-load their domestic problems, which flowed like running water. Their knitting resumed and they appeared to use the skill, the quiet and deep thinking it promoted, to deal with Mamie's new problem. With head bowed over the navy blue school jumper that was being knitted for me, they exchanged views or rather, through release and reassurance; they attempted to resolve their various dilemmas.

"Well Calvin now, he say no boss going to treat him like dirt, so he threatening to give up his work," said Mamie.

"Oh Gawd, eh? What's wrong with him? Their Grenadian Creole expressions took over the niceties of their ornamental Standard English and made their emotional responses seemed more natural.

"Well, he say he want to go an' study," Mamie told Aunty Mary.

"Study for what now? He's no child – leave that to the children, noh!"

"Girl, he want to be a solicitor," Mamie said half-laughing. "He say he doh want no factory work, and nobody telling him to sweep no floor for the hell of it," Mamie added.

"You mean he bust up with is Supervisor then?"

"Well it look so, dey give him a warning, so he take 2 days off, pretending to be sick; to punish them he said," Mamie said.

"Punish THEM!! What he playing? Who go feed his children? What about the rent? And he doh have no money save up!"

"Girl! Ah doh know but I could see trouble ahead," Mamie warned.

Aunty Marry shook her head in disgust, and remained quiet for a few minutes. Then she ventured again.

"I think you will have to study your head, you know. You have 3 mouths to feed, and if you doh look sharp, it seems it will be 4 mouths plus your own when they kick his backside outa the house, with that type ah attitude. So you have to keep your head on."

Aunty Mary's warning made me anxious and my heart pounded nervously. They had forgotten I was there.

"Look, you must join Matthew's little *su-su*. At least you will have something to fall back on when *things turn ol' mass.*"

"How much is the *su-su*?" Mamie asked with interest.

"It's one shilling. I know it's a lot but if you could close your eyes and struggle and pay it, at leas' you could keep your head above water and a roof over your children head. Otherwise, *dog eat your share*," Aunty Mary advised cautiously. "If not, whey you goin' to go with them?"

"Well ah tell him to go to the Labour Exchange to see what he could find before things get bad," Mamie replied, still whispering. "Girl, I don't think he even hear me yet. He just sittdung at home playing a guitar."

"Eh heh! He want to be a solicitor, but he sittdung there playing guitar! Look at me ass cross, noh!" Aunty Mary retorted.

I had stirred noisily, indicating my discomfort with the conversation by turning the pages of my book over and over, so Mamie signalled with her usual clearing of the throat. Aunty Mary was obviously getting angry by the minute.

The final pronouncements were made. Aunt Mary was disgusted by the whole affair and worried for her sister and family.

"We used to t'ink England life easy. Yes, we all want to be something great but we have to live, eat, and survive firs'. God smile on him and at least he *have* a job; he should count himself lucky."

"What the ass he playing?" said Aunty Mary, her voice getting louder. "Girl, he need a good planass to bring him to his senses!"

Then the loud stupes ended her annoyance. At least Mamie had begun to find an answer to her dilemma and Aunty Mary seemed determined to help her.

"You know something, Gladys told me about a job at the airport. She heard about it from a Guyanese friend. I'll ask her for the telephone number. This could be an answer to your prayer," said Aunty Mary.

"Well, Joanne going to school now and I need to change things up you know. I was thinking maybe I should get a day job, in case *things turn ole mass*," Mamie finally reasoned, with an air of hopefulness.

The women had begun to find answers to their problems, and intent on working immediately on their expressed resolutions, Aunty Mary took the lead.

"Well you off tonight. Why don't we go an' see Gladys and at the same time, pass and see Matthew about the *su-su*."

"Yes, because by tomorrow that job could be gone, who knows?" Mamie reasoned with relief.

Calvin learnt about the *su-su* much later. Mamie had been paying it for more than six weeks, and now it was her turn to get the total sum of money. It was a lot of money and the thought of this economic plan being done behind his back, made Calvin furious. Firstly, he saw it as treachery, the secret of hiding money which he said he had contributed to. Secondly, he did not approve of the plan to buy their own house; that was a foolish ambition, impossible by coloured standards, he said unconvincingly.

"Buy a house in England! Stupes! You crazy!" he asked Mamie.

"Yes buy a house, right here in England!" she retorted.

"Other people do it. There's nothing wrong with us putting money together to save and help one another out – that's the only way we going to make it in England."

"Ah don't know who put this crazy idea in you head," said Calvin, "But I cyan see it happening to us here in England."

"Yes, you keep saying this is England," she snapped. "Why you think we can't progress like others do? We have to make it right here." Mamie spoke as if she was scolding Calvin.

"Your children were born right here. If you ask me, I think it's a more crazy idea wanting to be a lawyer. At least my idea is practical. We all have to take our responsibilities seriously – like feeding, clothing *your* children and providing a roof over their heads."

The sound of a hard slap followed his charges.

"You saying ah have fancy ideas eh," he said squaring up to her. "You think you bloody better than me. Ah have me head on more than you think. I am a Black man in this hell of a place!" Calvin shouted, shaking slightly as he did so.

"If you think you can do better, go and work as a Black man out there. I was ah Overseer home, nobody treat me like dirt. Ah have me pride!"

"Go to hell, with your pride!" She snapped back and another slap sounded, followed by scuffling over the sound of the TV in the sitting room.

There was a noisy exchange through a tearful voice. Mamie had been crying and Calvin did most of the talking. During all this kafuffle, I was eavesdropping nervously, while the twins slept undisturbed during the whole episode. My parents continued quarrelling for at least 5 minutes with angry exchanges of hurtful words. They sounded as if they were carrying the problems of England on their shoulders, each feeling justified that their own problem was greater than the other. Each locked in a real battle; individually but together as a race.

Calvin made his final pronouncement as he prepared to head for the betting shop.

"I'm the bloody man in this family, what I say goes!" Calvin screamed. "And if you don't like it you know what you can do!" And with that, he left the house and the front door slammed.

The social ills of Caribbean life in Britain had long taken its toll on most black families. They seemed to be plagued with similar problems, whether they had migrated from Grenada, Jamaica, Barbados, Trinidad or Guyana. They were all faced with uprootedness, insecurities, the threat of joblessness, merciless Landlords, pressure of supporting families back at home, unplanned births in Britain, failed ambitions, and disappointment over previously misplaced perception of migrant life in Britain.

It was those deep developing problems which made 17 year old Peter, my British-born cousin announce one day, that he would never marry a black woman! Most times Peter was an observer and when he spoke he didn't have much to say, but one particular day he became quite talkative; he said quite a lot.

"Listen, Peter told me, I've got the answer."

Peter was often cryptic and gave the impression that he was often thinking out aloud when he spoke.

"OK, which answer?" I questioned, waiting for him to continue.

"I think I have examined and dissected the problems of our Caribbean parents."

A *'Man of Words'* he was not; certainly not like the talkative young men of his age in Grenada. That evening, I listened carefully to Peter's logic, when he said that he had looked at the status quo and came to one conclusion. Such a conclusion he had said, hinged on real progress as he saw it. Peter said that he was convinced that our progress or a way forward in England lay in "white power."

There was no interjection from me. I figured that since Peter knew about life in England more than I did, I should listen to him; after all, he was born here! So I listened. Peter made it clear that the kind of power he was referring to was the power he would gain in marrying a white partner, to help to pave the way ahead for him! This strategy, he felt certain, would help him to avoid the pitfalls of our older generation.

Chapter 11

"With lies and deceit they take way me land
Destroying the pride of an honest man
Leaving a ghetto for my children
Leaving below the standards of other men
Towards my race there's so much hate
Inevitably we will retaliate
The sun will dry the tears from my face
My people will find their rightful place."

Lord Shorty (Hollis Liverpool)

Mamie got the job which Aunty Mary had told her about. She remained there for 3 years. This helped her to survive Calvin's roller-coaster employment record, ensured we had food and a roof over our heads and reduced the anxiety of becoming homeless. She left the 3-year-old Airport job and had barely settled into the routine of a day job, when the usual jealousy, discrimination, and ensuing problems reared their ugly heads.

One dull, wet morning, she drove into her company car park, at 8.30am. With racing pulse, she squared her shoulders and sighed deeply before heading for the main entrance. Friday's episode, like countless other days previously, was still fresh in her mind. Once more her intense, melancholic silence was evidence that she was becoming less tolerant of her job's daily torment.

She was speedily promoted from Vending Machine Operator to Cashier within 2 months. With Mamie's meager promotion, came a sizeable and barely tolerant atmosphere; hence her lack of enthusiasm and repression of the hatred, she now felt for her fellow workers. Each day, she felt overwrought by the hard, nerve-taxing job. Her work demanded tact and a pleasing personality; qualities which she had managed to convince Mrs. Alexander, the Manageress, she had.

"Girls, this is Irene," Mrs. Alexander had announced. She is joining us a Vending Operator. Irene, meet Rose our Directors' Waitress; Shirley and Eileen and Christine or Chris; our General Assistants."

Then she turned to the only male among the staff and said, "And this is Ricky. He is our Chef."

The introduction was made cheerfully then Miss Alexander continued, "You'll find the crowd pleasing to work with and I certainly hope you'll like working here with us."

Mrs. Alexander was a thin, rather well dressed, elderly woman, with an air of confidence and authority. She upheld strict rules and a high standard of discipline, giving preference above all, to capability, diplomacy and punctuality at work. The girls, on the other hand, regarded Mrs. Alexander as old-fashioned, and looked forward to her forthcoming retirement with delight.

Mamie's first impression of her new working team was hopeful and she strove hard to do her best. The job of refilling vending machines and collecting their numerous coins was somewhat a comedown, in comparison with her former occupation, which had been, at any rate, loftier and more soul-satisfying. Her former Canteen Supervisor's post ended just like her marital status. Now she was a divorcee, house-owner and had total responsibility for her family. Clad daily in her blue-and-white overall, Mamie moved with confidence and vitality. Her way of dealing with any mistake or snobbery on the part of the General Assistants, was discreet and authoritative.

"Ee-rr! Listen to this!" Shirley called out to the others from across the kitchen.

"D'you know, Rose collected more money from the vending yesterday when Irene was away!"

This information was conveyed in Shirley's usual caterwauling manner. It made the women snigger and the eighteen year old felt her contribution gave her more importance in the group. Shirley was the youngest employee and this was her only job since leaving school two years ago. Like mum, at the start of her job, she was slightly isolated working amongst the others. The fact is, being placed in a group of women who were much older than her; Shirley felt she had to quickly adopt their mannerisms and attitudes in order to fit in.

Mum told me that one day she entered the kitchen unexpectedly to hear gossiping taking place about her. Unlucky for them, mum was able to surprise Chris and Rose with her timely entry. With red flushed faces they were about to leave the kitchen when mum said, "Then I take it, Mrs. Alexander asked you to pass this message on, Shirley."

Both Chris and Rose disappeared, leaving Shirley even more embarrassed for mum to deal with. Into the pause which followed came crisp, hard footsteps. Together mum and Shirley looked towards the direction of the sound and saw Mrs. Alexander's head appearing from around the corner.

"Ah, good morning girls," said Mrs. Alexander then she continued, "Irene, have you finished vending for today?"

"Yes, Mrs. Alexander."

"And the money, has it been bagged?"

"Oh yes. Ready for banking," replied the confident Irene.

"Splendid. Now, before you go to the bank, I'm going to show you how to do the invoices."

Mum and Mrs. Alexander left the red-faced Shirley standing, looking somewhat embarrassed, as she watched them in their tête-à-tête disappearing down the corridor. The girl was filled with envy and resentment so she stormed into the general canteen area to report this to the others.

Chris, who was wiping table-tops with little effort, was talking to Rose. Rose was sitting in a corner with eyes that revealed sleepless nights. She was staring idly out of a nearby window. Her coarse ginger hair was well tucked under her white cap and she looked exhausted. She did not stir as the girl approached her.

"That Irene's gone off with Mrs. A. again. Showing her how to do invoices, she is," Shirley announced.

"God! I hope she's not training Irene to take over when she retires!" Chris replied.

"Well, you never know," Rose said. "She goes around here thinking she's second boss anyway."

The girls remained quiet so Rose continued.

"I've been here longer than anyone of you. Seen them come and go, I have. No one's shown me how to do invoices. All I do here is just serve these gluttons who call themselves directors. Day in, day out; the same damn thing!"

"Ah come on Rose, steady now," Chris told her firmly.

"This is your job. Besides, you've said enough. We've got potatoes and carrots to peel - C'mon on."

Rose remained unmoved and a strained silence followed. Her eyes stared past them, filled with anger and hate for the situation she felt trapped in. The girls looked at each other puzzled. The atmosphere remained tense as Rose continued,

"Been working all my life, and I've got sod-all to show for it - a ruddy council flat, a man who's unemployed and...."

"O.K. Rose," Chris interrupted, "Since you won't snap out of it, who did you have a row with last night - Your old man or your boy?"

There was no reply.

Chris, the oldest amongst the General Assistants knew Rose well. She had consoled Rose on many occasions and even covered up for her on days when she arrived to work overtly depressed or showing signs of drunkenness.

Rose lit a cigarette. The glow from the light revealed attractive but angry features. She sucked and spoke over puffs but coughed when she took a draw on the cigarette while talking. She then stuck the thing in a corner of her lips, letting it hang there. Her features looked washed by misery which seemed to come from nowhere. Yet, here Rose was drowning in despair caused by pity for herself and this was noticeable by everyone. Rose continued, "Oh, I'm just fed up to the teeth. That's what I am - fed up!" she said, knocking off the ash with the emphasis on her last words.

It was not mum's place to wash dishes and pots, or mop the floor but the girls felt that is what she should be doing. In their opinion, the higher administrative duties were the prerogative of Mrs. Alexander; the trouble was, she often shared this with mum. Consequently, this situation became the root of the girls' growing resentment for mum.

Now and again, mum was given additional opportunities of doing the cashing up during dinnertime. The clients who bought food from the canteen, made it obvious that they liked Irene's pleasing personality and readiness to help. They publicly expressed their pleasure with, "Thank you, Irene," and this was often accompanied with a dazzling smile or a wink. Soon it was generally known that mum had become popular among general company staff. She knew that her popularity was causing conflict amongst the G.A.'s but confident that her new duties had not ousted them out of their jobs, mum continued cheerfully to befriend the girls.

In the meantime, Rose had elected herself as leader amongst the G.A.'s and indiscreetly began to taunt mum, especially since the addition of a new employee. The new worker was a Pakistani woman called Nadeen - another foreigner the GA's had said! They knew this before Irene did because Ricky used to pass on confidential information to the girls in exchange for his inclusion into their clan. On this particular occasion, after the interviews were final, Ricky informed the girls that the successful applicant was, "one of Irene's kind."

"See what I mean," Rose announced. "Get one in and they all come and take over!"

She began to instill in the girls the need for their collective disapproval of Mrs. Alexander's preference of mum over them and suggested they should protest against the continuing employment of foreigners. Though Chris did not wholly agree with Rose's instigation, she was told that only with everyone's full support, would the situation alter to their benefit.

Mum was finding it increasingly difficult to wear the right expression, since she became aware of her colleagues envy of her position. The hardest part to bear was the girls' continual efforts to conspire against her, which at one time was very nearly successful.

Following Mrs. Alexander's retirement, mum's skills and knowledge of the canteen's clerical duties became more prominent, despite opposition. However, by the time the notices of staff changes were circulated one morning, the girls gathered in the kitchen to await the outcome with malicious anticipation. Shirley announced that she might resign should mum become her new boss. Chris, who was leaning on a wall, looked ghostly white with her bottom lip drawn across her teeth. She was contemplating in silence. They were startled when Rose burst into the kitchen ecstatically.

"Ricky's got it! He's got it!"

She was unable to contain her excitement and they repeatedly questioned her.

"Got what?" they asked impatiently.

"He's got the job!"

Those words were the signal for a celebration.

"Ricky is our boss?" the girls asked in disbelief, but with delight.

Their sighs of relief and outburst of loud happy chattering was evidence that their earlier fears were allayed. Mum, they learnt, had gained the position of Cashier Control Clerk-cum-Secretary-cum-Assistant to Ricky.

Although mum's new position was not to their liking, the girls no longer regarded her as a threat. Mrs. Alexander's deliberations in preparing mum for the managerial post and not appointing her baffled them. However, it baffled mum the most.

Later, when mum heard the reason why she was not given the post of Manageress, she felt her world had descended into hell. She felt defeated in her daily battle to win with her personal attributes; knowledge, faith in her self and the ability to resist the girls' deliberate and destructive ploys. She was certain that in the midst of the prevailing racial resentment, justice would prevail. How foolishly she had visualized herself in charge of the canteen, and expected Mrs. Alexander to recommend her whole-heartedly! She recalled those distressful words she overheard between Mrs. Alexander and Ricky.

"Of course, Irene would be the most suitable choice for this position," Mrs. Alexander said.

"I guess so, though she's only been here for a short while," he replied.

"The problem is, I fear the girls would not want to take orders from her. I've made it known that not only is Irene the newest member of our team but she does know her work well and can be relied on to perform conscientiously. That's why I'm giving her to you."

It was then mum felt an overwhelming feeling of disappointment after the staff's orgy of joy and pleasure. She was now going to be used by the Company to do Ricky's job for him. This unfair concept of being the driver of a car, with someone else at the steering wheel was absurd. For mum, that awful descent into accepting her new post was more like a horror dance, whose success depended entirely on her single performance - a wretched plot!

Ricky had started work in the canteen as a General Assistant after leaving his orphanage at the age of 17. He got married a year after that to a girl of the same age. Although Ricky was confident as a youngster, his scanty education had not prepared him for such a post. This was clearly evident by his inability to write or spell correctly.

Now 27 years old, with two children and totally dominated by his wife, he found it rather difficult to relate to women. This Mrs. Alexander knew this only too well, hence her intention to team him with Irene, who would act as both his anchor and shadow.

Ricky knew too, that the structure of the new staff change although in his favour, was grossly unfair. However, the moment he had secretly yearned for all these years had at last come to him, so he was more than grateful for Mrs Alexander's consideration. This promotion was an answer to a secret longing he had; it was a long to control others, rather than be controlled. He would rule and dominate his staff - all of them women! He felt that mum would instill in him the know-how and confidence needed to be their "Boss." Yes, he would answer to the name of Manager; he would instruct the General Assistants in their duties and also be "their" Chef. He would delegate Irene to be responsible for the correct undertaking of all paperwork; the invoices and the daily banking of the monies. She would also control the stock and report to him. He was glad he would be "their boss."

However, the staff changes brought a swift change of the G.A.'s attitude not only towards mum but an unexpected disregard for Ricky's authority. Instead, Rose reigned as dictator with great delight, whilst Shirley and Chris heeded her every command. In the meantime, Ricky's eloquence faded, as did his ability to control them. To add to the canteen's general chaos, Ricky's marital problems, which stemmed from his wife's infidelity, was broadcasted by Rose to everyone. She had overheard Ricky asking for mum's advice on how to handle his wife's infidelity.

It was clear that the disappearance of Mrs. Alexander's firm managerial control of the staff, since her retirement had brought a lowering of the high standard of respect and service from the workers. Daily gossiping, bickering, and Rose's continuing misbehaviour dominated the environment.

Mum, who was now trapped by her necessity to remain in post until the twins had settled in college, felt that all storms in the form of such changes had to be weathered until her goal was reached. The collapse of several other large companies, together with the numerous job enquiries she received daily from people seeking work in their Company, was an indication that the time was not right to make job changes.

However, the height of her despair reached its peak, when Rose and the Girls succeeded in encouraging Ricky to dismiss Nadeen. It is true that absenteeism rated high in Nadeen's job appraisal because of her frequent days off sick. However, when Rose's neighbour, a retired teacher, enquired about a part-time job in the canteen, she was given Nadeen's cleaning job. This state of recklessness and corruption existed in the midst of mum's dissatisfaction and helplessness to curb Rose's reign of terror. Each day, mum witnessed Rose's husband's frequent visits to the canteen. He often remained on the premises throughout the day, with all his meals supplied freely.

Added to this, Ricky's marital problems drove him to seek mum's daily advice and moral support - this she handled tactfully and with confidence. Luckily, mum was a tower of strength to Ricky and a genuine friendship grew between them - another situation which Rose found threatening. This peculiar tension brought mum once more under constant attacks of racial abuse by Rose.

Rose's drinking habits increased. Her excessive alcohol consumption on the canteen premises went unnoticed. Ricky's marital problems worsened and increasingly, he lacked concentration, since he was unable to focus on the canteen's chaos. Mum also recorded the daily high percentage of stock shrinkage, while Ricky disregarded the girls' blatant swindling of the Company.

Situations came to a head when Rose's drinking demon overpowered her in making a final bid to place her husband in Ricky's post. Her inner conflict of insecurity at home and the threatened stability of her marriage escalated. In this desperate situation, her values of appropriate behaviour, of risk and loss became confused, and she sought continuous solace in the large quantities of alcohol that she drank.

In a raging drunken stupor one Friday afternoon, Rose verbally attacked Ricky as being a traitor among them.

"L-l-look at him!" she stuttered, pointing to Ricky, "Another nigger-lover!"

Chris held on to Rose to stop her from stumbling, while she pleaded with the woman for self-constraint. Shirley looked on, embarrassed at the outburst.

"Let me go!" Rose shouted, violently shrugging off Chris, almost causing her to fall.

"Send them all back!" She shouted, "Bloody foreigners!" Then pointing a finger at Irene and looking directly at her, Rose burst into tears.

"She won't be my friend!" The pathetic feelings were aired. She stood there crying amidst hick-ups.

"Hick! Take me home Irene, Hick!" she stuttered, whilst advancing towards Irene. "I only want to be your friend."

Rose's confused gibberish faded, as did her ability to remain standing. She promptly collapsed onto the ground. Mum, who had witnessed this strange dilemma, rushed to Rose's aid while Chris and Shirley watched their fallen heroine with pity. In the meantime, the panic-stricken Ricky telephoned their medical department for help. A sudden hush existed among them, while the rest of the G.A.'s looked on puzzled and somewhat ashamed of Rose's last words.

It was the mocked difference of Rose's deep-seated need for love and friendship, which contrasted her treatment of mum at the beginning, which puzzled them most. The G.A.'s were silent now. Yes, this was a stirring hour indeed. Thus, was the climax of the "gospel" and teachings according to Rose. It had produced a pathetic mixture of a strong need to belong and personal, emotional conflict, arising from her cultural conditioning.

Mum pitied the fallen leader and took the opportunity to openly advise Rose's confused 'disciples.' She told them that she hoped that the weekend, which lay ahead of them, would

bring sufficient moments of reflection: a time they should use
to personally examine the real causes of the day's episode.

Chapter 12

"Many West Indians are sorry now
They left their country and don't know how
Some left their jobs and their family
And determined to come to London City
Well they are crying, they now regret
No kind of employment that they can get."

Lord Kitchener (Aldwin Roberts)

Northend Girls School was five minutes away from my home and I relished every step to the prominent, high-gated building with twin playgrounds. Those months of waiting for a school had developed an increased intensity to learn so much, that I savoured each lesson as if it was a precious jewel. My only disappointment was my impatience and surprise at the lower standard of education in some of the classes, compared to my classes in Grenada.

I had to give up French because I had surpassed, in Grenada, the present level being taught in my French classes in England. Sadly, but realistically, I had to give up the much-loved subject, in order to fulfill the list of my ambitions with the least possible delay. The boredom of waiting for the class to catch up eventually, to my present advanced level, proved unbearable. Instead, the free period I was given as an option from French became an opportunity to do Shorthand instead, which I took up with a vengeance.

I became the best in my class within record timing. Every free second was spent taking down the words of all the vinyl records we had in a big gramophone at home. I became a constant bore to everyone, with the obsessive playing and replaying of Percy Sledge, Jim Reeves, Englebert Humperdink, Tom Jones and whatever songs I could lay my hands on.

The TV too, became more interesting. Every word uttered on the silver screen was documented in my shorthand, pencilled scrawl. Developing my Shorthand skill increased my zeal in church-going on Sundays too because the lecture-style preaching was perfect for my insatiable appetite to practise the crafty skill. I became like someone possessed by the need to pencil every word in symbols. Literally, sometimes mentally, I traced the Pitman symbols everywhere with my fingers, willing the passion for this skill's scholarly qualities to shine in me. My progress was rapid, much to the delight of Miss Edwards, our Shorthand teacher.

Miss Edwards was a spinster who, it was rumoured, had once loved a General but unrequited love and the years of separation during wartime, had made her resign to the lifestyle of a single woman. She was proud of my efforts to achieve and equally she pushed me with vehemence as her protégé who was capable of reflecting her own personal and secret ambitions.

"You know," she told Mamie, with admiration in her voice at a Parents' Evening in School, "Joanne is a very conscientious young girl." The word *"conscientious"* echoed in my mind, throughout the evening. It sounded big and important and at the first given opportunity, I delved into a dictionary to look up the word in our family dictionary. The meaning was good and this helped to fuel my passion to succeed even further. I worked harder to please her. Thankfully, I had found someone who believed in me, like Gran-Gran, and who could help propel me further and it was working very well.

Miss Edwards had put me in for the 130 words a minute Pitman's written exam; a first ever in our school's history.

The school staff had every confidence I would, like a beacon, shine through the rigors of this exam and make this a record for our School. Ever teacher admired my passion to soar in my educational endeavours and this was the talk in the staff room. In return, I had secretly vowed never to disappoint them. This was certainly the case, until I came face-to-face with a piece of homework which shook my confidence somewhat.

ع

"What is a High Tea?" I asked my mum.

I was stuck on that assignment for a whole evening after school. I had combed through the books in our home "library;" a cupboard filled with 5 shelves of second-hand books. Among them were Britannica Encyclopedias, medical books, showing real pictures of the human body and an assortment of Janet Frazer catalogues. I had dubbed the cupboard "the library" and pretended the books were mine. Only the Hoover vacuum cleaner, an unwanted occupant by my standards, lay at the bottom in its box. Each time this carpet cleaner was used it was carefully replaced there for lack of space elsewhere.

Mum did not know what a *High Tea* was. My library books, the pride and source of my knowledge thus far, had let me down. Aunty Mary did not know what a *High Tea* was either; though she had lived in England longer than anyone I had known.

Both she and Mr. Christopher, her neighbour, were the only ones I knew who were knowledgeable on matters relating to England outside of my school. Their knowledge was well-known among our migrant communities, especially as they had bought their own homes in England. Buying your

267

own home was one of the greatest ambitions of Caribbean nationals in England. It was the envy of many, since it gave the owner respect, a sense of power, a higher rank and a *rite-de-passage* to success, apart from book learning. But despite this, Aunty Mary and her neighbour did not know what a *High Tea* was.

Therefore, I had ceded defeat in the homework department with my Cookery teacher because I had no knowledge what a *High Tea* was. The embarrassment was met with a smirk smile and patronising platitudes from her but at least there were no reprimands.

As time went on our school become noisier generally. Miss Hubbard, our Headmistress, had warned us in Assembly one Friday morning, against showing interest in the boys who were beginning to congregate at our school gates. We were advised strictly not to encourage this behaviour as it was considered improper and was giving our school a bad name.

The blue-eyed, grey-haired, formal woman had threatened to punish us severely, if we were caught breaking the rules. Breaking the rules, she had stressed, included running through the corridors, chewing gum, a habit she abhorred and any kind of fighting on school premises. And whilst saying so, she deliberately looked in the direction of a known culprit called Jessica; a Grenadian girl, who was constantly in trouble, with a noisy group following her.

Jessica was branded a reckless ringleader and would think nothing of either bashing someone about if they had dared to look too hard at her. Worse still, if anyone was foolish enough to mimic her raw Grenadian accent, Jessica's violence was unstoppable. Therefore, Jessica did not last long at our school. It was rumoured months after she had disappeared, that she was sent to an Educationally Sub-Normal school. It was the dreaded kind of place which

Caribbean parents like Aunty Mary and others had feared the most.

When I had understood the full extent of ESN schools, I felt sorry for Jessica. I was more horrified by the fact that the standard of schooling in England could be so low that it became necessary for the government to create *"sub-standard schools."* I spent many weeks thinking about the fate of others like Jessica, about what Peter had vowed and the 'loss' of my best friend Emma.

I had written many letters to Emma's address in England but since no reply to my letters came, I wondered what had happened to her. Our childish ambitions and role-playing of our presumed style of living in England was farcical but we could not have known it; no one could - neither children nor adults. Seemingly, we had all been deluded into the belief that everything in the "garden" called England was rosy – how wrong! But we were growing up in a new home and life progressed from day to day. I had made some good friends. I ventured around the British Isles, learning of our English "homeland."

ع

One late spring, in a second floor flat, a group of ten of us discussed plans for our forthcoming summer holidays. For most of us, it was going to be our first holiday in the land where we had lived three-quarters, and for some, all of their lives. Indeed, we had only lived in one sector of the community and to get an overall picture, as well as to enjoy our "home," we decided to venture into other parts of the England.

The British Isles, we were taught from childhood, was full of hope, with green, pleasant lands that we had seen very

269

little of. Occasionally, our individual experiences had fallen short of our expectations but it was this very land we now sought to explore; to enjoy just as the "back home" a few of us had often spoken about.

A rich flow of talk went on in Burt and Rose's small living room, which was separated from the TV room by a thick-walled partition. Everyone in our group talked loudly, the most dominant sounds being the bass voices of the male amongst us. With gesturing hands and white teeth flashing against various shades of brown skin, we all spoke with vibrant expectation. Burt stood up to refill glasses with drinks, followed by Rose with a platter bearing cake and peanuts.

"Look we have enough brochures here to decide where to go without making a whole lot of noise about it!" exclaimed Derek.

"Let's go somewhere hot man!"

"Ain't nowhere here that's really hot. A hot country would have to be back-home preferably," Ken replied.

But then such a remark was always expected of Ken. He had lived in Brooklyn New York for many years and was greatly influenced by their sweltering hot summers, not to mention his most vivid memories of "back home" in Trinidad. This he felt made the British summer months, by comparison, a frustrated and anxious period.

"Well, ah doan know about you, it's not possible for Pat and me to go to the West Indies. Anyway, I thought this was supposed to be an English holiday. Even the Continent would suit us," Derek explained.

"Then let's go to Spain. That's a Continent and it's hot there!" Rose replied.

"Yeah! Then me and Kathy could speak Spanish," Theresa agreed, immediately launching into her samples of Spanish words.

"Buenos nochas."

"You mean the kinda Spanish you been learning in evening classes?" I asked her. "Didn't you two opt out half-way? Huh! Some tourists we would make, relying on your quality of Spanish," I said laughing.

"Nah, nah, nah! Spain's not a good place to go, not with the World Cup and all. Besides, I doan want to use me poyah on anyone!" Derek replied.

"Poyah, what's that?" Theresa asked.

"You doh know what a poyah is and you're a Grenadian?" he asked. "I take it you know what a cutlass is?" he continued.

"Of course, I know what a cutlass is."

"Well, then you know what a poyah is," Derek concluded.

Our conversation then wove in and out in a sort of confused debate regarding cutlasses, their uses and misuses.

"Wait a minute!" Derek held out his hand for silence.

"Comment una y," Theresa and Kathy continued in the corner of the room, refreshing their scanty Spanish and clearly, already in difficulty.

"We can't all talk at once. We came here to discuss a holiday and so far, we've hardly talked about that. What we need is a Chairman," Derek announced then he continued.

"Dave, you don't say ah ting yet, you best be Chairman."

Dave had hardly opened his mouth to reply when Burt held up his hand immediately, indicating that he wished to have his turn to speak first.

"O.K," Dave replied, looking at his digital watch, "You have two minutes."

So the planning was under way, with the occasional interruption from the three children, who were in the TV room, watching cartoons. Now and again, they fought over a single toy or crisps. With such a haphazard fashion, this meeting was clearly not going to be the only one. In fact, we had six such weekly meetings before our group finally decided that a caravan holiday in the West Country was the choice for our summer holiday. This holiday was going to be quite an occasion; an occasion which we had looked forward to with a strange urgency. It was going to be an occasion which had its own secret attraction - freedom.

Up to this point Verna had remained quiet as she listened throughout the discussions. She did not talk a lot but whenever she did, it was most dramatic - the kind that forces everyone to listen to her. Her quiet manner and confident disposition was almost mesmerizing. It was obvious that she was educated and well experienced. She had a saddened expression when she told us about an experience she had during a past visit to the West Country. During a day's visit she said that some children had exclaimed at them with scorn, "Look mummy, there's a black man!"

It was Verna's opinion that this occasion was perhaps the first time those unfortunate children had seen black people in the flesh. However, it had made her feel a little uncomfortable and sad for their ignorance. At any rate, the group silently noted Verna's experience but continued undaunted by her tales of woe and of past rain-soaked days in a chalet in the West Country. Everyone was determined that this holiday would and should be different.

"That's why a caravan holiday would be best," Derek said. He was a strong, medium-height, muscular fellow. The most travelled amongst the group was Derek. He had been on several Duke of Edinburgh Award Schemes and was very good at reading maps.

"Caravan holiday, that's no good for the kids," Kathy complained, "Just being cooped up in a caravan driving around all day. It's not fair on them."

Her husband Dave, or "Mr. Cool," as the group chose to call him spoke slowly and directly. It was as if to instill in the group a sense of quietness and calmness. It was obviously needed to get his point across.

"Look doll," he said responding to his wife's concern, "If we get a Do-mobile with all facilities on board, there should be no problem. They usually have toilet, shower and the usual gear on board - cooker, fridge, beds and so on."

His deliberations were successful, because everyone was now sitting quite still, listening to the voice of someone who had obviously done his homework. Dave continued, "I've found out we can either have a Class 1, Class 2 or Luxury Deluxe caravan. Here are the leaflets and prices. The Geezer who gave them to me said we could book one with a deposit of £100 - so it's a Tenner for each of us."

"That sounds O.K. but is that the cheapest price?" Derek asked.

He liked the idea, so he continued, "We need to have other prices to compare and a caravan holiday is a good idea because being mobile means we won't be stuck in one place. We could go to and from base each day. We could cover fresh ground and get to see more of everything," he concluded.

So the majority of the brochures were put aside while everyone thoughtfully studied and discussed the caravan terms of hiring. Dave suggested that each couple should scout around for details of other hiring companies during the week, in order to compare terms and prices, before the next meeting.

That was the end of our first holiday meeting, but not the end of conversations which followed afterwards. The various topics conveyed pride, prejudices and politics, and for some the disadvantages of their education in Britain.

Their differences of opinions were evident, because the debate became noisy again. Criticism followed criticism, of aspects of Britain they were dissatisfied with. They related past, unpleasant, experiences during which their expressions became defiant, showing a resistance to the adverse incidences they had experienced. Despite this, they showed a willingness to be positive about life. This was more than a feeling of triumph - it was the formula for conquering ignorance. Ours was therefore a positive outlook for the summer ahead.

Therefore, a couple of weeks after our final meeting, a pleasant May morning saw two of us from the group heading to the Caravan Showroom to book the Caravan. Ken had took his toddler and we were armed with the £100 booking fee for the holiday.

Ken was tall, with chestnut eyes set in a clean-shaven face, and a precise moustache. With lean cheeks and a pronounced chin, he wore his hair in a neat, well-rounded Afro hairstyle. He drove his car at a fast pace with constant complaints from me, about his speed and his apparent lack of regard for road conditions.

His three-year-old son, who sat in a seat at the rear, also complained that he wanted the car to be still, while he fixed his puzzles. Ken's driving was unchanged, he stressed repeatedly that we only had seven minutes to get to the showroom before it closed. He also reminded me that our lateness was due to my all day shopping spree in Shepherd's Bush market. By the time we arrived at the Show Room we were quite tense.

"There's no one here," I said.

"But the door's open. You think we should go in?" he asked.

We went in quietly then a voice bellowed from a closed room behind the counter.

"Take a seat. Be with you in a moment!" It was a man's voice and he sounded cheerful enough.

In the meantime, Ken browsed around the various caravans on display in the large reception area. His son rushed around to a nearby bright orange chair, sat in it and swiveled it madly.

"Come here!" I said, grabbing him. "You're not to go breaking up the people's place," I scolded, making him stand next to me.

Intermittently, Ken called out excitedly, informing me of the facilities on board the caravan he was examining.

"Now what can I do for you?" the gentleman who appeared from behind the closed door asked. He was leaning both arms on his desk, looking down at us with eyebrows raised in polite enquiry. This red-eyed, middle-age man appeared rather surprised to see us. He was secretly eying us as he rubbed his eyes and yawned. He then apologized for his obvious rudeness and questioned us further. He sat down in his chair, his hands clasped behind his head, staring at us as we relayed our intentions to him.

"I don't know if we can help you," the man replied. "When did you say you want it for?"

"July – the second and third weeks; for two weeks," Ken replied.

The man rubbed his mouth and sat up in his chair. He appeared to chew on his biro pen while he contemplated in silence. After a short while he yelled, "Pete! Can we spare two for middle June?" He was waiting for someone inside the closed door behind him to answer.

Ken stared at me. I stared back at him with a knowing glance. My eye language pointed Ken to the large calendar on the wall behind this man's chair. Second and third week in June, we could see, were not marked. The other weeks and months were clearly marked off in red ink which ran through the chart in the calendar. The man behind the desk waited for a reply from Pete.

Ken and I shrugged at each other and stood there waiting. Pete did not answer and the silence made us impatient. The room was a silent pressure. After the long interval which followed, the pressure was unbearable because there was no immediate reply. We stood there waiting still.

"'Scuse me for a sec," the man said, "Don't think Pete heard me." He disappeared through the door behind his desk, leaving us in the showroom.

Now we knew that this man's question seemed irrelevant and thought that it must be some sort of code between the two men because an open diary was also on the desk in front of him. The dates corresponded with crossed out dates on visible calendar on the wall.

"There we go again," Ken whispered to me between his clenched teeth.

It grew still all around us. We stood there waiting. There was no sound except for the intermittent roaring of vehicles' engines passing outside and Ken's son's shuffling on the showroom floor with his puzzles. Later we heard a muttering of voices, in fits and starts, from behind the door where it seemed a conversation was taking place.

"Thought you said this place closes half-day?" I asked, breaking the silence between us.

"That's what Dave said. Don't know what they're pissing about in there for, instead of dealing with this goddam thing out here!" Ken complained. His voice was becoming louder as he spoke.

The man returned. He looked at us as though he was trying to see beyond our faces, to read our thoughts. His eyes sank deep under his brow, giving his nose an owlish appearance. He kept his glance occasionally away from our eyes, as if he was too embarrassed to hide the lie he was about to tell. He shifted uncomfortably in his chair.

"Well - er - now," he said slowly, being careful not to say anything that might offend.

"You have to be at least twenty-five years old, with a clean driving licence," he said.

We both nodded and the man frowned. He seemed a little annoyed because he had presumed we were not old enough for such an undertaking - it was clear.

"There'll be ten of us going," I said.

"Ten!" the man repeated, rubbing his chin and hesitating.

"Where did you say, you were going?" The man asked.

"Cornwall, Devon - the West Country."

"Oh the West Country!" the man exclaimed, with a sigh of relief and a forced smile, which immediately wavered and disappeared.

"And five of you drive, eh?" he asked in disbelief.

There was silence as he turned our answers over in his mind. We noticed that he was not writing anything down and he seemed to be hesitating for too long. We both stood there waiting, still. Now and then, the effort this man made at relaxing, caused him to curl back his lips, baring white teeth to his gums. Then eventually he broke the silence.

"Ah, but you haven't got one hundred pounds to deposit now, have you?" he said almost delightedly, convinced that he had caught us out on this detail.

"Yes we have, here it is. We also know that the rest has to be paid to you twenty-eight days before we collect the vans," I replied.

His expression sank. He looked as if he had been beaten at his own game. Increasingly, Ken was seething with anger at this man's handling of what he thought was a simple procedure. I could see that Ken was barely controlling himself so he got up to look at the notice board behind us once more. He left me to deal with the form-filling and booking forms.

"West Country, did you say?" the man asked again, and on our repeated confirmation, his expression changed.

"I take it you're saying we can hire two caravans?" Ken asked, once I had signed the booking forms.

"Well, yes," the man answered, looking at the diary on his desk.

Surprisingly, this man began to show signs of enthusiasm, especially when each detail of every member of our group's occupation and marital status was revealed.

"A Chef, an Electrician and a Builder. You got a right combination here for this holiday," he mused.

Then turning to me he continued, "And what about you Missus, shall I put you down as housewife?"

"No, thank you! HCO will do. It stands for Higher Clerical officer," I stressed, irritated by his assumption.

The man scratched his neck uneasily. He continued writing out the form attentively with a measure of surprise that all was well! Having received the deposit and seen the driving licences, his attitude became almost cordial. He rubbed his eyes and stuttered an apology for his dazed appearance.

"Been drinking last night," he said, trying to invite conversation, "God what a head I have!" he said seeking sympathy. "Wife won't talk to me and the girls take her side. Got two girls and a boy," he concluded.

There was no reply from either of us.

"Is this the only one you got?" he probed further, pointing to Ken's son, who by now was sitting on my lap.

Yes," I lied deliberately.

The man rummaged his desk for a sweet and offered one to the three year old. Then I spoke rather perceptively, "I take it you don't have our kind of people coming here - you know black people, to hire caravans."

"Nah, nah not really! Had an Indian family though, and what a smell they left - curry, garlic. We had to air out the van for days. Cor, what a state it was in! Don't like Indians at all," he said finally shaking his head.

"Why not? They're people just like you and me," Ken replied.

"Ah, but you don't have to live next to them. Nah, don't like them at all."

Then he said half-laughing, "Not keen on foreigners and I'm a foreigner myself - Scottish," he said grinning.

He stood up and stretched. This man felt he had made friends with us by discrediting other foreign nationals. In a way, it was as if to reassure us that we were all right, albeit for the time being. We were disgusted so we stared at him a deep, ruthless stare then thanked and left him to his embarrassment. We walked away, consciously averting our eyes from our reflection in the showroom window. We recovered and it was not long when the day finally came to collect the caravans we had booked from the Showroom.

Saturday evening Dave drove with me and Ken accompanying him, to the Hire Company. We hurried to the showroom with a secret thrill that made talking easy. The Hire Company was expecting us; having agreed on the telephone, that Saturday evening would be better for us instead of the previously planned Sunday morning collection. There was a broad and tolerant atmosphere of excitement between the boys as they chatted to the man.

During the past two months, our group had spent time anticipating the novelty of places we would visit, with combined confidence. Now this was rapidly becoming a reality. Immediately, we were shown the two caravans on hire and having been given a brief explanation for use of the gas, fridge and heater, we were dispatched with courtesy. We went back to the group's meeting-place, where food, clothes, pots and all imaginable paraphernalia were ready for packing on board the vans.

Like children inspecting new toys, we all boarded the caravans, with glee. We surveyed them with instant satisfaction for our new achievement; not to mention the pride, we felt when neighbours also came out to admire the caravans. However, our excitement was short-lived with our gradual discovered that all was not well with the vehicles.

"Wait a minute! This van's got sleeping room for only four!" Burt exclaimed.

"There's no way we're going to get six people to sleep on this," he continued, as he tested the firmness of the cushioned mattress.

"And didn't we pay for a Luxury Deluxe six berth?" Rose asked. "Thought you lot said there'd be a toilet and shower. There's none on this caravan."

"Ours haven't either!" I shouted from the other caravan.

"Hey! Look at this sticker, says *"Tax in post*. Can't we get nicked for that?" Kathy added.

"Look, don't panic," Dave said, trying to calm them. "I know there's no toilet. We couldn't get one with toilet but the Geezer said that there's no need to have one anyway, since we'll be going to campsites. These sites are well equipped with all the facilities. Look, he's even given us his guide to caravan sites as a bonus."

"Nah, nah! Wait a minute! You can't expect these kids to wait each time, 'till we get to a site!" Kathy exclaimed. "You must be joking. S'pose we're driving down the motorway and they need to use the toilet?"

The silence which followed was an obvious agreement, an unspoken realization of what we were thinking and feeling.

"Looks like we've been had," Derek said calmly. "You mean to say you guys accept vans like this! You realise we're going a long way. We need one hundred percent comfort as well as our Right on the road."

Dave began reassuring them that the small matter of the tax was not so serious, since it is the Hiring Company who will be held responsible by law. His reassurances were not going to be accepted, everyone had told him so.

Meanwhile, Rose who had already begun loading her meat in the fridge was having difficulty in following Ken's instructions for getting it to work. The answer they had discovered was simple; the fridge was not in working condition. It was then that Ken informed us that his caravan had stalled on the way after the collection, though it was be a minor mechanical problem which, he had managed to put right himself.

Then, questions followed more questions. How was it we had not known, not even thought about checking these things? Why had we neglected to take the Agreement Form to tick off the facilities we were being loaned? We consoled ourselves with the idea that not having ventured on a similar holiday like this before, it was a mistake anyone would probably make.

Our excitement was transformed into regret, near panic and actual anger, because we all felt cheated by this man. We repeatedly questioned the reason for his deceit in giving us the two old vans; questions which became sharp mental agony. There was no logical solution and we could not have foreseen this. The hardest part, the part which followed, was almost unbearable. We hastened back to the showroom to complain and to insist on our rights, only to find the showroom was already closed.

How our hearts were set on it all! Now anger and frustration reigned where there was once excitement and happiness. This was especially intense because the next day being Sunday, meant that no one would be available in the Showroom to help us. Our holiday plans, it seemed, were going to be set back by a whole day and a half - a wretched thought. What a beginning! Like a bad dream, sitting around, counting the passing hours, blaming ourselves for not having been more meticulous in our detail, waiting impatiently for Monday.

The weather on Monday did not seem promising. A slight drizzle was falling beneath an overcast sky. The mood among the group members was no more promising. Our immediate ambition for the morning was to hasten to the Caravan Showroom, in order to express our dissatisfaction and extreme anger; having had the beginning of our holiday marred by deceit. This we did in no uncertain terms.

"We want what we've paid for!" Burt said angrily. "Why don't you give us those two vans over there?" he asked, pointing to two Luxury Deluxe caravans, the pride of their fleet.

"Not for hire. They're for sale! 'Sides, the guv'nor would never agree to that," the Showroom man replied.

"For sale?" Ken replied, "They were the two you showed us with the same facilities on board that we've paid for."

"I've told you before, it's not up to me to give you those vans; it's up to the guv'nor," the man repeated.

Then he insulted our feelings with his suggestion, "I'll try repairing those two for you but there's nothing more I can do," he argued.

"Then in that case we'll do you for misrepresentation. No doubt, the Director of Fair Trading would be interested in this kinda set-up you lot have here," Dave said.

"How does that grab you?" Ken added.

"Yeah, and if he says it's up to the guv'nor, then looks like we'll have to stay here 'till the guv'nor comes," Derek stated adamantly.

The boys were growing moderately aggressive in their demands when the man attempted to mend the fridge with no success. The toilet and shower he told us was really "an optional extra." Additionally, he stressed that the tax situation was the Company's problem, not ours.

A tense stillness followed our initial noisy protests while this man's face showed a feeling of stress; almost a sense of shame. He turned away as though he had not seen the five boys. He was almost unwilling to take the responsibility of this explosive situation. The truth is deep down he felt most uneasy. There was also the fact that he had revealed his prejudice previously towards foreigners - information which inflamed the boys' determination, was now putting his excuses in a different light.

The boys' conversations died down to a single voice - Dave's. He was encouraged by the others silence. He emphasized that the only solution to our problems was that the man had to give us the two Luxury Deluxe caravans we had paid for.

"Listen, Mr....er."

"Stuart," the man added quickly.

"Mr. Stuart, when you've saved and planned your holiday like the ten of us have done; currently have five young ladies and two children waiting and wondering what kinda set-up you guys have here; the fact that we've lost two days of our holidays because of you; and at this late time in the day, you still cannot agree with our Rights – we have to believe that you must all be stark raving mad!" His stare was fixed, his manner cool but he was resolute. He continued.

"Who is this guv'nor anyway, and why can't we talk to him ourselves, because I tell you there's just no way we're going to move from here, 'till we get what's rightfully ours." Dave's voice was clear and firm.

Mr. Stuart listened to the boy's complaints. His lips curled to one corner of his mouth, was drawn with a frown. He looked contemptuously at them. Then shrugging finally, he left us standing outside to use the telephone inside the showroom. Cupping his hand around the mouthpiece, for greater privacy, Mr. Stuart spoke rapidly with gesturing hands; clearly angry with the person on the receiving end. He avoided looking at us with mounting frustrations, sitting around outside.

Mr. Stuart returned finally looking more subdued. He stood for a moment and seemed more ready to deal with the situation at hand. The boys, who perceived what was happening, concealed their glances. Mr. Stuart apologised rather unconvincingly to us, and we all found it easy to show how we really felt about being duped.

Mr. Stuart checked the boy's Hire Agreement Form again, pretending to show some interest in our plight. His pride was wounded pride and the conflict between his feelings for us, and his duty as an employee, seemed a shameful defeat. There was now no contradiction in what was obviously our Rights, as customers. We were all amazed at the ease with which Mr. Stuart eventually yielded to the very demands we had spent half the morning wrangling over.

A strange undertaking indeed! This reckless, incredible event, full of blatant and discriminating practices stemmed from ignorance of the worst kind! Though the boys felt that just to drive away with the two caravans was simply not enough satisfaction for our present feelings, our two weeks of freedom, fresh and precious; enjoyment of the green, pleasant lands we had heard so much about; all were at stake here, so we quietly left the Caravan Showroom with the caravans we had paid for.

The morning had been an experience which some or most of us had been faced with before. No doubt, we would encounter similar types of senarios again. Our experience had been such a mental strain, so powerful, that throughout the holiday, it had brought hasty exchanges of angry words and anxiety among the group; who were worried about the welfare and safe return of the vans.

Our group had seemingly held on to a faint hope that Mr. Stuart and his guv'nor should see us as beyond reproach, unlike the foreigners he had criticized. Our holiday was transferred into the agony of conscious and obsessive sweeping, cleaning, polishing and airing the caravans that were commissioned for sale! Such was the power of our guilt, through no fault of our own, but being what we were - just plain ordinary, but unfortunate foreign people; the victims of corrupt stigmatism - the colour of our skin, our only crime.

For the next three summers our holidays around Cornwall and the West Country continued. Dave said that it reminded him of life in Grenada, something to do with the green landscape. We loved the driving up and down, the Cornish hills and the thick darkness at nights; not to mention the narrow country lanes with matted, stubbly bush on either side.

We relished the idea of using torches and seeing the real sky with stars at night. We attempted to have mock storytelling but nothing came close to the real thing in Grenada. For one thing, it rained a lot, day or night and it was cold and damp most of the times. The darkness was menacing but was not conducive to sustaining the "*crick-crack*" storytelling framework. However, exploring England became a mission and we planned our annual holidays with determination. Each year we were joined by other friends who were intrigued with our successes and inspired by our love for the English countryside.

Chapter 13

"Thousands of people are asking me
How I spend my time in London City
Well that is a question I cannot answer
I regret the day I left sweet Jamaica
I mean you would pity my position
Because I nearly die here from starvation."

Lord Kitchener (Aldwin Roberts)

My sister Darris, who had met an English boy called Tony after a year's courtship, decided she would go and live with him. She had just finished a Secretarial Course at Isleworth Polytechnic in Hounslow and decided she now wanted to spread her wings by moving out of the area. When Tony realised that Darris' intention was to flee the family nest, and seek the bright lights elsewhere, he somehow talked her into living with him instead.

Her dream was to go to America to be a secretary or a model, or both she had said. It was her ambition since the age of 12 years and this somehow had not changed.

Tony was a 21-year-old Northerner, who claimed to be motherless; a fact we were told, after mum's suggestion for a meeting with his parents. The frequency of his visits and the intensity of his relationship with Darris bothered mum.

"Not right!" Mamie had remarked, when the couple were preparing to go to a late night party at 10.30pm one night. Mamie was irritated and seemed nervous for my sister.

"Who goes to a party at this time? Vagabonds!" stated Mamie. "That's the time you should be coming back home.

Decent folks have respect for themselves. Your grandparents would turn in their graves with this kind of English slackness!"

She had ranted and raved for over twenty minutes after Darris and Tony had left that Saturday night, but not before she had tried to row with Darris for being too scantily dressed. She complained that Darris was not respecting herself enough and criticised her choice in a partner who would let her go out with her flesh on display like that!

"Behaving like a *nowherian*, giving people the impression you're not from a decent home!" Mamie had snapped.

But Darris had stood her ground firmly and determinedly. She was not going to be drawn into a verbal boxing matching. Instead she reassured mum that it was not as bad as she had made out, pecked her on the cheek to quell mum's rising anger; then she closed the front door.

"In my country," mum had told Tony one Sunday, after we had begun to delve into the rice and peas dinner, "Young women don't just go and live with a man, not before they get married anyway."

In the tense silence, which immediately followed mum's outspoken comment, I watched the steam rise from the bowl of rice and purposely lingered my eyes on the sparsity of peas that attempted to unite with the rice in the famous cultural dish. The brown mass was disturbed by the big spoon, which Darris had dug roughly into it, before depositing a heap on her plate. She quietly aimed for the meat, while she bit her bottom lips with her top teeth. Her small nostrils widened after she had rolled her eyes heaven-wards with the familiar, 'not again' as mum spoke.

"Meat?" she asked Tony curtly, breaking the strained silence which had trespassed on our customary talkative event. Her breathing fastened.

"I'll have some too," Darrin said, picking up the oval bowl by its metal ear-like handles.

She had tried to be jovial in the midst of the tension but her voice sounded understandably unnatural. Momentarily, the ticking of the clock was audible, as we continued to eat. Everyone became aware of the quarter-past the hour time, when the chiming drew attentive eyes to the swinging pendulum inside the decorated mahogany box on the wall.

Mum had become outspoken and anxious and her hairline had begun to show signs of graying at the temples. She had warned us against men wanting only one thing from women and dusting off, once a girl was foolish enough to allow herself to be used, before the sanctity of marriage.

Repeatedly, we were told that it was, and would always be her view as proclaimed by the church. This really meant her Grenadian church, which she literally grew up in. The open statement had surprised Tony and his nervousness showed when he seemed to have bitten his tongue but stifled the double pain to keep the peace. After he regained his composure, he stammered as he tried to reassure mum.

"You know, Mrs B, my mum would've liked you," Tony said, choosing his words carefully.

"She also had the same principles, and you know, I'd be the last one to take advantage of my D," he said, trying to reassure mum and at the same time seeking Darris' support with a fixed stare that said, *"Help me out here!"*

Mum already have the *not-before-marriage-talk* with them in the past. Each time, Darris had been defensively vocal as to why both she and Tony have decided to live together. They regarded mum's ideals as old-fashioned. Theirs, they told mum, was firmly established in the 1980's and a woman's 'Right' to find out if they want to live with a man before a lifetime commitment. Only last week Darris was confronted with an open barrage of straight, off the cuff, questions on this very subject.

"That's what you young people tell yourselves. It was good enough for us in our young days and nothing can change that," Mum argued then continued.

"Being used by someone is one thing and modern ideas about living can't change that."

Darris' reassurances were always repeated, "Mum, times have changed. I'll be all right! I have a job, my own money and I am independent and sensible, just like you."

Mum always fell for the last phrase but would often retort, "Not for long! I'm worried about you girls. Look at you in the prime of your life. What does Tony have? A Council flat! I didn't bring you up to go and live in a Council flat. What do you really know about him anyway?" mum questioned.

"We don't know a single person in his family – only what he tell us. I'm not calling him a liar but how d'you know his family will approve of him having a coloured girlfriend? Remember, from where I stand, we're the ones doing all the approving but we don't know the other side of midnight!" Mum reasoned.

There was some truth in her anxieties and no amount of reassurances could change her view. Darris' move was planned for the end of the month and nothing anyone said was going to change her intention either. In the meantime, Darrin, her twin, appeared to worry for her sister and often I caught her crying alone, pained by the impending parting of her twin sister. It was obvious that she did not want to interfere with Darris' sense of happiness and freedom. However, she could not help confiding in me what her grave doubts about Tony were.

"He is no good, I have my doubts about all this and maybe mum is right!" Darrin confided.

It was after quizzing her to get to the bottom of her resentment that I discovered Tony had once made a pass at her. He had pretended it was an error of mistaken identity with their identical appearance, but Darrin was not convinced.

Aunty Mary proffered a different view. She was quite ambivalent about Darris relationship with Tony and always seemed to console mum about the new generation's modern ideas. In fact, she told mum fact that parents needed to understand that England was different from Grenada. Her son, Peter's future goal to choose a white partner was probably supported by her too.

I felt neither Darris nor Peter knew exactly what they were letting themselves in for. Neither of them had argued for the future struggles of their union with children – offspring's of mixed marriage. Neither of them seem to care about the consequences of the added prejudices and discrimination on both sides of society's cultural and racial divide.

Aunt Mary, the mother of a male child, was very much placatory. She saw her role as constantly reasoning with her anxious sister over her niece's chosen path for the future.

I began to witness the pain and inner suffering on mum's face, as the day of the move drew closer. We had spent days packing Darris' things, in addition to equipment and bedclothes which mum had bought from the £1 shop in Northfield's Avenue. It seems that mum had been buying and hoarding secret purchases in preparation for a future wedding for her girls. She had anticipated marriage, it was obvious and had made no secret of the fact that she would have been happier planning a white wedding; than sending her child off to a stranger who she felt she really knew nothing about. It became clear that the anxiety was more to do with the fact that Tony was white, a sort of unknown quantity to mum.

She had asked all the questions mothers usually asked their daughters. She had also spoken to Aunt Mary. One night as we sat watching TV, as if to justify her right to worry about her girls, mum decided to recount her tales about a miscarriage she once suffered. We had come to the end of a *Val Doonican's TV Show* and after we had eaten coconut tart, mum spoke of her old doctor's misdiagnosis of her unusually painful stomach and heavy periods. She said that she did have a birth control coil put in place by her doctor, yet surprisingly, she became pregnant.

We listened to her tales of woe at the hands of the hospital doctors, who offered her a hysterectomy because they thought she was a single mother. We listened more attentively when she detailed stories of other people she had known, who she said had experienced the misfortune of this crime. Her overall view was that the hospital staff was racist and dangerous for thinking that, as a young black woman, she was going to populate Britain with lots of little black bastard children.

"Their solution for all of us," she said. "It's to make us incapable of having children in England, that way we're less of a bother in numbers."

Darris had immediately disagreed and accused mum of being paranoid. Darrin listened but said very little and when asked for my views, I said that perhaps it must be true, since it was not our experience. Mum had agreed with her final pronouncement: "Only those, whose backside is in the fire, know how hot it is!"

I know that deep down mum had felt disappointed that without Calvin, she had failed to make Darris do things "the proper way." It had been her goal and she was hell bent on showing the estranged father, how well she had done without his help, in bringing up her girls. She seemed weak and conquered by Darris' episode and I wondered about her life with Randolph in her youth when she was a fresh, youthful, determined, and ambitious daddy's girl.

ع

For years I had wondered what talking to her about hers and Randolph's past relationship would be like, especially with her new situation and her family in England. It was almost as if that relationship never existed. All my past childhood wonderings about my entry into the world and their reconciliation was never fulfilled. Mamie never talked about her past. She appeared to blot out the past happening, my conception and birth, as some non-event. The view that *"children must be seen and not heard,"* prevailed all those years, and had quite happily crossed the Atlantic Ocean from Grenada to England. That view still demanded silence from the young, as a matter of course, when it was convenient. It demanded answers or made pronouncements when it suited the adults, and claimed the authority to obliterate aspects of our lives at will.

The knowledge of Randolph existed in my mind like a shadowy ghost; popping up occasionally when questions demanded to be answered. When the picture of a face needed to be created, that picture would be a resemblance to me. Alternatively, it was either someone who was smiling, frowning, moving, talking or even sleeping. The contents of Aunt Meena's letters which I had read in Grenada would echo and re-echo in my mind during times of stress or when I felt sad. They resurrected a sense of longing and "loss." That "loss" was the missing piece of jigsaw puzzle needed to compensate for the world's best-kept secret.

But adults, I had decided many years ago, were perfect at playing the game of *"Hate-Till–Death."* It was an adult's intransigence, which contrasted a child's way of dealing with situations. In comparison, children's hurt expressions would evaporate within minutes, almost as the smoke from a freshly fired canon. It would explode, impact, and then diminish with the advancing seconds into nothingness.

That was a life-long wish for the mummy-Randolph scenario; the wish that it had all been a bad dream and I'd wake up to the reality of quite the opposite. However, time had tempered the many years of wishful thinking. Instead, it had schooled me, in the realities of what is seen and experienced; of accepting the inevitable, that Randolph had a new family. Then there was the possibility that he may just have other children to love. My fear was, perhaps he never really cared whether I had lived or died after birth.

I had held on to an idea that maybe once Randolph had made his escape from the embarrassing shores of Grenada, his knowledge of my situation would resurrect a secret need to find me. These thoughts which squeezed out momentarily, the romance of fatherly interest, of musing with thoughts of belonging to someone; who was somewhere, and who may have a secret interest in me, soon evaporated. There was nothing to help me keep this view of myself. It had been 30 years, the life-span of a generation.

I later told myself that it could all have been a terrible misrepresentation of the facts. After all, I had learnt of the details about Randolph from only *one* of Aunt Meena's letter. How sure can anyone be of the truth in those letters? There was never an outsider view or second opinion to their story. Furthermore, perhaps this whole notion of someone wanting me, the product of a loose sperm after childish passion, was a figment of my imagination. In my doubt, I wondered whether it may even have been the depravation of my mind to offer an alternative jug-saw piece, where nothing existed, that inspired my quest.

Life had been complicated, silent and pretentious and maybe best left alone to unravel its mysteries in the fullness of time, I concluded. This had become my prevailing thoughts. The very moment I had finally and consciously decided to lay the subject of Randolph to rest, was the day I became an independent thinker. It was also the day I became an adult who was the mistress of my own scenario and the teller of my own tale.

Nineteen years of existing in the wilderness, in search of tender care had ceased. I was now on the lookout for signs and signal which remotely resembled a repetition of this sad life-long scenario. The Jekyll and Hyde existence of extreme opposites that adults play, I decided, would be avoided at all costs.

Darris' departure with Tony to their Council flat had appeared to resurrect pain, sadness and a feeling of failure for mum. I guessed mum felt that once again, life had not ceded to her ambitions or requests of what she viewed as success and happiness, so I commiserated with her. Darrin too, affected by the loss, became more involved in church activities, perhaps to find spiritual strength to deal with her twin's departure and other emotional baggage. She had slowly come to terms with the eventual separation and saw her life's calling as being a missionary bound for a life abroad!

Once again, our residence was minus its second occupant and the three of us seemed somewhat weaker. As our numbers dwindled, so did our resolve. Initially, Calvin's departure was felt but we had somehow managed to cope. Mum's confidence that she could face raise her girls without a father was also strong to begin with. Like a mother hen, she had fussed and was vigilant over us. Overall, she seemed to have managed well but also to the detriment of her health. The punishing excessive extra working shifts to make ends meet had finally taken its toll. It had reduced mum to being a workaholic; someone who had become conversation-less, always-tired and frequently moody.

Church-going became less frequent, and watching TV became an instant lullaby for sleep, whilst general communication lessened. Instead, necessity became the mother of convenience and making do. We were all forced to adopt a busier lifestyle, each occupied in our own catalogues of strenuous tasks. However, increasingly we were bereft of excitement, laughter and the anticipation of good things. Aunt Mary's visits became infrequent too, since mum was rarely available. Our home was a house, where we seemed to pass by like visiting ships in the night, from which we ran away in the day.

ع

One day I received an emergency telephone call from the local hospital, informing me that mum had collapsed at work. It then became quite clear to me that things had deteriorated drastically. The severity of our punishing working schedules and maniacal lifestyles made me realise how vulnerable and weak the three of us had become.

"What happened? Is she alright?" I asked the Hospital Receptionist.

"She passed out at work, but is resting comfortably now. Doctor's running some tests. He'll be able to tell you more later."

I could ill afford the time off work, being in the middle of a financial inspection from Head Office. Therefore, my initial and subsequent visits to the hospital were only made possible because I had worked during all of my lunch hours. This enabled me to make the hour's train dash after work to get to the hospital before visiting hours ended.

Was I becoming like my mother, I asked myself, as I ate half sandwiches, drank cold coffee, missed lunches and refused our staff's usual after-work gatherings in a local bar. Entering the automatic sliding doors to the Accident and Emergency ward, the smell of antiseptic hit me. The Casualty Room was full of waiting men and women with children, and this slowed down my initial hastiness. I took quiet and deliberate steps as I approached the Reception desk. The white-coated robotic hospital staff showed various senses of 'emergency.'

An unemotional clerk asked me the usual questions, as loudly as she could, so that those waiting to be seen were forced to learn all our personal details from answers I was made to give equally loudly. I had noticed this kind of impatience and annoyance of Reception staff before. It was the time I visited the hospital to accompany Rose and Brian with their two year old, who had pushed a pea up her nose.

At that time, I had witnessed that some hospital staff was desperate to show whatever kind of authority they could. It was my view also that perhaps it was their only means of venting their personal frustrations and anger by bullying anyone who had the misfortune to walk through the hospital doors.

Today, it was my turn, and the extent of the embarrassment was doubled, because all attempts to whisper my information or demonstrate a sense of privacy to the Receptionist, made her bellow at me more.

Another enquirer, this time a staff nurse, evident by her thick blue ban in her nursing cap and the corresponding thick blue belt around her waist, told me to follow her. She was armed with a buff manila file, so I quick-marched behind her into a side ward with a single bed with mum, seemingly plugged into by a clear fluid intravenously feeding her right arm, she appeared to be sleeping.

"Try not to be long," the nurse advised, before checking mum's pulse and scribbling on the record chart at the foot of her bed. I sat in the chair next to the bed and before leaving mum's bedside the nurse dropped an unexpected clanger.

"There is concern for her heart condition. She'll need a lot of rest until we finish some more tests."

Later on, the doctor told me to prepare for the worst, as the two heart attacks mum sustained in less than 24 hours, had now put her on the critical list, adding that she was surprisingly lucky to be alive.

Sitting quietly next to the hospital bed with mum in it, brought home the reality of the situation. The information was surprising as mum did not complain of heart symptoms. She rarely took time off work and was hardly ever off sick. I sighed and looked at the pathetic figure of my slumbering mum. Watching her as I did, made my mind flash back to Grenada and Mark's funeral, when I had seen the 7 year old corpse lying in his coffin. He too, had looked asleep though lifeless.

Just then, memories of the traumatized village, adult sorrow and our extreme childish fears flooded my mind and I began to cry. I whimpered silently at first, then louder, so that my unchecked sniffles woke mum up. Surprisingly, she stirred then opened her eyes. Turning to look at me, she just asked for Darrin and Darris, then went back to sleep. She had ignored me totally. I sat there motionless, puzzled and feeling slightly hurt. She had not even acknowledged me.

My surprise was not due to the fact that she had, once again, appeared to ignore or reject me. The gravity of the situation was the fact that in this moment of crisis, when as the eldest, I had been regarded as the immediate and responsible next of kin; her preference was expressed for the others. It seems to me what I had long held as my existence of convenience, was no longer childish musings or paranoia.

However, Gran-Gran had taught me to be strong at all times, and I had held on to her advice and personal words of comfort, just as I had held on to the three beads she had given me. They were what I called my lucky charm and I believed that magically, they seemed to inspire me to accept what to others seemed unacceptable. They inspired me to hold visions of goals and aims thought impossible to achieve by others. Above all, their presence gave me a strong sense of confidence and unshakeable determination to get ahead. My overriding and unwavering drive was to accomplish Gran-Gran's long-term goals for my life; to get to the top, to be that *Woman of Destiny* - no matter what!

However, today, something in mum's eyes caused that firmly rooted feeling to shake. That feeling had gone beyond my presence to somewhere deep into an unknown. It had caused a feeling of abandonment, a sense of déjà-vu; an uncanny sense of unease, that I had felt and experienced before. Strangely, the atmosphere became cold, though not unusual for a March evening. This situation seemed to cause a tugging at my heart. It felt like a taut piece of string, which had been straining and stretching to breaking point, and had now snapped.

Loneliness overtook me like an orphan on Mars, and I felt the urge to leave the hospital immediately. Fast, then faster, I trotted down the corridor, quickly passing the red, yellow blue and green lines on the floor which led to X-ray, blood test and Pharmacy. I went through the heavy, swinging fire-check doors and eventually out into the open air of the car-park. There I stood, breathing deeply as I calmed myself down. It had become dark and I was exhausted from my day's work. I then took slow, purposeful, steps towards the waiting bus stop for the journey home.

As the days wore on, I became increasingly tired and the intensity of daily exhaustion made me also fear for my own life. There were never any enquiries from either of the twins. Excuses were frequent. They ranged from having their own family commitments – Darris a young baby, and Darrin had moved to Birmingham where she had met a Christian man. By all accounts, she was going to undertake missionary work in Africa. But I needed some sort of support from them too. I became annoyed with Darrin, since she should demonstrate charity at home, before setting sail to give charity on the African Continent.

This solitary bearing of burden and isolation in times of dire need would not have happened in Grenada I thought. As I sat in the E3 bus, drunk with fatigue, anger and frustration, I compared similar occurrences in Grenada. Certainly in the island was the unswerving bond and strength of villagers, those beyond the village; in fact support would come from anywhere in the island. There is a distinctive participation of people to support in the surrounding Parishes and seemingly the whole island, in times which need communal effort. Tradition dictates that everyone should rally around the burdened or bereaved in times of need, to soothe their emotional pains or grant material support without being asked.

Tears welled up in my eyes, and my throat tightened with a parched feeling of strain. My head ached at the nape of my neck, my ears pricked and hot tears readily filled my eyes. It covered my eyeballs, collected at the corners of my eyes then rolled down my cheeks. Sitting as I did on the bus, I bit my lip to hold back any public show of emotions; too embarrassed that people might stare at me. Right now, there was no particular attention that would be welcomed. Secretly, I brushed the tears as it appeared at the sides of my eyes then I blew my nose. I breathed deeply and cleared my throat before propping my chin on my right arm to deal with the *What-ifs* that were trespassing on my mind.

No one is particularly schooled for death in England, that unspoken never-to-mention, taboo subject, is like miasma to a healthy patient. The word "*dead*" was for goldfish, rats, mice and insects, not even pet dogs and cats. As for humans, strangely, the world's greatest secret was that it happens and when it does, you deal with it in your own way. More ridiculous is the fact that no one expects it to happen before old age. That fear of uttering the word "*dead*" and the cultural acceptance of the ignorance, associated with this secret, made me very angry. Momentarily, I shifted in my seat, squared my shoulder and cleared my throat intermittently, throughout the journey home.

It was not only a lack of knowledge on this subject that angered me but also the apparent ignorance of absolutely everyone, about how to cope with something which must affect us all at some time. Logically, I felt society's conspiracy to force individuals to experience extreme trauma at a time when knowledge of coping strategies could minimize that pain, was a farce that we all contribute to every day. I longed for the Grenadian tradition; that of togetherness, community spirit and a one-island-family feeling. This was the practice not only in time of troubles and woe, but was also available to celebrate the good times too.

The bus had sped through Ealing in no time. I had hardly been aware of the frequent stops and the exits and entrances of passengers, or the road traffic conditions. Locked in my immense world of fear for my own situation, as well as mum's, I became very pensive. I tried to deal with the private imaginings and mental monologues of how I would manage with more *what-ifs*, and *what-would-I-do* scenarios. I became more struck by the fact that the subject of death was not something you discussed with your best friend or neighbour and I had not seen any *Teach Yourself* handbook on Death either.

That nicer word "bereavement," euphemistically made more palatable, was mainly associated with the after-shocks and counselling. My ignorance was that I did not know what to do or where to start in practical terms. On the other hand, we had all promoted that "*pass away*" was more something you whisper to someone else. That someone would equally be embarrassed or frightened, to talk to you about your situation for fear that they too, would have to face up to the fact they had no real schooling about how to respond to life's most inevitable event.

On reaching home, I glanced at the clock, it was 9.30pm. I threw myself onto my bed, still dressed with the thought of resting for just a very short while, before tackling the domestic environment. However, the sight of my bed was never more welcoming and I knew that not only did I fall asleep instantly, but must have snored noisily as well.

Twelve hours later, still fully clad in work clothes, I woke up feeling ravenously hungry and still very tired.

EPILOGUE... *"So shall it be in the end."*

The silk cotton tree had witnessed years of grief. Standing there as it does now, in the middle of this cemetery, it was the symbol of fear for children, schooled in the folklore. It reminded some of stories of souls being pinned on it by Obeah men and of those kinds of trees which sucked innocent lives into its bowels via large, spider-like roots; to feed its insatiable appetite. Most importantly, some spoke of the necessity to appease the tree's bad spirits, in order to prevent violent harm to villagers.

This echo of Reverend Blackman's words, "As *it was in the Beginning, so shall it be in the end,"* rang true in my ears and I winced at the thought of coming to terms with the death of a mother who, at the same time, was a stranger in many ways. The quietness of such a placid spot made me doubt the silk-cotton tree's ominous reputation.

Here in this spot, I could reflect and welcome the peacefulness, in contrast to the many recent days with throngs of people who had literally taken on the seriousness of sending a loved one to that spiritual home. This was done with respect and precision, to traditional and cultural procedures. The Grenadian villagers took charge and I tried to follow automatically; though stupefied by unpalatable revelations about mum's own private world.

Life had sped past me in what seemed like a nightmare-moment. This nightmare was the revelation of mum's lifetime of woes, bitterness, ruin, secrecy and hate of an extraordinary kind. It made me realize that the many façades that protect our private world are often laid bare in death. It was indeed a time of reckoning for many; though for some, it was often too late, to give answers to questions, or deal with accusations and confessions.

Death for mum had revealed a web of deceit mixed with anger and her need to wreak pain and havoc on those she considered responsible for her life's adverse dilemmas. I had discovered many bundles of letters, mostly unopened but carefully preserved, that were hidden in mum's original suitcase or grip. The grip which she had travelled from Grenada to England in 1960 with was her secret hiding place. This little suitcase was cleverly hidden inside a larger modern suitcase. Its contents contained the information, rather like jigsaw pieces to complete what seems to be like the larger puzzle of my life because in those items I found answers to my questions.

Shocked by its revelation, Aunt Mary was my first port of call. There were the scores of letters, addressed to me from Emma. There were also letters to me from past boyfriends and most importantly to mum from Randolph, addressed to her from America. Revelations of their existence cut through my heart like the repeated stabbing of an uncured wound, causing fresh bleeding at each attack.

Aunt Mary did not have the answers to many of my questions. How could she? But she had tried her best to explain the enormity of the pain that mum had experienced at Randolph's initial denial of being my father. She related the family's shame 30 years ago, the village gossip and the sense of shame, that mum, a rising star, had become a fallen comet; once pregnancy had occurred. Worse still, was Randolph's parents' refusal to accept that their son had fathered a child out of wedlock, contrary to their expectations. This was coupled with the crashing blow of his paternity denial; it had galled everyone.

"Your mother almost went insane," said Aunt Mary. "I'm sorry but she didn't see how she could achieve her goals in life, which was to become a teacher, by being pregnant with you. She felt it was her duty to stop the pregnancy and attempted abortion several times. We all feared for her life, so we had to supervise her - your mother was never left alone. All we could do then was to pray for her and you - her unborn child."

"You see Joanne, people took advantage of this and ridiculed your grandfather; a very upright man in the village. He was proud and strict, a real God-fearing man who everyone looked up to. The irony is, he had saved many families from the same plight and felt pained by the fact that he was not able to do anything about his own situation. That is why after the disaster, he vowed never to preach in our church again."

I swallowed hard at the thought of me being considered "*a disaster,*" but I pressed Aunt Mary to continue. She noticed how hurt I was and this made her nervous, so that she stuttered with difficulty while trying to cut the story short. I probed some more.

"Didn't Randolph *really* want me?" I asked, stressing on the 'really' and almost fearing Aunt Mary's reply. She sat up, facing me so that my eyes and hers make four and she instructed me.

"Well, er- you see, er- these things Joanne were not as straightforward as they seem these days. Nowadays, it doesn't seem to matter much if an unmarried woman gets pregnant. Randolph was a boy. He was scared. In Grenada, the blight on families in this situation is not just for one but for all – gossip, talk, losing face, reputation, Christian living, family ties - all have their pressure to bear on individuals. Sometimes mistakes are made, not on purpose, but people move and react where pressure is greatest. You understand what I mean?"

I nodded. "You mean he was too scared to admit he had broken the rules?" Then becoming a little impatient with Aunt Mary's answer, I surprised her when I snapped.

"He was a bloody coward!"

"It's not quite like that Joanne. I mean, not so clear-cut," she insisted.

I launched into a semi-lecture, with questions, statements and rhetoric. Somehow it had seemed unfair for me to demand answers and explanations from Aunty Mary, but she was a willing listener and by all accounts, she was also the only person who could throw some light on most of the issues.

"But Auntie Mary, how can you explain Emma's letters to me? Dozens kept here unopened, it's as if I myself was dead; didn't exist! Randolph's letters too. He did try to make up. Look at the scores of letters begging for forgiveness, pleading to look after me, to help me, even offering schooling; something I could have done with in Grenada. Everyone I know with parents abroad had private school education except me. Everybody had something sent to him or her by someone. What was wrong with that?"

The tone of my voice had become a little higher and Aunt Mary clearly did not have the answers. She gently touched me in the shoulder as we sat next to each other, whilst she tried to explain a situation she was not the creator of. I did not ask Aunt Mary what her opinions then were, but I told her about Aunt Meena's letter that I had seen in Grenada; written to mum in 1963. I told her that Randolph had been pleading for a change of heart and had begged for mum's corporation in introducing me to his side of the family, especially his aging parents.

No one can explain the reasons for such behaviour. At present, there is no answer to that. There is also no understanding of why letters from Ian, a past boyfriend, had been hidden from me. Some were clearly opened and neatly folded back and filed in their bundles. There were responses to job applications I had made, which had come back to me offering me the positions that I thought had been refused. More devastating than all – the revelation of mum's *Will*. She'd left everything to *"my TWO children"* - Darris and Darrin! This was outrageous to say the least, since this rejection was added to by the mockery of condolences and cards of sympathy for mum's death form previous work places; they had come addressed to Darris and Darrin. In fact, one letter of sympathy had referred to me as *"the niece!"*

Of course, I didn't expect Aunt Mary to explain absolutely everything to me – what had been revealed had saturated my mind since then. Conversely, the situation was illuminating despite my demand for answers to my ultimate question - *Can a woman's tender care cease towards the child she bears?*

Almost as if I had experienced an epiphany, I arose from the tip of the mound which was covered in wreaths and bouquets and looked at the one shaped with the words *"MUM."* I pondered the meaning it now held for me, as I reflected on the current state of affairs. In the distance, the gathered few who had left the cemetery walked like lost souls but convinced that all will be well for mum, beyond this swollen, floral mound.

The wind blew cold and the rustling cotton leaves swayed and danced in the breeze, as my friend Yvette's little talk on Buddhism about cause and effect flashed in my mind. Faced with such perplexing dilemmas, philosophies are often examined, and decisions are made. So as Yvette had directed

I chanted to break the family karmic effects of the painful causes and left the cemetery to join the waiting cars.

I vowed that I would not to look back at the grave when I leave. This had a deep meaning for me, leaving the past behind, since the jigsaw puzzle was now fully pieced together. The search was over and life had come to another juncture. What it brings, would be up to me to make the causes for.

I rolled Gran-gran's beads between my fingers and pondered. Tomorrow is another day. I would be in another place, another time, and another world. I would be back in London, where I would reconstruct my present and look forward to my future. There, Kenneth my long-standing boyfriend, is waiting for me, for an answer to his nuptial question – Would I marry him?

GLOSSARY

Ale	(French origin): To go
All man jack and their brother	Absolutely everyone
Anancy	A character in Caribbean folklore, a cunning trickster generally depicted as a spider with a human head; the subject of many Anancy stories, the character has its origins among the Ashanti of W Africa
Awright	All right
Asham	A desert snack made by shelling dry corn, parching it in a hot pan and then pounding it in a mortar, then sifting it until it is fine
Bacchanal	Gossip resulting from some commotion: Originally associated with noisy, carnival revellery.
Bad eye	A dirty or evil look
Bay leaf	The leaf of the bayberry, *Pimenta racemosa*, used in making bay oil and bay rum.
Bon Je!	Patois (*pronounced Patwa – French Creole*), means '*Oh God!*'
Bon Je, look at me ass cross!	Patois (*pronounced Patwa – French Creole*), means '*Oh God, look at my troubles!*'
Beke	A white person, or white people
Belly wuk	Diarrhea

Big-shot	A high-ranking person; similarly a child playing "big" means, assuming you are mature or grown up.
Bluggoe	A tropical plant, *Musa paradisiaca,* of the banana family resembling the banana.
Bois den	The leaves of *Pimenta racemosa Myrtaceae* – the West Indian Bay tree used culinary and to produce The cologne called Bay rum.
Boli	A large round fruit from which calabash is made – *African origin – Wolof*
Bougainvillea	A large climbing shrub that is used as a hedge: It can be trained to climb other trees or on trellis
Bourgeois	Typical of the middle class or having a strong interest in money and possession
Breadfruit	A large fruit tree native to Pacific islands and Malaysia that was brought to the West Indies in the 18th century. The large round fruit is also called breadfruit
BWIA	Official acronym for the now defunct national airline of Trinidad and Tobago during the 1960s/70s
Buss ass	A good beating
Crayfish	Also called cacadoe *crawdad, cacadaw* any freshwater *decapod crustacean* of the *genera Astacus* and *Cambarus,* closely related to but smaller than the lobsters.
Calaloo	Also referred to as dasheen bush; edible leaves of the taro plant; used as greens or in making thick soups

Calypso	This word has several derivations: *A Carib Word *"Carieto"*, meaning a joyous song which itself evolved into *cariso* *A French archaic word meaning a drinking party or festivity *"carouse"*, transmitted orally sounding like *Kaiso"* *A Spanish word *"caliso"*, also used for a topical song in St. Lucia. *Alternatively, there is also a West African (Hausa) term *"Kaiso"*, itself a corruption of *"kaito"*, an expression of approval and encouragement similar to *bravo*!
Careila	(can also be spelt *Kareila*): A bitter herbal bush (called *bitter cerocee* in other parts of the Caribbean). It is a vine bearing a small bumpy skinned yellow or orange fruit. The leaves are used to make a bitter herbal remedy. It is used in tea, regarded for cleansing the blood and other blood related sicknesses.
Caribbean Orature	A fusion of the oral and written traditions of the region which embody *sound, words, performance, music, drama, and visual.*
Chick nor chack	Absolutely nothing
Cocoa	Used here as both the fruit and the plant. The fruit resembles a yellow or orange torpedo approximately a foot in length.
Comese	To be in a mess, melee, or confusion
Compere Tig or Zien	Caribbean folktales within the long tradition of proverbs, jokes, riddles and stories which people have

Coo-coo also cou cou	A dish made from corn meal enjoyed throughout the Caribbean from Trinidad and Tobago to Grenada and Jamaica. In Barbados, Coo-Coo is the national dish.
Couchon	Patois (*pronounced pat-wa – French Creole*), means *'pig'*
Crocus bag	A burlap bag, also called a croker sack in Southern U.S. (chiefly South Atlantic States)
Cushu	Cashew
Damsel	The tree and fruit of *Phyllanthus acidus:* The small sized tree produces small, flattened, multi-lobed berries
Dog eat your share	You will be in a terrible situation. Logically if a dog eats your share, you have nothing left!
Dougla	A person of mixed African and East Indian or white ancestry
Ent	Similar to American "*aint*" – is not
Fete	Party, revelry, celebration
Gade mize mwen non!	Patois (*pronounced pat-wa French Creole*), Means *'Look at my troubles or Look at the problems I have!'*
Galvanize	Galvanized sheets (zinc coated) of metal used for roofing
Gazoo cork	Drinks bottle tops that are pounded and flattened and used to make wheels for toys.
Gi' Jack 'e Jacket	(*Give Jack his Jacket*): Give credit where credit is due, and not assign it to others

Goat mouth	Idiomatic expression, meaning something someone says that comes true, it's usually something negative.
Good mahning	*"Good Morning";* generally the first greeting when you meet someone in the Caribbean, especially in a business setting, but even said sometimes when getting into a bus, walking into the post office and encountering the people in line.
Good-for-nuting	*Good-for-nothing* – a person considered worthless
Golden apple	*(Aegle Marmelos):* This is a hard shelled fruit about the size of a grapefruit that is used for food
Governor plum	The fruit of the *Flacourtia indica,* which is a species of flowering plant native to much of Africa and tropical temperate areas of the globe.
Griot	A person among the peoples of western Africa, whose function is to keep an oral history of the tribe or village and to entertain with stories, poems, songs, dances, etc.
Gros bete	Patois (*pronounced pat-wa – French Creole*), for *big beast or big animal – negative*
Gungo peas	Pigeon peas
Hefe	*"Big"* meaning important, like someone in a position of authority or power (From Spanish *jefe* probably absorbed into the Grenadian language through workers at the Panama Canal).

Horse's flesh	The real truth
Hurricane Janet	Hurricane Janet was the most powerful tropical cyclone of the 1955 Atlantic hurricane season and one of the strongest Atlantic hurricanes on record.
Il fait froid maitainent	Patois (*pronounced pat-wa – French Creole*), meaning *"It feels cold now, or I'm feeling cold/I feel cold."*
Jab-jab	Also called "devil mas" is a type of masquerade in the West Indian carnival
Julie mango	A mango cultiva that was made popular in the Caribbean: Also known as St. Julian.
Kata	A coil wrap worn on the head to cushion heavy loads (*African origin – Twi*)
Krapo-go-to-church	Illegible or bad handwriting
Ki servant sa?	*'What servant?'* (A mixture of patois and English), A question that suggests an impossibility
Ki read sa?	*'Reading? No way!'* (A mixture of patois and English), A question that suggests the person is pretending
La Bay	The sea or the bay – the name by which Grenville, Grenada's second town is known.
Lambie	(a class of mollusks): A local name that is applied to a number of different medium to large-sized sea snails
Limacol	A popular eau de cologne, used in the Caribbean

Look at me ass cross!	Look at my troubles! Look at the troubles I find myself in!
Lougarou	(Sometimes spelt *ligaroo*) - A being, in folk legend, resembling a ball of fire which humans turn into, in order to feed on the blood of their victims, though they don't usually harm them: (*Similar to the Dracula Legend*).
Lowdown	The gossip, the news according to hearsay
Mad ants	(*Nylanderia pubens):* A small ant that moves in a quick erratic manner.
Making sweet eyes	Winking at a person and showing affection
Manicou	A prehensile-tailed marsupial: *Didelphis virginiana*, of the Caribbean and eastern U.S.
Mwen	Patois (*pronounced pat-wa – French Creole*), meaning, '*me or I*'
Makome	Patois (*pronounced pat-wa – French Creole*), literally it means, '*My dear*' (familiar term of address to a woman friend)
Moless	Annoy
Mullato	A person of mixed white and Negro ancestry in the Caribbean
Nenen	Godmother
No-where-ian	Someone from no where, negative, indicating not a good person
Obeah	A form of belief involving sorcery, practiced in parts of the Caribbean, South America, the southern U.S., and Africa.

Ochras	Okra known in many English-speaking countries as *ladies' fingers*, bhindi, bamia, ochro or gumbo, is a flowering plant in the mallow family.
Oh ho!	*I see!*
Ole talk	Gossip
Ooman	Woman
Oui	Yes
Pale Patwa petite moun ka rive	Patois (*pronounced pat-wa – French Creole*),
Paliass	A mattress made out of straw
Papa met!	An exclamation (literally means, *Oh my father!*), but used also to mean, *My God!*
Paradise plum	A very hard fruity candy
Paren	A child's Godfather (as with God parents)
Patwa	(*pronounced pat-wa – French Creole; also Patois*): A mixture of French words and Creole or non-Standard English, the result of which is Grenadian French Creole language which retains some French words and sounds but with different word-order and spelling.
Pectus	Stately, proper
Planass	To beat someone with the broad side of a cutlass
Plantain	A tropical plant, *Musa paradisiaca*, of the banana family, resembling the banana
Pli mal	Patois (*pronounced pat-wa – French Creole*),

meaning '*It gets worse*'

Pli maliwel!	Patois (*pronounced pat-wa – French Creole*), *I put a bad curse on you!*
Poyah	A cutlass
Sa ki fe'w?	Patois (*pronounced pat-wa – French Creole*), meaning, '*What's happening? Or what's wrong with you? Or just what's wrong?*
Saracca	A ritual feast of African origin, held for a healing purpose, to bring good spirits and good fortune to a neighbourhood
Saga boy	A lady's man or sweet boy; a typical *Don Juan*
Se kon sa tout moun an famni-a ye	Patois (*pronounced pat-wa – French Creole*), negative – meaning, *Everyone in the family is like that/they are all like that!*
Sessay mwen	*My dear* - a familiar term to address a same-age friend
Shango	African religion, acknowledging the ancestral god of lightning: It is a vestige of African religion still in the Caribbean.
Shortney	A type of masquerade in the West Indian Carnival
Silk cotton tree	Also known as "jumbie or zombie tree" – *Ceiba Pentandra,* is a tropical tree of the order *Malvales* and the family *Melvaceae.*
Skin teet	Grinning or laughing
Smiley puss	Someone who smiles too much
Soursop	The large, dark-green, slightly acid, pulpy

	fruit of a small West Indian tree, *Annona muricata*, of the *annona* family. Also called *guanabana*
Sugar cake	A sweet treat made from diced coconut, sugar and spices. The mixture is boiled until thick enough to set and harden when cold.
Susu	A form of savings where a group of people pay an agreed sum of money on a periodic basis (weekly/monthly) and at the end of each period a member of the group gets the whole amount. When every member gets the whole amount; the cycle starts again.
Siddung	Sit down
Tabanca	Love sickness
Tania	Also known as eddo is the edible root of the taro or of any of several related plants.
Tay-tay	A girl's breasts
Thermogene	A medicated, heat-producing rub
Things turn ol mass	When the situation becomes extremely bad
Tout moun ka ale	Patois (*pronounced pat-wa – French Creole*), means everyone is going
Washicon	A canvas shoe with a rubber sole; gym shoe; Sneakers.
Wi/oui	Patois (*pronounced pat-wa – French Creole*), meaning, Yes
Yam	The starchy, tuberous root of any of various climbing vines of the genus *Dioscorea,* cultivated for food in warm regions.

Zaboca   Avocado or just referred to as 'pear': An edible pear-shaped or round fruit with an egg-shaped seed. The flesh is green inside and turns yellow closer to the ripening stage.

Note: English as spoken throughout the Caribbean, called *Creole, Jamaica Talk* or Nation Language, has no official orthography, spellings have been adopted and modified to represent the language phonetically. However, for further guidance on Creole English; See Dr. Richard Allsop's *Dictionary of Caribbean Creole* (1999), published by Oxford University Press.